THE VILLA

Jess Ryder is the bestselling author of nine psychological thrillers. Her novel *The Ex-Wife* was recently adapted into a Paramount+ TV series to the acclaim of critics and viewers alike, and her thrillers have been read by countless readers. She lives with her partner in London and has four grown-up children.

Also by Jess Ryder

Lie to Me

The Good Sister

The Ex-Wife

The Dream House

The Girl You Gave Away

The Night Away

The Second Marriage

My Husband's Lover

THE VILLA

JESS RYDER

PENGUIN BOOKS

PENGUIN BOOKS

UK | USA | Canada | Ireland | Australia
India | New Zealand | South Africa

Penguin Books is part of the Penguin Random House group
of companies whose addresses can be found at
global.penguinrandomhouse.com

Penguin
Random House
UK

Published in Penguin Books 2024
001

Copyright © Jess Ryder, 2024

The moral right of the author has been asserted

Typeset in 10.4/15pt Palatino LT Pro by Jouve (UK), Milton Keynes
Printed and bound in Great Britain by Clays Ltd, Elcograf S.p.A.

The authorised representative in the EEA is Penguin Random House
Ireland, Morrison Chambers, 32 Nassau Street, Dublin D02 YH68

A CIP catalogue record for this book is available from the British Library

ISBN: 978–1–804–94690–9

www.greenpenguin.co.uk

MIX
Paper | Supporting
responsible forestry
FSC® C018179

Penguin Random House is committed to a
sustainable future for our business, our readers
and our planet. This book is made from Forest
Stewardship Council® certified paper.

For Karen and Fiona

Prologue: Then

DANI

Dani moved her arm, feeling a hard, smooth surface beneath her. As she shifted her leg, a stabbing pain shot through her knee. She opened one eye – slowly and carefully – then the other. Her vision was blurry. The darkness was interrupted by blue and amber lights flashing rhythmically into the room. Where was she? At the nightclub? Perhaps she'd blacked out on the dance floor . . .

No. That was the night before last.

She tried to twist her head and look around but found she could barely move. As the lights pulsed through the gloom, she looked for familiar objects. Ah, yes . . . There was the rug, patterned in red and yellow, like the Spanish flag. And the statue of the Buddha on the shelves beneath the stairs.

She was at the villa, then. In the sitting room. Good. But that didn't explain the lights. Maybe they were in her head.

What had happened? She didn't have a clue how she'd hurt her knee, or how long she'd been lying here, splayed out on the floor. What time was it? It felt late. Where was Aoife? Surely she wasn't still outside, partying.

She wanted to get into bed. Or better, to stick her head in the toilet bowl. But their bedroom was upstairs, there was no way she could make it with this knee. It was unbelievably painful. And she'd never been thirstier in her life. She made a mental map of the route to the kitchen, imagined heaving herself up to the sink and running the tap, forcing her mouth under it to catch a few lukewarm dribbles. She had to get some liquid inside her.

I will never, never, ever touch a drop of alcohol again, she told herself. And this time, she meant it.

The blue and amber lights seemed to be flashing faster, more insistently. She could hear noises around her: people talking on the other side of the room, men's voices, the thrum of a vehicle outside, the loud thud of a closing door. A siren started to wail and suddenly she realised where the lights were coming from. What they might mean.

'I think she's come round,' a woman said. They approached, calling her name. She looked up. Beth was standing over her – wild-eyed, breathing heavily. Her party dress was soaked in blood.

Chapter One: Now

DANI

Dani lays her passport on the counter, trying to blink back tears as the border guard scrutinises her face. The unrelenting sunshine, the warm tarmac, the rapid fire of Spanish in the shuttle bus and even the scented disinfectant on the airport floors, whoosh her back in time. Three years have passed since she was last in Andalucia, and yet it's as if she never left.

From the moment she stepped off the plane, she's been overwhelmed with conflicting emotions: deep sadness for what happened the last time she was here; excitement that this weekend has finally arrived; anxiety and trepidation for how it might turn out. This is a huge risk she's taking, but she's tried every therapy available for dealing with her grief and so far, nothing's worked.

The guard stamps a page and hands the passport back with a quick smile. She glances behind to see where the others have got to. They stopped to use the toilets and are now at the back of the queue. A security officer hurries her on. She tows her suitcase through the barriers and enters the baggage reclaim hall, where fellow passengers on the flight from Stansted are assembling eagerly around the carousel.

The conveyor belt clunks into action and there is a murmur of anticipation as the first cases emerge.

Dani didn't put any luggage in the hold, but she lingers, half-waiting for the others, half-watching another group of women, wearing sashes and bunny ears, playfighting each other to grab their luggage. Hens. They were on the same flight, seated a few rows behind. One of the party – the bride herself, judging by the L-plate pinned to her bottom – loses her balance as she whips a large silver case off the belt and falls backwards, hitting the floor hard. She sits with legs akimbo, crying out for help, but the hens respond only with hoots of laughter.

Aoife refused to wear an L-plate, Dani remembers. She was hardly a learner, she said, given that she'd been living with Nathan for the past two years. But she was happy to go along with Tiff's idea to dress up as Disney characters, and to drink champagne for breakfast in the departure lounge. In her gold ballgown, Aoife had looked stunning as Belle from *Beauty and the Beast*. She and Dani had made an exhibition of themselves on the plane: talking too loudly, dancing in the aisle, flirting with the stewards, cracking dirty jokes. It usually required a lot more alcohol for them to behave like that, but they'd enjoyed playing up to the occasion.

Today's bride-to-be is helped to her feet by a young guy who demands a kiss in payment. She offers her hand, but he tries to snog her instead. The hens shriek with laughter and demand a reconstruction so they can put it on Instagram.

Dani stares at the group for a few moments. There are ten of them, double the number at Aoife's party three years ago. The women are strangers to her, yet she feels a strong

4

connection with them, a desire to warn and protect. She wants to go up and say, 'Have a great time, girls – get hammered, play silly games, do whatever you want – just make sure you all come back alive.' She doesn't, of course. It would sound weird. They wouldn't understand that actions have consequences . . .

Dani's chest tightens. Suddenly, the baggage hall feels suffocating and she moves on, heading for the automatic doors of the exit, beyond which there is no return.

She stands in the centre of the concourse, trying to breathe. It's as if she is the only fixed point and everyone and everything else is rushing around her. Uniformed travel reps parade with clipboards, taxi drivers hold up signs. Husbands, wives, boyfriends, girlfriends, grandparents and small children wave as their loved ones come through. The air is so full of joy, you can almost taste it.

Nobody is here to greet Dani. She's not expecting anyone, but it still makes her feel lonely. It's been *so* difficult coming back here, probably the hardest thing she's ever had to do in her life. She has huge ambitions for this weekend, which the others don't know about yet. Her secrets make her feel lonely and uncertain. She would have loved somebody to have met her with a smile and a warm embrace, to whisper in her ear that she's doing the right thing. Or conversely, to tell her to stop, turn around and get back on the plane. She's been single for over three years and no longer has a best mate – somebody who's always on her side, whose opinion she can trust. Aoife's death left a vacancy, and so far, nobody's come close to filling it.

'*There* you are,' says Celine, striding up to her. 'We've

been looking for you everywhere. Why didn't you wait for us?'

'Sorry. I – er—'

'Are you okay?' asks Beth.

'Yes, fine.'

'Sure? You seem a bit—'

'I'm just tired.'

'Really? It's not like you had an early start,' says Tiff. '*I* had a four-hour train journey to get to Stansted.'

'I sleep badly,' Dani explains. Badly is an understatement. She's forgotten the last time she slept through the night. This past week has been worse than ever, tossing and turning in bed, worrying about whether her plan would work, how the other hens would react when they found out what she was up to, whether she'd be able to cope if they turned against her en masse.

Dani's eyes flicker over her fellow travellers. When they met at the airport five hours ago, suitcases at their side, clutching their passports, they must have looked like a bunch of friends going on holiday together. Nothing could be further from the truth. Tiff and Beth are Aoife's old schoolmates, but before the hen weekend Dani had only met them a couple of times – Aoife's twenty-fifth and a New Year's party at the swanky apartment she shared with Nathan. Celine was Aoife's work colleague, a stranger to the rest of them. It was Aoife's forthcoming marriage that threw them together and, strangely, it's her death that has kept them in touch. They know each other better now, but Dani wouldn't say they've bonded over the tragedy, not in the least. As a group, they remain as loose and dysfunctional as they were on that fateful weekend.

Dani hasn't seen Tiff, Beth or Celine for almost exactly a year, when she'd invited them to meet in a pub in Soho to mark the second anniversary. Beth had travelled up from Kent and Tiff made a special trip from Manchester to join them. They drank wine and ate fancy burgers. Nobody knew whether to be jolly or whether to grieve. In the end, they did neither successfully. Before that, they'd had a similarly awkward reunion on the first anniversary, also organised by Dani.

Tiff sets down her suitcase and unzips the lid. 'Got to get rid of this jacket.' She takes it off, then lays it carefully on top of her clothes, which have been rolled and put into clear plastic bags. Everyone watches as she folds over the sleeves and tucks in the collar, mesmerised by her neatness. 'That's better,' she says, zipping up the case and putting it back on its wheels.

'So, what now? Taxi?' Celine rummages in her bag for her sunglasses.

'I've booked a hire car,' says Dani. 'I'm picking it up from here.'

'Oh, yes, you said . . . I'll come with you.'

Dani turns to Tiff and Beth. She always thinks of them as a pair, although they have very different personalities. Beth is soft and yielding, Tiff is brittle enough to snap. 'Do you want to wait outside? Find a café?'

'I'd rather stay here,' says Beth. 'In the cool.'

'I agree,' says Tiff. 'It'll be boiling out there.' When they left London, it was only fifteen degrees. Now it's thirty-one and rising.

'I'll be as quick as I can.'

Celine sets off with Dani. They take the lift to Level One and join the queue for Hertz. It's the first time the two of them have been alone today and instantly Dani feels nervous. Celine is very perceptive – you can't get much past her. She watches and listens, taking it all in, and when she does talk, she usually speaks her mind.

'This is so weird,' she says. 'You *do* know that, don't you?'

'I don't see what's weird about celebrating someone's life.'

'That's fine. I'm talking about having a hen party without the bride.'

'It's not a party,' Dani snaps. 'We're here to remember Aoife.'

'I still think it's a strange thing to do . . . coming back here . . . it's kind of morbid.'

Dani pretends to search her bag for the car-hire documents.

'I'll never understand why her family didn't have the body repatriated,' Celine continues, off on a new track. 'Maybe she wasn't insured. It's very expensive if you have to pay for it yourself. Apparently.'

'I don't know. Something to do with the investigation, I expect. Does it matter?'

'No. Just that it's awful to think of her lying alone in some foreign cemetery, miles from home, far from the people who love her. If it was my daughter, I'd want her nearby.' Celine pulls out a packet of tissues.

'Her parents usually come over for the anniversary, but her dad's ill so they can't make it this year,' says Dani. 'Nathan's been a couple of times, but he's tied up with work.

8

That's what Tiff said, anyway. She's the only one who keeps in touch with the family. They go way back.' She pauses for emphasis. 'Don't you think it's about time we paid our respects?'

'Yes, but it's completely different for us. We were *there*.' Celine dabs her eyes. 'To be honest, I'm going to find this weekend very difficult.'

'We all will. It's inevitable.'

'So why are we putting ourselves through the agony, all over again? I can't see the point.'

'I'm sorry you feel like that,' says Dani.

Celine sucks in a breath. 'At first, I was like, no way would you get me back to Marbella, not in a million years. Also, it's really hard for me now that I've got Felix. He's only thirteen months old. I felt so guilty leaving him, but I didn't want to let everyone else down.'

'Well, if it helps, I'm glad you decided to come.'

'All for one, and one for all, I guess.' Celine gives her a penetrating look. 'Why *are* we here, Dani? What is it you want from us?'

Dani feels her voice trembling as she fumbles for a convincing answer. 'I don't *want* anything. It's the third anniversary of her death, that's all. I just thought it would be good to mark it in some way. To show that we haven't forgotten her.'

'That's it? Nothing more?'

She shakes her head. 'What else could there be?'

'I don't know, I just feel like you're hiding something.'

'*¿Hola, señoritas?*' The rentals clerk beckons them forward. Spared, Dani steps up to the desk. Her university Spanish comes flooding back. *'Buenos días. Soy Daniela Harrington. Tengo una reserva . . .'*

'All sorted?' enquires Beth as Dani and Celine approach.

'Yeah. Just got to play hunt the car now.' They tow their luggage towards the multi-storey.

'I think it must be that one . . . over there.' Dani drags her case noisily across the tarmac, pressing the fob at a white Seat Ibiza. Beth and Celine follow, but Tiff stops in her tracks.

'Hey! That's the same car!' she calls out. Trust Tiff to remember.

Dani turns around. 'What?'

'The same car. As last time.'

Everyone stops. A shudder passes between them. This is the first time any of them has used that phrase – *last time.*

'Is it?' Dani feigns surprise. 'How do you know it's the same? Do you remember the number plate?'

'Of course not,' Tiff replies tetchily. 'What I mean is, it's the same colour, same make. It's just given me a flashback.'

'Oh. Sorry.'

'Can we change it?'

Dani hesitates. 'I don't know . . . I doubt it.'

'It's just a car, sweetie, it doesn't matter.' Beth gently strokes Tiff's arm. 'Let's get going, eh?'

Tiff shakes her off. 'Celine – what do you think?'

'I know what Tiff means. It makes me feel on edge – like it's déjà vu. To be fair, I've been feeling it ever since we got here.'

'Shall we get a different one, then?' Tiff looks at Dani.

'I can ask, but there might not be another option.'

'It's already hot out there,' adds Beth. 'The sooner we get going . . .'

Tiff huffs. 'Okay, leave it. Whatever.'

Dani takes their cases and stacks them in the boot, like a taxi driver. Celine climbs into the back next to Tiff. Beth goes to squeeze in with them, then thinks better of it and takes the front passenger seat. Dani pretends to be unaware of their manoeuvres, busying herself with the dashboard, checking that she knows where the indicators and wipers are, fiddling with the gear stick until she finds reverse.

'Everyone belted up?' she asks, turning on the engine. They chorus a reply. 'Okay, let's do this.'

Dani would never say, but she specifically asked for a Seat Ibiza – preferably white. Now they are installed, she realises it wouldn't matter what kind of car they were in. Any vehicle would have evoked a memory. Because the last time she drove away from Malaga Airport, there were *three* of them crammed onto the back seat – Tiff in the middle because she's the tiniest, with Celine and Beth on either side. As guest of honour, Aoife had sat in the front. Dani could see her now, resplendent in her golden Belle costume, her bride-to-be sash falling off her shoulder, a red rose tucked behind her ear, sipping duty-free champagne from a bottle secreted in her hand luggage. Everyone had been in such high spirits; eager to make the weekend a success despite the fact that some of them barely knew each other, or that rivalries already existed between certain members of the group. They were setting aside their differences for Aoife's sake. At least, that had been the intention.

Beth reaches forward and turns on the Sat Nav. 'Give me the address of the Airbnb and I'll punch it in.'

'No need.' Dani backs out of the space. 'I've memorised the journey.'

'Really?'

'Yes. I know exactly where I'm going.'

'Impressive,' remarks Tiff from behind.

Dani slowly follows the signs for the exit, preparing her brain for driving on the right-hand side of the road again.

'I'm glad we're staying in the resort this time,' says Beth, leaning back in her seat. 'It's better to be near things like . . .' she tails off.

Hospitals and police stations, thinks Dani. Nobody else comments but she knows Celine and Tiff will be finishing Beth's sentence in the same way. There are bound to be plenty of moments like this over the coming weekend. The ground is strewn with tripwires; it will be impossible to avoid them all.

She follows the signs for the toll road that takes them west. It's a scenic drive, with the sea to their left, lush mountains to their right – golf courses and thousands of apartment blocks scattered in between. They pass turn-offs for Torremolinos, Benalmádena and Fuengirola, climbing and descending, shooting through tunnels carved into the hilly landscape. The driving she can do easily – she worked in Seville for a year, ferrying schoolkids around in a minibus. It's the rest of the weekend she's worried about; how they're going to react when they find out where she's taking them.

Conversation dies away. Nobody seems to want to talk, their thoughts drifting back to the past, or forward perhaps, to the next couple of days. This time there will be no action-packed itinerary of workshops, karaoke, games and going out. Instead, it will be a quiet, reflective weekend, commemorating the life of a young woman who touched all their hearts in different ways. Dani has asked the others to bring a poem or a piece of music that reminds them of Aoife, and to write a speech about her for a candlelit ceremony to be held on the last evening, the closest Sunday to the anniversary of her death.

She drives on, revisiting the exchange she had with Celine in the queue. She *does* want more from this trip, something she can't achieve without all of them being here with her. This is not just about remembering Aoife – it's about bringing the past back to life.

Chapter Two: Now

DANI

It's late afternoon by the time they reach Marbella. Dani leaves the toll road and takes the Autovía del Mediterráneo, bypassing the Golden Mile of exclusive clubs and hotels. Her hands feel sweaty on the steering wheel, partly due to the heat, but mainly down to nerves. This is going to be a tricky manoeuvre; it could be the worst bit of the entire weekend. If the others refuse to go along with her plan, then this will have been a complete waste of time and money – money she doesn't have.

When she'd first proposed this trip, she'd been met by polite resistance. The others claimed to be sympathetic to the idea, but they had availability issues. Tiff had a conference, Beth had earmarked June for a holiday with her mother, Celine wasn't sure she wanted to leave her little boy for a whole weekend. A few weeks of silence went by, and Dani gave up hope. Then, within a day of each other, they each emailed to say they wanted to come.

They must have discussed it together, without her – by phone probably, as it would have been difficult for them to meet up. She wonders who argued for what, which reasons they gave for and against going. Dani had been expecting more debate about the details, but once they agreed to come, they let her arrange everything – flights, car-hire, accommodation – without argument.

Only Celine asked for the actual address of where they were staying – 'in case of emergency'. Dani sent a link to an apartment in San Pedro with communal grounds and a large swimming pool. Everyone seemed happy with her choice and there were no more questions asked.

Dani knows there will be plenty of questions soon.

The turn-off for Istán is coming up. If the others remember their geography, they'll expect her to keep going. San Pedro is an area west of Marbella, beyond Puerto Banús. She slows down and takes the slip-road. As they queue at the round-about, she waits for someone to question her, but nobody seems to realise that she's taking them away from the coast.

It's a winding climb up towards the Country Club – a development of large villas nestled in the foothills of the famous mountain that dominates Marbella, known as La Concha. To their left is Lake Istán, a reservoir set deep in the valley. Today, it looks like a long streak of blue paint, reflecting the brilliant, cloudless sky. The road is in good condition, but narrow. There are rugged red cliffs on one side and sheer drops on the other. Dani keeps to the right-hand side and tries to ignore a truck steaming up behind her.

'I thought San Pedro was on the beach,' remarks Beth after a few minutes. She turns round in her seat. 'Look! The sea's way behind us.'

'We've gone wrong,' says Tiff. 'Dani – you need to turn around.'

'Or just put the Sat Nav on,' Celine mutters. 'God, it's like being in the car with my husband.'

Dani drives on, pretending she hasn't heard them. To their left, dotted among the golf courses, are numerous apartment complexes – brilliant white boxes wedged into the side of the hill. The first time they saw them, Aoife said they looked like the tiers of a wedding cake. *I hope your cake is going to look better than that*, Beth had replied. Or had it been Tiff? She can't remember.

'Dani – say something,' Celine persists. 'This doesn't seem right. Do you know where you're going?'

'Yes. The turning is just a bit further on.' They pass the road for the Country Club and continue driving northwards. Dani lowers the gear as the road winds ever upward, as if they're travelling the wrong way up a helter-skelter. The dramatic landscape is breathtaking. She'd forgotten how remote and beautiful it is around here, how much they aahed and oohed when they first arrived.

'Dani . . .' says Beth, in a low voice. 'Where *is* this place?'

The turning she needs is half a kilometre ahead, just beyond the roadside shrine – a miniature house on stilts, with a plaster statue of the Madonna peering out from behind glass. Dani knows the others will recognise it immediately. Aoife, who had Irish roots and was culturally Catholic, had crossed herself every time they'd driven past.

'There's the shrine!' cries Beth on cue.

Dani says nothing but turns left down an unmarked track.

'Wait a sec! I know this road. It only goes to one place. This is the way to—'

'Villa Floriana,' finishes Celine.

'Stop!' shouts Tiff. 'Dani! Stop the car right now!'

She pulls over onto the thin strip of verge and cuts the engine. The car is close to the edge, with only a low barrier protecting them from a steep, wooded drop. This is the moment she's been dreading for weeks. She can feel her heart pounding.

'What's going on?' Celine demands.

'Just because you're driving, it doesn't mean you're in charge,' says Tiff crossly. 'We're not kids.'

'Too right,' adds Celine. 'You could at least have asked us if we wanted to see the place.'

'Well, I *don't* want to see it,' says Beth. 'I don't want to go there ever again. Can we just turn round and find the Airbnb, please?'

Dani drops the bomb she's been carrying around ever since they landed at the airport. 'There is no Airbnb,' she says. 'It was booked up. Everywhere was booked up.'

'That's a lie,' says Celine. 'I bet I could go online and find something in two minutes.' She huffs. 'I *knew* you were hiding something.'

'Hold on ... Are you telling us,' Tiff says slowly, 'that you have actually booked Villa Floriana?'

Dani nods. 'Yes. It was the only place that was available.'

'Bullshit,' declares Celine.

'I'm not kidding, it was.'

Tiff pokes her head between the front seats. 'So, you thought you'd book it without checking with us first? How could you possibly assume we'd all be happy to go back to the place where Aoife died – where we spent the worst night of our entire lives?'

'I'm sorry! But it was the only place around here that could take all of us. Maybe it was meant to be—'

'Meant to be? Have you lost your mind?!'

'Oh, Dani,' whispers Beth. 'Why didn't you ask us first?'

'Because we would have said no,' Celine says. 'She tricked us, that's the worst part.'

'You're right,' says Tiff. 'We can't stay here. I'm calling a taxi. Maybe there's an evening flight . . . Beth? You coming?' She tries to open the passenger door, but the child lock is on. 'Dani! Unlock this! Now.'

Dani presses the release button and Tiff and Celine get out, slamming their doors behind them. They wave their phones around in search of a signal. But to Dani's surprise, Beth stays in the car.

'We can't go back to the villa,' she says after a beat of silence. 'It's impossible.'

Dani rests her head on the steering wheel and starts to cry. 'I know it was wrong to trick you, but I *have* to go back there. It's my only hope.'

'What do you mean?'

'I know everyone was traumatised by what happened, but the three of you have come to terms with it somehow. You've all managed to move on with your lives.'

'Don't think for one second that it's been easy.'

'No, I get that, but you've all come through it, you're doing really well. Beth, you've qualified as a solicitor. Tiff's just bought a flat. Celine's got married and had a baby. I've done nothing. I'm stuck.'

There's a pause. 'People deal with grief in different ways,' Beth says carefully. 'Maybe we've been luckier, had more support. Celine has had her husband to lean on, and Tiff's been very involved with Aoife's family. My parents have been great, but mainly I've just buried myself in my work.'

Beth is right, Dani knows. She's been on her own these last years. Friends and family have tried to help, but they haven't been able to understand the loss she still feels, every single day. The emptiness. The pain. The guilt. She's done her best to put on a brave face. The others know she's suffered from depression, but not how badly.

Dani lifts her head. 'It's been tough,' she says. 'At one point in the year after Aoife died, I was drinking two bottles of wine a day. I lost my job. Now I'm turning things around. I've been dry for over five months, but I'm still walking a tight-rope. I can't go on like this. I need to start moving forward. And I've realised that the only way I can do it is by going back. To the villa. I have to find out what really happened that night.'

'But you already know what—'

'No, I don't. I only know what I've been told.'

Beth looks hurt. 'Are you saying, you don't believe us?'

'Not at all. But I still have so many questions, so many doubts.' Beth has no idea how hard it's been. Her sleepless nights are peppered with tormenting thoughts – if only she'd done this, if only she hadn't done that. 'What I'm saying is, I need to remember *for myself*.'

'But how can you remember something you didn't witness?' A flash of pain passes across Beth's face.

'I think . . . maybe he tried to attack me too . . . I have this nightmare I can't explain, I think it's a memory, but I can't be

19

sure. I think he went for me first ... but it's confusing ... doesn't make sense. There are gaps in that evening, big gaps I can't fill. Like, how did I hurt my knee so badly?' Dani grabs Beth's arm and looks directly into her eyes. 'And the blood on my dress. Aoife's blood! How did it get there?'

'It was transferred from one of us when we tried to wake you,' says Beth patiently. 'We've been through this a thousand times.'

'I'm sure there's something else ... Something I've forgotten. It could be the missing piece in the puzzle. Stay at the villa with me. Please! Help me put the picture together.'

'I can't see how it's going to help you, or any of us, to be honest. It could make things worse.'

'Talk to the others. Persuade them. Tiff will listen to you.'

'I can tell you now, she won't want to do it. I can't see Celine going along with it either.' They look through the car window to where the two women are pacing about, throwing up their arms in frustration at the lack of signal.

'Explain how much I need it,' tries Dani, desperation in her voice now.

'Look, we all want to help you, but we came here to honour Aoife, not to get sucked into the past. Being in Marbella is difficult enough, but staying in Villa Floriana? That's too big an ask.'

'All I need is for the rest of you to be there with me. We'll do everything as planned. We'll spend our time thinking about Aoife and how much we loved her. We'll visit the cemetery and put flowers on her grave. On Sunday we'll have the ceremony in the very place where she died. Then we'll go our separate ways and you'll never hear from me again, if that's what you want. No more reunions, nothing.' Dani looks at her imploringly. 'Just give me this one chance. Maybe it can be healing for *all* of us.'

Beth thinks for a few seconds, weighing it all up. 'Okay, okay . . . I'll talk to them,' she says, 'I'll try to explain.' She opens the passenger door. 'But no promises.'

Chapter Three: Then

TIFF

When anyone asked how long Aoife and I had known each other, we always said 'since we were in the womb'. It was true in a way. Our mothers were in the same NCT group and became close friends while they were pregnant. We were born in the same hospital, two days apart, spent our first months lying on the same playmat or being pushed around the same park. All my earliest memories included Aoife. We lived around the corner from each other, went to the same baby and toddler group, the same infant, primary and secondary schools. In the holidays, one of our mums would take time off work to look after the children. Then they'd swap over. Either my brothers and I were around Aoife's house, or she was around mine.

It wasn't until we got to secondary school that things began to shift. We were put in different forms and no longer had lessons together. Inevitably, we branched out and made other friends, although we were always firm besties. I met Beth and we got on really well. Aoife liked her too and our duo became a trio.

As we grew up, I realised that Aoife and I had very different, almost clashing personalities. She wasn't very interested in schoolwork, whereas I was a swot. She was chaotic, always forgetting her sports stuff or losing textbooks (sometimes deliberately), while I was the most organised student in the school. Aoife could be cheeky in class and often got told off for talking. I hated getting into trouble and went through my entire school career without a single detention.

At a parents' evening, my teacher remarked to my mum that she thought Aoife a surprising choice of friend for her daughter, not understanding that there'd never been a choice. In that respect, we were like family. Sisters. I loved Aoife because of who she was, and despite who she was too. Even when we went our separate ways at eighteen, choosing different universities hundreds of miles apart, it never occurred to me that she might find a more compatible, less surprising friend.

Aoife, Beth and I met up over the first Christmas break to exchange uni experiences. I'd had quite a tough term, feeling homesick and lonely, but Aoife claimed she'd had a blast. Every story she told me was full of this Dani person, who was 'wicked' and 'a rebel' and 'such a laugh' – my opposite, basically. I was immediately consumed by jealousy. I decided I didn't want to meet her. Ever.

For the next three years, whenever Aoife invited me to Birmingham, I made excuses, saying I couldn't afford the train fare or had too much work on my plate. After university, I got a place on a graduate training scheme with a large management consultancy and was sent to Manchester. Dani and Aoife went down to London together and flat-shared. It became increasingly hard to avoid Dani, and we ended up meeting at one of Aoife's birthdays. She was friendly towards me, but I could tell it was an act. We took an instant dislike to each other.

Usually, I'd suggest meeting up with Aoife in Hastings, our hometown, combining it with seeing our mothers who were still very close. Sometimes, Beth would come over from Kent, where she'd stayed after uni, and the three of us would go for long walks along the seafront. We'd talk about old times, particularly the teenage years.

I was so happy for Aoife when she told me that she'd met Nathan – 'the love of her life' as she called him. She'd had rather a chequered career with men up to that point which was something I put down to Dani's malign influence. And so I was delighted to hear that Aoife had moved out of her flat-share with Dani and in with Nathan. I invited them up to Manchester for the weekend and we got along really well. Nathan was my kind of person – hardworking, ambitious, full of energy and drive. He really cared about Aoife too. 'I'm "growing her up",' he told me. 'I've got massive plans for her future.' I also discovered that he didn't like Dani, so we instantly bonded on that score.

Over the next two years, I sensed that Aoife was growing apart from Dani and gradually coming back to me. I went to stay at Nathan and Aoife's lush apartment a few times and they visited me again in Manchester. When Aoife took Nathan home for Christmas, I made sure I was around. Beth would join us if she could, and Nathan would take us all out to dinner in Hastings's classiest restaurant. Dani, of course, was nowhere to be seen. Aoife still saw her, apparently, but they were no longer as thick as thieves.

When Nathan asked Aoife to marry him, I thought she was the luckiest girl in the world. A small, ungracious part of me felt she didn't deserve it, given how she'd wasted her twenties before she met him. I'd worked so hard and tried to make the best of myself, yet I was staring thirty in the face and was still single. Where was my knight in shining armour, come to sweep me off my feet? Maybe I'd meet him at Aoife's wedding, I thought. Surely Nathan would have some suitable mates . . .

If you'd asked me five years ago who Aoife would have picked as her Chief Bridesmaid, I would have said Dani straightaway, no question. But the balance of power had shifted, and she'd chosen me. It felt like the ultimate victory. I danced around my lonely sitting room, whooping and cheering. Later, I rang Beth to tell her.

'You do know that means you'll have to organise the hen party?' she said.

'Yes, no problem. I'm super good at organisation. That's my job.'

'You'll have to invite Dani,' she added.

'Yes, yes, I know,' I sighed. 'Let's hope she can't make it.'

'Come on, nothing will stop her, Tiff. Dani loves Aoife *and* she loves a party. If the stories are true about what they got up to at—'

'Aoife's changed,' I said. 'She's calmed down a lot since she's been with Nathan.'

'But once she's with Dani again—'

'I'll be in charge, so it'll be fine,' I assured her.

Aoife sent me a list of about twelve women she wanted to invite, and sure enough, Dani's name was right at the top. I went down the democratic route and asked everyone for ideas about where to go and where to stay. Naturally, I received lots of suggestions, so off I went, researching remote castles in Scotland, bargain breaks in Blackpool, holiday barns in the West Country . . .

Choosing the right destination was crucial. It was supposed to be a surprise for the bride-to-be yet also needed to be somewhere she'd definitely want to go. I wasn't sure of Aoife's tastes anymore. Before she met Nathan, she was a nature-loving hippy, who liked swimming in lakes and camping under the stars. Now, she was more inclined towards spa breaks in boutique hotels.

Then Nathan got in touch. He said he was coming to Manchester on business and wanted to see me in secret. Aoife had been dropping hints about where she'd like to go, and he needed to fill me in so that we could give her what he called 'the most amazing hen party ever'. It was so sweet of him.

I invited him to my flat for dinner. I was saving hard for a deposit to buy somewhere, but I pushed the boat out, buying two 21-day dry-aged steaks and a bottle of claret that I knew would impress him. Nathan was as charming as ever. He praised my cooking to the skies and asked me lots of questions about myself and my ambitions for the future. How did I like living in Manchester? Was there a special someone in my life? I told him there wasn't.

He opened another bottle of wine, an even more expensive one that he'd brought. 'I can't believe somebody hasn't snapped you up already, Tiffany,' he said.

'Tell me about Aoife's ideas for the hen party,' I replied, blushing.

He smiled. 'She desperately wants to go to Marbella. She's seen this place on the internet – Villa Floriana. It's in the mountains, just outside the resort.' He brought the website up on his phone and showed me the pictures. I could see why she'd fallen in love with the place.

'It looks amazing, but it only sleeps six,' I said. 'There are twelve hens. Where are the rest of them supposed to stay?'

'I don't know, they can find somewhere, surely. To be honest, twelve sounds like a big group. If I were you, I'd ditch the hangers-on and make it an intimate, luxury experience for best friends only.'

'How? We've already got a WhatsApp group, everyone's involved. Aoife's cousins, a couple of other friends from home, some London people, her uni crowd ... it's a very mixed bag. I've never even met some of them.'

'Say this is what Aoife wants, whack up the price tag and tell them places at the villa are on a first-come-first-served basis.'

'But *nobody* will be able to afford these prices,' I said, looking at the rental fees.

'Don't worry about that. If there's a problem, I'll chip in.' He rested his finger on his lips. 'Just don't let on to Aoife, okay? It's our secret. She's always telling me off for spoiling her, but I can't help it.'

'Well, that's very generous of you,' I said.

'Anything for her.' We raised our glasses and made a toast to Aoife. For a moment I wished it were me marrying Nathan and Aoife organising *my* hen party. He and I seemed so suited, so at ease in each other's company. We finished the second bottle of wine and carried on talking into the night.

Following Nathan's instructions, I announced the new arrangements to the WhatsApp group. Unsurprisingly, several of Aoife's friends objected to having to compete for places at the villa while others said they couldn't afford a luxury weekend in Marbella anyway and pulled out. By January, we were down to only three of us – me, Beth and Dani. I'd been hoping that Dani would drop out for financial reasons as I knew she didn't have a permanent job, but she was the first to sign up. I should have realised she wasn't going to miss a weekend of boozing and dragging Aoife off the rails.

The luxury weekend idea had backfired. I'd gone from having too many hens to not having enough. I knew Aoife would be upset when she discovered that so few people were coming, and I was worried that I'd get the blame. I asked Nathan what I should do. Bless him, he conjured somebody called Celine out of nowhere, but that still only made five of us, including Aoife.

It was incredibly stressful and took several evenings on the internet, but eventually I managed to organise a weekend that I hoped would be perfect for Aoife. We were booked into the area's most popular beach club for the Saturday afternoon and the hottest nightclub in the evening. I'd also scheduled some downtime for us to enjoy the delights of Villa Floriana itself as well as organising catering, bunting and sashes, party poppers and balloons. I'd put together a great playlist and made up a first-aid kit for any accidents. I even had a naughty surprise up my sleeve for Sunday afternoon. It was definitely going to be 'the most amazing hen do ever'.

Chapter Four: Now

DANI

Dani drives along the track. It's stonier and more overgrown than she remembers it. Nobody is daring to speak, but she can sense Tiff fuming, scarcely containing herself. She glances into the rear mirror and sees Celine staring into her lap, still trying to find a signal on her phone probably. It's the only reason she agreed to get back in the car: so that she can tap into the villa's Wi-Fi and order a taxi to take her to the airport.

It took intense, and at times tearful, debate for Tiff to agree to stay over, but she committed to one night. Dani knows that won't be long enough to recapture the past, but she has accepted the compromise for now. Beth bravely negotiated the whole thing under the glare of the afternoon sun, while Dani remained in the car – biting her nails down to the quick, hardly daring to breathe. When Beth climbed back in and told her the deal, Dani threw her arms around her neck and sobbed with gratitude.

'You have no idea what this means to me,' she said.

'It's going to be tough,' Beth replied, 'but if it helps you . . . hopefully it'll be worth it.'

They swing around the bend by the olive grove and the orchard, the only remnants of the small farm that used to be on the site. As they pass, unease flickers in Dani's stomach – a reaction she can't quite understand.

There's the villa, its walls whitewashed in the local style, with a pitched tiled roof and a terrace shaded by a canopy of woven rushes that runs the width of the house. Small rectangular windows, covered with wrought-iron grilles, peep out like eyes. The front door is painted brown to match the terracotta tiles. Nothing has changed, apart from the bougainvillaea which has spread further up the wall.

Dani pulls up in the courtyard outside the garage, parking in the same place as before. She switches off the engine and gets out. The others remain inside the sweltering car, unable, or perhaps unwilling, to move.

Glad to have these first moments to herself, she walks around the side of the villa to the back, where there is a lawn and a swimming pool surrounded by a terrace. The same bleached sunbeds are strewn about, and the water looks as blue and inviting as ever. Beyond the pool, rough ground tumbles down a hillside strewn with boulders. To the left, but out of sight, is the olive grove. There are no other villas nearby. The only buildings visible from here are far away, tiny white dots on the other side of the valley.

At the far end of the garden is the small, raised patio with railings on three sides, built to act as a mirador or lookout point, with incredible views every way you turn – the sparkling sea, the stunning lake, the lush dark Sierra. It is where she was interviewed by Inspector Mengual the morning after. The villa itself was a crime scene, swarming with people in white paper suits.

She can see the past superimposed on the neat and tidy

garden. Empty bottles and used wine glasses were scattered across the terrace. The candles they'd placed along the path and in the bushes were all spent. A pink sash, with the slogan 'Bestie of the Bride', was slung over the back of a chair. Several of the balloons they'd hung from the canopy had popped in the heat, apart from one that had escaped and floated idly in the swimming pool. Their dirty plates were littered about; discarded prawn shells and scraps of uneaten paella attracting busy flies.

Inspector Mengual sat her down at the mosaic table in the blazing sunshine, with not even a glass of water to drink. It had felt like torture.

'Tell me what happened,' he said.

'I don't know, I can't remember,' she replied. 'I'm really sorry, but it's all a blank.'

He gave her a curious look. 'Your friends say they were in the garden, celebrating, dancing to music. It was very loud, yes?'

She shrugged. 'Probably.' Tiff had put together the Ultimate Hen Party Playlist – 'Girls Just Want to Have Fun', 'I Will Survive', 'Going to the Chapel', 'Single Ladies'. She remembered dancing to it at some point over the weekend, Tiff belting out Beyoncé lyrics like they were a personal message for her. But they were inside then, weren't they? And that was Friday night, or maybe early evening on Saturday before they went out. Both, perhaps. The weekend had become one long blur.

'You'd gone for a walk,' Mengual continued. 'When you came back, you were hurt. How did that happen?'

'I've no idea.' She stretched out one leg. There was a

31

nasty gash on her knee. A lot of skin had been scraped off, leaving a raw, bloody cut. It was still stinging like mad.

'Aoife took you inside to help clean it up. Is that correct?'

'If that's what the others say happened, yes.'

'Aoife disturbed the intruder . . . Did you see him?'

She closed her eyes, screwing them up in concentration. 'Possibly. I think he might have attacked me too. I have this very vague memory, or feeling, of being pinned up against a wall, something like that. But I'm not sure where or when that happened.' She opened her eyes again. 'Or even *if*.'

'Either it did or it didn't,' the inspector said solemnly. He waited for her to respond, looking up from his notebook when she did not. His face was lined but he had beautiful dark eyes. 'Why are you telling me you don't remember anything?'

'Because it's the truth. I'd passed out.' He looked confused. 'You understand?' Dani tried to summon up the Spanish word for 'unconscious'. She knew it was similar, but her brain was in no mood for translating. Inspector Mengual probably understood anyway – you couldn't work on the Costa del Sol and not speak good English.

'Why? Did this intruder hit you, perhaps? Did he knock you out?'

'No, no . . . I'd had, you know . . . too much to drink.'

'You were in the same room and yet you saw nothing, heard nothing?'

'Not that I can remember, no.'

'To remember nothing at all – that's very bad,' he said. 'Too much alcohol. Not good for the health.'

32

'Yes, I know. We went too far, but it was a special occasion. Aoife's getting – *was* getting – married.' She'd suddenly thought about Nathan – how devastated he would be. She thought about all the wedding preparations and how they would have to inform the guests. Had anyone spoken to Aoife's parents yet?

While Mengual made some notes, Dani looked over to her fellow hens who were standing under some lemon trees in a thin patch of shade. They'd been up all night and had already been interviewed. Dani was still wearing the beach dress she'd worn the previous day. She couldn't understand why she hadn't changed into the floaty minidress she'd brought specially for Sunday night. The others had taken off their blood-stained clothes and given them to the forensic team. They were dressed for going home now: jeans and pale T-shirts, trainers instead of heels. Flights were booked for this afternoon, but they'd already been told they wouldn't be leaving today.

Tiff and Beth held onto each other, their mouths permanently half-open but saying nothing. Celine stood apart from the group. She looked more composed. Her stare zeroed in on Dani across the rectangle of turquoise water. Even from a distance, it felt accusatory, although she couldn't work out why. Their eyes met for a moment, then Dani looked away.

'So, miss, please tell me,' Mengual said, picking up his pen again. 'When did you wake from this "sleep"?'

'Not until it was all over. The emergency services were very late in arriving, they went to the wrong place apparently. I think they'd been here a while before I came round. I remember Beth coming up to me . . .'

'What did she say?'

'Um . . . that Aoife was dead.'

Mengual leaned forward. 'What else? I need to know precisely. Every word.'

She tried to remember. 'Just that she must have disturbed an intruder. He'd attacked Aoife, there'd been a fight and he'd thrown her onto the glass coffee table. The others tried to save her but . . .' The sunlight was frying her brain. Suddenly she felt dizzy and lurched to one side. 'Sorry. I was only half-conscious – couldn't take it all in.'

'Did they see this intruder?'

'No.'

The inspector looked across the garden to the other hens. 'Tell me. Was it a good party?'

'Um . . . yes, it was great. Brilliant.' She'd hesitated before answering and he'd sniffed out the lie.

'Are you sure? There were no problems? No arguments between you?'

'No . . . not really. The weekend was pretty intense, you know. There was the odd spat, but nothing serious.' She felt herself blushing and covered her face, pretending to shield her eyes from the searing light of the sun.

'What were these "spats" about? Who was arguing? Was Aoife involved?'

'Honestly, it was nothing, just the normal stuff you get when people are tired or have had too much to drink.'

She couldn't tell him the truth. She and her fellow hens had already agreed that there was no need to tell the police about some of the things that had happened over the course of the weekend. They were irrelevant to the investigation and would only upset Nathan and Aoife's family if they found out.

The inspector was looking at her, trying to read her thoughts. 'Do you have any idea who did this?' she said, in an effort to distract him.

He considered his reply. 'There is violent crime in Marbella, but most of it is between gangs, not involving tourists. And there are also break-ins at hotels and villas – for passports, credit cards, phones, jewellery. I'm sorry to say this is normal in the big holiday resorts. And yet nothing was taken last night.'

'Perhaps Aoife disturbed them before they had a chance.'

'That's possible, yes.' Mengual paused to look around. 'I think maybe they chose this place because it's so remote. There are no neighbours. No security. Also, you were young women, on your own. You were an easy target. Hmm . . . Even so, there's something unusual about this case. There is evidence of a fight. That doesn't feel like a burglary to me. It feels . . . how can I say? More personal.'

'Are you saying the others are lying about what happened?' she whispered, stealing a glance across the terrace.

'No.' He gave her a tight smile. 'But I think this case is complicated. There is much to investigate.'

'I'll do everything I can to help you find Aoife's killer,' she said. 'I was right there – I must have seen something. I've been wracking my brains, but my mind is a complete blank.'

'Now you are in shock,' Inspector Mengual replied. 'Soon, I think, when you are well, your memories will come back.'

But the detective was wrong. Over the years, she has tried to retrieve them – with counselling and CBT, even hypnotherapy – but they have always eluded her. That's why she's here; why she needs the other hens with her. She has to relive that weekend and make the memories come back.

Dani returns to the courtyard. Beth, Tiff and Celine have got out of the car and are waiting for her. She walks towards the front door. This is where the remembering begins, she thinks. That Friday afternoon, when they first arrived.

Chapter Five: Then

DANI

They wheeled their cases across the courtyard, approaching a tall woman with long black hair. She stood at the open door wearing green dungarees and a white vest. Her hands were clasped together excitedly, and her smile flashed in the sunshine.

'Welcome to Villa Floriana! I'm Marta, the owner. I'm so happy that you're here.'

Aoife stepped forward. 'So are we! Hi.'

'You are the bride, yes?' Marta pointed at her sash. 'Congratulations.'

'Aw, thanks. Yes, I'm Aoife. And these are my lovely hens.'

'*Encantada, mucho gusto*,' Dani said, when it was her turn to air-kiss Marta. '*Qué casa tan bonita*. This is an amazing place.'

'*Gracias*, I love it very much. It was my grandparents' farm. I've known it since I was a child.' Their hostess paused, looking wistful for a moment, before brightening. 'You had a good journey? You didn't get lost, I hope.'

Aoife touched Dani's arm. 'No, our chauffeur here did a brilliant job.'

'Yeah, I always drive better when I'm pissed . . . Joking!' Dani added, catching Marta's alarmed expression. 'Honestly, I'm okay. Only one glass of champagne since breakfast.'

Marta called into the house. 'John! Where are you? Our guests are here!' She turned back to us. 'My husband is British, so for more information, you ask him please. My English is not so good.'

'It sounds perfect to me,' said Tiff.

'A hundred times better than my Spanish,' agreed Beth.

Aoife nudged Dani. 'Dani's practically fluent.'

'No, I'm not! I studied it at uni and lived in Spain for a while, but I haven't spoken it properly for years.'

Marta smiled. 'John's Spanish is very bad, but it doesn't matter. Living here you don't need it.'

At that moment, her husband stepped through the door. He was equally tall and slim, deeply tanned with light brown hair and a beard that was sun-bleached at its tips. He wore a loose T-shirt, baggy khaki shorts and black flip-flops. Attractive if you liked the beach-bum look, Dani thought. She guessed he and Marta were in their mid to late thirties, a few years older than her.

'Hi,' said John. 'How's it going? You're on a hen party, right?'

'No, we always dress up as Disney characters,' said Dani, cheekily swishing the fishtail of her Little Mermaid skirt.

He grinned. 'Well, you've come to the right place. Marbs is the number one spot for hens and stags across the whole of Spain.'

'That's why we chose it,' said Tiff – a little snippily, Dani thought.

'The guy booked for your cocktail workshop is a mate of mine. Matt. He's great, all the girls fight over him.'

'Ooh, that'll be fun,' said Dani. 'Sharpen your claws, girls!'

Marta's face tightened. 'I'll show you around the villa – explain you everything. Please?' She led the way inside, and they trooped after her.

'What I really want right now is a swim,' whispered Aoife. 'I can't wait to get out of this ridiculous dress.'

'Same here,' said Beth, whose Cinderella costume was a puffy parcel of blue net and satin. Tiff had made a cooler choice with a miniskirted version of Snow White. Celine was dressed as Minnie Mouse – black T-shirt, red and white spotty skirt, black pumps, and round ears on a headband. Dani thought they looked like giant kids at a fancy-dress party.

Marta waved in the direction of the kitchen. 'If you want to cook, there's everything you need. Also, homemade lemonade in the fridge and fruits. Coffee, tea, many infusions. Tomorrow, if you like, I can come early with croissants and *jamón*, and make you fresh orange juice.'

'What do you think, girls?' asked Aoife.

'That sounds nice,' said Dani, 'as long as we don't have to get up at the crack of dawn.'

'Is there, like, a village nearby with a café?' asked Beth. 'I'm thinking eggs and bacon.'

'But we're in Spain,' Dani murmured under her breath, unable to hide her irritation. She'd only met Beth a couple of times before and had found her pleasant enough – friendlier towards her than Tiff had been, for sure – but it was becoming clear that they didn't share the same outlook on life. Beth seemed incredibly English, while Dani and Aoife regarded themselves – humorously – as 'children of the universe'. They'd done a lot of travelling together in their early twenties and had always sought out the most authentic experiences possible, breakfasts included.

'There is no village, but there's a roadside restaurant about eight minutes' drive away,' replied Marta. 'It's called Venta El Lago. There are beautiful views of the lake. The food is very typical. I'm not sure they will do your English breakfast, but I can show you on the map.'

Tiff intercepted, using her Chief Bridesmaid voice. 'All sounds lovely but we've got a packed schedule for tomorrow, so we won't have time to go out for breakfast. I actually already ordered the fresh croissants, remember? The Spanish ham sounds great. And some fruit and yoghurts, please, Martha.'

'Yes, of course.' Marta reddened. 'Sorry. Excuse me.'

'It's *Marta*,' murmured Dani as they moved on, unable to resist correcting Tiff's pronunciation. 'No h.' Tiff pretended she hadn't heard.

'This is where you relax,' Marta continued, gesturing towards two squashy sofas and an armchair arranged around a large glass coffee table. 'There is Wi-Fi of course, and the television has Netflix.'

'Great,' said Tiff, 'but we're not planning to stay indoors and watch films.'

'We're here for the beach,' said Beth. 'And the bars and the clubs.'

Aoife giggled. 'And the stags!'

'Definitely the stags,' Dani chimed in. 'I'm single so there'll be nothing stopping me. Obviously, our bride-to-be is out of the running, and Celine's attached.'

'That's not how I'd put it, but I have a partner, yes,' said

Celine. She'd chatted to Dani about her fiancé Farrell in the plane on the way over. They were planning to marry the following year, although their wedding would be far more modest than Aoife's.

Beth and Tiff weren't saying anything. That probably meant they were single too, thought Dani, reminding herself to check later with Aoife. She would give her the full lowdown. It was odd to be spending the weekend with people she knew virtually nothing about, other than third-hand snippets of information. She wondered briefly what Aoife had told the others about her, hoping she hadn't spilled too many secrets.

At the other end of the living area was an open staircase. Marta led them up to the master suite with its own shower room.

'For the bride, I think,' she said.

It was a lovely cool space – exposed beams, pale walls, polished floorboards, painted furniture, and simple white linen on the super-king-size bed. The room looked onto the courtyard at the front of the villa. No doubt, there were fabulous views of La Concha behind the closed shutters.

'It's enormous! I can't sleep here all on my own, Dani Girl,' said Aoife. Dani's nickname was an adaptation of 'Danny Boy', the Irish song Aoife's dad used to sing to her as a child. 'Will you share with me?'

'Sure,' Dani replied quickly. She'd been secretly worrying about the sleeping arrangements. 'It'll be like old times. Remember that trip to Greece – at the end of our second year? We shared a bed for three weeks.'

'Apart from when you were with the guy who ran the water-skiing,' Aoife reminded her.

41

'I only got with him because you'd abandoned me for that German guy!' They guffawed, and Dani noticed Tiff tensing her jaw.

'Tiff and I can take one of the twin rooms downstairs,' said Beth, stepping in. 'That means lucky Celine can have the third bedroom all to herself.'

'If that's okay?' she said.

'¡Perfecto!' Marta smiled. 'Let's go outside.'

They went back downstairs. Marta showed them the swimming pool and where the fresh towels were kept. Then they walked back around the side of the villa and looked at the small orchard – 'My grandmother used to make wonderful jam from the special Lunero lemons,' she explained. Lastly, she took them back along the track to the olive grove, leading them downhill through the old, gnarled trees to the bottom where the views were even more stunning than they were from the garden. There was a firepit there, roughly built from rocks and stones.

'I'm sorry, but we're not allowed fires in the summer months,' said Marta. 'It's the law.'

'Don't worry,' Beth assured her. 'We won't set the forest alight.'

When they returned, John was waiting for them in the courtyard, holding what looked like a bunch of tickets. 'I forgot to give you these,' he said.

'Thanks.' Tiff took them all. 'What are they?'

'Free drinks vouchers. For my bar.'

Beth looked impressed. 'You own a bar as well as a villa?'

'I wish,' he laughed. 'No, I just lease it off the owner. Me and Marta live in the flat upstairs. The bar is in Puerto Banús.

It's called Supernova – on the second line, behind the sea-front. Everyone knows it. Best karaoke bar in the whole of Marbs. Open from nine p.m. – check it out. You can have two free shots, a glass of wine or a beer. All you have to do is leave me a five-star review on Tripadvisor, okay?'

'Sounds like bribery and corruption to me,' said Beth.

'She's a solicitor,' explained Tiff.

'Solicitor *in training*.'

'I don't mind being bribed and corrupted,' quipped Dani.

Aoife laughed. 'Nor do I. Thanks so much. We'll definitely come down, maybe this evening.'

'We've got other plans for this evening,' said Tiff, 'but maybe tomorrow, if we can fit it in.'

'Whenever. I'll be there.' He studied each of them in turn, his gaze finally landing on Aoife. 'Anyway, have a great hen do, girls. Have fun with Matt, he really knows his stuff, but I warn you, his cocktails are fierce.'

Marta sent her husband a warning look. 'We must leave our guests to settle in.'

'Sorry, yeah, gotta go. See you tomorrow evening!' He turned and flip-flopped his way to the car.

'Hmm . . . he's buff,' Aoife commented once the couple had driven away.

'And married,' Beth reminded her sharply.

'Wouldn't bother me,' said Dani, although that wasn't true. She'd tried dating married men before and it had always ended in disaster.

Aoife laughed. 'Stop frowning, Beth. We're here to have a good time. What happens in Marbs, stays in Marbs, remember?'

Chapter Six: Now

DANI

Aoife's laughter still echoes in Dani's ears as she punches the code into the key safe by the front door. She retrieves a set of keys. Last time, Marta and John had been here to welcome them, but today not even the agent has turned up. When she went to book the villa, she found it on a large holiday website, described as 'converted from a traditional *finca*, now boasting luxurious modern amenities'. There was no mention of the couple who had lovingly carried out the renovation. Maybe they no longer own it, she thinks. Not that she'd blame them for selling up and putting the tragedy behind them.

The others hover behind her, holding their breath. Dani senses their anxiety about what lies behind the front door. When they'd left the villa the last time, pieces of broken furniture were strewn about and the floor was covered with shards of shattered glass. Aoife's blood was everywhere – spatters on the walls, stains on the floorboards, even footprints on the rug. In Dani's imagination, the mess has never been cleared up, the blood never washed away. It's as if time stopped three years ago and they're about to enter a crime scene, swarming with police and forensics.

'Are we ready?' Dani asks.

'As we'll ever be,' from Tiff.

Celine sighs irritably. 'Just do it.'

Dani turns the key in the lock and slowly pushes the door open. Instantly, a burglar alarm goes off and they leap back in surprise.

'Shit!'

'That's new,' says Beth.

'Sorry, they did mention it, but I forgot.' Dani starts scrolling frantically through her emails while the bleeps louden and accelerate. 'Can someone find out where the unit is while I look for the passcode?'

Their reluctance to enter is overridden by the need to stop the deafening noise. Beth charges in and looks around. 'It's in here,' she calls from the space under the stairs. 'What's the code?'

'Er . . . hang on . . . er . . . got it! One-two-four-nine.'

Beth enters the digits, and the bleeping stops. 'It's okay, you can come in now. All safe.'

Dani steps over the threshold. As her feet hit the flag-stones, an electrical charge shoots through her body, all the way to her fingertips. Her head is singing, her hands tingling. Feeling off balance, she leans against the wall and tries to calm her breathing. What's this about? She has never felt such a psychophysical response to anything before. Maybe it was a power surge of emotional energy, making her system temporarily cut out.

She turns around, expecting to see Tiff and Celine similarly affected, but they are just standing there, taking in the surroundings, letting the past sink in.

'You okay, Dani?' asks Beth, coming towards her. 'You look like you're in shock.'

'Yes, I think I am a bit.' She rubs her hands to get the sensation back in her fingers. 'I feel really peculiar.'

'It's all flooding back, isn't it?'

She nods. 'I was dreading this moment. I knew it would be the most difficult part.'

'I'm sorry,' Tiff blurts out, 'but I'm not sure I can do this.'

Beth puts a protective arm around her. 'It's okay,' she says softly. 'There's nothing to be scared of. Just stick with me.'

Dani pushes herself away from the wall. The numbness and tingling fade, her hands slowly coming back to life. She gazes around.

The place looks clean and fresh. Most of the furniture is the same – a dining table with six unmatching chairs, a bookcase stuffed with paperbacks, a heavy sideboard in dark wood, a small television on a stand, brightly coloured cushions on a bench seat leaning against the whitewashed walls. But there are framed prints and ornaments she doesn't recognise; replacements, no doubt, for the things that were smashed. The Buddha statue is still in its usual place, though – unscarred by the attack – sitting contemplatively in the alcove under the stairs.

'Not much has changed,' says Beth. 'Except for over here.' She walks to the seating area. 'New sofas. New rug. New coffee table – obviously. The walls have been repainted. You wouldn't know . . .'

Celine tries to access the Wi-Fi on her phone. 'This doesn't seem to be working,' she says. 'Can anyone else connect?' Glad of the distraction, they spend the next few minutes examining the router, entering and re-entering passcodes, switching their phones off, then on again. Nobody can get online, and there's no mobile signal at all.

'I'll see if the agency has given us a different passcode,' says Dani, returning to the emails. 'Hm . . . no. It just says there's free Wi-Fi, that's all.'

Celine groans. 'We have to go and find somewhere with internet.'

'I'd rather not do that right now,' Dani says. 'I need a rest and we've got to sort out rooms—'

'I told you, I'm not staying.' Celine folds her arms. 'You can't keep me here like a prisoner.'

'Please. We've only just got here.'

'So? I have to find a hotel for tonight, and I need to call home. It's important.'

'I could also do with making some calls,' says Tiff. 'And Dani, you should get in touch with the agent, tell them to fix the internet.'

'Yeah, okay, okay . . .'

'Look,' says Beth. 'Why don't we let Dani have a quick rest, then find the nearest bar, somewhere with Wi-Fi. We can look on the Sat Nav.'

Celine frowns. 'How long is a quick rest?'

'Twenty minutes?' Dani swallows her irritation.

'Okay.'

'Shall we take the same bedrooms as we had last time?' asks Dani, as casually as she can. The truth is, she *has* to have the bedroom at the top again. Everything has to be the same as before.

'Fine by me,' Beth replies.

'I'm not staying,' Celine reminds them for the umpteenth time. 'So nobody needs to share. Unless you want to, that is.'

'I think I'd rather tuck up with you, Beth,' says Tiff.

Beth smiles. 'Of course, sweetie. Whatever you want.'

Dani grabs the handle of her suitcase. 'Good. I'll take my things up then and have my quick rest.'

The master bedroom is unchanged. The horrors of that night never reached the upper floor so there was no need for any redecoration. Dani runs her fingers over the dressing table, picturing Aoife sitting in front of the mirror. She can almost see her reflection – short spiky blonde hair, blue eyes outlined in kohl, a slightly turned-up nose, small rosebud mouth. She always looked like a mischievous pixie although she was too tall for the part.

Dani remembers how chuffed she'd been that Friday afternoon when Aoife had asked her to share the master suite. It had gone some way to compensate for not being Chief Bridesmaid. She'd been really upset and hurt when Aoife told her she'd chosen Tiff.

'She's my oldest friend,' she said. 'We've known each other since before we were born.'

'Impossible,' Dani replied sulkily.

'Our mums are really close. We did everything together, we *had* to be friends.'

'You mean you were forced on each other.'

'Not at all. It's true, we don't have much in common, and we don't think the same way, but we know each other inside out. I love her to bits, she's like my sister.' That stung. As an only child, Dani had always longed for a sibling, preferably a girl. 'But you and I, we're twin souls,' Aoife continued, looking at her imploringly with those baby-blue eyes. 'I would much rather have had you, but Mum would have killed me if I hadn't asked Tiff. I didn't think it would bother you. At least you don't have to organise the hen party.'

But it *had* bothered her. A lot. As far as Dani was concerned, Tiff was a relic from Aoife's past. The few times they'd met over the years, it had been very awkward. Dani had tried to be friendly, but Tiff had always shrugged her off. It was as if she'd already made her mind up against her. Eventually, Dani had stopped worrying about it. She didn't care about being Aoife's oldest friend, as long as she was her best.

Dani unzips her case and lays her clothes on the bed. It all seems so pathetic now, that petty rivalry for the number one spot in Aoife's friendship chart.

At Birmingham Uni, she and Aoife had been inseparable, almost from the first day. They were on different courses but on the same corridor in their accommodation block, sharing a kitchen with six others. It was love at first sight. They quickly found out that they had the same attitudes, the same political beliefs, the same tastes in fashion and music, an almost identical sense of humour. They both did the minimum amount of studying to get by and spent the rest of their time partying. People said they were like twins, although they didn't look alike, and they laughingly referred to themselves as Double Trouble.

In the second and third years they rented a house with other friends, and after graduation, moved down to London together. They flailed about for a while, going from one dodgy flat rental to another, making stuttering attempts to launch their careers. They went clubbing at weekends, shared tents at countless festivals, drank a lot of alcohol, hooked up with a few unsuitable guys online. They were always there for each other when things went wrong, which they occasionally did, but for the most part it was fun. That was the London life – always broke, but never bored. They couldn't get enough of it.

Then Aoife met Nathan, and everything changed. Or rather, *Aoife* changed. Nathan said she'd been wasting her time since university and needed to grow up. She had untapped potential and hidden talents. With his help, she would blossom into this amazing superwoman and take over the world. Yeah, right, thought Dani.

The first time she was introduced to Nathan, she realised that they were going to be enemies, in competition for Aoife's love. Nathan blamed Dani for all Aoife's shortcomings, as he saw them, and decided that they should be separated, as if they were naughty kids in class. Aoife was besotted with him and went along with whatever he said. After a few months, she abandoned Dani and moved into his gorgeous riverside apartment in Canary Wharf. He wangled a job for her, working for a television production company that made reality shows.

That was where Aoife met Celine. They became yoga buddies. Yoga – what was that about? In all the years Dani had known Aoife, she'd never showed any interest in exercise. She started doing lots of new things after meeting Nathan. Like tanning her legs and having her nails done . . . Dani hardly recognised her. Whenever they met up – which wasn't often anymore – Aoife spent the evening extolling

Nathan's countless virtues, none of which were apparent to Dani. She didn't care for this new Aoife, but hung on, believing the relationship with Nathan couldn't possibly last and that, one day, she'd get her best friend back. It was a complete shock when the couple got engaged. Another blow when she was passed over for the role of Chief Bridesmaid.

Dani turns away from the mirror. There she goes again, stabbing old wounds, picking at the scabs of resentment. What's the point of competing for the attention of somebody who no longer exists? She's explored this in various therapy sessions, of course, and it's never been explained, let alone resolved.

'Were you in love with Aoife?' a therapist dared to ask her once. Dani still doesn't know the true answer to that one. She has always thought of herself as heterosexual and has never been particularly attracted to women, but the impact of Aoife's death has struck her so hard, she has started to wonder. They were never lovers physically, and yet it was much more than just a friendship. It was a union – they'd been bound to each other for years. Losing Aoife was like losing part of herself. She loved her, yes, of course she loved her. There are so many different kinds of love . . .

She hears the sound of someone climbing the stairs and quickly lies down on the bed, as if she has been resting.

Celine appears at the open door. 'Can we go now?' she says. 'Only if I'm going to have any chance of finding a hotel . . .'

'I wish you'd stay,' Dani replies, sitting up and leaning on her elbows.

'I don't want to. You shouldn't have brought us here, it's

cruel. Tiff is in bits. I'm sure Beth is struggling too, even though she won't show it.'

'I'm sorry . . . I know I should have consulted everyone, but I was frightened you'd say no.'

'Do Marta and John know we're here?'

'Doubt it. I don't even know if they still own the place. I booked online via an agency – it was all very impersonal.' Dani shuffles to the edge of the bed and slips her feet into her sandals. 'Please think again, Celine. I'm sure Tiff and Beth would rather we all stuck together. You still want to visit Aoife's grave, don't you?'

'I don't know . . .'

'Look, we'll go to the bar, get something to eat, you can make your calls, then we'll come back and have an early night. Then if you really don't want to stay, I'll take you to the airport tomorrow morning. How's that?'

'Hmm.'

'Please. Just give me one night.'

'I don't understand why you've brought us back here. What do you want?'

'I don't know, exactly. I suppose you'd call it closure.'

'Closure? It feels like you want to open everything up again.'

Dani stands up. 'Come on. You'll feel better once you've called home and checked on your little boy. Then you can decide.'

Chapter Seven: Then

CELINE

Out of all the hens on the weekend, I was Aoife's newest friend by far. I knew her from work. She'd turned up out of the blue eighteen months ago and had been put at the desk opposite mine. 'Aoife's our new Development Assistant,' my boss Charlie had said. 'Show her the ropes, please, Celine. Be nice!'

Initially, I hadn't felt like being nice. None of us had been told there was a job going, let alone been consulted about what extra support we needed. We all felt Aoife had been foisted on us. When I asked her how she'd got the job, she mumbled something about her boyfriend being an old mate of Charlie's and their having done some business together. That kind of thing happened all the time. There was no point complaining about nepotism. It was just how it was. Fortunately, Aoife was likeable and willing to learn, so nobody held it against her personally.

Although I was a few years older than her, Aoife and I soon became friends. We always had lunch together and I persuaded her to go to yoga with me on Monday nights. In return, she dragged me to the cinema to see romantic comedies that Nathan refused to watch. I think she liked that I was also in a serious relationship. We'd been on some double dates and our boyfriends got on well. In fact, Farrell had a bit of a man crush on Nathan. He had this idea (well, more of a fantasy) that Nathan was going to find investors for his new business venture – Caribbean sauces based on his grandmother's recipes. That's what Nathan did for a living, apparently. He made other people's dreams come true.

We'd been invited to the wedding, but only to the evening part when the oldies had gone home and fresh legs were needed for the dancing. Farrell was disappointed, but I was fine with it. Some of my work colleagues were going too, so I was expecting it to be a laugh. Aoife hadn't said anything about a hen do, so I assumed that either she wasn't having one, which seemed unlikely, or that I hadn't made the cut. Again, it didn't bother me. Aoife and I got on well, but we weren't close, and I didn't know any of her other friends. Also, I didn't want the expense of it.

About three months before the Big Day, Nathan and Aoife asked us out to dinner – they wanted to try a restaurant that had just been opened by the winner of some cookery show. 'My shout,' Nathan said. It was always his shout. True, he earned a lot more money than we did, but I was embarrassed about never even going halves on the bill. This time, however, I was relieved. The prices were off the scale.

The restaurant was the ultimate in pretentiousness. It only did small plates, which were brought out one by one – in an order decided by the chef – to be admired and photographed before they were tasted. Everything was for sharing and although the food was delicious, the portions were so small they could be eaten in a couple of mouthfuls.

There was a lot of boasting about the wedding, which

sounded like it was going to be extravagant. Floral arches, chocolate fountains, string quartets, high-end caterers, a nine-piece jazz band . . . Nathan did most of the talking. He seemed to have forgotten that we were only on the subs bench and wouldn't arrive until the cake had been cut. Then he moved on to the hen weekend. He clearly thought I'd been invited, asked me what Disney character I was going as. Aoife, bless her, immediately asked me to come and Farrell just as quickly accepted on my behalf. I was furious with him and we argued about it on the way home.

'She didn't really mean it,' I said. 'She was only being polite.'

'Maybe, but it's good to get in with them,' he replied. 'Nathan's got incredible connections.'

'He won't be there. Besides, it's a private party, not a networking event.'

'You still need to go. It's important. For me . . . For the business.'

'Do you have any idea how much it's going to cost?' I cried. 'It's not a pub crawl down the high street. It's Marbella – for three nights! We can't afford it.' I stopped short of reminding Farrell that he was currently freelance – otherwise known as unemployed – and that I was the only one with a permanent job, basically supporting both of us.

When I discovered there were only going to be five of us – a real besties-only affair – I felt embarrassed, but by then it was too late. I'd booked time off work, paid for my flight, and bought my Minnie Mouse costume. I'd even done the whole *No Carbs Before Marbs* thing and lost two kilos.

I met Tiff, Beth and Dani for the first time that Friday

morning, at the airport. Aoife had already filled me in with the basic details – Tiff and Beth were schoolfriends and the three of them had known each other forever, Tiff was a management consultant and Beth was training to be a solicitor. They sounded quite high-powered, and I was worried that they'd look down on me. Aoife had lost track of what Dani was doing but it was some kind of temp job. She'd been Aoife's best mate at university. I got the impression she was still her best mate, even though Tiff was Chief Bridesmaid.

Dani was very attractive – slim but with some curves. She had soft brown skin, beautiful brown eyes and curly dark hair that she wore loose. She was full of energy and appeared very confident. She was the friendliest of the three, sitting next to me on the flight over and making sure I was included in the silly games we were playing. The champagne breakfast certainly helped me relax. Before long we were joking with the stewards and even performed an impromptu duet of Diana Ross's 'I'm Still Waiting' in the queue for the toilet.

It didn't take long to suss out the deeper structure of the group. Dani and Aoife were a definite pair. They kept exchanging glances and laughing at private jokes. Tiff didn't like that very much. She and Dani started making sly digs at each other – there was definitely a rivalry between them, right from the start. Beth didn't get involved. She was like a cuddly teddy, all soft and easy-going. She had beautiful long auburn hair and very pale skin. I cast her as the peacemaker. Tiff in contrast was as snappy as a twig with not an ounce of spare flesh on her.

As Chief Bridesmaid, she was desperate to be in charge

at all times, but Dani was our only driver, and the only one of us who spoke Spanish. We couldn't do much without her co-operation, which created an extra layer of tension. Tiff had already found a supermarket on Google that was near the airport for us to pick up supplies. Dani said we should play it by ear and could find somewhere closer to the villa so that the frozen stuff wouldn't melt. It was a fair point. Tiff protested, saying we might not find anywhere closer. Dani said of course we would. In any case, she was prepared to take the risk. As the driver, she won.

We easily found a Mercadona on a roundabout in Marbella and did a supermarket dash, running along the aisles in our costumes, shouting out to each other as we hurled bottles into the trolley – wine, cava, vodka, gin, tequila. In went the cans of pre-mixed cocktails – Strawberry Daiquiris, Mojitos, Margaritas, Piña Coladas – the cheapest brands we could lay our hands on. Beth went wild in the deli section, piling into the trolley tubs of olives, sticks of bread, large packets of ham and several giant bags of crisps and pretzels to 'soak up the booze', as she so eloquently put it. We also bought a crazy amount of Häagen-Dazs. Nobody was interested in the list that Tiff had carefully compiled in advance, and she stomped out of the supermarket, refusing to carry anything.

We stuffed the shopping bags into the boot on top of our cases and got back into the hire car. Off we went into the mountains. I had my heart in my mouth as the route twisted and climbed, although I had to admit, Dani did a great job, quickly adjusting to driving on what I always think of as the wrong side of the road.

I was surprised that we were staying so far from the coast, but as soon as I saw Villa Floriana I was enchanted. I loved the uneven whitewashed walls, the tiled roof, the bulbous earthenware pots overflowing with colourful flowers, the stunning views across the valley that constantly drew my gaze. I'd been to Spain several times before but only to purpose-built holiday resorts on the coast. This was something else entirely. A different world. Hang the expense, I thought. This is going to be amazing.

After giving us the grand tour, Marta and her English husband left us to settle in. We unpacked the shopping and stacked the fridge with bottles of booze. The ice cream, which was already a bit soft from the heat, went straight into the freezer. Dani opened a bottle of cava and we found some champagne flutes.

'To Aoife!' she cried, raising her glass. 'And all who sail with her!'

When the whooping died down, Tiff announced that our next task was to decorate the space. There were balloons to blow up, candles to light, themed bunting to festoon on the terrace, battery-operated fairy lights to hang in the garden . . . Aoife said she wasn't going to do anything until she'd had a swim, and the rest of us were happy for her to lead the rebellion.

I was relieved to have a bedroom to myself – at the back of the house on the ground floor, next to Tiff and Beth's. It didn't take long to unpack. I'd only brought the minimum – a dress for clubbing, a black halter jumpsuit, a sundress for shopping or walking around, a pair of shorts and a couple of tops, two bikinis and a beach wrap. I hung the dresses in the wardrobe, then lined up my heels, trainers and Birkenstocks against the wall. The only thing left was a plastic carrier bag containing the novelty masks that Nathan had given me. I was worried about them. They had come with strict instructions that I didn't want to carry out. I flapped down the lid and zipped the case up, like I was afraid they might escape.

Choosing the bed nearest the window, I lay down for a few moments, resting my head on the pillow, which was a bit too flat for my liking. Outside, there was blazing sunshine, but the room was dark. Within seconds, I could feel my eyelids drooping. I was tired from travelling and the stress of meeting new people. This was supposed to be a quick pit-stop to change into our swimsuits, but I didn't want to move.

Just as I was about to fall asleep, my phone pinged. My heart raced for a few seconds, thinking it might be an email from Charlie, my boss. But it was a text from Farrell, asking if I'd heard any news. *No. Nothing yet,* I replied.

I'd had the job interview yesterday. It'd gone really well, despite my being nervous beforehand. The interviews with the external shortlisted candidates were taking place today. Hopefully, the panel would reach a quick decision and I'd hear confirmation before the end of the afternoon.

I lay on the bed, thinking about how far I'd come and feeling proud of what I'd achieved. I'd joined the media production company twelve years ago, when I was twenty. I was already a big fan of reality television but hadn't a clue about how it was made. The company was a start-up back then and couldn't afford to give permanent contracts. I began as a lowly runner, making tea and photocopying. As the company developed and expanded, so did my skillset. I progressed to receptionist, then PA to Charlie, who realised my potential. He let me make a sideways move from admin to creative, working as a Development Assistant. It wasn't well paid, but it was my big opportunity and I grasped it with both hands.

For years, I'd worked long hours, including bank holidays. I'd looked after Charlie's kids when he'd brought them into work. I'd donned wellies and cleared out the basement when the building flooded. I'd watched thousands of hours of content, kept up to date with what was hot and what not, and had a good nose for sniffing out future trends. Perhaps even more importantly, I understood the audience in ways that some of my graduate colleagues did not.

Eventually, I made it to Development Executive, not bad for someone who'd left school at sixteen. By now I had a lot of experience and had been involved in several successful commissions. Friends said I was underpaid – that I should spread my wings and look elsewhere. But I was loyal to the company, and to Charlie, who'd always believed in me.

When Jocelyn, our Head of Development, went on maternity leave, Charlie asked me to step up and cover for her. He'd said it was my chance to prove myself, and without wishing to sound arrogant, I made a great job of it. When Jocelyn decided not to come back, everyone – including me – thought I'd automatically be promoted, but the company had its own Human Resources department by now and I was told the post would have to be advertised. Charlie said not to worry, it was only for the sake of equal opportunities – the job was mine.

But when I read the advert online, my heart sank. It said the ideal candidate would be 'a graduate with a relevant degree', which I didn't have. Still my colleagues assured me I was a shoo-in. And not because I'd been with the company from the beginning, but because I deserved it.

My phone pinged again. An email, this time. Could this be it? Heart thumping, I opened my inbox. Unfortunately, it was a marketing email from an estate agent I'd signed up with years ago when I was looking for a new flat to rent. I sighed, exasperated with myself for getting worked up over nothing. Perhaps it was better not to know for now. Friday was nearly over, and I wouldn't hear anything now until Monday. *Just forget about it*, I told myself. *Relax. Have fun.*

Heaving myself off the bed, I reached for my swimsuit.

Chapter Eight: Now

DANI

Everyone has changed into summer dresses or shorts – a good sign, Dani thinks, as she does a three-point turn. There is a noticeable easing of tension as they drive away from the villa, escaping if only for a few hours. She turns right at the end of the track, then left shortly afterwards, heading in the direction of the coast. The nearest bar is only a few kilometres away, but you can't walk it. The roads are too narrow and twisty. There are no pavements, no lighting.

Venta El Lago stands by itself on the crest of a hill. Last time, Marta suggested it for breakfast, but they never went. Dani parks in front of the building, squeezing the Seat into the last available space. They get out and walk around the side of the building to a large terrace overlooking the valley with spectacular views of Lake Istán.

It's early evening, but the place is already buzzing. The architecture and the weather are Spanish, but the atmosphere reminds her of a British pub. Everyone is sitting outside. Dani can hear English spoken in a variety of accents – London, Northern, German, Scandinavian. Venta El Lago may be Spanish-run, but it clearly attracts all the expats who live in the surrounding developments.

'Is over there okay?' Dani asks, pointing to a table in the

far corner, by the condiments and cutlery stand. 'Not that there's much choice.'

'Suits me,' says Beth. Eyes follow them curiously as they weave between the tables. Everyone seems to know each other and clearly this is not a place that tourists normally frequent.

Celine has been studying her phone since they arrived. 'At last,' she says. 'Free Wi-Fi. I really need to call home. Can somebody order me a glass of white, please? Anything except Chardonnay.' She doesn't wait for a reply, just strides off back to the car park, the phone already against her ear.

'Actually, I need to make a call too,' says Tiff. 'The same for me if that's okay. Large glass. Won't be long.' She scurries inside the bar, almost colliding with a waiter who is coming out with a full tray of drinks.

Beth stares after Tiff, an expression of mild panic briefly crossing her face.

'Looks like it's just the two of us,' Dani says as Beth sits down. A waiter arrives and Dani orders in Spanish – a bottle of wine because it turns out to be cheaper than three glasses, and a Coke for herself.

They sit in silence, observing the scene. A group of expats are clustered around a table a short distance away, their voices loud enough for Dani to hear snatches of conversation. They are easy in each other's company, drinking hard. One of them is cracking jokes to groans and hoots of laughter. There's a thank God it's Friday vibe going on, although she doubts any of them have just completed a week's work.

'Don't look now but see those guys behind you?' whispers Beth, leaning across the table. 'I think they're drug dealers.'

'Really?' Dani resists the temptation to look over her shoulder immediately. 'How do you know?'

'They've each got a load of mobiles in front of them, in different-coloured cases. That's a sure sign. One of them is wearing a satchel thingy. And the manager is running in circles around them, like they're important customers.'

'It's a bit blatant, isn't it?'

'Yup. And they're watching us.'

'Shit. Don't let them catch your eye, Beth, for God's sake. Look away.'

'They're right in front of me.'

'Shuffle round then, but don't make it look too obvious.'

She leans forward and whispers, 'They remind me of those guys in the nightclub, remember?'

Of course she remembers. Only too well. But that memory is for tomorrow evening, not now. Dani wants to relive everything in the order it happened, not jump about.

'Do you deal with those type of people in your job?' she asks Beth.

'Good God, no. I'm a family solicitor. Wills, divorces, care orders, adoptions . . .'

'You've qualified now, is that right?' Beth nods proudly. 'Congratulations. I've heard it's a really long, tough process.'

'Yup. It is, and I made it harder for myself. I should have done Law at uni – it would have saved an awful lot of time and trouble – but at first I thought I wanted to be an accountant. I gave it a go, but it was too lonely. I'm a people person. I need human interaction, you know?' She seems relieved to have something to talk about. 'I'd thought about being a solicitor before, but I was frightened I wasn't clever enough.'

'You were holding yourself back,' says Dani, knowing the feeling only too well. She's the same. When she was at school, she had dreams of being a linguist, travelling the world, working for the United Nations or the EU. But once she started her degree in French and Spanish, she discovered that the top translating jobs usually went to highly educated people who had been brought up bi- or trilingual. Her dreams evaporated in an instant. She felt cheated, mis-sold.

Instead of working even harder to fight against the odds, she gave up. She and Aoife had encouraged each other to live for the moment and not worry about the future. It seemed so far away then. They had an amazing three years, and after they graduated with the inevitable 2:2s, they didn't want it to stop. They kept the party vibe going for a while, but quickly ran out of money and had to start looking for work. Dani went to Spain for a year, but she missed London and Aoife, so she came back. The two of them felt lost. They had no career, no money, unsatisfactory love lives. The party was well and truly over. *At least we have each other*, Dani used to think. Then Nathan arrived on the scene, and she was left to be a failure on her own.

'I admire you, Beth,' Dani says, returning to the conversation. 'Aoife's death must have knocked you for six. I don't know how you kept going, I really don't. I've achieved nothing these last three years, but you've turned your whole life around. That must have taken some guts.'

'Aoife dying made me more determined,' Beth says. 'I'd already spent a fortune and sacrificed so much . . . my social life, relationships . . . I couldn't just give it all up.' She looks away, biting her lip. Tears well in her eyes and she wipes them away with her hand. 'Sorry. Being back here brings it home – what a struggle it's been, for all of us.'

'At least you've done something positive,' says Dani. She reaches out her hand and places it tentatively on Beth's arm. 'Aoife would be proud of you.'

'No . . . don't say that.' The tears Beth has been trying to hold back roll down her face. She takes a serviette from the holder on the table and dabs her eyes. 'Please don't say that.'

Their drinks arrive, bringing the topic to a close. Dani sips her Coke, allowing Beth a breather. She didn't mean to make her cry, but she's glad that they managed to have this conversation by themselves – the second one today. Usually, it's impossible to peel Beth away from Tiff. They are the oldest and closest friends in the group, but there's more to it than that. It's as if they need each other's permission to express an opinion.

Tiff has been on the phone for a long time. She must be moaning to someone – a boyfriend perhaps. Does Tiff have a boyfriend? Dani has no idea. Their friendship, if they ever had one, doesn't operate at that level. Beth will know, of course, but Dani doesn't want to ask. It will seem like she's prying.

Celine reappears a few moments later. 'Thanks,' she says, coming back to the table and sitting down. She pours herself a glass. 'I got through. Finally.'

'How's things?' asks Dani.

'Good. There are no signs that he's missing me at all, apparently. Huh! You wait till he wakes up in the middle of the night.'

'You're very brave, leaving him for so long.'

'Or negligent.'

'No, not at all. I didn't mean that.'

'It's okay, I was kidding.' Celine takes a slurp of wine. 'Anyway, Farrell has persuaded me to stay at the villa tonight. He didn't like the idea of me going off to some hotel by myself. I suppose he's right.'

'That's great, I'm pleased,' says Dani. 'Much better if we all stick together.'

Tiff comes back a few minutes later, an inscrutable expression on her face.

'Everything okay?' asks Beth, putting on a smile. The tears are gone, but her eyes are still red.

'Yes,' Tiff replies. 'Thanks for the wine.'

'Who were you talking to?'

'My mum. Why do you want to know?'

'Er . . . just wondering, that's all.'

'She's not been well. I was checking up on her, is that okay?'

'Of course. I didn't mean to—' flusters Beth. 'How is she?'

'Hmm? Better, thanks.' Tiff sits down and immediately picks up the menu. 'I'm starving,' she says. 'Let's eat.'

Dani leans back in her chair and lets the others pore over their choices. There's no need for her to translate because everything's written in English. Her eyes flicker from one to the other. She feels a real sense of achievement to have brought everyone this far. It was a huge risk booking Villa Floriana and she's not surprised that they want to leave tomorrow. Whether they'll want to find a hotel and continue with the tribute to Aoife – the visit to the cemetery, the ceremony on Sunday evening – she doesn't know. Right now, it seems unlikely. She has to be grateful that they're staying at the villa tonight and make the most of it. Maybe she'll stay on by herself . . . if she dares.

There's so much to remember, so many incidents to reconstruct, and she hasn't even reached the end of Friday yet. The bustle of the restaurant recedes.

They stayed in that first evening, and let the party come to them. She casts her mind back, sees herself in the swimming pool, floating around on a lilo, a glass of bubbly in her hand.

Chapter Nine: Then

DANI

Aoife and Tiff were throwing a beach ball around in the pool. Tiff was pretending to have fun, but Dani could tell that she was worrying about something. The schedule, probably. They'd only just arrived and had already gone off-piste, having decided not to put up the decorations until they'd cooled off. However, Dani felt some sympathy for her. The weekend had taken a lot of organising, and Tiff clearly felt responsible for its success. But she was being such a pain about it. She was the complete opposite to Aoife, who was so easy-going and spontaneous. It was hard to imagine that they had ever been friends, not even as kids.

About twenty minutes passed before Celine emerged poolside. 'What's it like?' she asked.

'Divine!' Aoife shouted. 'Come on in!'

Beth sat on a lounger, daubing herself with sunscreen. Her pale, freckly skin already looked a bit pink. She glanced up at Celine. 'We thought maybe you'd gone for a siesta,' she said.

'No. I just had a few emails to see to,' she replied.

'Have you heard?' shouted Aoife. Celine shook her head.

'Heard about what?' asked Beth.

'Oh, it's just some job,' she said, embarrassed.

'It's not just some job,' said Aoife, swimming over. 'Celine is going to be our new Head of Development.'

They chorused their congratulations.

Celine held up her hand to silence them. 'Thanks, but it's not confirmed yet.'

'She's already been doing the job for a year as a mat cover. Honestly, this woman is brilliant, she taught me everything I know. The job's in the bag.'

'Hopefully,' said Celine.

'When are they going to let you know?' asked Beth.

'I was hoping I might hear this afternoon, but it's too late now.'

'Stop stressing, it's yours!' shouted Aoife, throwing a beach ball at Celine and hitting her in the stomach. 'Now get in the bloody water!'

Celine gave a half-smile, then took off her wrap and sat down on the edge, dangling her feet in. She seemed slightly annoyed by Aoife's revelation and Dani could appreciate how she might have preferred to keep it to herself, at least until she knew there was definitely something to celebrate.

The sun beat down on the pool's surface all afternoon. Celine gradually eased herself in and then doggy-paddled around, holding her chin up, grimacing every time she felt a splash on her face. Aoife and Tiff still chucked the beach ball around, not caring who got in the splash-zone.

Dani closed her eyes and let the alcohol seep through her veins. She hadn't minded doing the driving, but she was glad that job was over for the day. If they decided to go out later, it would have to be in a taxi.

'I think we should all get out now,' Tiff announced

suddenly. 'Do we want to put up the decorations before we have our showers or afterwards?'

Aoife said she'd rather do it before because otherwise she might get sweaty again. Beth suggested that, as the bride, Aoife shouldn't be doing the decorating at all. Celine said she was easy either way.

'Do we have to do it this evening?' Dani asked. 'Can't it wait until tomorrow?'

'Not really. The mixologist is coming at nine,' answered Tiff. 'I want the place to look nice for photos.'

Dani groaned inwardly. It was as if the photos mattered more than the actual experience. She slid off the lilo and ducked her head under. 'Okay,' she said as she came back up. 'Let's get it done.'

Tiff gave her the worst job – balloons. Dani was handed a spool of silver tape and a pump. 'Once you've blown them up, attach them to the sun canopy,' Tiff instructed. She turned her attention to Beth, who was untangling a long paper sign which spelled out *Bride to Be* in pink and silver lettering. They had a torturous conversation about where it should be hung before Tiff put her foot down and directed Beth to the front of the canopy.

Celine was entrusted with the job of erecting the fairy lights – Tiff had bought several boxes of them from a pound shop, along with a packet of cheap batteries. She wanted the lights woven through the bushes and trees. The flexes were quite short and their illumination was feeble. Tiff explained that they would look better once it was dark.

'No shit,' muttered Dani.

Aoife 'supervised' from the patio, where she sat with

her feet up on the outdoor sofa, scoffing pretzels from a giant bag on her lap and swigging premixed Mojito from the can.

'We're having proper cocktails later,' Tiff reminded her as she unpacked a box of candles.

'I know.' Aoife rolled her eyes, glancing up to the underside of the canopy. Dani tried to thread the balloon strings in between the rushes. The whole structure seemed quite fragile, and she was frightened of breaking it.

'Here, let me help,' Aoife said, standing up. She wobbled for a few moments, trying to find her balance.

'It's okay, I can manage,' Dani replied. 'You relax, Your Majesty.'

Once everyone had put up enough decorations to satisfy Tiff, they went off to shower and get changed. Dani took another bottle of cava out of the fridge and was sneaking it upstairs when Tiff stopped her.

'You shouldn't drink so much on an empty stomach,' she said. 'The pizzas aren't arriving until eight.'

Dani frowned. 'What pizzas?' Tiff sighed irritably. 'Don't tell me, it's on the schedule?'

'Yes, it is, actually. I pre-ordered. It's all under control.'

'Fine . . . Did you ask Aoife what pizza she wanted?'

'No. I ordered a variety, so everyone can pick and mix. I checked allergies weeks ago and nobody said they had any.' Tiff glared at her. 'Is that okay with you?'

'Yes, of course it's okay, I just didn't remember, that's all. Good idea. Makes things simpler.' Dani carried on up the stairs, the bottle of cava still firmly gripped in her hand.

*

They had barely finished eating their meal when Matt the Mixologist arrived. He didn't knock at the front door, just strode into the garden carrying two large cool boxes. He seemed very relaxed, like he knew his way around the villa.

Tiff leaped up and introduced herself. 'You're here – phew! That's brilliant. Thanks so much for doing this. I was having real trouble finding anyone. You're a friend of John's, right?'

'Yeah. We go way back. Anything for that guy.'

He was fair-haired with extraordinary green eyes, which stood out against his golden beach tan. When he smiled, which was most of the time, there were dimples in his cheeks. He wore a crisp white shirt and smart jeans. Nice bum too, Dani thought. She could see why John said the hens went wild for him.

'Shall I set up here?' he asked.

'Yes, please. We'll clear the table,' replied Tiff.

'I'll need five minutes to sort myself out.'

'Sounds perfect. We'll leave you to it.'

She ordered everyone to pick up their dirty plates and take them to the kitchen. Celine put the ice cream back in the freezer. Aoife, who clearly thought she was off duty for the entire weekend, remained seated, watching Matt as he lined up various bottles of spirits and brightly coloured mixers on the table. Dani picked up the empty pizza boxes and went inside.

'Everything can go in the dishwasher,' said Tiff. 'Dani – put the leftover pizza into one box and put it in the fridge, please.'

God, this woman was trying her patience. Dani shot

a furtive glance at Celine, but she didn't respond. Presumably, she wasn't interested in taking sides. Dani had only just met Celine, but she liked the way she held herself. She'd changed into a black halter-neck jumpsuit. Her long dark hair – carefully tonged – cascaded in gentle waves over her shoulders. The look was a bit sophisticated for a night in, but the transformation from Minnie Mouse was impressive.

Aoife came into the kitchen. 'He's ready for us,' she said.

'Really? I doubt it!' replied Dani. She took Aoife's arm, and they ran back out, laughing. They commandeered the rattan sofa while Matt opened a cool box and plunged a silver bucket into crushed ice. Tiff, Beth and Celine emerged a few moments later and took their seats.

Dani noticed that Matt couldn't take his eyes off Aoife. It was easy to see why. She wore an off-the-shoulder mini-dress with a frill across the front – it was bright red and barely covered her bum. She'd had her legs spray-tanned especially for the party, although the colour had faded a bit after she had spent most of the afternoon in the pool. On her feet were a pair of black sandals with block heels, her red toenails poking through. Beth and Tiff both wore floral dresses with puffy sleeves – Tiff's was very short, while Beth had gone for the expansive parachute look. Dani looked down at her simple cotton shift and wished she was wearing something more evening-y, to tie in with Aoife, but it was too late to change now.

Matt was full of jokey patter, every line of his routine laced with sexual innuendo. He said they were going to start with a Blow Job to get them in the mood.

'I'm really good at blow jobs,' Dani said, joining in the fun.

'Me too!' shouted Aoife, and a vision popped into Dani's head that she really didn't want to be there.

The Blow Jobs turned out to be shots – half Sambuca, half Baileys. Dani demonstrated how she could swallow the lot in one go. She let a bit dribble down her chin, which made Aoife laugh so much she got hiccups.

'Right, girls, no doubt you were expecting our first cocktail to be something dirty like Sex on the Beach,' said Matt, his green eyes glittering wickedly. 'But actually, I decided to prepare something more appropriate . . .' He paused dramatically. 'Sex by the Pool! Hah!' Everyone giggled accordingly, and Aoife seemed to find this particularly funny.

He showed them how to mix Sex by the Pool – vodka, orange juice, peach schnapps, a splash of grenadine and pineapple juice instead of the traditional cranberry, with a slice of orange and maraschino cherries to finish it off. Afterwards he asked for two volunteers to make the same cocktail for the rest of the group. Dani and Aoife leaped to their feet, and the others had to witness the spectacle of the two of them competing for Matt's attention. It was obvious that he preferred Aoife, despite her bride-to-be sash that made it clear she was off-limits. He stood right behind her, puppeteering her as she flipped the bottle over. They counted the shots in together, his mouth so close to her neck that he was almost kissing it. She was loving every second of it. Dani was left to make her cocktails by herself.

She didn't mind too much – she was used to Aoife getting all the attention. The few times that they'd been interested in the same man, Dani had lost out. It was perhaps a little unfair tonight, when Aoife was already spoken for, but Dani forgave her. There would be other Matts. This was Aoife's last chance to have a bit of harmless fun.

'Oh, shit, I forgot!' Tiff cried out suddenly. 'Hang on, don't drink them yet!' She bounded back indoors.

While they waited, Aoife flirted with Matt, asking him where he was from and how long he'd lived in Marbella – East London and about eight years were the replies. He said he used to work in the big hotels and beach clubs as a professional mixologist – juggling with bottles and shakers, putting on a bartender's dance for the punters. Recently, he'd given up the hen circuit and was concentrating on DJ-ing. Later tonight, he was doing a session at John's bar Supernova and another one tomorrow evening. They should come along, he said. Aoife was all up for going, until Celine reminded her that it wasn't on The Schedule and the four of them had a chuckle at Tiff's expense.

'What are you laughing about?' she asked, rejoining them. She carried a brown envelope bearing an Amazon sticker.

'Oh, nothing,' replied Dani. 'What have you got there?'

Tiff produced the 'goodies' she'd bought specially for the workshop. There were penis-shaped drinking straws, penis-shaped cocktail umbrellas, penis-shaped ice cube trays, even penis-shaped coasters. Matt wasn't surprised, or at all embarrassed. In fact, he continued the theme with the second cocktail – Penis Colada. It was getting beyond a joke, but Aoife seemed to love it. Dani took a video of her dancing around the patio, 'cock'-tail (hah-hah) in hand while Matt showered her with glittery penis confetti.

'Same penis forever!' she shouted at the phone camera.

'Same. Penis. For. Ever!!' From the way she was behaving, that seemed unlikely.

'Please, whatever you do, don't put that anywhere online,' Tiff said. 'Nathan will have a fit.'

Their hour was up. Matt posed for a group selfie, then packed up his bottles and glasses. Aoife decided to help him carry his stuff back to his car, even though everything fitted into the trolley. She was gone several minutes.

'Do you think we should go and rescue her?' asked Celine.

'Matt's the one who needs rescuing,' murmured Beth. She looked decidedly unimpressed.

Chapter Ten: Now

DANI

Dani is still thinking about Aoife and Matt as she drives back to the villa, almost missing the turn-off. She has to concentrate hard to keep to the narrow road and not stray onto the rough ground on the other side. Even though the lights of Marbella twinkle in the distance, the darkness up here is total apart from the beam of the Seat's headlights. She takes a sharp bend, and a large tree suddenly lurches into view – she has to swerve to avoid it.

'Hey, careful!' shouts Tiff, breaking the silence that has descended over them on the way back. Dani was starting to think they'd all fallen asleep. The track opens out and a few moments later the car sweeps around to the front of the villa, coming to a halt in the courtyard. Everyone gets out, pausing to breathe in the sweet night air and listen to the cicadas.

'Thank goodness this is just for one night,' mutters Celine as Dani unlocks the front door. Beth runs in again and turns off the alarm. Even so, Tiff and Celine enter anxiously, as if expecting somebody to jump out at them from behind the sofa. Dani switches on the light and they all sigh with relief.

'Anyone want a tea? Or a drink?' she asks.

'No, I just want to sleep,' answers Tiff, adding, 'if I can.'

Beth yawns. 'I'm tired enough.'

'Tell me about it,' says Celine. 'It's been a long day.'

They say goodnight and go to their rooms beyond the kitchen, leaving Dani on her own. She wanders around for a few minutes, trailing her fingers across the dark, heavy furniture before turning out the lights and going upstairs. It feels too late to shower, so she has a quick wash and cleans her teeth, then gets into bed. She lies naked under the sheet and listens to the buzz of a mosquito that has sneaked into the room.

The others are clearly relieved to be leaving the villa tomorrow. They were quite chatty over the tapas earlier in the evening, while Dani sat in silence, pushing her food around her plate until it became a nondescript tomatoey mess. They are probably gathered together in their pyjamas right now to discuss the situation, debating whether to look for new accommodation or to cut their losses and fly straight home. They may not have much choice. At this time of year, the Costa del Sol is crammed with tourists.

Dani expects to spend the rest of the weekend alone. It's going to be tough. She searches the other side of the bed with her fingers, wishing she could feel the warmth of Aoife's presence next to her. It's strange to think that Aoife was the last person she shared a bed with. There's been nobody since – no lovers, no boyfriends, not even a one-night stand. Her sex life used to be active and mostly uncomplicated. Other friends seemed to be constantly searching for 'the one' but she'd enjoyed playing the field. Now she's afraid of being intimate with anyone. It's connected to Aoife's death, she knows that. Something inside her changed that night. She has tried to explore the problem in therapy, but as soon as she talks about sex, she feels panicky and breathless. Sometimes she wonders if she'll ever be able to have a physical relationship again.

She can't go there, it's too painful. Instead, she lies in the darkness, trying to recreate the hen party in her head in excruciating detail – a feat she has attempted hundreds of times before. Never successfully. She has no trouble getting as far as Sunday evening, but that's where the memories run out. It's like trekking through a jungle and finally reaching a precipice. She can see the other side, where the memories start again, but has no way of bridging the gap. The jump is too far, too perilous. All she can do is stop and look down into the yawning chasm below.

It's 2.30 a.m. when she finally gives up trying to sleep. Dani gets up and pulls a beach dress over her head before going downstairs to make herself some tea. Typically for Spain, there's no kettle. She puts some water into a saucepan and heats it on the electric hob. The cupboards are well stocked with condiments and everyday ingredients such as tea, coffee, olive oil, pulses, rice, pasta. She finds a box of manzanilla teabags and pops one into a mug.

She hears a clattering noise outside, like something's been knocked over. She jumps in surprise, almost spilling hot water onto her hand. There must be an animal out there, she thinks, looking for food. An ibex, fox, wildcat, badger . . . She tries not to have any more worrying thoughts, but it's impossible not to think about what happened last time.

Her mind returns to the intruder who nobody saw, who arrived silently, killed Aoife then vanished, taking nothing with them and leaving no trace of themselves – not a fingerprint, not a hair, not a scrap of flesh caught beneath Aoife's nails. The forensic team made a detailed search of the villa but didn't find any DNA that couldn't be accounted for. There was no CCTV on site, nor on the surrounding roads.

If only she could remember what Aoife's attacker looked like – their height, their sex, the colour of their hair, what they were wearing. Did they have a mask on? Did she see their eyes? Dani has a very blurry image in her head of somebody dressed in black, but it seems too much of a cliché to be relied upon. And there's a smell that always accompanies the picture, which she can't identify. It's body lotion, or shampoo, or perfume, or possibly aftershave. It isn't unpleasant in itself but the memory of it in her nose makes her instantly feel frightened, as if she's about to be hurt. That's all she has to go on and she knows it's not enough.

There's another noise – louder this time. It definitely came from the courtyard outside. She climbs onto the kitchen counter and peers through the small grilled window. It's pitch-black out there, impossible to see anything. Her heart starts to thump in her chest. Maybe it's not an animal. Maybe it's a person. If so, what are they doing?

She leaves the kitchen and pads barefoot down the corridor, passing the bedrooms where Tiff, Beth and Celine are sleeping, the utility room, some storage areas, and the downstairs bathroom. It's a maze back here – dark and slightly damp – she doesn't like the atmosphere; it makes her feel uneasy.

Dani unlocks the back door and opens it slowly, wincing as it scrapes over the flagstones. She steps into the rear courtyard, the air cooling her bare skin. 'Who's there?' she calls out, her voice sounding tiny in the vast expanse of night.

She looks around, trying to accustom her eyes to the darkness. She listens for the sound of an animal rustling in the bushes but all she can hear is an outside tap dripping and the roar of a vehicle driving into the distance. The noise she heard earlier sounded like something metal being knocked over – a bucket perhaps or a waste bin or a wheelbarrow – but she can't see any likely candidates. Maybe it came from inside the garage. She goes up to the brown double doors. Last time, they were left unlocked. She remembers going inside to look for extra chairs and finding packing boxes of John's stuff. Now there's a large shiny padlock. Nothing could find its way in.

Dani slips through the gap between the garage and the external wall of the villa and walks around to the front of the house. All seems quiet now. The sky is studded with stars and the air is fragrant with jasmine. She breathes it in and tries to calm her nerves. It's okay, there's nothing out here – not anymore anyway. Just flowerpots and garden ornaments, a wooden bench, the ghostly white Seat parked in the corner. Turning on her heel, she retraces her steps. As she emerges from the side of the garage, she suddenly collides with somebody. They both cry out simultaneously, then laugh with relief as they recognise each other.

'Dani!'

'Tiff!'

'Jesus, I thought—'

'Me too.'

'You scared the life out of me.'

'Me too. Sorry.'

They recover, then Tiff changes tone. 'What are you doing out here?' she asks suspiciously.

'Couldn't sleep. I went downstairs to make a hot drink and I heard a noise outside.'

Tiff looks alarmed. 'What kind of noise?'

'Like something had fallen over. I went to see.'

'And?'

'It's okay. There's nobody out there, I checked all around. It must have been an animal.'

'Are you sure?'

'Yeah. It's wild up here in the mountains, there must be all sorts prowling about.'

'Hmm . . .' Tiff hugs herself. 'I couldn't sleep either. I got up to use the bathroom and saw the back door was open. I thought somebody had broken in!'

'No, it was me. Honestly, there's nothing to worry about. We're both just nervous, that's all.'

They go back indoors, being sure to lock the door behind them. Dani offers to make her fellow insomniac a cup of tea.

'As long as it doesn't have caffeine in it,' Tiff says.

The saucepan has almost boiled itself dry. Dani tops up the water and finishes making the *infusiones*.

'I feel wired. Shall we go into the sitting room and chat for a bit?' she suggests cautiously.

'No, I think I'm going to try sleeping again.' Tiff picks up her mug. 'Thanks for this.'

'Okay. Best of luck.'

Tiff goes back to her room, leaving Dani feeling strangely bereft. It's rare to be on her own with Tiff. On the hen, they were constantly sniping at each other, but the animosity between them seems to have lessened since Aoife's death. Or rather, they don't make it so obvious. She still finds Tiff difficult to be around and the two of them will never be friends, but Dani has stopped hating her. There's no point.

She sits at the kitchen table and drinks her tea, hoping it will do the trick. She feels physically tired, but her body is still flooded with adrenalin. After a while, she goes back upstairs, lies down, and turns off the light.

She closes her heavy eyelids, begging sleep to come. But instead, her mind wanders back to that Friday evening, after the cocktail workshop. They were still sitting outside on the patio . . .

Chapter Eleven: Then

DANI

Matt the Mixologist had left but the night was still young. At least, it felt young to Dani and Aoife. They were both up for calling a taxi and hitting Puerto Banús. The clubs didn't open until midnight so there was still plenty of time left for partying.

'Clubbing is tomorrow night,' Tiff reminded them. 'I've reserved a table and everything. If you turn up now, you'll have to join the queue and it could be two a.m. before you even get through the doors.'

'Okay, let's go to Supernova instead. Matt's DJ-ing there from eleven. And we've got free drinks vouchers,' said Aoife. 'Come on, Tiff! Ditch the schedule for once.'

'What? Have you any idea how long it's taken me to put this whole thing together?' she cried. 'Weeks! Things get booked up months in advance, you can't just go with the flow. Not in Marbella. You're not the only bride having a hen party, you know. There were at least three others on the plane over.'

'So? What difference does that make? I only want to check the place out.'

Dani chuckled. 'Check Matt out, more like.'

Celine winced. 'We had a very early start – we must all be

tired. Why don't we just chill here, listen to some music, get to know each other?'

'Aoife, Beth and I don't need to get to know each other,' said Tiff.

'Yes, I realise,' Celine replied steadily. 'But I don't know any of you, and Dani was telling me she's only met you and Beth a couple of times—'

'Oh, I think we know each other well enough,' Dani murmured. Silence followed. Celine picked up her phone and started scrolling.

'What do you want to do, Dani Girl?' Aoife asked. 'We could just the two of us go.'

Dani had been trying to keep out of it. She'd already crossed swords with Tiff a couple of times that day and didn't want it to become a habit. 'Maybe we should save Banús for tomorrow,' she said. Aoife pouted. 'Look, it's your hen do. If you really want to go down there now, I'll order a taxi. But it'd be a shame to split the group up. There are only five of us as it is.'

'Yes? Why is that?' asked Aoife, waving a glass of cava around like it was a cheerleader's baton. Fizz always made her tongue loosen. She said things that everyone else was thinking but keeping in their heads. 'Why did so many of my so-called friends drop out? Do they hate me?'

'Of course not,' soothed Tiff. 'You said you wanted to stay in this particular villa, and it only slept six—'

'I never said that,' Aoife retorted. 'When did I say that?'

Tiff went pink. 'You didn't, sorry. I meant, I thought it was the kind of place you wanted.'

'What I wanted was to be by the sea, as close to the action

as possible. This place is too small and it's in the middle of fucking nowhere. I don't know what made you choose it, Tiff.'

'I . . . er . . . thought . . . Sorry if I got it wrong.' Tiff looked away. Dani studied her curiously. She was definitely hiding something.

But Aoife wouldn't give up. 'Did you tell everyone there were only six places available? Did you tell the rest they couldn't come? Like my cousin, for example, and the other girls from school?'

'No, of course I didn't. They could have stayed somewhere else.'

'Like where? There's no other villa for miles.'

'I think they dropped out because they couldn't afford it,' intervened Beth quickly. 'Hen weekends are very expensive – people just don't have the money these days. It wasn't personal, Aoife. If you'd had your hen do down the pub, dozens of friends would have turned up.'

There was another silence. Beth put on some music. Tiff and Celine were looking at their phones. Aoife stood up and walked to the end of the garden, where she gazed longingly at the lights of Marbella twinkling in the distance. Dani wondered whether to go and talk to her, try to calm her down, but she was frightened of making it worse. They'd all drunk too much. It was too hot and sticky for a fight.

'Let's play some games,' said Tiff, eventually.

Dani grimaced. 'As long as it's not Monopoly.'

'*Hen* party games, obviously.'

'Okay. What have you got?'

Tiff put down her phone. 'Well, there's Pin the Penis on the Groom, Mr and Mrs, Two Truths and a Lie—'

'How does that go?' asked Beth. 'Remind me.'

'You say three things about yourself, two are true, one's a lie. If the others guess which is which correctly, you have to drink a shot. If they get it wrong, they have to drink one.'

'A drinking game – now you're talking,' said Dani, getting to her feet. 'Everyone happy with vodka?' They nodded. She went to the kitchen and found some glasses in the cupboard. Extracting an ice-cold bottle from the freezer, she returned and poured out the shots. Tiff rushed off to her room and came back with pencils and paper.

'No conferring,' she said, handing them round. 'Just write your answers down.'

'Right,' Dani said, sitting next to Aoife. 'Who's going first?'

'Me!' said Aoife. 'I've got three things! Two truths and one big fat lie.'

'Hold on tight, girls,' laughed Dani. 'We're in for a roller-coaster ride.'

They waited for Aoife to speak. She'd been in a strange mood all evening, and it was making Dani feel nervous. Maybe this game wasn't such a good idea after all, and they should have stuck to something boring like Pin the Penis on the Groom.

'Go on then,' said Tiff.

Aoife sat up. 'Okay. Everybody ready? Here's number one. When I was a kid, I stole a Creme Egg from a sweet shop.'

'That's a true one,' said Dani instantly. 'You love Creme Eggs, God knows why . . . I think they're disgusting.'

'You're not supposed to comment,' Tiff reprimanded.

'Just write down what you think. Aoife? Number two, please.'

Aoife looked skyward. 'Hmm . . . Number two is . . . I've snorted cocaine four times.'

'Interesting,' said Dani under her breath. It was true that she and Aoife had tried cocaine, years ago, when they first came down to London, but she couldn't remember how many times. Dani had played this game before. The best lies always had a grain of truth in them. She wrote 'lie' with a question mark against number two.

'We've never done drugs together,' said Beth, primly.

'I said, no comments!' Tiff glared at her.

'Number three! Number three!' chanted Dani. 'Come on, Aoife, make it a corker.'

'Okay. So . . . my number three truth or lie is . . .' She paused for a silent drum roll. 'Hmm, this one's a bit edgy . . . Should I or shouldn't I?' She looked up again at the dark sky, as if hoping the twinkling stars would help her decide.

'Careful,' Tiff warned quietly. 'It's just a game, okay? Take it easy.'

'It was your idea to play it, not mine.'

'I just meant—'

'Number three is . . . I've slept with one of your boyfriends.'

Dani let out an instant 'Ooh!' but the rest of them just sat there, their mouths fallen open.

'Past or present boyfriend?' Dani asked. 'Before, after or while we were going out with him?'

'Not telling,' Aoife replied. 'Could be either. Could be

neither.' She downed her glass of bubbly and laughed. 'I said it was edgy.'

Beth got to her feet. 'I don't want to play anymore. I'm going to bed.'

'But we've only just started,' Aoife cried, waving at the row of undrunk shots. 'First, you vote, then I tell you the answer!'

'I've a feeling I already know.'

'What do you mean, Beth?'

'I'm sure you once told me you'd shoplifted, and if you've done drugs – with Dani, I'm guessing – you've probably done it more than four times. Which means *that's* the lie. So, you have slept with—'

'Actually, I got it mixed up,' cut in Aoife. 'My bad . . . I said two lies and a truth instead of two truths and a lie. Doh!' She slapped her head. 'The shoplifting one is the only truth. I've snorted cocaine about half a dozen times, and obviously I haven't slept with anyone's boyfriend. As if!' Her arms opened wide, ready to embrace them in a group hug. 'You're my best mates, I love you all . . . Sorry, I'm too drunk for this game.'

'Yes, you are,' agreed Beth. 'I'm going to bed.'

'Me too,' said Celine. 'Goodnight.' She followed Beth to the ground-floor rooms.

'Awkward,' said Dani. She helped herself to a shot.

Tiff threw up her hands. 'Why did you do that, Aoife? That was way out of order.'

Aoife grimaced. 'I told you, I got confused. Anyway, why did Beth get so upset?'

'You *know* why . . . Zach.'

Aoife gasped. 'Jesus! Was *that* who she thought I meant?'

'Who is Zach?' asked Dani, intrigued.

'Beth's ex,' Aoife answered. 'She was waiting for him to propose, then found out he'd been cheating on her for like forever. So she dumped him – about three years ago now, wasn't it, Tiff?'

Tiff frowns. 'We shouldn't talk about it behind her back.'

Aoife turns to Dani. 'I never had sex with Zach. Beth knows that.'

'It was still an insensitive thing to say,' says Tiff.

'Honestly, it never occurred to me. I'd forgotten all about it.'

'But *she* hasn't.' Tiff rose to her feet. 'I'd better go and check how she is.'

She went after Beth, leaving Dani and Aoife alone. Dani thought about ordering an Uber and going down to the marina, just the two of them, but it didn't feel right somehow. Aoife turned the music off and went upstairs. Dani followed, eager to dissect the evening with no danger of being overheard.

'What was all that about?' she asked, shutting the bedroom door.

'Oh . . . I don't know . . . people getting tired and emotional.' Aoife carefully wiped around her eyes with a cotton-wool pad. She never used to bother about removing her make-up after a night out, but with the wedding only a few weeks away, she wasn't taking any chances with spots.

Dani started undressing. 'Come on, tell me what happened with Beth's ex.'

Aoife let out a lengthy sigh. 'Zach and Beth started going

out in sixth form. They stayed together all through uni, moved in with each other after graduation, started saving up to buy a house. Everyone assumed they'd be the first in our group to get married. Then Beth discovered he'd been cheating on her. With loads of women. For years. She was absolutely devastated. They started having counselling and in one of their sessions, he claimed he'd had sex with me.'

'And had you?'

'No!'

'You sure? I always know when you're lying.'

Aoife lowered her voice. 'Okay . . . The truth is, we were at this party a few years back. Beth wasn't there, she had flu or something. Zach and I shared a bottle of vodka and ended up rolling around together on the bathroom floor. Fortunately, I came to my senses and stopped it just in time. Much to his annoyance.' She shuddered. 'I'm not proud of it. It was a shitty thing to do. I love Beth.'

'So, you denied it completely?'

Aoife pulled a face. 'Of course. It's always best to keep these things simple. I knew Beth was having a rough time and I didn't want to make it worse.'

'Right. And who did she believe?'

'Him at first, then eventually me. Zach's a cruel, lying bastard. She realised he was just trying to hurt her. Poor Beth . . . She was so pleased with herself for having a "partner", so desperate for him to propose. But in the end, she chucked him out and turned her life around. Good on her too.'

'No wonder she got upset when you told that "lie".' Like the lie about the drugs, there was an element of truth in it, thought Dani. And Beth had known that.

'It was stupid of me, I didn't think. Beth and Tiff take everything so seriously. Celine hasn't got much of a sense of humour either.' Aoife sighed. 'You're the only one that gets me.' She swivelled around on the stool to face Dani. 'Thank God you're here.'

'Yeah. I feel like it's a bit Us and Them already,' she said. 'Tiff's really uptight and Beth's like a little puppy dog, trailing after her.'

Aoife laughed. 'That's so mean!'

'Sorry. But it's true.'

'You're right. I never really noticed it until tonight. It's been years since the three of us have been together for a whole weekend. People change,' she continued, 'and yet they don't, do you know what I mean? Tiff and Beth will always be Tiff and Beth. They can both be a pain in their own way—'

'As can you.'

'As can *all* of us,' Aoife reminded her. 'That's what friendship means, isn't it? Accepting people for what they are. It's only lovers we try to change. Or who try to change us . . .'

'Can we stop, please?' Dani lay on the bed and stretched out, forming a starfish shape. 'My brain is too pickled for a philosophical debate.'

Aoife stared at her. 'If you're going to sleep like that, I'll make you share with Celine.'

'No, no!' Dani immediately curled into a tiny ball. 'Please, can I stay? Please, please, O Bride-to-be, don't banish me downstairs with The Stranger.' She put her hands together.

Aoife threw a rolled-up piece of tissue in Dani's direction. 'Celine's not a stranger. She's a good friend and a lovely person, actually. And she's like my line manager at work. At least, she will be if she gets this job.'

'Well, she's a stranger to *me*,' continued Dani. 'You've only ever mentioned her once or twice. Obvs, it's up to you who you invite to your hen, but if I'm honest, I was surprised when she turned up.'

Aoife applied the ridiculously expensive cleanser that she'd bought in Duty Free. 'Promise you won't say anything to the others?'

'Of course.' Dani zipped her mouth with her fingers.

Aoife lowered her voice to a whisper, even though they were well out of earshot. 'I *had* to invite Celine. Nathan invited her and Farrell out to dinner. He dumped me in it – said something like, "Oh, Celine, I bet you can't wait for the hen do." It was really embarrassing. I had to ask her, there and then.'

'What an idiot!'

'I think he did it deliberately.'

'Why?'

'He approves of Celine. Thinks she's a good influence on me.'

Dani raised her eyebrows. 'And I'm not, I suppose?'

'I'm afraid I told him too much about our time at uni.'

'Oh, so that's why he doesn't like me.'

'He *does* like you.'

'He so doesn't.' She didn't add that she didn't like him either.

'You need to get to know each other better, that's all.' Aoife paused. 'I have a sneaky feeling he wanted Celine here so she could keep an eye on me.'

'Really? That's a bit controlling.'

'Yeah. Sometimes it makes me want to do something completely reckless, just to prove to myself that I'm still free.'

'Is that why you made a play for Matt tonight? What happened when you went off to his car? You were gone a long time, everyone noticed.' She looked at Aoife's reflection in the mirror and saw her cheeks redden. 'Did you have a snog?' No reply. 'You *did*, didn't you?' Dani cackled. 'Unbelievable. Did it go any further? Did you stop it at the last minute, like with Zach?'

'Shh! No. It was just a bit of flirting, that's all.' Aoife smiled nonetheless, as if picturing the scene in her mind. 'I said we might see him tomorrow evening in the port. We exchanged numbers.'

'Woah! Slow down, Miss I'm-getting-married-at-the-end-of-the-month!'

'He said he'd give us some tips.'

'I bet he did.'

'Places to go, I mean.'

'Well, don't tell Celine he's got your number. She's probably sitting up in bed right now, writing a report for Nathan. Totting up all the cocktails you had.'

'I hope not. Nathan hates me getting drunk.'

Dani snorted. 'Well, tough, because tonight was just the beginning, my friend. Tomorrow is clubbing night, and we are going to get off our heads!'

Chapter Twelve: Then

BETH

It was only Friday night, but I was already wishing I hadn't come. I'd had some misgivings about joining the party, and everything that had happened so far had confirmed them. My long friendship with Aoife was reaching the end of its shelf life. There'd been a few incidents in recent years that had made me wonder whether I should cut ties altogether, but Tiff had always patched things up between us.

Aoife and I were opposites – The Wild Child versus Little Miss Sensible – and in the past we'd been a good foil for each other. I'd reined her in and kept her safe, while she'd encouraged me to be more adventurous. That had been fine during our schooldays, when there'd been little at stake, but as the years had gone by, our differing outlooks on life had become increasingly problematic. It sounds melodramatic, but I felt Aoife was potentially a danger to me.

At the time of the hen party, I was in the first year of a training contract with a firm of solicitors. The last thing I needed in my life was someone who wasn't that bothered about staying on the right side of the law. Not that Aoife was a criminal, but she occasionally took recreational drugs, did jobs for cash, drank too much in public . . . Normal misdemeanours in many people's eyes but all out of bounds for me. I'd always been a natural goody-goody; now I needed to be a professional one. Aoife didn't seem to appreciate my position, she wanted to behave as she'd always behaved.

The last time there'd been an issue was when we went up to Manchester to celebrate Tiff's thirtieth. I'd been studying hard and was looking forward to letting my hair down. Tiff took us to a nightclub, where we planned to party the night away. At first, it felt great, like being teenagers again – all girls together, dancing and having a laugh – but as the night wore on, Aoife became more lairy and out of control. I don't know whether it was the alcohol, or whether she'd secretly popped a pill, but she got into some stupid argument with a woman in the toilets, which spilled onto the dance floor. Tiff and I tried to calm things down, but the other woman's boyfriend got involved and the next thing I knew the bouncers had thrown us all out. The boyfriend and his mates carried on verbally abusing Aoife on the street. Aoife hit him – she barely made contact actually – he hit her back and it turned ugly. Tiff got into a tussle with the woman, and I tried to stop the boyfriend laying into Aoife. Luckily – but also unluckily – the police were close by and arrested all three of us.

I'd never sat in the back of a patrol vehicle before and felt sick with shame. Tiff and Aoife were really angry, protesting to the uniforms that we were the victims, not the perpetrators. I kept quiet, terrified that I'd be charged with drunk and disorderly behaviour or even assault and would end up with a criminal record. Any conviction for violence would wreck my dreams of a legal career.

The three of us spent the night in the cells. I'd never felt so anxious in my life. We were released the following morning – Aoife with a caution, and a reprimand for me and Tiff for not keeping our friend under control. Aoife begged us not to tell Nathan. He hated her getting drunk, she said, and would go crazy if he found out she'd got into trouble with the police.

I'd escaped, but it had been a close shave. I couldn't afford to get myself into a similar situation on the hen weekend. When I heard it was being held in Marbella, I told Tiff I would have to drop out, but she begged me to come. Nothing bad would happen, she promised, she'd make sure of that. But she needed my support to cope with Dani. She was very anxious about spending three days and nights in the same space as her and wanted us to present a united front.

'We may live in different parts of the country and lead very different lives,' Tiff declared, 'but you, Aoife and I will always be close.'

I wasn't so sure about that 'always', but I allowed myself to be persuaded. I couldn't refuse Tiff. We'd been friends since day one at secondary school. She'd been my rock throughout the horrible break-up with Zach. The hen weekend could be our last hurrah as a trio, I thought. After the wedding, I would let things drift. I felt even more certain of that now.

I was already in bed when Tiff came into the room. I'd turned the main light off and was lying with my face to the wall so that she couldn't see I'd been crying.

'Sorry about that, hon,' she said. 'I shouldn't have suggested the game. Aoife can be such a klutz . . . always says the first thing that comes into her head, never thinks.'

'Do you think it was a genuine mistake?' I asked. 'You

know, telling two lies and a truth instead of two truths and a lie? It felt kind of pointed, like she was trying to wind me up.'

''Course it was a mistake! She was pissed.'

'Hmm.' I turned over to face Tiff, watching as she took off her Chief Bridesmaid sash and laid it carefully over the back of a chair.

'She didn't sleep with Zach. I know that for a fact.'

'Not for a fact,' I said.

'I know Aoife better than she knows herself and she would never have betrayed you like that,' Tiff assured me, hanging up her clothes.

'But Zach said—'

'Zach was a cheat and a liar. Anyway, he's ancient history. You've moved on. Look at you now. Amazing.'

'But bits of me are still raw. When Aoife said—'

'Put it out of your head,' Tiff insisted. 'There are far more important things to worry about.'

'Like what?'

'Oh, you know, like everything going smoothly. People behaving themselves.' Tiff cleaned her teeth in the washbasin. 'It's Dani's fault,' she said, scrubbing away. 'She eggs Aoife on.'

'To be fair, she didn't need much egging tonight,' I said. 'She was all over the cocktail guy.'

'So embarrassing. I know it's her hen do, but she needs to dial it down. We're going clubbing tomorrow night – she'd better not pick a fight with anyone like last time.'

'Hopefully, she's learned her lesson.'

'I wouldn't bank on it, not with Dani around.'

'What do you make of Celine?' I asked, changing the subject.

'I like her. She's friendly but not too pushy. Seems very sensible, like you could trust her. Unlike some people I could mention.' She spat into the bowl.

'Stop going on about Dani. She's not too bad, you know.'

'Huh.' Tiff got into bed. 'I just feel she's mocking me all the time, trying to trip me up and make a fool of me in front of Aoife.'

'That's not true. She wants the weekend to be a success just as much as you do.'

'I'm the one Aoife chose to be Chief Bridesmaid. It's my responsibility.'

'But you're so nervous it's making you snappy,' I said. 'Try not to be so sensitive,' I added cautiously.

'You can talk! You just stormed out of the room over a game.'

I sighed. 'I know, you're right. We're both overtired. Let's get some sleep.'

We said goodnight and turned off the light. I lay in the dark, unable to stop myself thinking about Zach, even though I hadn't had anything to do with him for over three years. We'd been together for nine though, and he'd had a huge impact on my life.

It turned out that he had cheated on me with dozens of women – fellow students at university, work colleagues, strangers he'd met online. After I chucked him out, I became obsessed with infidelity. I read books and blog posts, joined an online support group for victims. I dug into my own pain and took on others' misery as well. It wasn't just the cheats I hated, it was the people they cheated with. I couldn't stop thinking about all the women who'd gone to bed with Zach, knowing he had a partner. I felt that they'd betrayed womankind.

Tiff brought me out of my despair. She told me to get a grip, start valuing myself and make some changes in my life. The time I'd spent poring through tragic stories of failed marriages inspired me to think of ways I could help others. I would retrain to be a family solicitor, I decided, specialising in divorce. I had one more year to go before qualifying. I was almost there.

Chapter Thirteen: Now

DANI

When Dani opens her eyes on Saturday morning, she has a splitting headache, even though not a drop of alcohol passed her lips the previous night. There are no sounds coming from downstairs. She checks the time on her phone – it's 7 a.m., which is only 6 a.m. really (a weekend isn't long enough to adjust to a new time zone). No wonder nobody else is awake yet. She lies there for a few more minutes, deciding what to do. Go for a swim, perhaps?

She puts on her bikini and ties a sarong around her waist, then tiptoes down the stairs. Needing a glass of water, she crosses the living room and goes into the kitchen.

'*Buenos días*,' says a female voice from behind the door of the fridge.

'Ah!' Dani jumps back.

'*Perdóname*. Did I surprise you? I've brought your breakfast. Sorry, I meant to come last night but—' The woman shuts the fridge door, breaking off as she sees who's standing before her.

'Hello, Marta,' says Dani.

Marta peers at her through the gloom. '*Madre mía* . . . I can't believe it. Dani, is that you?'

'Yup,' she replies, feeling self-conscious in her bikini and sarong. 'Good to . . . er . . . see you.'

Marta shakes her head in disbelief. 'I don't understand. Why didn't you tell me you were coming?'

'I booked through an agency. Your name didn't come up. I thought you must have sold the place,' Dani flounders. It's a poor excuse and she knows Marta's not buying it. The truth is, she'd been relieved not to have had to go through John and Marta. 'I'm sorry,' she adds. 'I didn't mean to shock you.'

Marta looks older, unless the dark circles beneath her eyes are a sign of sleeplessness rather than age. She twists her hands together as if wringing out a cloth – Dani remembers her doing it when she came to the villa on the morning after the murder. She was incredibly upset – not just that one of her guests had been killed, but that her grandparents' house had been so violated.

'This is very strange,' says Marta. 'When did we last meet?'

'At the inquest. Two and a half years ago. I'm surprised you recognise me.'

'I'll never forget your face. When I came to the villa, the morning after, you looked so shocked, so upset. It was like your world had ended.' She inhales sharply. 'I need a coffee. Do you want some?'

'Er . . . yes, please.'

Marta goes to the cupboard and takes out a packet of coffee beans. Neither of them attempts to talk above the noise of the grinder, but as soon as it finishes, Marta ventures a new question.

'So, tell me, Dani . . . why have you come back here?'

She shifts uncomfortably. 'Well, it's the third anniversary of Aoife's death. We wanted to mark it with a celebration of her life. Me and the other hens – Tiff, Beth, Celine.'

'They're here too?'

'Yes. Still asleep.' She nods in the direction of the down-stairs bedrooms.

'*Madre mía* . . . All of you – why?'

'To tell you the truth, I misled them. They thought we were booked into an apartment in San Pedro. They wouldn't have agreed to come back otherwise.'

'I see.' Marta spoons the ground coffee into the maker, pressing it down firmly. 'But why did *you* want to come back?'

'Because the case has never been solved. We still don't know who killed Aoife or why. The police have given up. Aoife's family and Nathan seem to have accepted that they'll never be found. The other hens too. Sometimes it feels like I'm the only one who still cares.' Tears surge behind her eyes, but she takes a deep breath and refuses to give in to them.

'It was some kid trying to prove himself to a gang. I promise you, Dani, he would have been taken out of the country a few hours after he killed your friend.' Marta puts the coffee maker on the hob.

Dani lowers her voice. 'The thing is . . . I don't believe it *was* a burglary. Nothing was taken.'

'Because Aoife disturbed him, no?'

'That was the theory.'

'He attacked her and she fought back?'

'Yes . . .'

'So?'

'I just don't think it was a burglar, that's all.'

'I remember, at the inquest, you said he attacked you too.'

Dani bites her lip. 'I said I thought he might have, but I wasn't sure. I'm still not sure.'

The coffee maker hisses and Marta immediately switches it off. She pours the coffee into two mugs and hands one to Dani.

'That's why I'm retracing my steps. There's so much about that night I can't remember—'

Marta waves her hand dismissively. 'You're lucky. I have too many memories. Everywhere, I see blood. On the walls, on the floor. We scrubbed and scrubbed but the stains wouldn't go away. Now everything is painted again, and the furniture is new, but still I see it.'

'I'm sorry, that must be awful.'

'Yes, it is. My home has been poisoned. It will never be the same.' She sighs. 'Search for Villa Floriana online and you'll find stories from your British newspapers. They called it the "Henhouse of Horrors".'

'Yes, I remember, it was disgusting.'

'Since that time, very few guests. When I saw there was a booking this weekend, I was pleased. I thought maybe things were getting better, but no . . . the business is still ruined.' Marta sighs.

'I'm so sorry to hear that. How is John?' Dani asks tentatively.

'We separated. More than two years ago.'

'Oh. Did he go back to the UK?'

'No. He still lives above the bar in Puerto Banús. I moved back here. It's a big place for one person, but it's my home now. If there are guests, which is very rare, I stay with a friend.' She sips her coffee, then stares into the mug. 'It's difficult with John. We have many problems to sort out.'

Dani visualises Marta's ex: flip-flops and baggy shorts, sun-bleached hair. 'Did the, er, split have anything to do with . . . what happened?'

'¡Claro! The murder changed everything. Our relationship, our business, our lives . . .' She hesitates, then adds, 'I admit, before that the marriage was not good, but Aoife's death was the finish.'

Dani feels awkward. 'If it's any help, I know how you feel. I was changed by it too. Now it's like I'm stuck in time, I can't move forward, can't get on with the rest of my life. That's why I've brought everyone back here. If I can work out what really happened that night, maybe we'll all find some peace.'

'Maybe,' says Marta, but she sounds unconvinced. She picks up her bag and car keys. 'I wish you luck, Dani, but to say the truth, I think you'll only find peace when you give up searching for it.'

'I can't give up. Not yet.'

'I have to go now. I only came to bring breakfast.'

'Muchas gracias.'

'De nada. And I forgot to ask you – is everything okay for your stay? Do you have everything you need?'

'Yes. It's all great. Apart from the Wi-Fi – it doesn't seem to be working.'

'Really? That's strange. I'll take a look at it.'

Dani follows her into the sitting room. Marta crouches down to inspect all the leads and sockets. 'I think maybe the router was knocked. It's fixed now.'

'Thanks. And sorry about not telling you we were coming. I hope you don't mind us being here.'

'You're welcome. It's difficult for me to see you again, but to be honest, I need the money.' And with that, Marta leaves by the front door.

Chapter Fourteen: Then

TIFF

I didn't exactly spring out of bed on Saturday morning. I hadn't slept well. I wasn't great with hot weather and my brain had been buzzing all night – not with Beth's worries but my own. All the other hens thought I was stressed about the schedule and everything being perfect for Aoife, but there was much more to it than that. I was experiencing an unbelievable amount of anxiety and had nobody to confide in. I had a terrible headache and my neck was a solid block of pain.

Last night, Aoife had sworn that she knew nothing about Villa Floriana, that she'd wanted to stay somewhere less remote and nearer the coast. I cast my mind back to my meeting with Nathan. I was sure he'd told me that she'd specifically asked to stay here. Had Nathan misunderstood? Had Aoife forgotten? I couldn't quiz her any further about it because Nathan had made me promise not to tell her that he was involved in organising – and to some extent financing – the hen party. We had other secrets from Aoife too.

It didn't help that he kept texting me to ask how things were going and whether Aoife was 'behaving herself'. How was I supposed to reply? I couldn't tell him that she'd flirted outrageously with the guy running the cocktail workshop and had disappeared with him for a suspiciously long time. If Aoife found out that Nathan and I were in cahoots, I would be in big trouble with both of them.

I got up, threw on some shorts and a top and went to see about breakfast. To my relief, Marta had followed my instructions to a tee. There was ciabatta bread and a bag of fresh croissants sitting on the kitchen counter, still warm from the bakery. She'd put out jars of jam, plus peanut butter and Marmite. In the fridge, she'd left a large hunk of watermelon, some tomato mixture, Spanish ham, a six-pack of yoghurts, and a jug of fresh orange juice. She must have popped in very early because I hadn't heard her coming or going.

I don't usually eat until lunchtime, but for some reason I was feeling hungry that morning. I stood in the kitchen deliberating whether to lay the rattan table outside or the dining table inside where it was cool; whether it was too soon to make a pot of coffee (answer, yes). The villa was quiet. Beth was still putting on her make-up and there were no signs that the other three were awake yet. I checked the time. It was only nine o'clock, early by most people's standards although not mine. But even *I* knew I couldn't go around waking people up. Not yet anyway.

As I sliced up the watermelon, I found myself feeling slightly pissed off with my fellow hens. I'd formed a secret plan to make a diary of the weekend, including photos, funny comments and affectionate messages. I was going to have everything printed up as a book to give to Aoife as a wedding present. So far, I'd taken shots of us in our costumes, swimming in the pool and eating pizza. I also had pictures of Matt teaching Aoife how to make cocktails, although I wasn't sure any of them would be usable.

This morning, I'd envisaged the five of us sitting around the patio table raising glasses of Buck's Fizz and posing for a group selfie with the caption *Bride-to-be Breakfast!* Or something wittier, if I could think of it. Now, the more likely scenario was that the others would crawl out of bed at various intervals during the morning, bleary-eyed and smelling of stale booze, groaning as they reached for the coffee pot, and shooing me away if I got anywhere near them with my camera.

My stomach rumbled. I snapped off a yoghurt and took it outside. As I sat there in the warm Marbella sunshine, I thought back to the dozens, probably hundreds, of times that Aoife and I had shared a meal together when we were kids.

Our mothers were always meeting up, sometimes in cafés but mainly in each other's houses. It was easier to stay at home and let the kids go off and play. They'd get out the white wine and sit in the kitchen, talking non-stop. We'd go up to my bedroom and play boardgames or dress up and act out stories. Aoife was quite bossy, even when she was the guest. She was a lot taller than me and behaved as if she was older, when in fact *I* was older than her by two days. I let her get away with it. Eventually, our mums would call us down for tea. It was always rubbish-food they knew we would eat without arguing – meatballs and spaghetti, garlic bread, chicken nuggets and oven chips, ice cream from the freezer dripping with chocolate sauce. They'd carry on drinking their wine, eating olives and crisps, nibbling at our leftovers.

Their laughter would grow louder and coarser. Afterwards, we'd go back upstairs or watch a Disney video in the sitting room.

Eventually, my dad would come home from work and Aoife and her mum would leave, like they suddenly had to be somewhere else. Dad was always cross because there was no dinner ready and the place was a tip. Mum would stand up for herself and sometimes it turned into a row. The white wine didn't help. I think Dad was jealous of our mothers' friendship. Of course, I didn't realise any of that at the time. I just felt sorry for Mum crying in her bedroom, and angry with Dad because he wouldn't let me watch my video to the end.

I'd always assumed that Aoife and I would be like our mums when we grew up, meeting for a good gossip while our daughters played together upstairs. Now I wasn't so sure.

'Hi, Tiff. How's it going?' I came back to the present with a jolt. Dani was standing at the threshold, biting into a slice of watermelon, juice all around her mouth. 'The stuff you get in England is always tasteless,' she said, 'but this is really yummy.'

'I was hoping we could wait to have breakfast together,' I said. The remark came out more pointed than I'd intended.

'Oh, really?' She spotted my empty yoghurt pot but didn't comment. 'Aoife's awake,' she said instead. 'It might be a while before she drags herself downstairs, though. Any sign of the others?'

'Beth's already up. Would you mind laying the table, please? I think we should bring everything outside.'

'Wouldn't it be easier to help ourselves from the kitchen?' Dani called after me. I pretended not to hear.

I didn't mention the breakfast selfie but sat drinking coffee, which I'd made far too strong. Beth munched her way through two croissants – one more than her allocation – while Dani made a show of eating Spanish-style, smothering her toasted ciabatta with olive oil and the garlicky tomato mixture Marta had provided. Celine, who turned out to have been doing yoga in the garden, only wanted a banana and Aoife didn't come down until after I'd put everything away.

Sensing that everyone was about to scatter, I tried to rally the troops. 'I hope you're up for a short quiz,' I said. 'It's just a bit of fun. And there's a prize for the winner!'

'Not sure my brain's up to much this morning,' said Dani, 'but I'll have a go.'

'What's it about?' asked Aoife, warily.

'How well we know you,' I replied. 'You can't do the quiz, obviously, but you can call out the questions. And, of course, you're the only one who knows the answers!'

After a short delay, I managed to get everyone assembled on the shaded terrace. I gave Aoife the list and handed around paper and pencils.

'Where did you get these questions from?' she asked, reading the list I'd compiled.

'Mostly off the internet, but some weren't relevant, like "What's your best sport?" so I deleted them and added a couple of my own,' I said.

'You mean, you rigged it to make sure you knew all the

112

answers,' remarked Dani. 'Only teasing,' she added quickly. 'Although as Aoife's oldest friend, you're bound to win.'

'And I'm going to come last for sure,' said Celine.

Aoife motioned for us all to be quiet. 'Okay. Here goes. Number one! This is so easy. What is my star sign?'

'No conferring or shouting out,' I reminded them. 'Just write it down.'

She carried on through the list. Who was her favourite celebrity? How did Nathan propose? What was her mum's maiden name, her shoe size, her karaoke song? We scribbled down answers obediently. Beth and Dani were making jokey comments and even Celine was joining in.

'Ooh, this question is interesting,' Aoife said, pausing. 'Hmm. Not sure I want to ask this one.'

'Oh, go on,' said Dani. 'Test us!'

'Okay . . . What is my greatest fear?'

'I know,' said Beth immediately. I glanced over to see what she'd written. *Spiders!* She must have remembered that night Aoife had hysterics over a spider in the bath, when we were having a birthday sleepover at my house. I couldn't think of anything else, so I wrote down the same.

Aoife carried on. How did she and Nathan meet? What was her favourite place, her favourite food, her favourite colour, her best and worst subject at school? Where was she going on honeymoon? What was her official job title? Had she ever had a pet?

'That's enough!' she cried. 'Pencils down.'

'Everyone swap papers,' I instructed, 'so there can be no cheating.'

I ended up marking Dani's paper, while Beth marked

mine. As Aoife called out her answers – hesitating as she tried to decide between purple and red, pepperoni pizza and Balti chicken – I realised I'd made a terrible mistake choosing this game.

Celine came bottom, as was expected, and Beth didn't do much better. I was the only one who knew Aoife's mother's maiden name, and I remembered she'd had a tortoise once (two of the questions that I'd added), but I didn't get any of her favourites right. Not one. Whereas Dani knew all of them.

To add to my humiliation, she was the only person to guess what Aoife's greatest fear was.

Being betrayed.

Chapter Fifteen: Now

DANI

'Dani!' She opens her eyes and sees Tiff standing at the poolside, looming over her. 'We've been looking for you everywhere. We didn't realise you were *swimming*,' she says, making it sound like a criticism.

Dani paddles to the shallow end and climbs out. 'Marta was here,' she says.

'Really?' Tiff's brow furrows. 'I didn't hear anyone.'

Dani grabs a rolled towel from the basket. 'She brought us breakfast. Like last time.'

'Oh. Yes, I remember. They still own the place, then?'

'Yeah, but she and John have split up.' Dani dries herself vigorously, then puts her sarong back on.

'Oh, dear. Did she say why?'

'Not exactly, but I think Aoife's murder had a lot to do with it. They can't rent the villa out – people are scared to stay here. I think they've got money problems.'

'That's bad . . . I bet she was surprised to see you.'

'Yes. It was a bit awkward, but we got over it.' Dani switches tone. 'So, have you recovered after our middle-of-the-night encounter? Did you manage to get back to sleep?'

'Eventually. Sorry about that. I was feeling jumpy, hearing strange noises. Couldn't stop imagining intruders.'

'It's understandable,' concedes Dani. 'So, what are your plans?' She wraps the towel around her head and wrings her hair.

'It depends,' answers Tiff, pursing her lips. 'We need to look at the options. Flying back today or staying and finding somewhere else to sleep. Do you mind taking us back to that restaurant? We need somewhere with Wi-Fi basically.'

'Sorry, I forgot to say. Marta fixed it.'

Tiff looks relieved. 'Oh, great. That's *something*.'

Dani lays the damp towel on one of the sunbeds. 'I'm going to have a shower now. Let me know when you've decided what to do. If you need a lift anywhere, just ask.' She walks back up to the house, her footprints drying instantly on the warm tiles. Tiff follows. They part ways in the living room, Tiff running off to Beth and Celine while Dani goes upstairs.

She shuts the door of her bedroom and lets out a breath. For once, she feels like she handled Tiff well. She doesn't like being pressurised, wants to feel like she's in charge even if she's not.

After her shower, Dani gets dressed and goes back downstairs, finding the others on the patio, huddled together on the sofa in the shade. Celine has her tablet on her lap and Beth and Tiff are either side of her, peering at the screen. Beth tries to shield it from the sunlight with one hand.

'How's it going?' asks Dani, adopting a careless tone.

'Hopeless,' concludes Celine. She looks up. 'No direct flights, the indirect ones take about fourteen hours.'

'I'm not surprised. It's high season.'

'And there's no accommodation. A couple of hotels in Malaga, but their reviews are terrible.'

'Airbnb?'

Beth wrinkles her nose. 'A few places out in the sticks, but none of us drive. All the hotels on the coast are fully booked.'

'We're trapped, basically,' says Tiff, staring hard at Dani. 'Of course, you knew we would be. It was all part of your plan.'

'That's not true.'

'Let's not fall out,' pleads Beth. 'It is what it is. We've just got to make the best of it.'

Celine grunts. 'I'm still not happy about being here. You lied to us, Dani.'

'I know, I've already apologised. I don't see what else I can do. I can't conjure up a plane.'

Beth stands up. 'We came here to celebrate Aoife's life, remember? So that's what we'll do. I think we should just relax today, get our breath back. Tomorrow we can visit the cemetery and do our little ceremony and think about how much we all loved her and—'

'Okay, we get it,' snipes Tiff. 'We'll pretend everything's perfect and that we're having a lovely time.'

Beth's face clouds over. 'I'm trying to be positive, that's all.'

'I know, hon, but it gets a bit wearing sometimes.'

Beth looks like she's about to burst into tears. 'I didn't want to come on this weekend any more than you did,' she says. 'I hate being here. Every room, every piece of furniture, even that amazing view, reminds me of what happened. It's like she's here with us. Like there's a ghost in the house. It makes me want to throw up.'

'It's the same for me,' interjects Celine.

'Of course it's emotional being here,' says Dani. 'Perhaps we just need to escape for a bit.'

Celine turns off her tablet. 'Fine with me, but where do we go? To the beach? Shopping? That doesn't feel right to me. We're not here for a holiday.'

'I didn't mean that,' Dani replies. 'But like I explained to Beth yesterday, as well as paying tribute to Aoife, I want to retrace my steps. You know, like in a crime investigation, when they stage a reconstruction? Except I want to relive the whole weekend, not just the bit at the end I can't remember. And you were with me, so it kind of makes sense if we . . .' She looks at them appealingly. 'What I'm trying to say is, I'd really like you to come to Puerto Banús with me this afternoon, like we did last time.'

'No way am I going back to that beach club,' says Tiff, crossing her arms.

'I wasn't going to suggest it. We probably wouldn't get in anyway. But I do want to go to Supernova later. And to the nightclub.'

'That's plain creepy,' Tiff says.

'And pointless,' adds Celine.

Beth nods. 'Sorry, Dani, but I agree. There's no connection between Saturday night and what happened on Sunday.'

'We don't know that for sure,' Dani argues. 'There *could* be.' Their faces are blank.

'I suppose Aoife could have told someone where we

were staying,' says Celine, shutting her tablet. 'But even if you managed to remember that detail, what are the chances of bumping into the same people again? Virtually zero. Anyway, the police probably know who attacked her – they just can't prove it.'

'Are you trying to play amateur detective, Dani?' asks Tiff. 'Because that's how it sounds.'

She tries again. 'No, not exactly. I know it seems like I'm clutching at straws, and I suppose I am, but I can't think of any other way to resolve this. I was with Aoife the whole weekend, and yet I don't know what happened in those last few minutes of her life. I should have been a witness! I have these odd snatches of memory, but I can't put them together, can't make sense of it all. Everything's so tangled up. This is my only chance of sorting it out in my head.'

'But why do you feel the need to sort it out?' asks Celine. 'It won't change anything.'

Dani looks at them hard. 'Things happened that weekend. Things we've never spoken about. To anyone. Not even the police.'

'They weren't relevant, that's why,' says Tiff.

'And they would only have upset Aoife's parents,' adds Beth. 'Mike and Kate have really suffered. The situation was bad enough, we all agreed there was no point making it worse.'

'Yes, but they still happened! We can't blot them out of existence.'

'More's the pity,' says Celine under her breath.

'I know it's uncomfortable, but we owe it to Aoife,' Dani carries on. 'At least . . . I do. I can't bring her back, but if I can find out who killed her, it'll be something. For her family, for Nathan.'

'If that's what you need to do, go ahead, do it,' says Tiff. 'I'm not going to stop you, but don't expect me to join in this – this pilgrimage. It'll be too painful and, ultimately, it's a waste of time.'

'I agree with Tiff,' says Beth quietly. 'Sorry, Dani.'

'What about you, Celine?' Dani asks.

'Being at the villa is uncomfortable enough. I don't want to go back to Supernova, I'm afraid. Or to the club. Sorry.'

'That's okay.'

Celine turns to the others. 'Mind you, if we don't go with Dani, we'll be stuck here all day, which feels even worse.'

'We could go into Marbella and mooch around while Dani's doing her thing,' suggests Beth. 'Not to have fun or anything, just to pass the time.'

'Okay with me,' says Tiff. 'Anywhere is better than here.'

Dani's spirits lift. 'It'll be impossible to park in the old town,' she says, 'but as I'm going to Puerto Banús, why don't you go for a walk along the *paseo marítimo*? It goes on for miles. You could find somewhere for lunch . . .'

'I'd be up for that,' says Celine. Beth and Tiff nod in agreement.

Dani smiles. 'Great. When do you want to leave?'

'In about twenty minutes? I need to make a call first,' Tiff says. She exits quickly in the direction of her bedroom.

'She's as bad as me,' Celine says, looking after her. 'Who does she keep calling? Has she got a new man?'

'I think it's her mother,' replies Beth. 'She's very invested. She was like a second mum to Aoife.'

When everyone's ready, Tiff goes round, making sure all the windows are closed, locking the patio doors. The others go to the car while she sets the alarm. Dani unlocks it and they get in, Celine taking the front passenger seat this time.

The Seat Ibiza is as hot as a pizza oven. Dani starts the engine to get the aircon going. This is fine, she thinks as they wait for Tiff. Maybe it will be better without the other hens. Supernova will be closed until 9 p.m., but John might be around. There's something she needs to talk to him about, and she can't do it if the others are with her.

Tiff appears and climbs into the rear seat, next to Beth. 'Sorry about that,' she says. 'Had a few problems setting the alarm. I hope I got it right.'

Dani doesn't need the Sat Nav to get to Puerto Banús. They went back and forth last time and it's a simple route to remember. She drives down the narrow bumpy track and turns right at the end, onto the main road.

A little way ahead, a motorcyclist is parked up in the layby next to the shrine. The ground around it is covered with offerings: flowers – real and artificial – candles flickering in jars, photos, messages, snippets of what look like Christmas decorations. A feral cat noses around, hoping to find something to eat. As they pass Dani sends up a silent prayer for Aoife, even though she doesn't believe in God. In her rear mirror, she sees the motorcyclist jump on his bike and join the road.

'Are you sure the aircon's working?' asks Beth. 'I'm sweating buckets back here.'

'Yes, it's on full blast,' says Dani. 'It just takes a while to kick in.'

Nobody chats, preferring to look at the scenery. It's stunningly beautiful around here. They can see the sweep of the Costa del Sol and the Rock of Gibraltar in the hazy distance. Down in Marbella itself, the roads will be gridlocked, but up in the Sierra there is very little traffic. Dani makes the descent to the coast, rounding bend after treacherous bend, drawing ever closer to the madness below – the crowds, the insane wealth, the glitz and glamour. She had never thought such a world would collide so strangely and so violently with her own.

The motorbike is still behind them as they pass the entrance to the Country Club – in reality an upmarket housing estate – with an electronic barrier across the road and a uniformed guard stationed in a little office. Security is tight in these places, and it needs to be. Dani is reminded of how vulnerable Villa Floriana is, perched on the mountainside, all by itself. Calling it a villa is a bit pretentious, really. It's a far cry from the marble monstrosities here, or the huge white cubes with enormous windows that must be impossible to live in during the hottest months.

'There's a turning, isn't there?' asks Celine from the back. 'Have we missed it?'

'No, it's on this road, should be coming up soon,' says Dani, slowing down. Glancing in the rear mirror, she spots the motorbike again. He must be sweltering in those leathers, she thinks, as she turns right at the junction.

They crawl their way to Puerto Banús, navigating roundabouts featuring ridiculous waterfalls and extravagant planting, passing retail parks and luxurious apartment blocks. Dani cruises around the port, almost running over several pedestrians and not seeing a single space to park.

'Nobody look, but I think we're being followed,' says Celine.

Beth instantly leans forward. 'What? Which car?'

'It's not a car, it's a motorbike. You must have noticed him, Dani? He was parked up by the shrine, he's been behind us ever since.'

'Um . . . yes, I did notice,' she replies. 'But I don't think he's been following us, as such, just going in the same direction.'

'Why would anyone be following us anyway?' says Tiff. 'You're being paranoid, Celine. Like Dani last night. She heard noises outside. Gave me a right scare.'

'I know, I'm sorry about that.'

'And was anyone out there?' asks Celine anxiously.

'No! An animal maybe, nothing else. We're all on edge. It's hardly surprising.'

Dani takes one of the boulevards that rise up from the seafront. Sure enough, the bike keeps them in its sights, although at a distance. She carries on driving around, looking for a space. Here, there is less traffic but there are more restaurants, more boutiques, more real-estate offices, more roundabouts. She finally manages to park on a very steep street, a long way from the beach.

'Sorry, but this is the best I can do,' she says, leaving the car in gear as she turns off the engine.

'He's turned around and driven off,' Celine announces. 'See? That confirms it.'

'Not necessarily,' says Tiff. 'I expect he's still looking for somewhere to park.'

Celine frowns. 'You can park a motorbike virtually anywhere.'

'That's true,' comments Beth.

'It doesn't matter, he's gone now,' Dani says, not wanting to discuss it further for fear of frightening them. But she can't deny to herself that Celine's right. The motorcyclist definitely followed them here, although she can't think why anyone would do such a thing.

Tiff tugs at the child-locked door handle. 'Well? Are we going for a walk or what?'

They get out and plod in single file down the hill. The pavement is steamy, and the palm trees offer only intermittent shade. When they reach the promenade, they are confronted by swarms of people – holidaymakers, kids on electric scooters, parents pushing buggies, elderly people with walking frames, glamorous women with pooches. There are parties of hens too – trailing white veils, bobbing bunny ears, flashing learner signs . . .

'Oh my God,' murmurs Celine. 'I'd forgotten what it was like.'

The beach is so packed Dani can barely make out the colour of the sand. They shuffle along the *paseo*, trying to carry on a serious conversation, but it's hard to stay together and almost impossible to hear each other's voices above the din.

They pass a sign for the Blue Oceania beach club. The logo – words written in the shape of a frothy wave with a golden sun forming the O – is enough to shake up her memories. They twist and turn like fragments in a child's kaleidoscope. Dani stops, unable to move with so many colourful images crowding inside her head.

There's Aoife standing next to her, in purple shorts and a yellow crop top, a red-and-white-striped bag on her shoulder, a pair of blue-framed shades perched on her nose . . .

Chapter Sixteen: Then

DANI

According to Tiff, who had done extensive research, the Blue Oceania beach club was one Marbella activity that they couldn't miss. Dani had taken a sneaky peek at the website herself and realised that the club was essentially an outdoor swimming pool with a fancy restaurant and bar. It wasn't really her thing, she decided, being more of a put-a-towel-down kind of girl herself, but When in Marbs . . .

The taxi dropped them off promptly at two o'clock in the afternoon. There was a small queue to get in. The security guard insisted on searching their beach bags for alcohol. When he was satisfied they weren't smuggling anything in from the Mercadona, they were shown to their sunbed – also pre-booked, for the extortionate sum of four hundred euros. It came with a 'free' bottle of champagne, for which they were obviously supposed to be grateful.

The sunbed was way back in the third line from the pool-side, tucked against the wall. It was round and white and strictly for a maximum of four people. They'd had to buy a separate 'general entrance' for the fifth person. Beth had heroically taken the single ticket, but Dani assumed they were going to take it in turns to stand around like a lemon while the others sipped fizz and worked on their tans.

'Do we have to be stuck back here?' complained Aoife, plonking down her bag. 'That big one at the front is free. Can't we have that?'

'Yeah, if you want to pay over a thousand euros,' said Tiff. Aoife flapped her hand in front of her face, as if to say the price was too high. She took off her shorts and top, revealing a stunning bikini – plain black with a plunge bra and the smallest of bottoms.

'Who's for a swim?' she asked.

'I'll come,' replied Tiff straightaway. 'Just let me get my kit off.'

Dani sat down next to Beth and Celine. She wasn't sure how they were supposed to share the sunbed without draping their limbs over each other. It seemed made for two couples rather than four friends and they weren't even friends – not really. Dani let Beth take the corner that was shaded by the striped parasol. She looked around self-consciously and still wore her shirt, even though it was incredibly hot. It was easy to feel intimidated by all the slim, scantily clad women swanning about, silver studs twinkling from the belly buttons of their flat tummies, flicking their hair over their shoulders and taking endless pouting selfies.

Dani pulled her dress over her head and was about to hang it over the rails of the parasol when a passing waiter gave her a warning look. Not allowed, apparently. She rolled it up and put it in her bag instead. She glanced over at Aoife and Tiff who were standing in the water, looking bored. Nobody was actually swimming. Perhaps that wasn't allowed either, she thought, adjusting the straps on her bikini.

The atmosphere wasn't as relaxed as she'd hoped. The bouncers were ever-watchful, and the high metal fencing around the back of the club made her feel like they were in a luxurious prison.

Their waiter arrived with champagne in an ice bucket and four glasses. He set it down on the little table in the centre of the sunbed, under the parasol.

'Don't forget, there's an additional minimum spend of five hundred euros,' he said in a camp Liverpudlian accent. 'You pay now, alright? If you go over, I'll let you know.'

'What!?' cried Celine. 'That can't be right.' She stood up and summoned Tiff to get out of the water.

'Five hundred euros more?' said Tiff, when she heard. 'We already paid four hundred for the sunbed.'

'Food and drink not included. It's the Saturday surcharge, everyone has to pay.'

'It didn't mention it when I booked.'

He waggled a finger at her. 'Yep, it did. It's in the Ts and Cs. You must have ticked the box or you wouldn't have been able to book the bed.'

'Well, it wasn't made clear enough,' Tiff carried on, hotly. 'That's outrageous.'

He sighed as if he held the same conversation ten times a day. 'Look, babe, nobody wants a scene. Not good for the vibe. Either you pay the five hundred euros now or you have to get off the sunbed. Your choice.'

Tiff turned to her fellow hens. 'I'm really sorry about this. What should we do?'

'A hundred euros each, that's a lot of food and drink,' said Beth.

'Not at these prices,' Dani muttered, looking at the snack menu.

'Are you going to pay or not?' the waiter asked. ''Cos I've got a long waiting list . . .'

Tiff looked across at Aoife. She was still in the pool, chatting to some muscly guys with tattoos. Dani nodded reluctantly. She didn't want to spend another hundred euros in the place – or any money in fact – but neither did she want to be dragged off the sunbed by security. Other people were looking at them. It was embarrassing.

'Um . . . okay then,' Tiff sighed, handing over her credit card.

When Aoife emerged from the pool, Tiff explained what had happened. Aoife wasn't really listening, she was too busy towelling herself down, making sure her spray tan hadn't gone streaky.

'You should have read the small print,' Dani couldn't stop herself from saying.

'Yes, thank you. I *know.* If you don't want to pay your share that's fine, but don't expect any food or drink.'

''Course I'll pay my share,' Dani growled. 'It's just a piss-take, that's all. I could have two weeks in Greece for what this weekend is costing.'

'We've got to bloody well make sure we spend the whole five hundred,' said Aoife, sitting down next to Beth. Immediately a bouncer came over and told them off for being too many on the bed. Not wanting another fuss, Dani stood up and said she was going to have a wander around to see what else Blue Oceania had to offer.

All the sunbeds were occupied now, and the queues at

the bar were four deep. At 3 p.m. the DJ suddenly ramped up the volume. Dancers appeared as if from nowhere, all wearing identical blue-and-white bikinis and ridiculously high heels. They strutted up and down the catwalk that intersected the swimming pool, wiggling their butts and striking sexy poses in time to the club sounds blasting through the speakers. On the other side of the pool, two handsome mixologists were performing a show, balancing bottles upside down on their arms, flipping and catching, juggling ice cubes, squirting drink into the mouths of the most attractive women nearby. Dani had to admit that everyone seemed to be having a great time, not caring in the least that they were being mightily ripped off.

They stayed for several hours, taking it in turns to sit down, ordering burgers with extra fries, fizz and more fizz, ice cream sundaes and tropical fruit salads. Tiff kept a strict tally of how much they were spending, determined to reach the five hundred limit and not go a euro over. By the end of the afternoon, they'd spent four hundred and ninety-seven euros. Their stomachs were bloated with food, their heads singing with alcohol. Dani had had enough sun and was tired of playing musical sunbeds. Annoyingly, they still had a third of a bottle of fizz left. Tiff wanted to take it back to the villa, but it was – unsurprisingly – against the rules.

'Drink up, everyone! We're not leaving it,' she said, passing the bottle round. Eventually, it was emptied and placed upside-down in the bucket in a triumphant gesture. They felt as if they'd cheated the system, although in fact the system had cheated them.

Chapter Seventeen: Then

CELINE

As soon as we returned from the beach club, we went off to our rooms to get ready for the night ahead. In an hour's time we'd be going down to the port yet again. As I stood under the shower, I wished we weren't staying so far away from the clubs and bars of the town. The villa was beautiful, and I loved the spectacular views, but the taxi fares were exorbitant.

The beach club had been an enormous rip-off, and we'd already had to pay extra for the activities because we were such a small number. I didn't want to tot up the full cost of the weekend because I knew it would make me feel sick. At this rate, I would have to borrow money to pay Tiff back my share.

The thought of putting on going-out gear – high heels and evening make-up – made me want to lie down in a heap. But there was no choice, I couldn't duck out, as much as I wanted to stay at the villa with a bag of pretzels and Netflix. Although we'd got through the afternoon without anyone having a tantrum, I hadn't forgotten the previous evening. Talk about soap operas ... First there'd been Aoife's unbelievable behaviour at the cocktail workshop, then that game that had made Beth so upset. Aoife had definitely touched a sore spot, maybe even a couple of sore spots, from their past. I sensed there was a lot more going on under the surface that I didn't understand. It made me feel distanced from the rest of them.

Naturally, I hadn't stopped thinking about when I might get confirmation of my new job. It came with a much-needed salary uplift too. I knew I wouldn't hear from HR over the weekend, yet I couldn't resist the temptation to check my emails, just in case Charlie had been in touch informally. He knew how anxious I was about it and would want to put my mind at rest if he could.

Predictably, there was no message. I was still in limbo, although I was pretty sure that I *was* the new Head of Development. My insides were skipping with excitement. I couldn't wait to get back to work and move into my new office with its own sofa and coffee table. When Jocelyn had been away on maternity leave, I'd taken over her work but hadn't been allowed to take over her office. HR said I wasn't the official maternity cover, and they couldn't offer me any more pay. Farrell was livid on my behalf, but I was cool about it. I was being given a chance to show what I could do. I'd proved my worth, now it was time to reap the rewards.

It would have been nice to celebrate over the weekend, but it looked like I was going to be made to wait until I got home on Monday evening. That was fine – better to celebrate with Farrell than with people I didn't really know. I'd take him out for a meal, I decided, maybe even to that posh restaurant that we'd gone to with Nathan and Aoife.

As I applied my make-up, I contemplated the evening ahead. Pre-drinks at a bar, hopefully our host's place.

Super-something it was called. It would be good to use the vouchers. Then once we were suitably tanked up – I sighed inwardly – we'd move on to the famous, or should I say infamous, Pesadilla nightclub. There were no plans, as far as I could make out from Tiff's schedule, for an evening meal, although we had already stuffed ourselves at the beach club, so maybe we could skip that.

There was just one more thing to consider. The masks. They were still lying in their carrier bag at the bottom of my suitcase. I couldn't ignore them any longer. Going to the corner of the room, I crouched down and unzipped the lid. I took the offending items out and laid them on the bed in a row.

Four larger-than-life-sized masks of Nathan's face, each stuck onto a long plastic stick stared at the ceiling. The photo that had been used was terrible – sausage-pink and fuzzy. I couldn't decide whether he was grinning or snarling. Either way, it wasn't a pleasant expression and made me wonder why he'd picked such an unattractive shot of himself. The masks were truly hideous, printed on glossy card that made his skin look sweaty. What *had* he been thinking?

Expect a package, Nathan had texted me a week ago. *It's coming directly to you.*

What is it? I asked.

Something for the hen party. A surprise!

I'd never seen groom masks before, but when they arrived, I googled them and saw that they were quite a popular thing. Why any bride would want her hens to go around wearing masks of her fiancé, I couldn't understand. Presumably they were meant to be funny, but I found them sinister. And the fact that Nathan had gone to the trouble of having them specially printed made me feel even more uneasy. I wished he hadn't given them to me. I wanted to send them back, but Farrell said I couldn't because it might cause offence.

Nathan had already messaged me three times that day, asking for pics. I couldn't carry on ignoring him. The masks would have to make an appearance tonight. We didn't have to wear them in Puerto Banús. All I needed was a photo at the villa – Aoife grinning with her four Nathans at her side. That should be enough to satisfy him, I thought.

I heard Beth and Tiff leaving their bedroom, their shoes clipping across the tiles of the corridor to the kitchen. The evening was beginning, whether I liked it or not. I put the masks back in the carrier and followed them outside.

Dani and Aoife were already sitting on the terrace, lolling about on the rattan sofa, tearing their way through a six-pack of premixes. Was that strictly necessary when we were about to go out? I had no idea how they managed to absorb so much alcohol into their blood and still stand up straight. They'd really gone overboard with their make-up tonight, with dark sparkly eyeshadow and matching glitter transfers on their cheeks. With her long legs, a white dress and a pair of massive false lashes glued to her eyelids, Aoife looked like a startled ostrich.

'What's in there?' Tiff asked me, immediately alert to the carrier bag.

'Well . . .' I began, dipping my hand in. I drew out one of the masks, with Nathan's head facing away from her. 'Nathan

gave me these. He thought you might like them for tonight.'
I turned it over and waggled it in her face.

'What the—?' said Aoife, snatching it off me.

Dani squealed. 'Oh my God, that is so creepy! Take it away!'

'*I'm* supposed to be in charge of accessories,' said Tiff after a few moments. 'What's going on?'

'Nothing to do with me,' I replied. 'Nathan had them printed. He sent them to my flat. He *made* me bring them.' I took the other three masks out of the bag. 'Apparently, everyone's meant to wear one except the bride.'

'Weird,' was all Beth had to say on the subject.

'No way am I parading around Marbs with a bunch of Nathans prowling after me,' Aoife announced. 'It's obscene.'

'We don't have to take them with us,' I said. 'All we need is a photo. We can do it by the pool, with the mountains as a backdrop.' Aoife looked unconvinced. 'Please? I virtually promised Nathan.'

'Take a photo of *this* then,' said Aoife, standing up and marching across the lawn to the pool, mask in hand. 'No, take a video!'

'Uh-oh,' said Dani, sensing trouble.

I looked at the others, wondering whether they were going to follow, but nobody moved. Taking my phone, I went after Aoife.

The sun was starting to go down and the sky was streaked pink and orange. Aoife stood right where the hillside fell away steeply. When she heard me approach, she turned around and held up the mask.

'Ready?' she asked.

I nodded, although I wasn't sure what I was meant to be ready for. I pointed my phone at her and pressed start.

'Fuck off and leave me alone, Nathan!' she shouted. She tossed the mask over her shoulder, into the valley below. Then, slapping her hands together as if to say 'Job well done', she stuck out her tongue to camera and strode past me, back to the terrace.

I stopped recording and deleted the video immediately. Now what was I supposed to do? Try later, when Aoife was too pissed to care? Ask Tiff to talk to her and explain? I still needed that photo. I went to see where the mask had fallen, thinking maybe there was a chance I could retrieve it, but it had dropped some way down and caught on a rock.

I peered at it. Nathan stared back up at me – shiny skin, dead eyes, a twisted expression on his face.

Chapter Eighteen: Now

DANI

'This is hopeless,' Celine says, side-stepping to avoid a skateboarder. They've been trudging along the crowded *paseo* for about half an hour and haven't managed more than a few hundred metres. 'Can we stop? Please?' She points to a patch of ground behind an ice cream kiosk and they wander over there, gathering in the shade of a tree. Wasps are swarming around a nearby bin overflowing with rubbish.

'What shall we do?' asks Beth, removing her sunglasses to wipe sweat off her forehead. 'Give up and go back to the villa?'

'No,' says Tiff firmly. 'Not yet.'

'We could do the cemetery visit,' Celine muses. 'I know we'd planned it for tomorrow, but—'

Dani interrupts. 'Sorry, but I don't want to do the cemetery today. I've other stuff I need to do here. Anyway, I'm not ready for it.'

'Nor am I,' says Tiff, for once agreeing with Dani. 'Perhaps we should go somewhere quieter, you know . . . into the Sierra.'

'And do what?' asks Celine. 'Go on a bloody hike? We're supposed to be celebrating Aoife's life and all we're doing is trudging along like a bunch of tourists.'

'Then suggest something else.'

'I already did.'

There is a long, irritable pause. Nobody knows whether to carry on walking or sit down or what.

'Do you think it would be alright if I had an ice cream?' asks Beth quietly. 'I know we're not on holiday but I'm so hot—'

'Of course it's alright,' says Tiff, adding a few moments later, 'Aoife loved ice cream. Salted caramel was her favourite.'

'No, it was chocolate,' Beth says.

It was pistachio, thinks Dani, but she doesn't get involved.

'Okay, have one scoop of each,' says Celine. 'In memory of her.' Beth smiles at Tiff tentatively, waiting for her nod of permission. She gets it and the four of them laugh gently.

Dani shifts her feet. 'Well, I'm going down to the marina,' she says. 'I may be a while. Text me when you decide what you're doing, okay? When I've finished, I'll come and find you.'

She leaves them queuing at the ice cream kiosk and heads in the direction of the port, relieved to have got away. But as she walks, she can't stop her mind returning to the mysterious motorcyclist. She keeps looking around to check that she's not being followed, although it's hard to know with these crowds. The hairs on the back of her neck spike in fear as she imagines a figure walking behind her, slowing as she slows, speeding up when she starts to panic, threading his way through the people until he's close enough to tap her on the shoulder.

Her heart leaps into her throat. Suddenly halting, she

spins around and stares accusingly at the sea of anonymous faces coming towards her. But nobody takes any notice of her; they are gazing into the distance or talking to their friends or looking down at their phones. They're not even aware of brushing her as they pass by.

She tells herself to calm down, take some deep breaths. It's okay.

Ever since Aoife's murder, Dani's been nervous of strangers getting too close. A few times, when walking home by herself at night, she's been convinced that somebody has been following her. It has sent her heart racing uncontrollably and she's become dizzy and fearful. She's also had nightmares in which a man is wrapping his arms around her, pushing himself against her so that she can't breathe. She wakes up screaming, tangled in her sheets, fighting the air. Her therapist thinks they could be flashbacks from the night that Aoife died, and that what she's experiencing is PTSD. Dani has no idea if that's the case because she can't remember. She's worried that she might have invented him as a way of explaining what happened to Aoife. Now she needs to know the truth either way.

Her eyes scan the vicinity – the packed beach on one side of the *paseo*, a strip of public garden on the other with benches and small kiosks. As far as she can tell, there's nobody lurking in the shadows, throwing her surreptitious glances. Maybe it was just a coincidence that a motorbike followed them all the way from the shrine to their parking spot. Then she remembers the noises she heard outside last night. Had somebody been snooping around?

Dani turns and continues walking in the same direction.

139

It's taken months of planning to get to this point, she can't run away now.

She reaches the port. Luxurious yachts gleam in the sunshine – stark white against the intense blue of the sky. Designer boutiques sit between exclusive bars and super-pricey restaurants. It's where the rich, beautiful people hang out and where the tourists go to watch them.

Dani heads for the infamous 'second line' that runs behind the seafront. It's another world entirely, known to Spanish locals as La Calle del Infierno, the Street of Hell; narrow and pedestrianised, with the back entrances of the premier venues on one side and the frontages of more downmarket bars, clubs and fast-food joints on the other. Puerto Banús is a night-time place, the daytime reserved for sleeping off the excesses of the evening before.

The last time Dani was here it was dark and the strip was heaving. At this time of day, it's relatively quiet. Most people are on the beach, or doing a boat trip, or gawping at the luxury yachts, or fainting at the prices in the boutiques.

She finds Supernova immediately, wedged between a kebab shop and a strip joint with blacked-out windows covered in giant posters of girls in sexy lingerie. As she had suspected it would be, the bar is closed, the graffiti-covered metal shutters rolled down.

She walks around the corner, looking for a service entrance, and finds a small door with a bell. She presses it and waits, not expecting it to be answered, but not knowing what else to do. Just as she's about to give up, she hears the sound of somebody running down the stairs. The door opens and there's John, the same gorgeous, sun-bleached mess that he was before, right down to his tatty flip-flops.

'*Hola*,' he says cautiously.

'*Hola, ¿qué tal?*'

'Er . . . *muy bien. ¿Y tú?*'

'*Bueno, así así*—' She breaks off. 'Why are we speaking Spanish?'

'Sorry . . . er . . . do I know you?'

'It's me! Dani.'

'Dani?'

'Daniela Harrington. Don't you remember? I was one of the hens.'

He shakes his head. 'Sorry. We get a lot of hen parties here.'

'I was Aoife's friend. Aoife Byrne. Who was—'

'Yeah, yeah, yeah, I'm with you now. Shit.' He scrapes his fingers through his hair. 'Sorry, of course I remember. I just didn't – out of context and all that. Dani. Yes.' He blinks at her through bleary eyes. 'Hi. What are you doing here?'

'It's the anniversary – three years since Aoife was killed.'

'Is it? Yeah, suppose it must be.'

'The other hens and I are staying at the villa.'

His mouth falls open. 'Not Villa Floriana?'

'Yes.'

'Why?'

'It's complicated. Can we talk?'

'What about?'

'What happened.'

'There's nothing more to say, is there?'

'I think there is. Please?'

'Okay. You'd better come in then.'

He stands back for her to enter. 'This way,' he says briskly, taking her down a narrow corridor, past crates of beer bottles, multipacks of toilet rolls, cartons of booze, bins overflowing with empties, and boxes of miscellaneous rubbish. He unclips a bunch of keys from his belt and unlocks the door that leads into the bar itself.

A cocktail of alcohol, sweat and cheap perfume permeates the room. He flicks a switch and all the lights turn on at once.

The scene is laid out before her, like a theatre set. Dani blinks, trying to adjust her pupils to the sudden brightness. The place is a tip. Empty glasses are lined up on the counter and the purple vinyl floor is covered with litter – limp foil balloons, paper napkins, karaoke microphones, a battered headdress with penises for antennae.

'We closed at four this morning,' John says by way of apology. 'I've been asleep, not had a chance to clear up yet.'

'Don't you have staff to do that for you?'

'Not anymore. Trying to cut down on my overheads, see. These are difficult times, Dani, difficult times.' He goes behind the bar. 'What can I get you?'

'Just water, thanks.' His brows shoot up. 'I don't drink.'

'That's not how I remember it.'

'People change.'

'Do they?' He takes a bottle out of the chill cabinet and hands it to her. 'So, why exactly have you come back?'

'To remember,' she says.

'Remember Aoife?'

'Yes, but mainly to remember what happened that night. I was completely out of it, you see. I'm going back over what we did that weekend, recreating it step by step. Like that Saturday night, when we came here, and afterwards, at Pesadilla.'

'You're going back to Pesadilla?'

'Later, yes.'

'Watch yourself. That place is full of baby gangsters.' He goes back to the bar, pulls himself a pint of San Miguel and brings it over to the table. 'So, what do you want to talk to me about?'

Dani unscrews her bottle of water and takes a slurp, momentarily wishing that it was a gin premix. 'Marta mentioned you'd split up,' she says.

'She chucked me out on my arse, but yes.'

'She said Aoife's murder changed everything. Destroyed your marriage.'

'She likes to be dramatic.'

'Some couples get closer in times of crisis,' Dani observes. 'Others pull apart.'

'We're definitely the second type,' he says with a wry smile. 'According to her, it's all my fault. We were supposed to be aiming at couples and families, not groups. When I took the hen booking, Marta said it was asking for trouble. She was worried you'd get drunk and break her stuff.'

Dani is surprised. 'Really? I remember she seemed quite welcoming when we turned up.'

'She was being professional, that's all. Afterwards, she was convinced you must have met some dodgy guys over the weekend and told them where you were staying.'

143

'I don't think I did,' says Dani. 'Maybe it was one of the others. Aoife could be a bit stupid like that. Thought everyone was her new best mate. She was always swapping numbers with strangers.'

'Yeah, I remember how friendly she was getting with people that Saturday night.'

'Including you.'

He doesn't respond, pretending to take more interest in his pint of lager.

'Does Marta know about that?' she asks after a pause.

'About what?'

'I thought maybe it was a factor in your splitting up.'

'Sorry, Dani, I don't know what you're talking about,' he says, looking at her with a bewildered expression.

'Oh, come on, John.' The memory of that night starts to creep up on her.

'Seriously, I don't know what you mean.'

'You and Aoife.'

'What about me and Aoife?'

'You had sex with her in your flat.'

He gapes. 'She told you that?'

'Yes.'

He puffs out his breath, setting his glass down on the table. 'Okay . . . She was hitting on me – really strong, that's true. I was a bit shocked. You *do* get flirty brides, but usually when it comes to it, they back off. Not that I'm in the habit of . . . you know . . . but when I was single . . .' He clears his throat.

'Why did you go off with her?'

'I didn't. She was offering herself on a plate basically, and

144

I was worried she was going to take it too far – not with me, with some other guy. I took her upstairs, made her a coffee, and tried to talk some sense into her. She was our guest, I felt kind of responsible.'

'That's not what Aoife said happened.'

'It's the truth. I tried my best, but she didn't want to listen. Started taking her clothes off. I mean she was obviously incredibly attractive, but I was like, really horrified. I told her to get dressed and go back to the bar. Virtually had to push her down the stairs.'

'No, you carried her into the bedroom and stripped her naked. That's what Aoife told me, and she never lied to me.'

She pauses. Aoife lied to other people, she remembers – mainly to cover up her mistakes and avoid getting into trouble. She was never very good at taking responsibility for her actions. But she and Dani never lied to each other. Never.

'I'm sorry but in this case, she *did* lie,' John goes on. 'We can't ask her, so you'll have to take my word for it. What does it matter now, anyway?'

Dani balks. 'It matters because it matters. I protected you. I never told anyone. Not the other hens, or Aoife's fiancé, or her family. Not your wife . . . I didn't even tell Inspector Mengual. I kept your secret. Not for your sake – for Aoife's!'

His tone suddenly hardens. 'I did not have sex with Aoife. Don't you ever dare tell *anyone* that because it's not true. It didn't happen, alright?' He looks at her strangely. 'What the hell are you doing back here anyway? Have you just come to make trouble?'

'No,' she protests. 'I want the truth.'

'I just told you the truth.'

'I mean the truth about what happened to Aoife.'

He frowns at her. 'It was a break-in that went wrong. That's what the investigation concluded.'

'Maybe it was, maybe it wasn't. There's so much crime here, it's easy to jump to conclusions. But my gut is telling me the police may have been looking in the wrong place.'

'Or turning a blind eye,' he says. 'Has that not occurred to you?'

She flames with indignation. 'No, it hasn't. Mengual is a good guy.'

'You have no idea how things work around here,' he cuts in. 'It's like the fucking Wild West. Burglaries, kidnaps, murder . . . it's all going on in Marbs. People rarely get arrested, let alone convicted. Half the police are corrupt. It's a bad idea to shake this case up again. A really, really bad idea. I'd go so far as to say, it's dangerous.'

Her mind flits briefly to the guy on the motorbike. Should she mention it? Suddenly, she feels like she can't trust John.

'I just want to know what really happened,' she says instead.

'Let me give you a word of advice.' He grabs her hand. 'Go home and get on with your life. Don't try to remember, try to forget. Don't say a word to the police, not even your precious Mengual. You don't know who's in whose pocket. Just keep your head down, okay?' She looks away. 'I mean it, Dani.'

'It sounds like you know who was behind Aoife's death,' she says under her breath.

'I don't, I swear. But if I did, I'd keep my mouth shut. Please. Go back to the UK. Before something worse happens.'

She glares at him. 'What could be worse than your best friend being murdered?'

He gives her a pitying look. 'Believe me, you don't want to find out.'

Chapter Nineteen: Then

DANI

John greeted them personally as soon as they arrived, all dressed up. Tiff waved their drinks vouchers in his face just in case he'd forgotten. He showed them to a table opposite the stage – the VIP area, as he described it, although no professional footballer or TOWIE celebrity would be seen dead in such a place. That didn't matter to Dani – she liked its cheap cheerfulness. This was where the expats hung out, where hens and stags came for cut-price pre-drinks and a spot of karaoke before hitting the clubs.

In the end, everyone had been up for ditching the schedule and coming here, even Tiff. Having been stung by the prices at the beach club earlier in the day, they were keen to save a few euros. Supernova seemed to be the perfect first stop on a journey that would last all night.

The crowds were already streaming in. Dani and Aoife were put in charge of keeping the seats warm, while Celine and Beth went to the bar. Tiff decided to check out the karaoke. According to Beth and Aoife, she had a really good singing voice, but would only attempt songs that were in her range.

Two blonde girls dressed in white were owning the stage, crucifying a Whitney Houston classic. Their friends stood on the dance floor, swaying in time, air-pumping the chorus. Normally, Dani and Aoife would have watched them, giggling and making arch comments, but Aoife was just sitting there, glum-faced, wincing at the singing like it was hurting her teeth.

'I can't do this,' she said suddenly.

'Yes, you can,' Dani replied. 'You're a way better singer than they are.'

'I didn't mean the karaoke.' Aoife looked away, staring into the middle distance.

'Are you okay? You've been in a weird mood all day.'

'I can't marry Nathan,' she said.

'What?' Dani wasn't sure she'd heard correctly. The wannabe Whitneys had just attempted the climactic top note, to loud cheers of support.

'I can't marry him,' Aoife repeated, louder and more decisively.

Dani ran her tongue over her lips as she searched for the right response. For the last two years, she had struggled to get beneath Aoife's loved-up veneer. Every time they met up, which had become less and less frequent, she'd only ever talked about how amazing her life was with super-boyfriend Nathan. He'd taken her in hand – given her the stability she'd been craving, fixed her up with a job that was perfect for her skillset and personality. He was kind, generous, thoughtful, attentive. Great in bed. 'I'm so happy,' Aoife kept insisting.

Dani had smiled and listened, somehow not convinced, although she couldn't put her finger on exactly why. Happiness was not something Dani fully believed in. In her view, it was a mood, not a constant state of being, and it had worried her that Aoife felt the need to keep going on about it. More to the point, Dani didn't like Nathan, or the way he was trying to change her friend's personality.

Beth and Celine were still queuing at the bar. 'Why the sudden change of heart?' Dani asked.

'It's not sudden. I've been feeling like this for a while.'

'How long?'

'Weeks. No, months . . . On and off since we got engaged.'

'Why didn't you tell me before?'

Aoife shrugged. 'I don't know. It felt awkward. Embarrassing.'

'Have you talked to Nathan about it?'

'Of course not.'

'But – surely – I mean – for God's sake, Aoife, the wedding is in three weeks!'

'Yes, I know! I can't decide what to do. Sometimes I think I'm the luckiest woman in the world. But there are other times when I think I can't go through with it, that I just don't love him enough, or as much as he loves me, and that makes me feel really guilty because he deserves—'

'Woah! You've got to talk to him about this. The minute you get home. Don't leave it till the wedding day, and definitely don't leave it till the day after. You've got to sort this out as soon as you can.'

Dani looked across, wondering what had happened to their drinks. She'd been drinking all day, but this was a crisis moment; a fresh hit of alcohol was needed, and fast. Dozens of people were crowding before the bar. Celine's black glossy mane of hair was just visible, but she couldn't see Beth at all.

'Yes, I know, you're right,' Aoife sighed. 'But if I tell him I've got doubts, even little ones, he'll be devastated. He won't understand. Everything with Nathan is black or white, there are no in-betweens. Either I want to marry him or I don't. I've got to decide one way or the other, then tell him. That's what this weekend's about.'

'That's not what it said on the invite,' Dani joked.

'It's not funny, Dani.'

'I know.' She leaned back in her seat, feeling slightly sick. 'It's just hard to enjoy the weekend if I know you're having second thoughts. We're supposed to be celebrating your future happiness.'

'We still are. I just don't know what my future happiness looks like yet.'

Tiff was singing now, belting out 'I Will Always Love You' with a quality to her voice that sounded almost professional. She couldn't have picked a less appropriate song if she'd tried. Dani stood briefly. 'Whoop-whoop! Go, Tiff!' she shouted, then sat down again. 'You can't do this,' she said, turning back to Aoife. 'You can't expect your friends to fork out well over a thousand euros each—'

'They don't need to know.'

'You think you're hiding it? Last night you were all over Matt, you spent this afternoon chatting up guys at the beach club, and then you had a meltdown over the groom masks.'

'I can't talk to the others about it. Only you. You know me like no one else does.'

Dani threw up her hands. 'When are those drinks coming?'

'Tiff and Beth think they know me, but they don't,' Aoife continued. 'Maybe when we were kids, but not anymore.

We've gone off in different directions, had different experiences. Every time we get together, I realise how far apart we've drifted. And as for Celine: she's a nice woman but she wasn't supposed to be here.' She shuffled closer and gave Dani a desperate hug. 'I'm in trouble, Dani. Please help me.'

'Of course – you know I'd do anything for you. I just don't know how I can help at this point.'

'I want to have a blast tonight, forget it's my hen, forget about Nathan. I want it to be like the old days. You and me. We had some wild times, remember? In Greece—'

Dani pulled away. 'Not sure we should go that far.'

'This is my last chance, Dani!'

'Last chance for what?' she replied, already knowing.

'I've been thinking, if I could … you know … get together with somebody tonight, it would help me test my feelings for Nathan.'

Dani grimaced. 'No, no, no, no, no. That is the worst idea ever. That's pressing the nuclear button, there's no way back. Even say you found somebody to oblige – I assume you're thinking of Matt – what if you wake up tomorrow and realise you love Nathan after all? Do you keep it a secret for the rest of your life, or do you confess? What if he doesn't forgive you? What if he finds out later and finishes with you?'

'I know it's a big risk. But it's the only way I can solve this. I've been texting Matt on and off all day, but he's not messaged back for a few hours. It'll have to be somebody else.'

'Like who?'

'I don't know.' Her eyelashes fluttered. 'That John's lush, exactly my type … I think I'm his as well. Yesterday, when we arrived at the villa, he couldn't take his eyes off me.'

Dani grabbed her hands. 'Please, I'm begging you. Don't go down this route.'

'Here we go! Sorry for the delay, it's a rugby scrum at the bar,' said Celine, resting a tray of wine glasses on the table. She and Beth sat down. Tiff, who had been persuaded to sing a second song, finally returned and claimed the place next to Aoife. They raised their glasses to a stonking night ahead.

At the start of the weekend, Dani had been the loudest in the group, the biggest drinker, the most up for partying. Now she was quiet, refusing to join in the casual bitching about the other singers' voices and what they were wearing. The others could tell something was up, but nobody probed, assuming perhaps that the two of them had had a falling out.

Tiff seemed to be enjoying this supposed rift hugely. She snuggled up to Aoife, cracking in-jokes and making pointed toasts of 'Friends for life!' With the obvious implication that life meant from birth to death – a claim on Aoife that only she was entitled to make. For once, Dani didn't rise to the bait. She was too busy trying to work out what to do. Should she bundle Aoife into a taxi and take her back to the villa? Lock her in the bedroom until she agreed to behave?

The singing was raucous. About eight women had climbed onto the stage and were doing an impersonation of the Spice Girls, three of them lunging forward with their tongues out, competing to be Scary Spice. People were jerking around, singing 'Wannabe' at the tops of their voices with no care for the melody. Despite the mayhem, Beth and Tiff decided they wanted to dance. Celine said she'd stay and keep the table, although actually there was no need as it was reserved. She was increasingly distancing herself from the rest of the group.

'Come on!' Tiff stood up and dragged Aoife off the seat.

'You too, Dani!' shouted Aoife. 'I'm not dancing without you!'

Dani didn't want to dance but she felt compelled to stay close, so she peeled herself off the banquette and followed, much to Tiff's irritation. They found a tiny space on the floor, wedged between a group of stags and another hen party. The whole room shouted out the lyrics. Dani knew what Aoife really wanted – or rather, what she *thought* she really wanted. She needed to stop her from getting it.

But Aoife had already launched her campaign to get laid – grinding her hips, sticking out her boobs, twirling around and deliberately bumping into guys, then feigning a kind of sexy innocence. A display of girl power it was not.

Then John reappeared. He made a beeline for their group and thrust himself into the middle, jiggling about with all of them in turn, like a good host should, but all the time staring at Aoife, working his way slowly towards her. Surely he wasn't interested? He was married, and he was the co-owner of the place where they were staying.

A couple of songs later, he caught her. Some guy was bawling out a ballad. They danced together like a couple who already knew each other intimately, faces close, thighs touching, fingers intertwined. Dani's heart was in her mouth; she could see it happening, right there on the dance floor – Aoife's future unravelling. And there was nothing she could do about it. Not without making a huge scene.

An upbeat song took over that was a Eurovision entry from a few years back, though she didn't remember whose; only that it involved people forming a chain and careering around the room, holding onto sweaty strangers. John put his hands around Aoife's waist and they joined the end of the line, melting into the crowd. The chain quickly broke up and the groups re-formed but Aoife and John didn't return.

Tiff and Beth had already gone to join Celine back at the table, leaving Dani stranded on her own. After waiting on the dance floor for a few minutes, she went to look for Aoife, but she was nowhere to be seen. Nor was John. Maybe they'd gone outside, Dani thought, making her way through the heaving throng to the front. She stood on tiptoes at the entrance but couldn't see beyond the queues of people on the pavement. She imagined John and Aoife up against a wall, snogging and groping each other like a couple of teenagers. Or worse. She started to feel panicky. Should she try to find them and pull them apart? Aoife wouldn't thank her for it now, but maybe later, when she'd sobered up . . .

Dani went to the toilets, but her friend wasn't there. Nor was she back on the dance floor. Perhaps she'd simply returned to their table. No such luck.

'Where's our bride?' Beth called out as Dani approached.

'Um . . . not sure. Gone to the loo, I think.'

'Is she okay?'

'Yeah, as far as I know.'

Dani sat down next to Tiff, feeling the vacant space between them. Celine went back to the bar to order a bottle of fizz and the rest of them sat there waiting. Dani tried not to look too anxious, pretending to watch the karaoke but all the time scanning the crowd for a sign of Aoife's blonde pixie haircut.

'Maybe I should go and see if she's alright,' said Beth after about ten minutes. 'She's been gone for ages. I hope she's not being sick.'

Tiff looked cross. 'You should have stayed with her, Dani.'

Aoife finally turned up twenty minutes later. Her hair was sticking up and she sounded breathless.

'Hey, where have you been?' asked Tiff.

'Outside. I needed some fresh air.' She grimaced. 'The doorman made me queue up again to get back in. Tosser.'

Dani knew she was lying. Her eyes glittered with secrets.

It was later on when Aoife confirmed her worst fears. 'We went upstairs,' she whispered while they were walking to the nightclub, tottering along the Street of Hell, the others walking several metres ahead and thankfully out of earshot. 'We had sex on their bed. Oh my God, it felt so transgressive, it was amazing.'

'Oh, Aoife,' Dani hissed. 'What have you done?'

She stopped and turned to face her friend. 'Promise me you'll never tell anyone? No matter what happens, not for the rest of your life?'

Dani promised.

Chapter Twenty: Now

DANI

Dani steps into the brilliant sunshine. Her insides are burning with anger on Aoife's behalf, but there's no way to release it. She replays the encounter with John in her mind, assessing it from every angle. When she turned up, he behaved like he didn't recognise her, but that makes no sense. They saw each other during that weekend, and in the few days following the attack, then again at the inquest. She has a strong sense that he was pretending and already knew the hens were back. He'd lied to her about not having sex with Aoife, so he could easily be lying about other stuff. Maybe he was even prowling around the villa last night.

He knows something about Aoife's murder, she's sure of it. Maybe he even knows who killed her. That's why he told her to stop digging around, why he tried to frighten her with stupid talk of gangsters – he was worried for himself as much as her.

She walks the few metres to the harbour front and sits down on a concrete block beneath a lamp post, concentrating her gaze on the gleaming yachts and the bluer than blue water, her vision smeared with furious tears. She doesn't dare go anywhere near another bar right now or she'll order a double vodka. Then another, and another. Her body is begging to feel ice-cold alcohol shoot through her system. These are the most difficult moments, intense desire coupled with immediate availability.

Today is her one hundred and fifty-eighth day without a drink. That's a real achievement, she's got to hold onto it. Can't give in now. She has to convert all this negative energy into positive action. It's the only way. Usually, it's running or going to the gym, or housework or even cooking. Today she'll be saved by doing the right thing. She's going to contact Inspector Mengual and tip him off about John.

She must still have his mobile number. He rang and messaged her a few times in the first months after Aoife's death, but she never added him to her contact list. Dani moves into the shade and runs her thumb down the screen, looking for a Spanish phone number. WhatsApp lists contacts in order of the most recent communication – the new group she created for this weekend, her mother, a couple of friends, various therapists, her buddy at AA, colleagues from her last job. Further down, the names and profile pictures become less familiar and the date of her last contact with some people shocks her. Has she really not been in touch with them for over two years?

Aoife's murder made the tabloids. It wasn't long before Dani was inundated with email and texts from their uni friends. They knew how close the two of them always were. A couple of women had even been on the original hen list but had pulled out when Tiff announced it was taking place in Marbella. No doubt they felt they'd had a lucky escape. People were sympathetic but also curious. They wanted the full lowdown but were too embarrassed to pick up the phone or meet Dani face to face. *If there's anything I can do . . .* She read that phrase so many times. It felt empty then and feels even emptier now. She didn't know how to respond to them. It was too raw. Too soon. No wonder so many of those friendships have wasted away.

She continues scrolling down the list, going back in time, finding mysterious numbers and profile pics of people she doesn't recognise. Soon she will reach the year of Aoife's death. If there are messages from Mengual they should appear in the first few weeks after . . . She slows down, looking for the Spanish international code.

Result. She finds her chat with him and, without further thought, makes the call. She leans against the wall, waiting for him to pick up. It rings and rings. She sends him psychic messages down the line, begging him to answer. Eventually, she gives up and sends him a voice message instead, telling him that she's back in Marbella, staying at the villa with the other hens.

'I have some information that could be important,' she whispers into the phone. 'Please, please get in touch with me as soon as possible. *Muchas gracias.*'

There. She's done it. Of course, there's a chance that Mengual is corrupt, but she doubts it. Although he was tough on her during her first interview that Monday morning, as the investigation proceeded she grew to trust him, even to like him. Spanish police were notoriously brusque, but Mengual showed real understanding and compassion.

Her phone rings. Her heart leaps, thinking it's the inspector ringing straight back, but it's Beth. 'Are you okay?' she asks. 'You've been gone ages.'

'I've just been walking around,' she lies.

'We're in a place on one of the streets behind the *paseo*. Come and join us. I'll text you the location.'

Dani finds her fellow hens sitting outside a large restaurant, sheltering under an expansive cloth awning. They've obviously eaten lunch and drunk a bottle of wine between them. She sits down and orders a Coke, the urge for alcohol having thankfully subsided.

'What have you been doing?' asks Tiff, an edge of suspicion in her voice.

'Nothing much,' she replies. 'I went to take a look at Supernova – it was closed, of course.'

Beth puts her head on one side, thinking. 'Funnily enough, Supernova wasn't on the schedule and yet it was the best bit of the whole weekend,' she says. 'It was really good, remember, Tiff? You even got up and sang.'

'How can you talk like that?' Tiff looks disgusted. 'Like it was a perfectly normal hen do that just went a teeny bit wrong at the end?'

Beth blushes. 'I'm sorry. I didn't mean to be insensitive. I thought this weekend was about celebrating Aoife's life? Surely that means remembering the good times as well as—'

'There *were* no good times, not at the hen,' Tiff rages. 'Before, yes, there were loads of them, but that weekend – no. It was the worst weekend of my entire life.'

'Calm down, Tiff,' says Celine.

'Don't tell me to calm down!' She almost explodes. 'I don't even know what we're doing here. Dani seems to be taking some kind of horror trip down Memory Lane. It's ghoulish.'

'I already explained, I'm trying to remember what happened,' she says gently.

'If you hadn't got so drunk you wouldn't *need* to try,' Tiff snaps.

'Tiff . . .' says Beth warningly. 'We agreed we wouldn't go there.'

'Yes, I know, but I've had enough of The Dani Show. We all know why she's brought us here. It's not to celebrate Aoife's life, it's to help her deal with her own guilt. She wants us to tell her we forgive her and have a big group hug.'

'No, I don't,' Dani mumbles.

'Aoife's death wasn't Dani's fault,' says Celine firmly.

'Wasn't it? What kind of person drinks so much they black out?' Tiff points a finger at Dani. 'If Aoife hadn't been looking after you, she wouldn't have gone indoors and disturbed the burglar.'

'I'm not sure it was a bur—' Dani starts, but Tiff barges on through.

'You didn't try to stop him attacking her – you just lay on the floor, conked out.'

'I know.' Dani shrivels inside with guilt.

'We needed your Spanish to call the ambulance, and when it didn't come, we needed you to drive her to the hospital, but you did nothing!' Tiff pushes back her chair and stands up. 'You let her die!' The chair clatters to the ground as she storms off.

They watch her go. There's a long, painful pause. Beth restores the chair to its upright position.

'Tiff doesn't mean it,' she says. 'I agree with Celine. It

wasn't your fault, Dani. Nobody could have saved her. We tried everything, but . . .' Her eyes fill with tears.

'Please stop! None of this is helping anyone,' says Celine.

There is another very long silence.

Finally, Celine turns to Dani, changing her tone. 'We need to get out of here. Before you arrived, we were looking at Benahavís. It's a little town inland, not too far. We thought we'd hang around there until we've had enough, then go back to the villa as late as possible.'

'Okay,' says Dani, grateful for the respite. 'Like I said, I'll be here until the clubs open, so you'll need to get a taxi there and back. Sorry.'

'Are you sure about staying, Dani?' Beth asks. 'It's such a long time to wait. And you don't want to be on your own in Banús at night. Most people on the streets will be pissed out of their brains. The drug dealers and prostitutes will be around. It's not safe. And the car's parked a long way out, you'll have to walk back to it in the dark.'

'Don't worry about me. I'll be fine.'

'Beth's right,' says Celine. 'You shouldn't be by yourself. Why don't you come with us to Benahavís? I'm not just saying that because I want a lift,' she adds. 'I'm concerned about your safety.'

'No. I need to do this. It's important to me.'

Beth and Celine exchange a glance. 'Okay,' Beth says. 'But stay in touch, and don't come back too late. I don't want to lie awake all night, wondering where you are.'

They settle the bill. Beth scoops up Tiff, who has been fuming on the corner, and the three of them walk towards the taxi rank. Dani stays behind, staring after their retreating figures until they merge with the crowd. Then she sets off in the opposite direction, back where she came from. She keeps turning around suddenly to see if anyone's behind her, as if she's playing Grandmother's Footsteps, but there's nobody there. It's important to stay calm, she thinks, and not let John's warnings spook her.

She stays on the beach for a bit, staring at the sea, then finds a tapas bar in the back streets, where she sits in the corner, ordering one dish at a time in order to while away the hours until midnight.

Dani stabs her fork into a pork cheek, braised in sherry. *Carrillada Ibérica* is one of her favourite tapas dishes; you only get it made like this in Spain. It's strange, she thinks, going back to the argument with Tiff, that she should envy her fellow hens their memories of the attack. But she does in a way. They have no idea how painful it is *not* to be able to remember. She has spent the last three years feeling disconnected, not just from what happened to Aoife, but from her own life. It's as if a wire was cut that night, plunging her into darkness. She has been fumbling about for too long, unable to see. This weekend is supposed to be about reconnecting, illuminating the past so that she can move forward into the future.

Tiff's right. If she hadn't been so drunk, she might have been able to save Aoife. Maybe it's also about coming to terms with her guilt. Receiving the forgiveness of others. Forgiving herself.

She checks her phone. Still no reply from the inspector.

Several hours later, Dani joins the queue for one of Marbella's most popular nightclubs: Pesadilla. She feels underdressed in her strappy top and short denim skirt; what little make-up she applied this morning has long since been sweated off in the sun. Her hair needs sorting out too, but there's nothing much she can do about that. She's not the type of woman who carries a hairbrush around with her. Once she's out, she's out. She never even takes a lipstick.

But she's made it to midnight without giving up or falling asleep or succumbing to alcohol and now she's here, queuing up with all the losers who either forgot or left it too late to book a table. There are hens in their sashes and bunny ears, stags in their personalised T-shirts, sporting wigs and false moustaches. One guy has a dildo sticking out of his forehead like a Dalek. Another appears to be dressed as a giant vagina. Dani suspects they may not be allowed in. This is an upmarket club. Last time she was here, nobody was wearing silly costumes.

The security guards are passing along the queue, weeding out the rejects in advance to save arguments at the door.

'No flip-flops,' one says, pointing at her feet. Her heart sinks. She'd forgotten about that bit of the dress code.

'Please!' Dani begs. 'I'm on my own. I'll stay in the background, I won't dance.'

He looks her up and down, unimpressed by her appearance. 'No sex workers inside the club,' he says.

She flushes hotly. 'I'm not a sex worker!'

'Hmm. You can't come in anyway. Girls have to wear heels.'

'That's ridiculous. And sexist.'

'I don't care what you think, it's the rules. Go find somewhere else.' He makes as if to shove her but she steps back first, relinquishing her place in the queue. The gap closes, like she was never there.

Dani wants to give his face a good slap with her flip-flop. She shouts curses at him as he carries on down the line, dismissing the silly costumes and the guys in trainers, confiscating sashes and headdresses.

'It's so unfair. I've been waiting all day!' she says to nobody in particular. 'How come they allow criminals in but not guys with penises strapped to their heads?'

But her fellow rejects are no longer there to sympathise with her. They've already shuffled off in search of a venue less squeamish about taking their money. Dani sits down on the edge of the kerb with her elbows on her knees and her chin in her hands. She knows there is another way to get in around the back – a small courtyard where the staff go to smoke or vape in the few minutes they're given for breaks. Whether she could use it as a way to get in is another matter. Dare she try?

Dani looks up and sees a group of young women standing in the queue. They are talking loudly and laughing. There are no sashes or veils in sight, but they are hens for sure. There's something familiar about them too. Maybe they were on the same plane over. If only she could hide among them and smuggle herself in.

New memories start to filter through. She transposes Aoife's image onto the woman she suspects is the bride, then places Tiff next to her. Beth and Celine had been behind, she remembers, while she'd been standing slightly apart. With a leap of her imagination, she whisks them all inside the nightclub.

Chapter Twenty-One: Then

DANI

They arrived at Pesadilla almost bang on midnight. As Tiff had pre-booked, it didn't take long to get through the queue for security checks. Inside, the music boomed, the dancers posed on their platforms and the lightshow was aggressive, but it was still early and the party hadn't really got going yet.

They were shown to their table, tucked away at the back near the cloakrooms, a long tedious trail to the dance floor with no view of the DJ. Their waiter, an English guy who introduced himself as Seb, brought them the drink that came with their package – two 70cl bottles of gin and vodka with giant sparklers attached and a large bucket of crushed ice. Mixers were extra. Seb poured their first drinks and Tiff proposed yet another toast to Aoife's future.

Dani joined in, but her heart was in her stomach. After the disastrous game on Friday night, the rip-off beach club and the weirdness over the groom masks, she'd thought the hen do couldn't get any worse. But Aoife had just screwed a guy and was now saying that she didn't want to marry Nathan. There was only one thing to do in such circumstances – hit the bottle hard.

She downed her vodka and tonic in one, then sat back to

survey the scene. The clientele included holidaymakers, large single-sex parties, couples, small mixed groups of friends. Everyone basically looked the same, like the club had a uniform. Virtually all the women wore skimpy dresses and were very heavily made-up – enormous false lashes, painted-on eyebrows, long pointy nails shiny with shellac. The men were dressed smart–casual – short-sleeved white shirts or tight black Ts, and black chinos (no jeans). Every exposed chest was hairless. Most arms, and some necks, bore tattoos.

Dani and Aoife had gone to considerable efforts with their hair and make-up that night, not wanting to look out of place. They wore intestine-crushing tube dresses and high heels that were going to be almost impossible to dance in. Fully embracing the Marbs vibe was all part of the fun. You couldn't turn up at Pesadilla looking any other way.

Then there were the guys wearing sports gear – oversized hoodies, baggy sweatpants, flashy trainers. (She thought they were banned?) Their clothes were plastered in logos from competing designer brands like Dior, Vuitton, Gucci. Gold chains hung around their necks, and showy rings sparkled on their fingers. A few wore sunglasses, despite the club being so dark, and had small satchels slung across their chests. Some looked English, possibly Dutch or German. Others were probably from North Africa – Morocco or Algeria at a guess. Whatever their nationality, they looked like parodies of themselves, and they made Dani want to laugh. She was fascinated by them, so much so that Beth had to tell her to stop staring.

'You'll get us into trouble,' she said.

'Sorry, can't help it,' Dani replied. 'I'm obsessed.'

Later, she thought it might have been her fault that one of the groups sent a bottle of champagne to their table.

'We didn't order this,' Celine said firmly.

'I know. It's compliments of table seventeen,' Seb the waiter said, digging into the wrapper with the end of his corkscrew.

'Really?' Aoife grinned. 'That's nice. Which is table seventeen?' She stood up and scanned the room, a wave of thanks at the ready.

'Sit down,' Celine said sharply, pulling her arm. 'I don't think we should accept this.'

'Are you mad? We can't turn down a free bottle of fizz!'

'We don't know who sent it.'

'We do!' Aoife insisted. 'Table seventeen.'

Seb bent forward. 'Sorry, ladies, can't take it back.'

'Yes, you can,' Celine replied haughtily. 'Say thanks very much, but we don't accept gifts from strangers.'

'Celine!' Dani rolled her eyes in exasperation. 'Don't be such a, such a—' She searched in vain for the word. 'Just lighten up.'

'You have to accept it,' said Seb. 'There's no choice. Not with these guys.'

'That's ridiculous,' Celine snorted.

'I'm on commission here. If this gets sent back, I'm in a world of pain.'

'Which guys are we talking about?' Dani asked.

He nodded slightly behind and to his right. 'About four tables along, next row down.' He lowered his voice, even though there was absolutely no chance of anyone else hearing him above the thumping music. 'You don't want to mess with them, particularly not the guy in the Balenciaga jacket.'

'Why not?' asked Aoife.

'They're foot-soldiers, you know?'

'What do you mean?'

'Just be careful, okay?' Seb removed the cork. It made a satisfying pop, but nobody whooped in response. He poured out five glasses, handing them round.

'Make sure you drink it,' he said. 'They'll be watching.'

Dani tried a surreptitious glance across to table seventeen, where four guys dressed head to toe in black leered over at them. The guy in the jacket that looked about six sizes too big for him shouted something at her she couldn't hear, let alone understand.

'This is not good,' said Celine once the waiter had gone. 'Those guys are real sleazebags. They'll be expecting to join us next – you wait.'

Aoife shrugged. 'Fine by me.'

'Don't be an idiot,' Tiff said. 'You know what foot-soldiers are? They do the dirty work for gangsters. We don't want to hang out with criminals.'

'No,' agreed Beth. 'We definitely don't. What if there's a scene, like in that club in Manchester? I can't afford to get arrested again, Aoife.'

'Good point,' said Tiff.

Aoife groaned. 'Come on, it's my hen party! We can't let a few jerks stop us having a good time.'

'I wouldn't call them jerks, not to their faces,' said Celine. 'We should leave while we can.'

'Yup,' said Beth. 'It's a shame, but it's the safest thing.'

Celine seemed to be taking charge. 'We need to slip out, one by one,' she said. 'Make it look like we're going to the loo or want to dance. We'll meet outside, at the end of the queue, and I'll call a taxi straightaway.'

'I don't want to go,' said Aoife, slugging down her champagne.

'You'll be expected to pay for that drink,' warned Celine. 'One way or another.'

'But this is the highlight of the whole weekend! Please, let's stay. It'll be okay.'

'It won't,' said Tiff.

Dani didn't know what to do. Normally, if anyone had influence over Aoife, it was her, but her advice at Supernova had been ignored, so there was no guarantee that her friend would comply now. Most importantly, Aoife mustn't be left alone with a group of gangsters, however wannabe. She'd already done something she was going to regret tomorrow. Dani had to make sure she didn't add anything else to the list.

Finally, she spoke up. 'I'm with Aoife. We've only just got here. We've still got the best part of a bottle of vodka to finish, we've hardly touched the gin and we haven't even had one dance. No way am I wasting another five hundred euros.'

'It doesn't matter about the money,' said Beth. 'It's about being sensible.'

'Sensible?!' scoffed Aoife. 'I didn't come here to be sensible!'

'That's up to you, but I'm not going to hang around,

waiting to be assaulted,' Celine said, grabbing her clutch bag and standing up.

'Nobody's going to get assaulted,' Dani replied, trying to calm the situation. 'We're in a club. There are security guys everywhere. Nothing bad is going to happen. And if they *do* try something on, we'll handle it.'

'Yeah. We've got this,' agreed Aoife.

Celine leaned forward, tapping her polished nail tips on the table. 'What if they insist that you go somewhere else with them? Like to a party in some luxury villa or on a yacht?'

Aoife laughed. 'Sounds good to me!'

'You don't understand. I've read about this kind of thing,' continued Celine. 'It starts out like fun. Then the next thing you know, you've been drugged. You wake up naked next to a total stranger and you can't remember what happened. It's dangerous!' She looked from Tiff to Beth and back again. 'You're Chief Bridesmaid, Tiff, you're in charge. What do you think? Say something.'

Tiff put her hands together. 'I don't know.' Dani could see her weighing up the options, trying to work out whose side it was best to be on. 'It may not be so bad,' she continued. 'They haven't made a move yet. Maybe we should just wait to see what they do and if we don't like it—'

'If we don't like it, *what*?' demanded Celine. 'It could be too late by then. You can tell by the look of them, they're nasty criminals.' She drew herself up to her full height. 'If anyone wants to share a taxi back to the villa, they need to come now.'

Tiff turned to Beth. 'What do you want to do?' she whispered.

'Get out of here.'

'But I don't trust Dani to look after Aoife.'

Unfortunately, her remark was overheard. 'I don't *need* looking after,' Aoife said. 'You've done nothing but boss me about ever since we got here. You're just like Nathan, always trying to control me. I can't stand it anymore. I'm not a child, I know what I'm doing!'

Dani couldn't let this carry on. 'Stop it, Aoife, that's not fair. Tiff has worked really hard to pull this weekend together.' She turned to Tiff. 'Sorry. Ignore her. She's pissed and talking shit, that's all. Please stay.' She really meant it. 'Let's forget all this and start again. And if we get any hassle from over there, we'll just ask for help.'

'No, I want to go now,' Tiff said, almost crying.

Beth nodded. 'Me too.'

'I'll try calling a taxi,' said Celine.

'No, stay! Please,' Dani pleaded. 'All of you. This is Aoife's big night.'

'Oh, let them go if they want to,' she said. 'They just want to stop me having fun.'

'No, they don't,' Dani soothed. She turned to the others. 'Come on, guys, we'll be okay if we stick together. There's safety in numbers.'

'I think we should *all* go back to the villa together,' said Beth. 'Have some coffee and sober up. Sort it out calmly, like grown-ups.'

'I already told you, I'm staying.' Aoife frowned stubbornly.

'Fine, whatever,' responded Tiff. 'You only want to hang out with Dani anyway. You should marry her, not Nathan.

He loves you so much and you don't deserve him!' She stood up and stormed out of the club with Celine and Beth following close behind.

'What was all that about?' said Dani, gazing after them. 'Has Tiff got a thing for Nathan?'

'Who knows? Who cares?' Aoife waved at the bottles. 'All the more booze for us!'

Chapter Twenty-Two: Now

DANI

She shakes herself free from the memory and opens her eyes. The queue for the nightclub snakes around the block. There is a babble of excited chatter, punctuated with sudden bursts of laughter. Somebody walks up and stands right in front of her.

'Hey . . . Dani? Is that you?'

Her gaze sweeps upwards, taking in a pair of expensive shoes, dark chinos, a pale blue shirt. Tanned skin. Blond wavy hair. Action Man features.

'Matt!'

'You remember me.'

''Course I do. You're Matt the Mixologist. What are you doing here?'

'Working. I'm Matt the DJ now,' he says with that winning smile of his. 'I do a session here, between two and three. Must say, I didn't expect to see you.'

'I've just been chucked out of the queue.'

He runs his eyes over her. 'Hmm. Flip-flops?'

'Got it in one.' She grins up at him, relieved to see a friendly face. 'It's been three years. How come you recognised me?'

'Never forget a face.'

'Wow. But you must meet so many people. And you remembered my name. That's impressive.'

'Not really. I'm a mate of John's, remember? We talked about that weekend a lot. I'll never forget the cocktail workshop. It's locked away in here' – he taps the side of his head – 'forever.'

'I know what you mean.'

'Are you okay?'

'Not really.'

'Fancy going somewhere for a quiet drink?'

'Um . . . yeah, that'd be good.' She feels tired and could do with a coffee before driving back to the villa. 'Sure you've got time?'

'Loads.' He holds out his hand and she lets him pull her to her feet.

They walk away from the club and find a bar overlooking the sea, at the far end of the marina. Its terrace is festooned with coloured umbrellas hanging from a pergola covered with fairy lights. The diners have largely gone and there are lots of empty tables. They choose one on the front row.

'So how come you're back in Marbs?' Matt asks once they've ordered a pint of lager and a double espresso. 'I would have thought this was the last place you'd want to be.'

'That's what everyone says.'

'Everyone being . . . ?'

'My fellow hens, Marta, John . . . we're staying at Villa Floriana.' Matt looks astonished. 'Yeah, I know. It's a bit weird. We're doing a kind of memorial thing. A tribute to Aoife.'

'Right.'

'And I've been trying to relive the hen do.'

'Oh.' He starts to look uncomfortable. 'Why?'

'Because I spent most of that weekend completely wasted. I'm trying to reconnect. Fill in the gaps. We went to Pesadilla on Saturday night, you see.'

'Doesn't surprise me. Most stag and hen parties end up there eventually.'

Their drinks arrive. She unwraps the tiny biscuit that comes with her coffee and dips it in. It disintegrates immediately, sinking to the bottom of the cup. 'Things happened that shouldn't have happened,' she says. 'I let Aoife down.'

'It wasn't your fault.'

'Wasn't it? I don't know, that's the problem. The hours before her death are a complete blank to me.'

He drinks his lager and gazes into the darkness – black sea, black sky, and no way of telling where one begins and the other ends. Dani can almost see him thinking, trying to work out whether to say something or keep quiet.

'What is it?' she asks.

'Oh, nothing. Just that Aoife's death really cut me up. I felt like shit because I'd been flirty with her and, when she came on to me, I didn't resist. I knew she was the bride, and I just let it happen. Afterwards, the fiancé's picture kept coming up on my feed and he looked so . . . destroyed. *He* was the person who should have kissed the bride last, not me.'

'Yeah . . . well . . . he never found out, so . . .'

'Didn't he?' Matt looks relieved. 'But *you* knew?'

'We all did. It was obvious that you had the hots for each other. But you weren't the last person who kissed her, so you can dump your guilty feelings.'

'I wasn't?' He whistles. 'Jesus, what kind of hen party was it?'

'The worst,' she replies.

'It ended in her death, so yeah . . .'

Dani takes a sip of her coffee. 'Aoife was hoping to see you on Saturday night, but you blew her off.'

'I thought better of it,' says Matt. 'So who took my place?'

She hesitates, wondering how much to reveal. 'Oh, just some guy she met in Supernova,' she says.

'And Nathan? That's the groom's name, right? Did he find out?'

'Good God, no. There was no point in rubbing salt in the wound. He was in a bad enough way as it was.'

'Yeah, I can imagine. That was a good call.' Matt nods slowly as he drinks. He drains the glass, then wipes the foam from his top lip.

'Aoife always had a wild streak,' Dani continues. 'She did some outrageous things when she was young, kissed a lot of frogs, you know? When she met Nathan, she said she'd finally found her prince. She settled down a lot, which I guess was a good thing, but she didn't seem like the same person anymore. Nathan was moulding her into something she wasn't. I didn't like it. But Aoife wouldn't hear a word against him, so there was no point saying anything. I assumed she was fine about it, that it was all happy ever after.' She takes a breath.

Matt leans in. 'But it wasn't?'

'No, not at all. Once we were on the hen, she started behaving strangely, drinking too much, saying weird things, putting out. She told me she didn't want to marry Nathan, that she was sick of him controlling her. It was like she'd pushed the self-destruct button. I was worried about her, but also relieved. I *wanted* her to call the wedding off.' She has a slug of coffee. 'Sorry, I don't know why I'm telling you this.'

'It's okay. Sometimes you need to talk to a stranger. I'm not a total stranger, but . . . I think I understand.'

'That's more than I do.' She takes a breath. 'Can I just ask you one thing?'

'Of course.'

'What do you know about John? What kind of people does he hang out with?'

Matt shrugs. 'Normal people. Expats, mostly. It's quite a small community here, everyone knows everyone.'

'Okay.' She tries a different tack. 'These expats . . . are any of them . . . you know . . . involved in stuff they shouldn't be?'

'That's more than one thing.'

'Please.'

'Depends on what you mean. There are tax dodgers out here, for sure. And there's one guy who's served time for fraud. But most of us are simply here for the lifestyle – sea, sun and sangria. Why are you asking?'

'It's just that I saw John earlier and he gave me a really fierce warning. Told me to stop digging around into Aoife's death, said Marbella was dangerous.'

'It *can* be. If you're in with the wrong people.'

'Is John in with the wrong people?'

'Nah, he's a beach bum at heart.'

'I've got a horrible feeling that he knows who killed Aoife. He insisted he didn't, but I think he was lying. He seemed genuinely scared.'

Matt ponders this for a few seconds. 'As far as I know,

178

John's straight. But he may have heard stuff on the grapevine or gossip in the bar. Like I said, Marbs is a small place. Best thing is to keep out of it. Keep John out of it too, okay? You'll only make it worse.'

Dani makes an exasperated noise. 'But what about justice for Aoife?'

'I know it's tough, but the chances are you'll never get that. There's a lot going on here. The case is ice-cold. The police have got enough to do with this week's crimes, let alone something that happened three years ago. Sorry if that sounds harsh, but John gave you good advice. Just let it go, Dani. Let it go and live your life again. Here, give me a hug.'

She lets him hold her for a few moments, fighting back the tears, feeling stupid and helpless.

'Let me walk you back to your car,' Matt says. 'It's not safe for a woman on her own, not at this time of night.'

'Are you sure you've got time?' she sniffs.

'Yeah, just about.'

'Okay, thanks, I'd appreciate that.'

Matt takes her arm and guides her through a maze of alleyways, avoiding the Street of Hell. They follow the main road cutting inland, back up the steep hill. The pavements are busy with drunken pedestrians, most of them heading in the opposite direction. On the way he chats easily, pretending the previous exchanges never took place. He points out various bars and restaurants where famous footballers and TOWIE celebrities are known to hang out, and where the more upmarket prostitutes ply their trade.

'Here you go,' he says as they arrive at the white Seat. 'Do you know your way back to the villa?'

'I think so. Thanks.'

He kisses her on both cheeks, Spanish-style. 'Keep your head down,' he murmurs in her ear. 'Do nothing, speak to nobody, and you'll be okay.'

She gets in the car and shuts the door. He bangs the bonnet the way men do, as if the car is a horse and they're telling it to canter off. She watches him head off down the hill, but instead of going back down the road they came up, he slips around the next corner and vanishes into the night.

Dani puts her seatbelt on and starts the engine. The clock display tells her it's 1.34 a.m. Matt had better hurry. He's going to be late for his DJ set if he's not careful. She still feels cross about not having been allowed into the club. If he hadn't happened to be passing, she might well have dived into the nearest bar and ordered a large vodka . . .

She sits there, not moving, distracted by a strange thought that's forming in her brain. Something's off kilter, but she can't put her finger on it. Something to do with Matt. His last words to her almost sounded like a threat. It was quite a coincidence that he found her on the pavement. Would he realistically recognise her so quickly when they'd only met once before at the cocktail workshop? John didn't. And because he owned the villa they'd seen each other a few times in the aftermath of Aoife's death.

Then she realises what's really bothering her. At no point this evening did she tell him that she was driving or where she'd parked the car.

Chapter Twenty-Three: Then

DANI

A few minutes after Tiff, Beth and Celine marched out of the club, the gangsters swaggered over to their table. At least, Dani assumed they were gangsters – she wasn't planning on asking for confirmation. Their leader, a tall, slim-hipped guy with a long nose and very arched eyebrows, sat down next to Aoife, put his arm around her and immediately started nuzzling into her neck. They didn't say hello or introduce themselves. The broadest one, who was dressed in monochrome camouflage sweatpants and an Under Armour vest, signalled at Dani to shift along so that he could squeeze next to her. The other two sat in the tub chairs opposite, presumably wondering what had happened to their dates.

Dani felt a hand grip her bare thigh and she shivered inwardly. Celine was right, they should have got out while they could. But Aoife had been adamant that she wanted to stick around, and Dani wasn't prepared to leave her on her own. The others had turned it into a battle of wills, which never worked with Aoife. She hated being bullied. If you wanted her to go along with you, you had to make her think it was her idea – manipulate her, basically. Dani was surprised that Tiff didn't know that. Although Aoife had been really mean to her, so it wasn't surprising that she'd stormed off, Beth in tow as usual. Dani liked Beth, but she was such a sheep. As for Celine . . . Dani had taken to her at first, but now she was behaving like she was their mum.

Another bottle of champagne was called for. Dani didn't want to drink anymore. She needed to have her senses about her. She had talked a good game about fending off predators, but doing it was another matter. These guys were seriously scary. Their leader looked like a dangerous character with his crazy black clothes and spider earrings.

Aoife was still being mauled by him. Dani tried to catch her eye but the guy was all over her, blocking the view. Aoife was in a wild mood tonight, but surely she didn't want this? Wasn't having sex with John, a virtual stranger, adventure enough?

'Where you stay?' the broad one asked Dani. 'Hotel? Villa?'

'Yeah, great,' she replied, pretending not to understand.

'Which hotel?'

'Can't remember.'

'Tell me! Where are you staying?'

'We're in a villa actually,' she said. 'Bella Vista, in San Pedro.' She had no idea whether there was such a place – she hoped not – but it was the first thing that came into her head.

'Bella Vista. Beautiful view,' he said.

'That's right. Hey, good English!' She laughed nervously.

He leaned over and said something to his mates in a language Dani didn't understand. There was a short conversation between the four of them, then the leader declared something and they all nodded in agreement.

He turned back to Dani. 'Where are your friends? Three girls. Where are they?'

'Um . . . one of them felt sick, so they left.'

'And now they are at Bella Vista, yeah?'

'Not sure. Possibly. No idea.'

'We go there now, yeah? We go find the others, yeah?'

'Um . . . maybe later. We like it here. Drinking. Dancing . . . Do you like dancing?'

'We go soon. Bella Vista. Beautiful view.'

She started to feel panicky. The evening had already gone wildly off the rails and who knew where it was heading next? Certainly not to a non-existent villa in San Pedro – that could get very tricky when they found out she'd lied.

Dani needed Aoife's help but she looked dazed, like she was barely conscious. Dani gave her what she hoped was a meaningful stare – *we need to get out of here* – but Aoife didn't react. Dani wriggled free from her own captor under the guise of pouring herself another drink. The champagne tasted sour.

She kept fidgeting – leaning forward, looking around as if expecting to see a friend, but in fact searching for a way to escape. It didn't help that her head was reeling. She wished she wasn't wearing heels. Even if she tried to run away, she wasn't sure she'd make it across the dance floor without falling over.

The chunky guy started stroking her back. It made her flesh creep, and it took all her mental strength not to flinch away. Realising he was about to kiss her, she grabbed her champagne glass.

'¡*Salud!*' she cried, drinking it so fast that the bubbles went up her nose, making her cough.

The tough-looking guy in the Balenciaga jacket was snogging Aoife again, gripping the tuft of hair at the back of her head so that she couldn't pull away. Dani saw her friend's eyes scrunch up in discomfort as she struggled to breathe. Finally, he let her go, flinging her aside with a flourish. One of the spare guys poured him a shot of vodka.

At last, Aoife caught Dani's eye. She looked scared. Dani knew she had to get them out of the club before they were pushed into a black Range Rover and driven off God knows where.

She wracked her brains for a plan. They'd been in similar situations before, but not with anyone remotely as dangerous. The best way to deal with unwanted guys hitting on you was to ask them to buy you a drink while you went to refresh your make-up. It lulled them into a false sense of security. While they were queuing at the bar, you could bolt out of the door and hail a cab. It was almost exactly the same move that Celine had proposed earlier. But now it was going to be a lot more difficult to execute. It was waiter-service so there was no need to go to the bar and the guys might not let them go off to the loos together. Not unless it was for a good reason . . .

Aoife's guy dived in for more, this time groping her with his free hand. Aoife's body stiffened with disgust, fingers clenching on the edges of her chair. This had to stop. Dani took a unilateral decision. She turned to her partner in the Under Armour vest and mimed snorting coke. He instantly understood.

'You want do some C?' he asked.

She nodded. 'Yes. And my friend too.'

'Okay.'

'How much?'

'You pay me later, yeah?' He swept his eyes over her body and licked his lips.

'Oh, right. Yeah, of course,' she giggled, trying to sound like she was well up for the blow job, or whatever other act he had in mind.

He turned around and fiddled with his bag, then turned back. He took her hand and placed a tiny plastic baggie in her palm, folding her fingers over it so that it couldn't be seen.

'Thanks. *Merci.*' Moroccans spoke French, didn't they? Was he even Moroccan? She had no idea. Her mind was rambling, she had to get a grip. 'Won't be long!' She wriggled past him, deftly grabbing her handbag on the way. He spotted it and suspicion briefly flashed across his face. 'Can't leave it here. Pickpockets.' He didn't seem to understand the word, but he let her take it. 'Come on!' She pulled at Aoife, dragging her to her feet. 'Bring everything,' she hissed.

She kept hold of Aoife's arm and steered her through the drinkers and dancers. The atmosphere was livelier now, the whole place throbbed with activity. Waiters carried flaming bottles, sparks shooting into the crowd. On the podiums, leggy girls wafted huge diaphanous capes while others waved light sabres around in a vaguely sexy manner.

'What's going on?' Aoife asked. 'You're not going to snort that, are you?'

185

'Of course not. I'm looking for our waiter. Can you see him?'

'Yes. Over there.'

Dani surged forward, cutting through the dancers. 'Seb! Hi, Seb!' she called urgently.

'Hi. Sorry, be right with you,' he said, only just recognising them. 'You're table . . . er . . .'

'Twelve!' Dani shouted into his ear. 'Those men who sent over the champagne are hitting on us big time. Is there another way out?'

He pulled a face. 'They won't like it if you don't come back. They'll come after you.'

'That's why we need help.' She opened her hand and showed him the cocaine. 'You can have this if you like.'

He shook his head. 'You wanna get me the sack? Come on then, follow me. There's a staff door next to the bar.'

'Perfect.'

They slipped away, out of the back exit and into a small tatty courtyard. There were two security guys on the gate, but they were more concerned about people getting in than out.

'Sorry, excuse me,' Dani mumbled, pushing Aoife forward.

They emerged in an unlit side street. Dani wasn't sure which direction they should go in, and she didn't have time to check her phone for directions. She took her heels off and ordered Aoife to do the same. They ran across the dirty cobbles, not knowing or caring if there was dog shit or broken glass underfoot.

The street came out on one of the main thoroughfares

leading to the marina. The place was heaving and it was easy to lose themselves in the crowd. After a couple of blocks, they sat down on a low wall and put their shoes back on. Finally, it seemed safe to speak.

'Oh, fuck,' said Aoife. 'That was horrendous. I thought he was going to suck my blood.'

'Yeah, I thought they were going to cart us off to some castle and turn us into brides of Dracula,' Dani laughed.

'Not funny.'

'At first, I couldn't tell whether you were enjoying it or not.'

'What? He was disgusting. Stank of fags and cologne. Yours looked even worse.'

'He was! Oh, God.'

'At least we got away. Good plan, Dani Girl!' Aoife attempted a high-five but she missed.

'We'd better not hang around. It's not a great move to humiliate a bunch of gangsters.'

'They weren't real gangsters. I mean, you couldn't rob a bank or make a getaway in those clothes. Did you see my guy's trousers? They were so baggy and way too long!'

'Come on,' said Dani, hauling Aoife to her feet. 'Are you okay to move on?'

'Feel a bit sick, but yes.' They carried on walking. 'I don't want to go back yet. Tiff will only say, "I told you so."'

'Where do you want to go then? Nowhere expensive. We've just blown five hundred euros, and we'll have to pay for a taxi.'

'Back to Supernova?' Aoife said. She had a sneaky look in her eyes. 'It's free to get in. John will give us drinks.'

'Hmm ... do you really want to go back for second helpings?'

'Stop it.'

'I'm serious. I don't know what you're doing, Aoife. I thought you wanted to get married, that Nathan was the love of your life and all that shit. This is very confusing.'

Aoife leaned into her. 'I'm okay,' she said. 'I know what I'm doing.'

'Good,' replied Dani, 'because I sure as hell don't.'

Chapter Twenty-Four: Now

DANI

The road back to the villa seems narrower and more twisty in the dark. Dani grips the steering wheel and tries to keep her mind on the driving, but her brain sparks off in all directions. Memories from three years ago won't leave her alone. Who were those guys at the nightclub? Did they pursue them, maybe even find out where they were staying? She and Aoife always assumed they'd got away scot-free, but maybe they were wrong. Dani feels that she can't discount any possibility now. People are lying to her. Nothing is as she originally thought.

Neither can she shake off the conviction that her encounter with Matt wasn't by chance. She remembers telling John she was going to Pesadilla – he could have sent Matt there to find her. Her blood freezes at the thought that she's been played. Matt did a good job. She let her guard down, opened up to him, let him hold her, comfort her. Now it seems like he and John could be working together, trying to frighten her and prevent her from talking to the police.

'Too late, mate,' she says under her breath. Not that Mengual has replied to her voice message yet.

Dani drives into the total darkness, her head rocking with tiredness. As she passes the turning to the Country

Club, a motorbike swings around the corner and starts to follow the car. At least that's how it feels because there are only the two of them on the road, nothing behind or ahead. Nobody is coming from the opposite direction, there's room to overtake, but he's clearly not interested. Just sits on her tail. Her heart starts to race.

It's the same bike. And even though the rider is dressed in black leathers and is wearing a helmet with the visor down, she knows it's the same guy. Could it even be Matt? Did he follow them earlier? He definitely knew where she'd parked the car. After he dropped her off, he said he was going back to the club, but he could have jumped on his bike and taken a back route. He obviously knows all the short-cuts and he would have had just about enough time.

Her palms sweat. It feels like there's no air left in the car, like someone has sucked it out. She glances intermittently at the dashboard while she negotiates the bends, looking for the aircon or side window buttons, desperate for air. But all she can see is a confusing mass of orange lights. She fiddles with the sticks by the steering wheel, clicking them up and down. The rear windscreen wipers come on. The blades judder and squeal on the dry screen. She tries to turn them off, jabbing at the symbols, switching the wipers off and putting on the haz-ards instead. She can feel the rider bearing down on her. He'll realise she's driving erratically. Panicking. The hazards are tick-ticking. She reaches for the off switch just as the car hits a pothole and lurches across the road. The radio suddenly comes on, a tinny voice singing in Spanish. She curses loudly. *Concentrate!* She clenches the wheel and looks ahead, eyes boring into the beam of the headlights.

After a long bend, the road straightens out for a few hundred metres. Dani allows herself a quick glance in the wing mirror. He's still there. Looming over her like a dark cloud. Whoever he is, he's riding intimidatingly close. She speeds up, trying to put distance between them, even though she's sure he can take these bends faster than she would ever dare. She tries to keep as tight to the scrubby rockface as she can. The car brushes noisily against the dry branches of a bush and she swerves away in response. Her heart is pounding. She can hardly breathe. Why won't the windows open?

Not much further to go now. Her body fills with dread as she thinks about the bike following her down the track to the villa. What's going to happen when she gets out? She might not even make it that far. He could be trying to kill her, and the possibility makes her throat tighten with panic. She imagines the bike clipping her bumper, sending the car flying across the road, toppling over the barrier into the chasm below. It would be certain death.

She can't let that happen.

They drive on, testing each other's skill, as if they're playing some video game, not driving along a real road in real darkness, putting their lives in danger. As she passes the shrine, she whispers a few words. '*Santa María, Madre de Dios*, don't let him drive me off the edge.'

The turning is just ahead. She doesn't indicate, just swings across. He must know where it is because he pulls back, letting her go. She bumps onto the track, expecting him to follow, but instead hears the bike screeching its brakes, then whizzing round and roaring away, back down the road from the direction they came. As the sound fades into the distance, Dani finally lets out a breath. He's gone. She inches the car along, skirting around large stones and the deep, hard furrows once made by a tractor.

She parks up and turns off the engine, staying inside the car for a few moments to slow her heart rate and take stock. That was terrifying. Thank God she hadn't drunk any alcohol or she'd be lying at the bottom of the ravine by now.

To her surprise, the lights in the villa are on. How come the others are still up? Dani peers into the dark, checking the surroundings before opening the car door and stepping out.

The air is quiet save for the click of cicadas. Dani runs to the front door of the villa. It's slightly ajar. She halts on the threshold, suddenly frightened of what she might find on the other side.

'Hello?' she shouts, her voice thin and squeaky. 'Everything okay?'

'Dani? Is that you?' Tiff's voice sounds strained.

'Yes!' she calls, walking in. 'I'm glad you're still up. I've just had this horrific experience—'

Dani enters the sitting room, recoiling when she takes in the scene before her. Beth, Tiff and Celine are still up but in their dressing gowns, sitting awkwardly at the dining table as if waiting for a meal that's never going to arrive. The room has been trashed. Furniture has been upended and thrown around. Pictures have been taken off the wall, their glass smashed against the flagstones. Ornaments are broken, including the Buddha who has been dragged from his home under the stairs and hurled to the floor. The contents of the sideboard have been emptied out. The cushions are torn and tossed around as if there's been a pillow fight.

'What the . . . ?' gasps Dani.

'It was like this when we got back,' Celine explains. She looks tired and shaken, her face devoid of make-up.

'Why didn't you call me?'

'We did. We rang, texted, WhatsApped you about a hundred times. Nothing.'

'Really? You sure?'

'Yes! Didn't you even check your phone once?'

'Er, no . . . I needed some time to myself, so I put it on silent.' She reaches into her bag and pulls out the mobile. The home screen is dotted with alerts. She slides the volume back up. 'I'm so sorry. I didn't realise.'

'We've been waiting up for you,' cuts in Beth. 'We thought you should know in advance – didn't want you to be shocked.'

'Thanks.' Her mind is racing, trying to join the dots.

'Nothing seems to have been taken,' says Tiff. 'We had our purses and phones on us. Our passports are in the safe.'

'How did they get in?'

'The back door was forced,' Beth says.

'Was the alarm ringing when you arrived?'

'No.'

Dani turns to Tiff. 'But you set it, didn't you?'

She pulls a guilty face. 'Hmm . . . I did have a few problems with it, remember? I *thought* I'd set it properly. Unless it rang for ages and then cut off. Nobody would have heard it, not out here.'

'We were gone for a long time,' says Beth. 'It could have happened just after we left.'

Dani nods. 'Have you called the police?'

Beth shakes her head. 'No. Not yet.'

'The really creepy thing,' says Celine, 'is that the damage looks almost exactly the same as last time. Like somebody's copied it from a photograph.'

It's true. The scene looks staged. Dani realised it as soon as she stepped through the door. Different objects, different pictures. Same wanton destruction. It can't be a coincidence.

An image interposes itself in front of her eyes for a second – Aoife's body under a plastic sheet, the white walls spattered red like a vast abstract painting. She shoves it away but it refuses to go far, lingering at the edge of her thoughts.

'The other thing is . . . a motorbike tried to run me off the road just now,' she says quietly. 'It was fucking terrifying, I thought he was going to kill me.' They all turn to look at her, eyes wide, jaws slack.

'Are you serious?' asks Tiff.

'Totally.'

'Was it the same bike that followed us down to Banús?' asks Celine.

'I think so.'

She slaps her hand across her mouth. 'I knew it!'

'I knew it too,' Dani replies. 'I kept telling myself it was only my imagination, but what happened just now was more than real . . .'

'I don't understand. Why is this happening?' Celine looks at them one by one.

'I've no idea,' says Tiff.

Beth shrugs. 'Me neither. But I don't like it. It's freaking me out.'

Dani swallows. 'I have a feeling John's involved. And Matt – the cocktail guy, remember? I went to see John earlier at Supernova, asked him a few questions.' Tiff looks to the ceiling in irritation. 'He acted like he didn't know we were staying here, but I think he was lying.'

'Maybe Marta told him,' suggests Beth.

'Yes, that's the obvious explanation. Anyway, he seemed quite rattled that we'd come back, warned me to stop digging around, told me to go home. Then later, Matt "bumped into me" outside Pesadilla. He pretty much told me the same thing. I didn't tell him where I'd parked the Seat, but he took me straight to it. I've a horrible feeling that it could even have been him on the bike.'

'And he could have done this,' says Celine, looking around at the devastation. 'He could have followed us earlier to check that we were out of the way, then come back here. The timeline fits.'

'Or John could have done it,' says Tiff.

'Whoever it was knew exactly what this place looked like when Aoife was attacked,' Dani adds. 'And they could only know that if they were there at the time.' There is a collective shiver.

'Yes, either of them could have done it, or it could be somebody else,' says Beth impatiently. 'The big question is *why*?'

'It's a warning,' says Dani.

'But about what?' Beth holds up her hands.

'I don't know, but I'm assuming they know who killed Aoife and they don't want us to find out.'

'This is your fault,' accuses Tiff. 'How could you do this to us – after all we've been through? You've made the situation a hundred times worse.'

Dani casts her eyes over the broken chairs, the shattered pictures and ornaments – the carefully curated, almost theatrical vandalism. 'I've always known in my heart that it wasn't just a burglary,' she says. 'Mengual said it seemed more personal. This proves it, doesn't it? John is shitting bricks – he got his mate Matt to scare us. All this was done to make us stop, shut us up.'

'To make *you* stop,' says Tiff. 'We're not doing anything.'

'You should never have gone to see John,' says Celine. 'You've put yourself – and us – in danger. *You* may be on your own, Dani, but I've got a family to go home to. I've got a little boy who needs me.'

'Yes, I know, I'm sorry.' Dani feels stung. They fall silent for a few moments, then she reaches for her phone. 'I'm going to call Inspector Mengual. He'll know what to do.'

'Hold on,' says Celine. 'I can't believe I'm saying this, but do we definitely want to involve the police?'

'Somebody tried to kill me just now!'

'Exactly. That's why we need to think very carefully.'

'We need protection, don't we?'

'Celine's right. Calling the police could put us in more danger. We don't know who we can trust,' says Beth.

Dani arches her brows. 'I can't believe you – a solicitor – could say that.'

'The law doesn't seem to apply much around here,' Beth responds. 'I'm scared.'

'Let's not make any rash decisions now. We'll work out what to do in the morning,' announces Tiff. 'We need to sleep.' Celine and Beth agree, scraping back their chairs and standing up. 'And no more going it alone, okay, Dani? This situation affects all of us, so we need to act as one.'

'Okay.'

It's late. Dani strokes her bare arms. She's starting to feel chilly, although that could just be utter exhaustion creeping over her. Or Aoife's ghost perhaps, wandering around, inspecting the damage, tiptoeing through the broken glass, trailing her fingers through the dust.

Dani goes upstairs. Her bedroom is as she left it this morning, the sheets dishevelled, her discarded bikini lying on the floor. She turns on the bedside lamp and pauses to stare at the empty mattress, remembering Celine's cruel jibe earlier. It's true, she's on her own and has nobody to go back to. Nobody who would really miss her if something happened and she didn't return – nobody apart from her mother. Her father died some years ago, before she went to uni. Aoife would have been the one to grieve her most, but obviously . . .

She goes into the bathroom. She's feeling so tired that she doesn't see it at first, not until she has put the toothpaste on and is holding the brush to her mouth. There's a message scrawled on the mirror in what looks like her ruby-red lipstick.

YOU'RE NEXT

Chapter Twenty-Five: Then

TIFF

Plenty of taxis were arriving at Pesadilla to drop clubbers off, but they weren't allowed to take our fare because there was no official rank. Celine got straight on to Uber. The news wasn't good. The prices had been severely hiked and there were waits of up to an hour. Beth checked Google Maps and told us the nearest taxi rank was outside the department store, which was about ten minutes' walk away. We set off in hope, following the spoken directions, although it was difficult to hear them above the noise of the crowd.

It was a hot, sticky night. The heat of the day had been trapped in the ground and the pavements were still warm. A cacophony of music blared out from the numerous bars. We walked with our heads down, weaving our way through the throng. Drunken tourists were staggering about, shouting, swearing, throwing up in doorways, bursting into tears. The atmosphere was charged and not in a good way. It felt as if something could kick off at any moment. A fight. A brawl. A full-scale riot.

I must admit, I was doing a fair bit of crying myself. Aoife had really upset me, but there was more to it than that. A lot more. It was as if I was being held together by an extremely tight elastic band that was ready to snap, sending bits of me flying off in all directions.

'She didn't mean it,' Beth said, clutching me by the arm and dragging me along. 'She was so pissed she didn't know what she was saying.'

'I know,' I muttered. 'I'm okay.'

'You don't seem okay.'

'I'm fine, just need to get back to the villa.'

Celine was walking ahead, eyes down, checking taxi apps on her phone.

'What is it?' Beth pressed, tightening her grip. 'There's something else, isn't there? Something you're not telling me. You're so uptight! I thought it was just because you were worried about everything going smoothly, but—'

'Yes, that's all it is.'

'Hmm . . . don't believe you.' She gave me a quizzical look. 'Is it something to do with Dani?'

I shrugged. 'Yes and no.'

I wasn't surprised that Beth had detected something odd about my behaviour. We'd known each other since we were eleven years old, after all. I'd done my best to imply that my anxieties were related to the organisation of the weekend – and people not wanting to follow my schedule. But although all that was annoying, it was way down on my list of problems.

I'd been in a terrible state for weeks, feeling like I was living on a knife-edge, but it had come to a head the moment I saw Aoife at the airport. The sight of her in the golden Belle gown and bridal sash, looking so happy and excited, had made me want to throw up. I nearly blurted out the truth there and then, but – luckily – the words had stuck in my throat like tiny bones. Otherwise there would have been no flight to Malaga, no hen party at all.

We'd reached the department store by now, but there were no taxis at the rank. Maybe one would turn up in a minute, I thought. We joined the long queue of partygoers and waited.

'This is why we needed to be based down here,' said Beth, 'not up in the mountains.'

'Don't you start,' I snapped. 'If you must know, it was Nathan who told me Aoife wanted to stay in Villa Floriana. That's the only reason I booked it.'

Beth frowned. 'How odd . . . she didn't seem to know anything about it.'

'I could have misunderstood.'

'It must have been difficult choosing the right place when it was supposed to be a surprise,' said Celine, picking up the thread of our conversation. 'Maybe she said somewhere *like* Villa Floriana.'

'He was only trying to help,' I said, feeling the need to defend him. 'He asked her lots of questions, showed her places online. He was behind the scenes, guiding me.'

'He seems to do a lot of "guiding",' Beth said wryly. She turned to Celine. 'Like with those masks.'

'Yes, that was awkward.' She pulled a face. 'Sorry about that. He insisted.'

Beth smiled. 'Not your fault.'

A steady stream of taxis drew up and we'd finally reached the front of the queue. As our ride approached the rank,

Celine cancelled the Uber booking and we dived into the back seat. Within minutes, we'd left the bright lights of the coast and were winding our way up into the mountains.

We appeared to have had enough of talking. Celine gazed out of the window, although there was nothing to see, only darkness. I rested my head on Beth's shoulder and closed my eyes, my thoughts drifting uncomfortably towards Nathan . . .

I'd hardly stopped thinking about him since our meeting in Manchester. He was so charming and attractive. Confident without having too much swagger. Generous too. When I mentioned that I was worried about the mounting costs of the hen party, he immediately offered to put some cash into the general kitty. 'That's between the two of us, okay?' he said.

He got in touch again a few weeks later, saying he needed to be in Manchester for work. 'I want to thank you for all you're doing for my girl,' he said. 'Let me take you out to dinner. Aoife doesn't need to know – it can be our secret.' He booked a table at one of the most expensive restaurants in the city centre and told me to be there for eight o'clock.

I'd been single for over six months, and all my evenings out since had been with work colleagues or girlfriends. Now here I was, sitting at a table for two in my sexiest dress – black and short with thin straps crossing at the back. My feet ached in the shiny high heels that made my legs look longer. Worst of all, I'd made sure to wear new, matching underwear. What was I thinking? I was meeting my best friend's fiancé to discuss the arrangements for her hen party, not going on a romantic date.

Nathan had asked me to keep it a secret because he didn't want Aoife to know that we'd been working really hard to make sure everything was perfect. Given that the hen party was supposed to be a surprise for the bride, it seemed like a perfectly reasonable request. Even so, I felt guilty about meeting him for dinner. Guilty and excited, if truth be told. I couldn't wait to spend another evening in his company – just the two of us.

'Wow! You look amazing!' he exclaimed as soon as he walked up to the table. 'Sorry I'm a bit late. I've been running around all day. Had to nip back to the hotel and freshen up.'

It pleased me that he'd showered and shaved. I could smell his cologne – I think it was Gucci. He wore a sharp navy suit with a white shirt, open at the neck, and a pair of designer trainers. When he kissed me on the cheek, my stomach flipped over, and afterwards, I couldn't stop myself from touching the spot where his lips had been. I think he noticed.

He sat down opposite me and reached for the menu. 'So good to see you, Tiffany,' he said. 'I've been looking forward to this all day.'

All day? It had been all week for me.

I was too nervous to eat much. He ordered a rib-eye steak with twice-cooked fries, while I picked at a salad. We had the best part of two bottles of red wine, which wasn't great for me as I was drinking on an almost empty stomach.

To my disappointment, he mainly wanted to talk about Aoife. How had we become friends? What had she been like at school? The more wine he drank, the bolder his questions became. He started probing about her previous boyfriends, asking me how many men she'd slept with, whether she'd ever been with a woman or had a threesome. When I balked, he explained that Aoife had refused to talk about her previous sexual experiences, and it worried him.

'I don't know,' I said truthfully. 'You'd have to ask her friend Dani about that kind of thing.' He made some disparaging remark about Dani, which I enjoyed. 'Yes, she's a bad influence,' I agreed. 'I know they got up to stuff at uni. And afterwards – when they shared a flat.'

'What kind of stuff?' he pressed.

'I don't know exactly.'

'Like hook-ups with strangers?'

'Maybe . . . not sure, to be honest.'

'Don't tell me they were cam girls.'

I laughed. 'No, no, nothing like that. They liked to party, that's all. If you feel anxious about it, you should talk to Aoife.'

'I'm not anxious,' he retorted. 'I just hate the thought of her being with another man, that's all. It torments me. Makes me fucking angry.' I noticed his jaw was locked and his fists clenched.

'You must have history too,' I said. 'I bet you've had loads of girlfriends.' He shook his head. 'Come on, a man like you. You're good-looking, well off . . . You must have girls hitting on you all the time.' I felt my cheeks reddening.

'Yeah, I do okay,' he replied. 'But it's different for guys. Aoife says she doesn't care about my past, but I need to know about hers. I get really jealous, you see. And when she won't tell me, it makes me suspicious.'

'Best not to think about it.'

Nathan sighed. 'I can't help myself. I keep thinking she's probably had more men than I've had women and that doesn't seem right to me. I feel like I should even up the score a bit.' He fixed me with a look. 'You know, before it's too late.'

'Oh,' I replied weakly.

'Because once we're married, we're mates for life, you understand? I'd never cheat on my wife. I hate men who have affairs. It's despicable. Especially if there are kids on the scene. But before you tie the knot, well, the same rules don't apply. A guy finds himself having dinner with a beautiful woman six weeks before his wedding ... they're obviously very attracted to each other ... they both know it's only going to be for one incredible night. There's no harm in that, is there?' He leaned forward. 'What do you think, Tiffany?'

I looked down at my plate. My insides quivered. If I'd been standing, I would have buckled at the knees. I knew deep down that it was wrong, but oh, my God, did I want him! His twisted logic was working on me. The truth was that Aoife *had* had sex with lots of guys, I didn't know how many exactly because we never had those kinds of conversations, but it wouldn't have surprised me if she had more notches on her bedpost than Nathan did. Like he said, it would be making things even and it would only be for one night. One *incredible* night, as he'd put it. Did I dare to have sex with a man, knowing that he was about to marry, with no hope or expectation that our first night would lead to another? I'd never done anything like it before, never been asked, never had to consider it. I didn't go seeking that kind of thrill. I even argued to myself that it would be better if Nathan cheated on Aoife with me rather than some other woman because he could guarantee that I would never tell her. Such were the mad thoughts that rushed through my veins, along with the red wine and my overwhelming desire for him to touch me.

Nathan took my hand across the table and pressed it against his mouth. 'Well?' He gently caressed my finger with his tongue and my body shuddered with pleasure.

'I hope Aoife and Dani are okay,' said Beth, suddenly cutting into my memories. 'I'm feeling a bit bad about leaving them with those men.'

'What? Oh, yeah.' I removed my head from her shoulder and sat up straight with a jolt.

'They'll probably be okay in the club, where there's security. It's getting home safely that worries me,' said Celine.

Ibiza club sounds poured out of the car radio. I pictured Aoife and Dani dancing with the drug dealers. The guys had looked faintly comic in their oversized designer sportswear and gothic commitment to the colour black. Could they be as dangerous as Celine suspected? The waiter had been very firm about our needing to accept the champagne, but had fleeing the premises been an overreaction?

Just before we left the UK, Nathan had called and made me promise to look after Aoife. 'Don't let her get into trouble,' he said. 'She's precious. I'm counting on you to keep her safe.' He'd been in touch several times since that night in his hotel – which was, as promised, incredible – but hadn't once mentioned what had gone on between us. He behaved as if it'd never happened, instead going on and on about the hen party, asking for precise details about what we'd be doing and when. I played my part and said nothing about the fact that I thought about him every waking moment and dreamed about him at night.

I'd made a deal and now I had to stick to it. I stupidly hadn't accounted for the fact that Nathan was a business-man who made deals all the time and made sure they were to his advantage. I was way out of my depth. Not only was I obsessed with a man I couldn't have, I was now consumed with guilt over what I'd done to my friend. I knew that if I told Aoife the truth, I'd lose her love. Even if she dumped Nathan, he would be utterly furious with me and there would be no future for us.

Celine instructed the driver to take the first turning after the shrine. We trundled down the track in the pitch-dark, then swept into the courtyard.

The villa was dark and stuffy. Beth flung open the patio doors to let in some fresh air. As soon as we put on the lights, all sorts of insects flew inside. There would be mosquitoes among them, I thought, but I didn't say anything.

Celine went straight to her room, while Beth went to make herself some tea. I walked onto the terrace and stared at the stars, feeling ashamed and conflicted and generally worked up. Nathan would be cross with me for abandoning Aoife at the nightclub. I looked at my phone and, sure enough, I'd received several texts from him, asking if we were still at Pesadilla. *Yes all fine,* I tapped onto my screen, then pressed to send the message back to London. I felt sick, couldn't take any more.

'Do you think we should wait up for them?' asked Beth, coming outside with her mug of tea.

'No.' I turned off my phone. 'I'm exhausted. Let's go to bed.'

Of course, I didn't sleep.

Chapter Twenty-Six: Now

DANI

Dani has a quick wash at the basin to wake herself up, although she hardly slept. She studies her reflection, eyes red-rimmed, skin sallow in the light, her features partially obscured by the terrifying words written on the mirror.

The message taunted her all night. She turned the light off and shut the bathroom door, but she could still see it on the back of her eyelids. She won't wipe it off the mirror. It's evidence. The vandalism downstairs was for show, but this is personal.

YOU'RE NEXT

Walking back into the bedroom she surveys the mess, most of it her own creation. Her passport is lying on the dressing table in full view; she hadn't even bothered to put it in the safe. That's how they knew it was her room. God, she made it so easy.

Last night, Tiff said that they needed to make a collective decision about what to do next, meaning *she* was going to decide – as if she was still Chief Bridesmaid. If anyone's in charge of this weekend, I am, Dani thinks. For better or for worse.

She picks up her mobile and goes to the window. The shutters have been open for hours and the morning sun has just hit the room. She lets it warm her bones for a few seconds, it's the closest she's going to get to a hug today. Her fingers hover over the keypad. Should she call Marta first, find out what she wants to do? It's her villa, after all. She may well have a view about whether or not they should involve the police. She rings Marta's mobile number but there's no answer. Dani sends a brief text instead. *Big problems here. You need to come over.* There, it's sent, no going back now. She doesn't care whether the others approve.

As she finishes getting dressed, her thoughts turn towards Inspector Mengual. He still hasn't replied to the voice message she left yesterday. Now it's even more important that she speaks with him. The trashing of the villa and the message connect unambiguously to Aoife's death. She was the first victim. Dani could be next. That's what is meant, pure and simple.

When Dani arrives downstairs a few minutes later, she finds Tiff and Beth working diligently – putting the furniture back in place, sweeping up shards of glass from the smashed pictures. Beth collects pieces of the broken Buddha and puts them carefully on the coffee table. Dani doesn't bother to reprimand them for destroying the crime scene, doesn't even allude to what they're doing. They had further cross words last night. When she showed them the message on the mirror, they were unsurprised and unsympathetic. 'See? *You* did this,' said Tiff. 'You and your meddling.' Dani's not going to consult them anymore, there's no point.

Tiff pretends she hasn't noticed Dani, while Beth looks

up from the Buddha jigsaw and gives her a half-apologetic, half-embarrassed smile. None of them says a word. Dani tiptoes past the debris and goes into the kitchen to fix herself some breakfast. She can hear muffled voices coming from Celine's room down the corridor. She must be talking on speaker with her husband and little son. God knows what she's telling them. *We almost had a repetition of the attack last night. Nobody's been killed. Yet. But someone left a message saying Dani's next on the list.*

She sits at the cramped table and shovels in some cereal. The milk tastes odd, makes her feel a little sick. Or maybe it's that message upstairs. She knows it's written in lipstick, but it looks like blood. She remembers the scene in the sitting room the morning after Aoife was killed. You could have written a novel in the blood from the wound. Is that what they have in mind for her too? She gags. What a disgusting thought. She needs to go outside, get some fresh air. She dumps the bowl on the drainer and leaves the kitchen, taking the back way out of the house to avoid Beth and Tiff.

It's still relatively early. Opening the back door, Dani walks around the side of the building and reaches the rear courtyard. She stands in the shade cast by the garage, breathes deeply, and tries to stop her mind from skittering. She's got to talk to *somebody* or she'll spiral. She can't hang around waiting for other people to decide her fate – *she* is the one who needs to decide. Without further thought, Dani calls Inspector Mengual's number. She paces about as it rings and rings, then the call is rejected. Either he's not on duty or he doesn't want to talk to her.

*

An hour later, Dani is lying down in her room, trying to sleep, when she hears a car outside, its wheels crunching over the gravel in the courtyard. She drags herself up and goes to the window, throwing open the shutters.

Marta gets out of her tatty old car. A sinking feeling hits Dani's stomach. This is going to be hard.

Marta looks up. 'Hi. I got your message,' she says, slamming the driver's door. 'What's the problem?'

'Wait! I'm coming down.'

They meet at the threshold. Dani bars her way. 'Don't be shocked,' she says. 'Most of it's been cleared up.'

Fear springs into Marta's eyes. '¿*Qué pasó?* Dani? Tell me!'

'Somebody broke in last night and trashed the place again.'

'¡*Madre mía!* I don't believe it! When? How?'

'Yesterday evening, we don't know exactly. Nobody was in.'

Marta strides past Dani, through the small hallway and into the sitting room. The place looks a lot better since Tiff and Beth cleared up, but Marta still puts her hand to her mouth when she sees the broken pictures and the pieces of the Buddha statue on the coffee table. She picks one up and holds it to her chest, pressing down on her emotions.

'I have this since when I was a teenager,' she says quietly.

'I'm really sorry, Marta.'

'Did you call the police?'

'No.' Dani decides not to mention that she tried Mengual. 'The others were frightened. We thought—'

'*Bueno.* You did the right thing. This is my problem – I'll deal with it. How is the rest of the house?'

'Fine. The upstairs is okay, apart from a message they left on my mirror.'

Marta's brow creases. 'What sort of message?'

'Come and read it for yourself.'

They go upstairs and squeeze into the tiny bathroom, staring at the mirror, which takes up the whole of one wall. The message screams at them.

'I think this is for me,' Marta says. 'Normally, this is my bedroom, my bathroom.'

Dani is stunned. The thought hadn't occurred to her. 'Really? But it's in English. And I'm sleeping here, so I assumed it was for me.'

'No, no. They're trying to scare me only, nobody else.' Marta picks up a cloth and wipes the message off. 'There. It's gone.'

'What do you mean? Who's trying to scare you?'

They leave the bathroom and go into the bedroom. Marta sits down on the unmade bed. It feels strange to Dani that this is really Marta's room, not hers.

'I don't understand,' Dani says, trying again. 'Tell me, Marta.'

'It's nothing. A stupid joke.'

'Come on, it's a lot more than that. Did John do this?'

'No. Someone else.'

'Who?'

'I can't talk about it. It's nothing to do with you.'

'But it totally is! Other stuff has been happening this weekend. I was nearly killed last night by a guy on a motorbike. He's been following us. I think it might have been Matt, John's friend. And when I saw John at Supernova, he got very nasty, told me to go home. What's he so worried about?'

'I can't tell you. Don't keep asking me.' Marta starts to sway. 'Sorry, it's so hot in here. *No me siento muy bien . . .*'

Dani feels exasperated. 'Lie down. I'll fetch you a glass of water.'

'*Gracias. Tengo un abanico . . .* a fan *. . . abajo . . . en el cajón de la cómoda . . .*'

'Chest of drawers. It's okay, I understand.'

Dani rushes downstairs to the kitchen. Her brain is doing triple somersaults as she tries to work out why Marta is so frightened. She takes a bottle of water out of the fridge and pours two glasses, then drinks one down.

Remembering the fan, Dani goes back into the living room where there is a large chest of drawers. The fan is in the third drawer down, next to a bunch of keys. Dani takes both out. They look like spares for the villa. She runs her fingers through the keys, which are all individually labelled in Spanish: front door, back door, patio, annexe, storage room . . . Another one has its own mini fob, a giant S against a star. Supernova. A thought enters her head, but she puts the keys back in the drawer and takes the glass of water and the fan up to Marta.

'Here you go,' Dani says.

'*Gracias.*' Marta drinks the water and fans her face. 'Sorry, you should not have to experience this. I must go. I'll sort it out, talk to John. I'm seeing him this afternoon.'

'How come?'

'He called me this morning. He wants to speak to me urgently.'

213

'What about?'

'I don't know. The divorce, perhaps.'

'Are you sure it's safe? If he's behind all these threats, if he did this damage . . .'

'No, it's okay. We're meeting at Venta El Lago.'

'What time?'

'Four o'clock. Honestly, Dani, there's nothing to worry about. I can handle John. Leave it to me. And, please, no police.'

Marta gathers herself and leaves. Dani goes downstairs and sees her out of her own house. She watches her drive away then returns to the chest of drawers in the living room. She takes out the bunch of keys again, twists the ring until the one for Supernova slips off.

She doesn't know whether that lipstick message was meant for Marta or for her, but one thing's certain: John has been spooked. He's clearly terrified of the murder case being opened again. If Dani can get into his apartment while he's meeting Marta, maybe she'll find out why.

Chapter Twenty-Seven: Then

BETH

I woke up on Sunday morning feeling hungover and vaguely depressed. Despite my best efforts, the mozzies had got into our room overnight and my forearms and legs had been bitten to pieces. Mosquitoes love me. I sat up and reached for my tube of antihistamine ointment, blobbing it in all the appropriate places until I looked like a strawberry cream gâteau.

Tiff sat in the other bed. She made a low groaning noise and rolled onto her back, rubbing her eyes with her fists. Her sheet, which she'd kicked off in the hottest part of the night, lay crumpled on the floor. She wore a cutesy pyjama set – grey elephants on a pale blue background – which made her look about seven years old.

'What'sertime?' she mumbled.

'Just gone nine.'

She groaned again. 'It's like somebody's drilling a hole in my head. I didn't even have that much to drink last night.'

'The evidence is against you,' I quipped.

'Don't start your lawyer stuff on me . . .'

'You need to rehydrate. I'll get us some water.'

I took two chilled bottles of mineral water from the fridge and returned to the bedroom. 'Come on, sit up,' I said, passing one to her. 'You need to recover fast. There's a lot going on today.'

'Tell me about it.' She twisted the cap off and gulped half the bottle down in one go. 'That's better . . . Well, a bit.'

I sat back on my bed with my knees up, sipping water and examining the bites as if they were battle wounds. 'They got back safely,' I said after a pause. 'Dani and Aoife. I heard them arriving at about four.'

'Yes, me too,' Tiff replied stiffly. 'I hardly slept a wink.' She pushed herself to the edge of the bed and stood up, groaning for the third time as her head lolled forward. 'Shit . . . If I'm this bad, God knows how those two must be feeling.'

'They're probably still comatose,' said Beth. 'Celine's not up either.' Tiff unhooked the shutters and opened them wide. 'What time are the caterers coming?'

'Not until this afternoon. They cook the meal from scratch in front of us – a sort of demo, you know. "Learn to cook traditional paella". I paid extra for it. Not that Aoife will be the slightest bit interested. She hates cooking.' Tiff sighed and returned to her bed, downing the rest of the water. 'I've got everything wrong.'

'That's not true,' I quickly reassured her.

'Oh, stop being so kind. The weekend has been a spectacular fail so far.' Her voice began to tremble. 'The villa is lovely but too remote, the beach club was a rip-off, the nightclub was full of dodgy men—'

'Not *full* of them.'

'And worst of all, the group has split. It's Dani and Aoife versus you, me and Celine. I should never have agreed to be

Chief Bridesmaid, it was a colossal mistake saying I'd organise the hen. Colossal.'

'No, it wasn't.'

'It was. One of the biggest mistakes of my life.' Tiff started to cry, roughly swiping the tears away with the back of her hand – as if she was angry with herself for showing emotion.

'What do you mean?' I sat down on her bed. 'What is it, Tiff? Why are you so upset? I know you're hiding something from me.'

She punched the pillow in frustration. 'I've messed up, Beth. Like, really messed up.'

'How?' I waited for her to explain. 'Have you done something wrong at work?' She shook her head. 'What then? If it's not work, it's got to be a man.'

'I can't talk about it.'

So it was a man then. 'What's the problem? Is he married?'

'No.'

I looked at her doubtfully. Tiff knew how I felt about women who slept with other women's husbands. 'Whatever it is, you can tell me,' I said. 'I won't judge.'

'I'm just upset about the hen party, that's all. There is no man.'

I didn't believe her for one second, but there was no point in pushing her further.

'Stop feeling sorry for yourself,' I said. 'You've worked incredibly hard on this weekend, and I think you've done a brilliant job.'

'I haven't, but thanks.' She reached out and squeezed my hand. 'I don't know what I would have done if you hadn't been here.' Tiff heaved a sigh that seemed to go through her entire body. She leaned over the side of the bed and picked up the sheet, then lay back down again, draping it over herself. I felt sorry for her, but if she wasn't prepared to tell me what was wrong, I couldn't help.

I showered and got dressed, then went back to the kitchen in search of breakfast. Celine was there, pouring herself a large glass of orange juice from a carton. 'Morning,' she said in a gravelly voice. 'How's things?'

'Not too bad,' I replied. 'Tiff is trying to sleep it off. I think Dani and Aoife must still be in bed.'

'Oh. So, they decided to come home then?'

'Yes. All safe and sound. They weren't trafficked or anything.' I attempted a feeble laugh, but Celine didn't find it amusing.

I put a couple of day-old croissants in the oven to heat through.

'So . . . what's the schedule for today?' asked Celine. 'I'm presuming there *is* a schedule.'

'Of course. The morning is free time, to spend how we like. Paella party at lunchtime, then the "surprise". It's all happening in the garden, where the decorations are. Better for the pics.'

'Of course. The pics.' Celine rolled her eyes.

'Tiff's put a load of effort into this party,' I said pointedly. 'I for one think she's done a great job.'

Celine let out a wry laugh. 'Are you going to be a defence barrister or a prosecuting one?'

I was taken aback by her question. 'I'm training to be a solicitor, but usually barristers do both. Why are you asking?'

'Just that you spend your whole time sticking up for other people, so I'm guessing, if you were a barrister, you'd rather defend.'

'Interesting,' I replied. 'Did you know, over eighty per cent of defendants are found guilty? A case doesn't get to court unless it's basically sound. If you're interested in trying to get criminals off the hook, be a defence lawyer. If you want to see them brought to justice, prosecute.'

'Wow. I hadn't thought of it like that.' She sounded genuinely surprised.

'I'm making a massive generalisation of course. There will always be innocent people who need defending.' I smiled at her, appreciating her interest. It was good to be having a proper conversation for a change. 'I'm not tough enough to be a barrister. Or bright enough.' I explained that I'd turned to legal training late, after realising that a career as an accountant was not for me. 'It's been a long haul, but I've done my exams and managed to get a training contract. One more year then I'll be fully qualified. Nothing's going to stop me.'

'I admire you,' she replied. I blushed. 'No really, I do. You go for it.'

'Thanks. Have you heard about your new job yet?' I asked, keen to reciprocate her interest in me.

She shook her head. 'No. I'll probably get a call first thing tomorrow.'

'Best of luck.'

'Hopefully, I won't need it. My boss has said all along that it's mine.'

I frowned. 'Then why make other people apply for it? That's not fair to them. It contravenes equal opps.'

'Well, I've already been doing it for a year for no extra money, which isn't fair either,' she pointed out.

'Hmm. Sounds like a dodgy company to me,' I said.

Celine's cheeks flamed. 'They're not dodgy, not at all. It's just that money's tight and it's a highly competitive business.' Her eyes welled with emotion. 'It's a defining moment in my career, you know? Everything I've been grafting for over these past twelve years is finally coming good. I didn't go to university, you see. I had to start at the very bottom and work my way up. I've seen people leap-frog me before, it's been so frustrating, but now it's finally my time.'

'Fingers crossed,' I said, wishing I could brush the chip off her shoulder.

The croissants were warmed through by now. I ate one and took the other to Tiff. Unfortunately, she'd gone back to sleep – or was pretending she had. I left it by her bed, grabbed my swimming things and tiptoed out of the room, hoping the extra snooze would improve her mood. I didn't like seeing her so down. I promised myself I would keep an eye on her for the rest of the weekend and, most importantly, keep her away from Dani. I didn't have a problem with Dani – in fact, I quite liked her – but I could see how she rubbed Tiff up the wrong way.

I went straight to the pool. To my amazement, Aoife was there, floating on a lilo. She was lying on her tummy, unaware of my presence. I stood under a parasol and applied lashings of factor fifty before easing myself into the water and doggy-paddling over.

'Hey, Aoife,' I said, gently tapping her on the arm. Her eyes opened and she turned her head towards me.

'Oh, you,' she answered.

'Yes, me. I didn't see you come down. How long have you been here?'

'Ages. Couldn't sleep.'

'Have you got sunscreen on?' She made a noise, something between a yes and a no. 'You'll burn up if you're not careful. You should get out and put some on. Now.'

'Don't nag, Beth. I've got a thumping head. Can't move a muscle . . .'

I squinted upwards at the raging sun. The sky was a solid seaside blue, with not a cloud in sight. I let go of the lilo and swam to the other end of the pool.

'How are my lovely hens?' she called out, trying to make amends.

'Hungover!' I paddled back. 'Tiff's asleep. Celine's having breakfast. I'm covered in mozzie bites but apart from that I'm good. Don't know about Dani.'

'She's dead to the world,' Aoife said. 'We went on a bit of a bender last night.'

'With the wannabe gangsters?'

'No way!' She laughed. 'We gave them the slip, ran back to Supernova and danced the night away. It was great actually, much better than the club. You should have been there. I missed you.'

'You were quite mean to Tiff,' I said, doing my protective act again.

Aoife rested her cheek on the lilo pillow. 'Was I? Sorry.'

'She's worked really hard pulling this weekend together, trying to please you. I think she needs to hear some appreciation.'

'Yeah, you're right. I'll make it up to her.'

'And, of course, she's incredibly jealous of Dani.'

Aoife made a noise of agreement. 'I know they don't get on, but I couldn't leave either of them out. To be fair to Dani, she's trying her best, but Tiff's constantly jumping down her throat. She's so tense, it's ridiculous. I mean, it's just a hen party, for God's sake.'

'There's something else going on,' I said, checking to make sure nobody was around. 'Tiff has got herself into a mess of some kind. I think it's quite serious. Usually, we tell each other everything, but this time she's refusing to share.'

Aoife lifted herself onto her elbows. 'Shit. What sort of mess? Like she's broken the law?'

'Don't think so, it seems more emotional. My guess is it's to do with a man. Maybe she's seeing someone married. Her boss perhaps? I don't know. She's denying it but I can't see what else it could be.'

Aoife sighed. 'Bloody men, they spoil everything.'

'She hasn't said anything to you?'

'No,' said Aoife. 'Not that there's been much chance for a heart-to-heart. Do you think I should try and talk to her about it?'

I frowned. 'Maybe leave it until after the weekend. I know she won't want to bother you with her problems. The best way you can help Tiff is to act like you're having a good time.'

'I *am* having a good time.'

'Are you?' I looked at her closely. 'You've been behaving strangely too. I know it's normal for everyone to flirt at hen parties, but the way you were with Matt on Friday night was . . . I hope you don't mind me saying, but it was a bit shocking, to tell you the truth. And you were getting very close with Marta's husband at Supernova. What was that about?'

Aoife looked away from me, towards the mountains. 'We were just dancing,' she murmured.

'I saw you go off with him. Where did you go?' She didn't answer but I felt I'd struck a nerve. 'What's going on, Aoife? You're about to get married. Nothing happened last night, did it? With John? Or those men at the club?' She shook her head, but still refused to look at me.

'To be honest, Beth,' she said finally, 'Tiff's not the only one in a mess. But don't worry about me, I'm sorting it.'

'If I can help—' I began, but just then her mobile phone, which she'd left on a sunbed nearby, bleeped.

'That'll be Nathan,' she said wearily. 'Checking up on me as usual.' She didn't attempt to answer it, just drifted away from me, closing her eyes and trailing her fingers in the water.

I swam about for a bit, then climbed out. Aoife's phone bleeped again so I picked it up. I wasn't meaning to snoop, I just wanted to stop it making such an irritating noise. Maybe I had it in mind to hand it to her, I don't know. I remember picking it up and opening the cover. Aoife didn't have a passcode. It was hard to see the screen in the harsh sunlight, but I could tell she'd had a WhatsApp text from a Spanish number – no name given. I stepped into the shade of the parasol, my back to Aoife. The message was short and suspiciously sweet.

Last night was hot. Got to see you again xx

It could be from anyone – Matt, John, the guy who'd been all over her in the club, somebody else she'd met up with at Supernova. The taste of the croissant instantly rose into my mouth. She'd lied about what she'd got up to last night, and I hated being lied to.

I turned around and looked across the water. Aoife still had her eyes closed and hadn't seen me. I put her phone back on the sunbed, seething with rage.

Draping a towel around my shoulders, I walked over to the other side of the pool, as far away from her as possible. I stared at the incredibly blue lake and the deep green mountains, the ribbon of sparkling sea and the smudge of Gibraltar just visible in the far distance, using the scenery to anchor my surging emotions.

Aoife had never had any trouble finding boyfriends. She wasn't especially beautiful, but she had a lively personality and knew how to make herself desirable. Unfortunately, the relationships rarely lasted beyond a few months. Either the guys were too intense, or they were complete tossers who treated her badly. Nathan was different. He was lovely – kind, funny, emotionally stable. He didn't have a secret child or a needy ex-wife. He earned very good money and had his own flat. It was true that he dominated Aoife, which surprised me because she wasn't an easy person to dominate. But his intentions were good, and it was obvious that he adored her. Since being with him, she'd grown up and seemed finally to be taking life seriously. With his help, she'd got an interesting job with a real future. So why was she mistreating him like this?

Aoife had it all. That's how it felt to me on that hot Sunday morning. Not content with an exciting job and a rich husband and a huge wedding that would cost tens of thousands, she seemed to think it was okay to spend her hen party getting wasted and hooking up with other guys. It wasn't fair. It wasn't right.

Maybe it was my over-developed sense of justice that made me act, or because I finally had a chance to get my own back on her for Zach. She'd always hotly denied having sex with him, but I knew in my heart that something had happened at that party a few years ago. Why else had Zach confessed? Tiff had always insisted Aoife was innocent, and I'd tried my hardest to believe it, but the doubt had never completely left my mind. All the hurt I'd suffered then came flooding back. There'd been other women, not just Aoife, but at the moment she symbolised all of them.

Over the hen weekend, I'd realised that Aoife was easily capable of betraying people she was supposed to care about. If she could do that to the man she was about to marry, why not me? I was brimming over with self-righteousness, allying myself with Nathan as a fellow victim. It felt like my duty to let him know what was going on.

Chapter Twenty-Eight: Now

DANI

Dani puts the key to John's apartment in her pocket. There are several hours to go before he'll definitely be out and she can let herself in. She has no idea what she's looking for. Proof of criminal connections, perhaps? And she doesn't know how she will manage to go there without the others knowing. This is so out of her comfort zone and yet she feels compelled – or does she mean *pro*pelled? Some other force is driving her, that's for sure. Aoife's spirit hovers at her side, nudging her in the ribs, grinning mischievously. *I dare you, Dani Girl*, she says. *Do it.*

God, Dani misses her.

She goes downstairs. The place seems so quiet. Where are the others? She wants to talk to them, find out how they're feeling, what they want to do. On the schedule – *her* schedule this time – is a visit to the cemetery, followed by a ceremony for Aoife this evening in the garden. It's the last place they were all together, drinking fizz, singing and dancing, eating cold paella leftovers, having a wonderful time – at least, that was how everyone described it to the police. She can't remember it herself, but she knows the atmosphere must have been far more tense than that. By Sunday afternoon, they'd all fallen out with each other.

It's been a long process – reconstructing the whole weekend, reliving it in her head as best she can. She's been working up to this evening from the moment she stepped back into the villa. She can't stop now, not when she feels she's getting so close to the truth.

Where are the others? Dani tries knocking on their bedroom doors, but there's no reply. She ventures inside a room. Tiff's side is pristine and tidy, clothes hung up on the rail, bed neatly made, toiletries lined up on the dressing table. In contrast, Beth's side looks like a Tracey Emin installation. Relieved that they haven't moved out, Dani quickly checks Celine's room but she's not there either.

Something is happening. She feels strange, as if her brain is unwinding. Maybe it's the heat and she's dehydrated. She tries the back door. It's stiff but it opens, scraping across the slabs. She enters the small courtyard. The paving stones are flecked with white paint, wildflowers growing in the gaps. An old wheelbarrow is propped against the wall. An outside tap drips.

She slips through the passage by the garage, arriving at the front of the villa. The heat intensifies. This is no weather for hide and seek. Marta's car has gone and only the white Seat is visible. Maybe the others have gone for a walk, she thinks, starting down the track that leads to the road. Her feet scuff up the dirt. The sunlight is blinding, she's not wearing shades or a hat.

She pauses at the start of the olive grove, which stretches away down the hillside. The trees are wizened and twisted, clinging to the slope. Suddenly, she senses something in her inner vision – something small but significant crawling out of the cracks in her memory, scuttling purposefully towards her . . . She gasps, her mouth drying instantly. What is her brain trying to remember? She feels attracted and repelled all at once. She wants to enter the olive grove, but her feet won't allow it. She can hardly breathe. Something happened down there . . .

She jolts back to the present as she sees Tiff, Beth and Celine coming round the bend. They walk towards her.

'Oh. There you are,' Dani says weakly. 'I've been looking for you everywhere.'

'Sorry,' says Beth. 'We weren't trying to avoid you.'

Dani doesn't believe her.

Tiff explains, 'We went to the shrine. Beth wanted to put some money in the box. For Aoife.'

'Oh, right . . . nice.'

'We're going to have some lunch now,' says Celine. 'Just whatever's left in the fridge. You coming?'

'Yeah, I guess.' They are behaving as if everything's totally normal. Dani finds it unnerving. Half an hour ago, Tiff and Beth were happy to ignore her. Now it's like they want to be friends.

'Can I ask you something?' she says.

Tiff looks irritated. 'What?'

'Did we go down there?' She points to the olive grove. 'I'm not sure when, maybe on the Sunday evening?'

'No, we only went down there when Marta gave us the tour on the first day,' Tiff replies.

Dani looks towards the trees again, their silver leaves like fingers, pulling her in. She shudders. 'There's something about that place that gives me the creeps. I almost had a panic attack just now.'

'This whole place gives me the creeps,' says Tiff. 'The sooner we get away, the better. Come on, I'm hungry.'

'Yes, Dani,' Beth says, quickening her pace to catch up with Celine. 'Have some lunch with us.'

They walk back to the villa.

'Marta came over while you were out,' Dani tells them. 'She was very upset by the damage, understandably. And she saw the message on the mirror. She thinks it was for her, not me.'

'Oh. That's interesting,' says Tiff. 'Is she going to call the police?'

'No, and she doesn't want us to, either.'

Celine looks surprised. 'Why not?'

'She's frightened . . . I think John might be involved in some dodgy stuff,' says Dani.

'We're not safe here,' says Celine. 'I'm starting to wonder whether we should just go back to the airport and wait overnight.'

'No, please don't do that,' says Dani. 'We haven't been to the cemetery yet, and we're supposed to be having the ceremony tonight.'

Tiff twists her mouth. 'I don't want to spend all night at the airport.'

'Neither do I,' says Beth. 'And we promised Aoife's parents that we'd visit her grave, remember.'

'I'm not sure I can cope with going to the cemetery, but Beth's right,' Tiff says. 'We can't let Mike and Kate down.'

'And tonight's ceremony is important,' adds Dani. 'We've all prepared stuff, right?'

'Okay, okay . . . if that's what everyone wants,' says Celine reluctantly. 'But we need to be careful.'

Beth, Tiff and Celine go inside to gather some bits for lunch. Dani stays on the terrace. She puts her hand in her pocket and runs her finger along the jagged edge of the Supernova key. She'll have to find some excuse to go back to Puerto Banús by herself after they've been to the cemetery. In the meantime, she has to do more remembering. It's Sunday lunchtime and she's way behind. She hasn't even got to the end of Saturday night yet.

She closes her eyes and thinks back to the early hours – running barefoot through the streets with Aoife, breathless with excitement and a smidgen of fear. Giggling about the gangsters' absurd clothes, mimicking their accents, bursting into Supernova, dancing with their hands raised, gyrating, smiling at each other giddily, mouthing 'love you, babe' as the music thrummed. Aoife and John had a quick smooch on the dance floor and even sang a karaoke duet together. After that, he was called to help out behind the bar and Aoife had returned to Dani. They'd danced the rest of the night away, and Dani had almost forgotten this was supposed to be her best friend's hen party. It had been a great night overall, like the good old days. Just the two of them without a care in the world.

It was only in the taxi on the way back to the villa that reality had struck home. Aoife had decided she didn't want to marry Nathan. That was big. It made a mockery out of the rest of the weekend. And they'd fallen out badly with the other hens, particularly Tiff. Would they be waiting up for them, ready for another confrontation? But no, everyone was in bed when they finally snuck in at around 4 a.m.

Chapter Twenty-Nine: Then

DANI

Dani reached out for her phone and checked the time. It was nearly noon, no wonder it was so hot. Her mouth felt scraped dry – she took a swig from the bottle of water on the side table. She reached out, expecting to see Aoife lying next to her, her long limbs tangled in the bedclothes, her bright pixie hair on the pillow. But she wasn't there.

Dani hauled herself out of bed and went to use the bathroom. She was not a pretty sight. There were puffy bags under her bloodshot eyes. Her skin looked rough. Her hair was matted, resisting all her efforts to comb it through.

What was on the schedule for today's entertainment? She wracked her brains. Oh, yes . . . the paella party, with a cooking lesson thrown in for good measure. The perfect activity to help everyone recover from their hangovers. Not.

What was the atmosphere going to be like today? Dani wondered, as she showered and dressed. Aoife was already up and had gone downstairs. How brave of her to face them on her own.

There were noises outside. Dani opened the shutters and looked out across the courtyard. A van had drawn up next to the hire car and two guys were busy unpacking crates of equipment and cooking ingredients. Tiff was talking to them, using a mixture of English and improvised sign language to explain what she wanted them to do and where they should do it. Dani briefly considered running downstairs and translating, but she held back. There was no doubt in her mind that Tiff would blame her for the argument last night. She seemed to think that Dani was the ringleader, egging Aoife on to do bad things, when in fact it was the opposite. Dani had been trying to stop her.

Anyway, they weren't necessarily bad things. You could see her having sex with John as a cry for help, a way of forcing the issue, of making it impossible to continue with her marriage. Realising that you didn't want to be with someone was extremely uncomfortable and calling off the wedding was going to upset a lot of people, most of all Nathan, but it would be far better to go through that pain now than endure years of an unhappy marriage. It was going to end badly, either way, so get it over and done with – that was Dani's take on the situation. She wouldn't try to persuade Aoife to go through with the wedding just because the venue was booked and the dress bought, and the menu had already been tasted.

Speaking of menus . . .

Dani went downstairs. She could hear the clanging of pans in the kitchen and Spanish being spoken in a very strong Andalucian accent. Desperate for a glass of orange juice, she went in and said hello, hoping that Tiff wouldn't still be ordering them about. She wasn't. There was a main chef, who was complaining about the cooking facilities, and an assistant, who was doing a lot of vegetable chopping. Dani engaged him in some Spanish chat. The chef told her that lunch comprised a selection of tapas followed by paella mixta, which contained chicken and seafood. Dani also found out that Tiff had cancelled the cooking demonstration.

Interesting, she thought. While she was relieved not to have to sit in rapt attention while pans were rattled and knives flourished, it was a bad sign. Tiff was almost certainly still in a huff. Dani helped herself to a glass of juice and took a banana from the fruit bowl.

She went into the sitting room and looked out of the small window next to the patio doors. Tiff was outside on the terrace, trying to drag a heavy table into the shade all by herself. She had a martyrish air about her. Again, Dani thought about going to help, but didn't. She was happy to make up with Tiff but wanted to talk to Aoife first to find out what the deal was – as in, who was apologising to whom, or were they all going to do it? Aoife was bound to be at the pool, but the only way down there was via the terrace, where Tiff was now laying the table.

Neither Beth nor Celine was in sight. Were they still in bed or also swimming? It was odd that Beth wasn't fluttering around, being Tiff's assistant, passing knives and forks, folding napkins.

Dani didn't want to talk to Tiff on her own. Feeling cowardly, she fled upstairs. She would wait until Aoife reappeared, she decided. They needed to present a united front.

But Aoife didn't come back to the room all morning. Dani tried texting her, but she didn't respond. In hiding with her feet up on the bed, playing with her phone, it was nearly time for lunch before Dani decided to go back downstairs and face the music. In any case there were some fantastic smells rising from the kitchen.

Celine and Aoife were already seated, talking quietly to each other. As Dani stepped onto the terrace, Aoife gave her a sly wink, but it was impossible to guess what it meant.

Tiff hovered at the head of the table. 'Oh, so you're awake then,' she snapped.

'Yeah. Sorry. It was a very late night.'

Aoife waved at the scene. 'Doesn't this look amazing? Thanks so much, Tiff.'

'Somebody had to make the effort,' she responded grumpily.

'Well, I really appreciate it,' Aoife said, smiling her best.

She was obviously trying to make up for last night, but she wasn't lying, the table did look splendid. Tiff had found a tablecloth, a North African print in earthy reds and yellows. The posh cutlery was out, as were the fancy wine glasses. The tapas starters – stuffed peppers, *croquetas*, olives, Iberian ham and Manchego cheese – had been artfully arranged on rustic wooden plates and were already beckoning flies. Three jugs of sangria were waiting to be poured. Only the pink Bride-to-Be bunting spoiled the authentic Andalucian vibe.

'I just wanted to say something.' Aoife grabbed Tiff's hand. 'I'm really sorry if I upset anyone last night. I know it's no excuse, but I was completely wasted. You lot were right, of course, those guys were nasty, but we managed to ditch them and there was no harm done.'

'That's a relief,' said Celine.

'We really missed you back at Supernova, didn't we, Dani?'

Dani hadn't missed the others one bit, but she nodded in support. If apologies were the order of the day, she would do apologies. 'I'm sorry too, if I offended anyone.'

'Let's just forget it and move on,' said Celine.

There was a long pause while Dani and Aoife waited for Tiff to make a similar gesture, but she remained stony-faced.

'Where's Beth?' Dani asked, keen to change gear.

'She was with me at the pool, then she went off some-where,' replied Aoife. 'We had a good chat earlier, she seemed fine.'

'We're not waiting,' said Tiff.

Just at that moment, Beth appeared from the side of the villa. Her face was red and she was dripping in the heat.

Tiff looked her up and down. 'Where the hell have you been?'

'Just for a little walk,' she replied defensively.

'Where?'

'Just around.'

'Why?'

'Because I felt like it.' Beth read Tiff's expression. 'What's the matter?'

'I needed you.'

'To do what?'

Tiff searched her brain. 'I don't know. Stuff.'

'You could have asked me,' said Celine.

Tiff tossed her head. 'That's not the point.'

'Isn't it?'

'No. Not really. I'd already spoken to Beth about helping.'

'It's okay,' said Beth, sitting down. 'I'm here now.' She picked up a napkin, using it to wipe the sweat off her face. Tiff winced. There was a tense silence.

'Everyone start,' Tiff commanded. 'The caterers have another hen party to go to this afternoon, so they need to be away by three.'

'They must be raking it in,' remarked Celine, handing round a rustic platter. 'How much did you say all this was?'

'Five hundred euros, give or take. Everything this weekend has cost five hundred euros, it's like the minimum.'

Dani hoped the caterers hadn't been listening, because almost immediately the chef – a stocky guy with a shaved head – made a theatrical entrance with an enormous pan of paella, which he rested on a small side table, brought in specially for the occasion. A heady aroma of smoked paprika and saffron rose into the air. Black mussel shells gleamed in the sunshine, giant prawns and wedges of lemon poked cheerfully out of the bright yellow rice. Nobody oohed or aahed and Dani had to lead the applause. The chef bowed and wished them '¡Buen provecho!', then retired to the kitchen to clear up.

People *did* eat. The food was too delicious to ignore completely, but the atmosphere was extremely strained. Tiff didn't eat any of the seafood and spent most of the meal chasing grains of rice around her plate. Beth, who normally had a good appetite, wasn't eating much either. There would be an embarrassing amount left over, thought Dani, heroically helping herself to another plateful. Only the sangria seemed to be going down well.

Dani tried to make conversation, recounting the various paellas she'd eaten while she'd lived in Seville. She could tell that nobody was interested. Tiff clearly still hadn't forgiven her (although for what, she wasn't sure) and Beth was in some kind of huff. God knows what that was about. Celine had got over the row last night, but she seemed preoccupied. Dani guessed she was probably dreaming about her amazing new job as Head of Something, she couldn't remember what.

Aoife was the only one pretending to listen to Dani's stories, but she didn't comment, and it was obvious that her thoughts were also elsewhere. Dani watched her pick the shell off a king prawn, slowly licking the sauce off her fingers. What was she remembering, exactly? The joy of dancing last night, perhaps. Or, more likely, the feel of John's body pressing against hers. She was certainly hitting the sangria with a vengeance, but whether it was because she felt liberated or scared by the enormity of what she'd done, Dani couldn't tell. Both, probably.

They limped to the dessert course, saying almost nothing. Tiff took out her phone and demanded a selfie with the chefs. Everyone managed to force a smile for the camera, fixing the lie forever.

The caterers collected the empty jugs and the giant paella pan, scraping the leftovers into plastic boxes. Then they picked up their crates, said *adiós*, and hurried away.

'We'll clear up properly later,' said Tiff. 'Things are running a bit behind. Now we've got to prepare for the surprise.'

Dani sighed before she could stop herself. Not *another* activity, she thought. Couldn't they just relax? 'What *is* the surprise?' she asked.

Tiff pursed her lips. 'Sorry. Can't tell you.'

'If we don't know what it is, how can we prepare for it?'

'It's not difficult. Just find some chairs and put them out in a circle, okay? Somewhere outside but in the shade and away from the main villa.'

'Like in the orchard? Or the olive grove?'

'No, it has to be somewhere flat. Maybe on that little terrace over there.' She pointed to it.

'But it's in full sunshine.'

'It won't be by the time we get there.'

'Okay. What chairs do you want me to use? These ones?'

'No, they're not suitable. We can't have anything that will spoil.'

So, the surprise was messy. 'Okaaay. Do you know where there are some extra chairs?'

'No,' Tiff said, turning away. 'You'll just have to look.'

'I'll help you,' said Celine, rising from her seat.

They went to the garage. Dani's eyes wandered over the miscellaneous junk – an old lamp stand, an office chair with an arm missing, a table football set, a dartboard that had been punctured to death. A plastic crate full of balls and frisbees. A pair of table-tennis bats. Even a surfboard. Large cardboard boxes – the kind you get when you move house – were stacked up against one wall. They were printed with the name of a removal company in North London and variously labelled in English: *books, DVDs and photos, kitchen, bits and bobs, memorabilia.*

'This must be John's stuff,' Dani said. 'Brought over from the UK. I wonder why he's never unpacked it.'

'Well, they don't live here, do they?' answered Celine. 'They live above the bar. There probably isn't room in their apartment.'

'True. Everyone carts too much stuff around with them. When you put things in storage for a while, you realise how little you actually need.'

They found some canvas fold-up chairs, which they dragged into the courtyard. Dani brushed off the dirty cobwebs with an old cloth. She picked up three of the chairs and tucked them under her arm. Celine did the same with the other two and they were carrying them around to the viewing platform when they heard a phone ringing.

'Sorry,' Celine said, instantly dropping the chairs. 'Got to take that.' She ran back to the terrace and snatched up her mobile. Beth had moved to the sofa and Tiff was clearing the table. Celine obviously didn't want to have her conversation in front of them, so she went inside.

'Perhaps it's about the job,' Dani said to Aoife, who'd come to take over the chair shifting.

'I doubt they'd call her at the weekend,' she replied. 'It's probably just Farrell. He's almost as bad as Nathan for "checking in".'

'Have you spoken to Nathan today?'

She shook her head. 'I can't. I'm frightened I'll say something.'

'Something you'll regret later?'

'Not regret necessarily. But I need to tell him face to face. It's only fair.'

'You still want to call it off, then?' Dani whispered. 'You're sure?'

Aoife nodded. Her blue eyes were bright and clear. 'Yes, I'm sure, but don't let on to the others. I just need to get through the rest of the weekend, then I'll deal with it. You and me, we're going to put on a show, okay? We're going to pretend everything's just fine.'

Chapter Thirty: Now

DANI

The Spanish *cementerio* is like nothing Dani has encountered before. She expected an open space with green grass, rows of grey headstones, statues of angels – in short, an English cemetery. But this is like a massive outdoor mausoleum, with everything above ground. The coffins and urns are encased in marble niches, stacked one above the other. There are walls and walls of them, about three metres high, forming a grid that seems almost never-ending. The floors of the narrow passageways are made of marble too, slippery underfoot from almost constant hosing down.

Beth holds onto Tiff's arm as she walks, scanning the inscriptions for Aoife's name. Dani is surprised that Tiff agreed to come. She seems on edge, looking around all the time as if frightened that somebody's going to jump out at her. They don't know where Aoife rests. There is no map to guide them.

Dani trails behind the others, listening to Beth reading out the names engraved on the doors in her terrible Spanish accent, while Celine comments on the strangeness of some of the items in the shrines: a plastic model of a man on a motorbike, a tractor made out of Lego, a faded picture of a dog. The sun bounces off the white marble, giving it an other-worldly – dare she say, heavenly? – atmosphere.

There was a huge fuss, she remembers, about the funeral arrangements. Aoife had had no travel insurance. When the Chief Bridesmaid made the bookings, she assumed everyone was already covered. None of them queried it in advance, so they were all to blame. There was talk about repatriating the body, but it took ages for it to be released, and in the end, Aoife's parents decided she should be buried in Spain. This location is beautiful, thinks Dani. It's the right home for her.

'Shall we split up?' says Celine after the four of them have slowly traipsed down the middle pathway of the cemetery. 'The whole place is enormous and it's really hot.'

'Good idea,' says Beth. 'I'll go left. Tiff, you go right. Celine and Dani, do you want to take the horizontals? Text if you find her.'

They set off in opposite directions. Dani walks slowly, still processing the fact that Beth, Tiff and Celine are here at all. Their attitude towards her seems to have flipped. It's as if they've stopped the clock and reset the game. She should be feeling pleased but instead she's suspicious. They were definitely plotting something on their walk to the shrine this morning. Rather than fight, they're trying to disarm her.

She carries on, looking in a criss-cross motion, up and down, side to side. Nearly all the names are Spanish, but occasionally she finds a foreigner – most often German, interestingly. Her heart quivers when she finds an English name, momentarily deceived by its familiarity. The letters dance before her eyes, she can hardly read them in the dazzling sunlight. She looks and looks and looks. Has she missed it? When she reaches the end of one section she goes back to the beginning and searches again.

Suddenly, there she is, halfway down the wall, wedged between a Concepción and a Martín. Dani blinks several times to make sure she's not imagining it. She reaches up and traces her finger across the brass lettering. Aoife Mary Byrne. The inscription says nothing about the circumstances of her death – why would it? The fact that she was only just thirty when she died tells its own story.

Dani contemplates the memorial, feeling the weight of its meaning. She is glad to have these few moments alone, just the two of them. When she's ready, she takes her phone out of her bag and sends a message to the group. *Found her.* She gives them directions, then waits.

Celine is the first to arrive. She appears in the gap between the next aisle and walks towards Dani. A few seconds later, she hears footsteps behind her. It's Beth, half-running, half-skating across the polished marble.

'Well done, Dani,' she says. 'I thought we were going to have to give up.' She stops and stares at the memorial. 'Oh, God,' she says under her breath. 'It's like it's suddenly real.'

'Where's Tiff?' asks Dani.

'She went all the way over to the other side,' says Celine. 'She said something about us needing to search logically.'

'Of course.'

They keep staring at the memorial, reading the inscription over and over again, not knowing what to say. Dani checks her phone to see whether Tiff has responded to the message.

'Maybe it didn't get through,' suggests Beth. She and Celine offer to go and round her up.

'You stay put, Dani. Don't move,' orders Celine, 'or we may never find her again.'

They go off in the direction that Tiff was last seen. Dani stays where she is. It's baking hot now and she's standing in full sunshine. There's only a ribbon of shade from the opposite wall, too thin to stand in. She feels thirsty. What the hell is Tiff playing at? So typical of her to go to the furthest extreme of the cemetery to start looking.

Beth and Celine seem to have been gone for several minutes. Dani starts to feel irritable. It's like everyone's run away to play a trick on her. She texts them again. *Where are you???*

When they return, Tiff is not with them.

'We've looked everywhere,' Beth says, 'but we can't find her.'

'It's like losing somebody at the supermarket,' Dani says. 'You know, you turn the corner just as they disappear down the next aisle.'

'I'll try calling,' says Beth. They huddle around her phone, listening to Tiff's number ringing out. 'This is ridiculous. Why won't she pick up?'

'Perhaps she put her phone on silent,' offers Celine. 'You know, out of respect.'

'I doubt it. Where on earth is she?' Beth sighs impatiently. 'It's like she's vanished into thin air.'

'We've got to search for her systematically,' says Celine.

Dani rolls her eyes. 'I thought you just did that.'

'Perhaps she's just gone to buy some water or something,' suggests Beth. 'Actually, I think she mentioned she was thirsty when we were in the car.'

'So why isn't she answering her phone?' says Dani. They both shrug. 'This is really annoying of her.'

'She wasn't too keen on coming in the first place,' says Beth. 'I had to persuade her. I hope she's alright.'

The sun beats down, burning their shoulders, catching the brass lettering on the memorial. It's as if Aoife's part of the group again, listening to the conversation.

'So, what do we do?' asks Dani. 'We can't stand here all day.'

'I think we should go back to the entrance and find some shade to sit in,' says Celine. 'Hopefully, Tiff will return Beth's call.'

Dani glances at the time on her phone. She was supposed to be in John's apartment twenty minutes ago. He should still be with Marta at Venta El Lago, but she doesn't know how long their meeting will last. She needs an excuse to get away for a short period.

'I'm going to drive around the streets, see if I can spot her,' Dani offers, hoping neither of them will want to come along.

'That's good of you, Dani,' says Beth. 'We'll stay here in case she comes back. I've a feeling she might be upset. She was so close to Aoife – they were like sisters. I know she's found this whole weekend extremely difficult. Perhaps coming here just tipped her over the edge.'

Dani glances at the time again. She really has to get going. 'Yeah, well, that's certainly a plausible explanation. I'm still going to look for her.'

'Okay.' Beth gives her a grateful smile. 'Keep in touch, eh? If you find her, let us know.'

Chapter Thirty-One: Then

CELINE

When my mobile rang – Farrell's special ringtone – I was keen to speak to him, even though we'd already talked earlier that day. I'd poured my heart out to him about how badly the hen weekend was going, and how much I longed to get home. He'd basically told me to grin and bear it and we'd parted on bad terms. We hardly ever argued, and I hated having negative thoughts about him.

'Sorry, babe, nearly there,' I said, rushing into my room and closing the door. It was lovely and cool at the back of the villa, where Marta's grandmother's pickles and jams used to be stored. I kicked off my Birkenstocks and jumped onto the bed. 'Ready now! I'm so glad you rang back,' I began. 'I'm sorry we fell out.'

'We didn't fall out,' Farrell contested. 'I tried to give you some advice, that's all. Coping mechanisms.'

'Yeah, but you don't know what it's like here. Honestly, we've just had this enormous paella – cost a bloody fortune, like hundreds of euros – and you could have cut the atmosphere with a knife. Now we've all got to do some other ridiculous activity. A surprise one. God knows what Tiff has booked! It'll be something naff. I can't bear it.'

'Yeah, I know.'

'I'd so much rather sit here and talk to you.'

'Hmm . . . Celine, hon?'

'I know, I know, I can't hide here all day,' I prattled on. 'I *will* stick it out. Promise. I know how much you want that investment. I mean, we have to be honest, it's still an outside chance, but I'm not going to wreck it for you. Are you still there?'

'Yup.'

'Only you're not saying anything.'

'You're not giving me a chance.'

'Hey, don't be like that. I thought you'd rung to make up.'

'Not exactly.' He hesitated.

'Oh. So, what have you rung for? Please don't give me more advice!'

'Nothing like that.'

'What's up? Has something bad happened? Is somebody ill?'

'Look . . . maybe I'm doing the wrong thing here by telling you, but . . .'

'But what?'

'Only I thought you'd be mad at me if I didn't and then you found out later. I know how you hate being kept in the dark.'

I felt my body completely tense up. 'What's wrong, Farrell?'

'Nathan called me.'

'Nathan?'

'Yup. He rang to ask me if I knew how the hen do was going. Apparently, Aoife's not been answering his calls or replying to his texts. He's worried about her. Is she okay? Has she lost her phone or something?'

'No,' I replied curtly. 'She's been too busy getting drunk and making a fool of herself. What did Nathan say?'

'Well, it came about in a strange way. He said he wanted to speak to Aoife because he had some exciting news to tell her.'

'Oh. Okay. I'll try asking her to call him if you like. No promises. If she doesn't want to talk to him, that's her lookout.'

'Don't worry. The thing is . . .' Farrell hesitated. 'The thing is . . . he went out for dinner last night with your boss – did you know they were mates?'

'Charlie and Nathan? Yeah, I think Nathan's been involved in some production funding – you know, finding investors. And that's how Aoife got her job in the first place, of course. You know how cosy it is in the media world.'

'Sure is,' he muttered.

'So, what is this exciting news for Aoife?'

'Well, Nathan said he was really chuffed with himself because he'd persuaded this guy to promote her.' Farrell gulped.

'Wow! To Production Executive? There'll be an empty slot once I move up. I mean, she's only been doing the job for eighteen months, and she's not the best, but—'

'Celine, listen to me,' he interrupted. 'Nathan said she's going to be Head of Development. That's the position you went for, yes?'

It was as if he'd dropped a large stone into the pit of my stomach. 'You know it is,' I said dully.

'And there's definitely only one of them up for grabs?'

'There can only be one Head, Farrell.'

'Shit. I thought so. I'm really sorry, babe. It's so unfair.'

'You're telling me!' It was as much as I could do to keep my voice down. 'I was told it was mine, that the interview was just a formality! There's no way that Aoife is ready to be Head of Development. She's barely experienced enough to be an Executive. I had to wait eight years before I got that. It's outrageous! I've never heard anything so ridiculous in my life. How could she do it to me?'

'Hold your horses,' Farrell said. 'I don't think she even knows about it, babe.'

'I bet she does,' I replied, boiling up. 'She probably asked Nathan to take Charlie out for dinner while we were away and wangle it for her.'

'You don't know that. I mean, she didn't actually apply, did she?'

'No, but she obviously didn't need to! It's all about who you know, not what you know. She was hopeless when she started – I took her under my wing, taught her the job, covered up her mistakes . . .'

He sighed heavily. 'Oh, God. I shouldn't have told you. I should have waited until you got home.'

'No, no, I'm glad you did. It's good to know who's your friend and who's your enemy.'

'She's not your enemy, Celine. She's just a woman with a powerful fiancé. I'd do the same for you if I could.'

'No, you wouldn't. And I wouldn't let you. I'd rather succeed on my own merits.'

There was a long silence between us.

'What are you going to do?' Farrell said, breaking into my troubled thoughts.

'I don't know. Ask her what she's playing at, I suppose.'

'Don't go out there all guns blazing. Aoife may be innocent.'

'Hmm,' I said, not believing it for a second.

'Don't wreck this, Celine.'

'What the hell are you talking about? I haven't done anything wrong. I've just lost the job of a lifetime. No other company would even look at me for a job like that. You have to have a stupid degree in film or TV production or parents who work in the industry, preferably both. You have to be—'

'Hey, hey! I know it's unfair but look at the big picture. Nathan is right on the brink of investing in my idea. You know how much we need that money. If you fall out with Aoife, he will take her side and it'll be dead in the water.'

'For God's sake, stop going on about your bloody investment. My career has just been flushed down the toilet,' I said.

'Not necessarily.'

'Yes, my time there is over! I can't carry on as her junior. It's obscene. I'll have to resign.'

'You can't do that! How would we pay the rent?'

'Maybe you could get a job for once,' I snapped.

He sighed. 'Look, I know you're upset, but don't make any hasty decisions. Get your facts straight, don't jump in feet first. Better if you don't say anything, to be honest. Just leave it until the weekend's over.'

'Don't keep saying "don't". *I'll* decide what to do.'

'Best of luck. Love you,' he said lamely.

We ended the call. I took a few moments to gather myself then left the bedroom and went back outside. I didn't want to wreck the weekend, but I couldn't pretend nothing was wrong. I had to talk to Aoife.

Chapter Thirty-Two: Now

DANI

Relieved to have got away from Beth and Celine, Dani unlocks the car and climbs in. The seats are hot, and the steering wheel almost burns her hands. She's not sure how to get to Supernova from here, but decides to follow her nose rather than set the Sat Nav. As she drives through an endless succession of roundabouts, she thinks about Tiff's strange disappearance. It was really annoying of her to run off like that. Why didn't she just say if she needed some time to herself? Why wasn't she answering her phone?

She changes down a gear to cope with the steep descent, hitting Puerto Banús at the end of the marina, more by luck than judgement. To her added surprise, she manages to find a parking place in a side street only a hundred metres from the bar. As she walks towards it, her heart rate starts to speed up. She's never done anything like this before. It feels scary. What if she is spotted letting herself in to the apartment? There could be CCTV. She hasn't got a mask or a hoodie, isn't wearing gloves. She'll leave her DNA and prints everywhere. She doesn't even know what it is she's looking for.

She stands in front of the door, clutching the key in her pocket, reviewing her plan. Either John trashed the villa himself last night or he and Marta know who did and they're scared. It's clear that they're in some serious trouble and Dani has a hunch that it's connected to Aoife's death. Maybe she'll find evidence on John's computer – if she can get into it. She hesitates. Is this a stupid thing to be doing?

No, Dani Girl, says Aoife's voice in her head. *You carry on.*

The Street of Hell is not as hellish in daylight. In fact, it seems pretty normal. Most of the shops and bars are closed, but there are still several tourists wandering along, chatting, licking ice creams. Checking behind her just in case someone is watching, she approaches the door to the apartment. It's 4.40 p.m. Could John already have returned? Unlikely but . . .

She rings the bell then ducks around the corner, her heart going like the clappers. Her ears strain for telltale noises, the door opening, the sound of John's voice calling into the street, but there's no response. Good. He's gone out. She peeps round the wall, checks again, then walks back to the building and stands in front of the door. Carefully sneaking the key out of her pocket, she slides it into the lock. Her fingers feel sweaty with fear as she turns it one way, then the other. Finally, it bites, and she feels the lock releasing. She looks around then quickly lets herself in, shutting the door behind her.

It's dark, but she's reluctant to turn on the light. She tries to calm her heart rate, but if anything it has speeded up. What if he didn't go to meet Marta? What if he's upstairs, asleep, and didn't hear the doorbell? No, she reminds herself. He was the one who wanted to meet Marta, not the other way around.

Slowly, she climbs the narrow staircase. The concrete

steps curve round, half-lined with traditional Andalucian tiles – blue, gold and white. At the top, there are three doors leading off a square landing. The apartment is small and compact, it won't take long to search it. She picks a door and finds herself in the kitchen. There's another door on the far wall, leading to a roof terrace perhaps, or down to the back yard, possibly both. It could provide a way of escape if needed.

She looks around, careful not to touch anything. Dirty plates are piled up in the sink. The worktop is covered with saucepans, packets of dried goods, bottles of oil and vinegar. On the small table there's a breadboard covered with crumbs, a string of garlic, an open pack of ham, drying at the edges, a half-drunk glass of water. She recognises it as the home of somebody who lives alone, with nobody to clear up for, nobody to care. Her tiny flat in London often looks the same.

Leaving the kitchen, she goes back onto the landing and takes the second door, which leads into the bedroom. It's only just big enough to accommodate the double bed and a table on which stands an alarm clock and another half-drunk glass of water. The walls are bare, and the grey metal shutters lend the room the atmosphere of a prison cell. The T-shirt John was wearing yesterday lies on the floor next to some shorts and several pairs of used boxers. The bed is unmade, and the undersheet looks like it could do with changing.

Dani stares at the mattress for a few seconds, picturing Aoife and John having frantic sex here on that night – Aoife's eyes staring at the white, cracked ceiling, the smell of their sweaty bodies as he thrusts into her, finally collapsing onto her bare breasts. She can almost feel the weight of him . . . No, this is horrible. She dismisses the image, banishes it from her mind. There's nothing to see here.

She turns around and leaves, goes back to the tiny landing. Of course, the room she wants is the last one she chooses.

She goes into the sitting room. It's long and thin, furnished from IKEA, the surfaces covered in a film of dust. There are empty beer bottles lying on the rug and the smelly remains of a kebab are festering in a polystyrene tray. Last night's dinner, by the look of it.

John hasn't always lived here by himself. Three years ago, he was sharing the apartment with Marta. Dani scans for signs of her influence – some Spanish art on the walls, a patterned throw, a cushion, an ornament perhaps – but there's nothing.

His laptop lies on the sofa, a blue two-seater that has seen better days. She sits down and lifts it onto her knees, noticing how her hands shake as she opens the lid and presses the on button. She's greeted with a stunning photo of pink misty mountains in Asia. There's no four-digit code required to get to the home screen and then his Gmail account connects automatically via Chrome. Easy.

John has over two thousand read or unread messages in his inbox. She quickly scans the names of recent senders, hoping something will catch her eye. But most of the mail is junk – newsletters and special offers from websites John probably never meant to subscribe to. The rest are notifications from various suppliers – electricity, internet, credit cards, breweries, cash 'n' carry, cleaning products. Very few personal emails, which she finds striking. Is John a lonely guy or does he communicate with friends and family through other channels? Does he use Instagram maybe? Not that she's going to find anything incriminating on a public platform. Come to think of it, if he has dealings with criminals, he's unlikely to do it by email. He probably uses burner phones, not that she knows what they are exactly.

Her own phone bleeps at that moment. She jumps nervously, fishing it out of her bag. It's a message from Beth, asking whether she's found Tiff yet. They've had no word from her. Dani texts back a quick reply, saying she'll meet them at the cemetery entrance, and puts her phone away.

Time is passing quickly. The whole enterprise starts to feel pointlessly risky. Unease ripples through her. Why is she doing this? She doesn't even know what she's looking for.

She scours the room, hoping for inspiration. On the shelf next to the magazines is a framed photo of an older couple, who look like John's parents. It makes her wonder if there might be pictures of John's associates on his laptop. They might be known to the Spanish police. If she took copies and sent them to Inspector Mengual, he might just recognise them and be able to put a name to the face. Okay, it's a long shot, but she might as well take a look.

Luckily, John uses Google Photos. Hundreds of images come up immediately, stretching back over several years. She starts scrolling through, looking for likely candidates to play the role of expat money launderers – older guys perhaps, with beer-bellies, outdated tattoos, and an evil look in their eye. Sadly, there's nobody that fits the stereotype.

She scrolls down further until she finds photos of John and Marta together. There are heaps of them – on the beach, on a boat, partying with friends, dining on the terrace of what looks like Venta El Lago, at the marina posing in front of a gleaming super-yacht, comically pretending it's theirs. Next, she finds shots of Villa Floriana taken during the refurbishment. John laying hardcore for the new patio. Marta standing in the freshly dug hole for the swimming pool. Lots of photos involving buckets and paintbrushes.

Then she comes across their wedding pictures, which bring a lump to her throat because they look so happy together, so fresh and hopeful for the future. She moves swiftly on, going further back in time and finding several photos that look as if they were taken at John's stag do. A large group of guys in silly costumes hold beer glasses up to camera. They look as if they're standing outside Supernova. She peers into the shot. There's Matt, very fetching in a Marilyn Monroe wig; an older guy who could be a brother. And whose half-face is this, leaning out from behind somebody's shoulder? He looks familiar. She expands the photo.

Her heart leaps into her mouth. This can't be true. The photo is too fuzzy, she must be mistaken. She hasn't seen him for so long, she's almost forgotten what he looks like. It's only half a face anyway, you can't tell from half a face.

Except she knows it's him. And that this changes everything.

Chapter Thirty-Three: Then

BETH

I popped into the bedroom to splash my face and compose myself. The paella party had been an ordeal. Usually, I have a good appetite, but I'd hardly managed a morsel. I'd spent the entire time watching Aoife out of the corner of my eye, trying to work out what was going on inside her head, and why she'd behaved so abominably the previous night. The anger that'd been burning inside me all morning hadn't fizzled out. If anything, it was stronger now.

I felt like I didn't know her anymore. Maybe I'd never known her . . . not properly. In truth, it was a long time since we'd been really close. Although at the time I'd tried to accept that she *hadn't* slept with Zach, the incident had left a scar. Her behaviour over the weekend had made me realise that the wound had never properly healed. I'd wanted so much to believe her, but the nagging feeling that she'd betrayed me was still there.

As I made a few repairs to my melting make-up, I kept thinking about the WhatsApp message Aoife had received earlier. Who had it been from? It was a Spanish number, but that didn't mean it was a Spanish person. Marbella was bursting with expats. I wished I'd memorised it. Thoughts flew around my brain for a few seconds, hovered over Matt, then landed firmly on John. There were other candidates, of course – the guys at Pesadilla and other men she might have met when she and Dani returned to Supernova. Even so, John was the one I was putting my money on. I'd definitely seen them going off together while the rest of us were dancing. When she'd returned, there'd been an excited glint in her eyes, a different energy coming off her like steam.

Tiff had left her phone on her bedside table and it kept ringing relentlessly. She was outside, getting ready for the 'surprise' and obviously couldn't hear it. Who was so desperate to speak to her? I wondered. I hoped there wasn't some emergency back home. I picked up the phone and typed in Tiff's birthday as the passcode – it was a guess, but it worked. I wasn't planning to go beyond her home screen, but when I saw that she had fifteen WhatsApp messages – then sixteen, then seventeen – my curiosity got the better of me.

They were all from Nathan. Aoife hadn't been in touch with him since Saturday evening; she wasn't responding to his texts or picking up his calls. Was Aoife sick? Had she had an accident? Was she pissed off with him over the groom masks? Had she run out of juice on her phone? Where was she? He needed to talk to her. He wanted Tiff to *make* her call him. Now. It couldn't wait until tomorrow. He had some exciting news and wanted to tell her on a video call, so he could see her reaction.

I was tempted to reply on Tiff's behalf, but I knew she'd be cross if she found out that I'd been snooping. One good thing about the hen party was that it had given our friendship a new lease of life and I didn't want to spoil that. Tiff was already upset about something, although she was refusing to explain precisely what. She blamed herself for the hen party going so badly. I kept telling her it wasn't her fault, but she wouldn't listen. It was obvious that she was keeping some big secret from me, but I couldn't imagine what it was. I suspected a man was the problem. They usually were, in my experience. She'd flatly denied it but I knew the signs. She needed to share her troubles, and I wanted to be the one she shared them with, but so far, she'd been a closed book.

The mobile continued with its annoying refrain. It was Nathan calling, yet again. I know I should have rushed out with the phone and found Tiff, but the truth was that I wanted to talk to him myself. There were several things I needed to get off my chest. Things I felt he needed to know.

I let the call ring out. Then I transferred Nathan's number to my own contacts list. I clutched my phone to my chest, debating whether to call him or to leave things be. If I told him what had really been going on this weekend, he would be devastated and probably very angry. He might even call the wedding off. I thought of the chaos and upset that would be caused, not just to Nathan and Aoife but their families and friends – people who'd already invested a lot of time, money and energy in their relationship. Was I going to be the Bad Fairy and wreck all that? It wasn't a role I relished playing. On the other hand, I felt Nathan deserved to know the truth about the woman he was about to commit to for the rest of his life. For me, fidelity is the most important thing in a marriage. Without it, there's no value in the relationship. I was a victim of cheating myself. Only too well I remembered how hurt and lost I'd felt when the scales fell from my eyes, and I realised that Zach had never truly loved me. It was nine years before I faced reality, nine wasted years that I could have spent building my career or in a better relationship with someone else. I genuinely didn't want that for Nathan. And I didn't think Aoife should marry a man she didn't love either. How *could* she love him when she'd spent the weekend throwing herself at every passing stranger?

I went through the arguments again, trying to be as objective as possible, like any good solicitor would. My decision was made. I pressed the green button and he answered after two rings.

'Hello?' he said. 'Who is this?'

'Beth,' I replied, keeping my voice down. 'Aoife's friend. One of the hens.'

'Oh, yes, I remember. Beth. From school. Is Aoife okay? Is something wrong? Why are you calling?' He sounded very anxious.

'She's fine, nothing's wrong, we're all at the villa, but I'm not with Aoife right now.'

'I've been trying to get hold of her all weekend. I tried Tiff too but she's not replying. Why are they avoiding me?'

'I don't know.'

'I really need to speak to her. Can you just go and grab her for me?'

'I'm sorry but not really.'

'Why not?'

'I don't want her to know . . . I was hoping we could have a private conversation.'

There was a pause. 'What about? What's been going on?'

'I'm worried about Aoife,' I said, moving to my side of the room and sitting down on the edge of my bed. 'Her behaviour's been . . . odd. All weekend.'

'How do you mean, odd?'

I told him about the excessive drinking. About how she'd stayed behind at the club with a bunch of men. I could almost sense his jaw dropping.

'On her own?' he asked.

'With Dani.'

'I might have known. Can't stand that woman.'

'I don't think it's all Dani's fault, not at all. Aoife's gone a bit wild. I think she's gone too far.'

'Too far,' he repeated. 'Like how?'

'You know, drinking and flirting.'

'Yeah . . . and? Give me specifics. What was she doing? Who was she with? Where did they come from?'

I felt myself growing hot with embarrassment. 'I don't know, I wasn't there, but last night, she got together with someone,' I said. 'He sent her this . . . well . . . this message, wanting to see her again. It was a Spanish number. We're not going out tonight, so they won't be able to meet up, but . . . it just doesn't seem right to me when she's about to get married and . . .' The rest of the sentence escaped before I was able to speak it. 'Sorry,' I added lamely. 'This must be difficult for you to hear. Maybe I shouldn't have told you . . .' I tailed off, a bad taste in my mouth.

The silence stretched between us. 'Right. I'll deal with it,' Nathan said finally. 'This conversation never happened, okay? Just between you and me.'

'Okay,' I answered in a whisper. I was about to apologise

again, maybe even backtrack a little, but he ended the call before I could say anything else.

Guilt was coursing through me as I got ready for the evening party. My dress seemed to stick to my skin, and my fingers fumbled with the strap on my silver sandals. I felt uncomfortably hot and my cheeks were bright pink. Poor Nathan. How must he be feeling? Aoife had been blocking him all weekend. Now he knew why.

He'd seemed more angry than upset. I wondered exactly how he was going to deal with it. I didn't want to think about the ugly scene there would be once Aoife got home tomorrow. She would want to know how he'd found out, but it sounded like Nathan was going to protect me. Maybe Tiff would get the blame. Aoife knew she and Nathan had been in touch over the arrangements. I didn't want to land Tiff in the shit, but it was all beyond my control. I still thought Aoife had behaved appallingly and that Nathan deserved to know, but now I'd done the deed, the thought of the possible consequences made me feel uneasy.

The prospect of spending the evening with Aoife added to my nausea, but I couldn't hide here. I had to get away from Tiff's phone – which had finally stopped bleeping – and my own company. There was no way Aoife could know that I'd told tales. I'd have to give the performance of my life as the happiest hen in the party. Copious amounts of booze would be necessary to get me through. I wasn't sure I would be up to the task.

Chapter Thirty-Four: Now

DANI

She needs to take a copy of the photo. John's laptop screen is smudged with fingerprints; she angles the lid forward to reduce the glare and takes a shot with her phone. Click.

There's the sound of a key turning in a lock, the hinges of the front door squeaking as it swings open. It must be John, already back from seeing Marta. She slams the lid of the laptop shut. Remembering the fire exit, she grabs hold of her bag and darts across the upper landing into the kitchen. The key is in the door. She unlocks it, but it won't pull open. It's bolted at the bottom. Her fingers tremble as she tries to slide the bolt up. It's heavy, reluctant to budge. She can hear footsteps coming up the stairs. He'll be here any second—

The bolt comes free, catching her fingers. She flings open the door and bursts out, running quietly down the metal staircase into a yard full of crates and broken furniture, then leaping onto an upturned box and vaulting over the wall. She lands in the street. As she runs off, she can hear John, shouting and swearing from the top of the fire escape. Did he see her? She doesn't dare to look back.

She should have realised! They're all in it together. There's nobody she can trust. But she can't think about that too much now, can't even begin to understand what this discovery means. Just needs to get back to the car and lock herself in. Not that John seems to be running after her. Why would he? He knows where to find her.

YOU'RE NEXT.

Dani's hands tremble as she starts the Seat's engine and reverses out of the space. She drives straight back to the cemetery. Celine and Beth were supposed to wait at the entrance for her, but now they seem to have vanished too. She fires off a WhatsApp message to the group chat.

Where are you? Found Tiff yet?

While she waits for a reply, she checks to see how the photo came out. It's hard to see at all in this bright sunshine. Looks a bit fuzzy. She's still sure it's him, though . . . She's not making this up.

After a few minutes, Celine calls to say that she and Beth are at a café in the next street. There's been no word from Tiff.

'I'll come and find you,' Dani says, 'then we can make a plan.'

She drives around the corner and parks up. Beth and Celine are sitting on the pavement under a stripy umbrella, drinking coffees.

'So, what do you think is going on?' Dani says, taking a seat. 'You know Tiff better than we do, Beth. Does she have a habit of going AWOL?'

'Not really,' she replies. 'I know she didn't want to go to the cemetery. Maybe it all got too much for her.'

'We think she could be having a bit of a breakdown,' says Celine, stirring her coffee thoughtfully.

Beth nods. 'I sent her a private message saying it was fine if she needed some time alone and to let me know she was okay, but she hasn't got back yet.'

'Maybe she's somewhere without a signal,' Celine suggests. 'Or her battery has died.'

'That's not like Tiff,' says Beth. 'She's super organised about that kind of thing. My guess is she's gone off to have some time alone and she'll get in touch when she's ready.'

Dani fishes her phone out of her bag. 'Okay, there's something I have to show you. When I left the cemetery earlier, I wasn't really looking for Tiff. Well, I was, but . . .'

'I had a feeling you were up to something,' Celine interjects. 'Where did you go?'

'To John's apartment.'

'You broke in?' asks Beth, horrified.

'Not exactly. I found a key at the villa.'

'That's still trespassing,' says Beth. 'I don't understand, what were you looking for?'

'Evidence.'

'Evidence of what?' Celine presses.

Dani takes a breath. 'That John's a criminal, I guess. Instead, I found something far worse.'

'Worse?' gasps Beth. 'How can it be worse than that?'

Dani takes out her phone and finds the picture. 'Sorry, it's not very easy to see properly. It was taken at John's stag do. Everyone's wearing costumes and wigs and stuff, but I'm pretty certain it's him . . .' She passes the phone to Beth.

'What do you think? The guy in the middle with the stick-on moustache.'

'I'm not sure,' says Beth, squinting.

'Show me,' demands Celine. She takes the phone and stares at the screen. 'Oh. My. God.'

'Sorry, it's not a great shot, I didn't have time. I haven't seen him for over two years but—'

'It's Nathan,' confirms Celine. 'I haven't seen him for ages either, but I knew him quite well.' She hands the phone back. 'What does this mean?'

Dani stares at Nathan's face. Even in the silly photo, he has a mean, arrogant look. She'd never been able to see what it was about him that Aoife found so attractive.

'John and Nathan are friends?' asks Beth in a disbelieving voice.

'Yeah. Close friends, by the look of it. Matt's in the same picture.' Dani points. 'See? There. Seems like they're all mates. Do you remember where Nathan's from?'

'London,' answers Beth.

'Big place,' Celine murmurs.

'East. Hackney, I think.'

'Perhaps they were at school together.'

'But they never mentioned they knew each other,' says Beth. 'Not to us, anyway.'

'And I don't remember them speaking to each other at the inquest,' adds Celine.

'They avoided each other. I assume it's because they fell out, remember?' says Dani. 'After Aoife died, Nathan turned up at the villa and went ballistic at John about the lack of security. There was nearly a fight – Mengual had to break it up.'

'But why did they keep their connection a secret?' asks Celine.

Dani frowns. 'There has to be a reason.'

'Nathan was heavily involved in the hen party, behind the scenes,' says Beth. 'Remember, Celine? When we were waiting for the taxi on Saturday night, Tiff told us that he'd virtually insisted she booked Villa Floriana. He said it was what Aoife wanted, but she knew nothing about it.'

'Yes. Tiff thought she'd misunderstood, but he'd been lying to her,' says Celine. 'He could be quite controlling. He was always telling Aoife what she ought to want or like, how she should dress for work, what wine she should drink . . .'

'I wonder if the police were aware of the link between John, Matt and Nathan,' Beth considers.

'I doubt it,' says Dani, 'but I think we should tell them. They'll need to reopen the case, interview all three of them, check alibis.' She shudders. 'Maybe *this* is why we've been followed this weekend, why the villa was trashed? That message on the mirror might have been meant for me, after all.'

'Hey, let's stay calm and not jump to conclusions,' says Beth. 'It *is* weird that they kept it quiet, but it might be for some other reason. I'm not sure opening up the case again is going to help anyone. Least of all Aoife's parents. They've suffered enough.'

'That's for the police to decide, isn't it?' Dani says.

'I think we should check with Tiff first,' Beth argues. 'She knows Nathan better than us, she dealt with him over the hen party and—' She stops herself. 'Anyway, she'll know more about what was going on.'

'Except she's done a bunk,' says Dani, feeling her irritation rise.

'It's really out of order for her not to tell us where she's gone,' Celine remarks. 'There's no point in hanging around. I think we should go back to the villa. Tiff might even be there.'

Dani drives them back. As soon as she parks, Beth flings open the car door and rushes over to the house.

'Tiff can't be indoors,' she calls, holding up the key. 'Because this was still in the safe.' She unlocks the front door and hurries to disable the alarm. After a few seconds it stops, leaving an ominous silence.

'Maybe she's outside,' suggests Celine. She and Beth go back out through the front door and around the side of the house, calling Tiff's name.

Dani walks into the sitting room. And then there were three, she thinks, a shiver running through her. She studies the rearranged furniture, the freshly swept floor, the stack of broken picture frames leaning against the wall. She stares and stares, trying to understand the message that was sent last night, wondering how Nathan fits into the puzzle of Aoife's death. Because he *does* fit in somehow, she has no doubt about that.

She paces about, wracking her brains for reasons why Nathan would want – or need – to hide his friendship with John and Matt. Was he embarrassed about trying to control the hen party without Aoife knowing? Ashamed that he'd failed so spectacularly to protect her? Neither of those reasons seems strong enough. It has to be something very important for him to have kept it from the police and Aoife's family. A feeling of dread seeps into her veins . . .

'Tiff's not by the pool,' says Celine, coming back in and interrupting her thoughts.

Beth follows close behind. 'I'll try her again,' she says, taking out her phone and dialling. Instead of ringing out, this time the call is rejected. 'Hmm, that's odd.'

'I hope she's okay,' says Celine.

'Yes. Me too.'

'I expect she'll turn up when she's ready,' Dani says curtly. She doesn't want to think about Tiff right now. She needs to concentrate.

Stepping outside, she walks down to the little terrace that's set apart from the main garden, the place she always associates with her interview with Mengual, although it featured in other aspects of that weekend. She drags her chair into the corner, where there's a small patch of shade, and sits down at the mosaic table. Now she knows about Nathan, she has to revisit everything in her head, see it through different eyes, look in different places for new clues.

According to Beth, Nathan was involved in the organisation of the hen party. It sounds like he manipulated Tiff into booking this villa. At the time, Dani was surprised that she had gone for a place that was so off the beaten track and only slept six people. It had caused a lot of ill feeling when she'd announced that places at Villa Floriana were limited and that those not lucky enough to bag one would have to find alternative accommodation. That was why so many women had dropped out. It had really upset Aoife, who'd thought that her friends didn't care about her. She'd had no idea that Nathan was behind the choice and had blamed Tiff, who – somewhat mysteriously – hadn't betrayed Nathan and had taken the rap. Why? Dani knows she would never have done that. Not that Nathan would have attempted to boss her about. But Tiff was no pushover, and she was always desperate to be in Aoife's good books. It was strange . . .

There had to be a particular reason that Nathan wanted the hen party to take place at Villa Floriana. Did he do it simply to put some business his mate's way? Perhaps. If their friendship went back a long time. John and Marta had only just started out renting, maybe they were short of money. All of that seems possible, but it doesn't tie in with what little Dani knows about Nathan. She's always had the impression that he's not a generous man. He was generous to Aoife – bought her designer clothes, sent her to the top hair salons in the West End, encouraged her to have beauty treatments – but that was different. That was because he was shaping her into the wife that he wanted for himself. Dani can't help but conclude that he needed them to stay at the villa so he could carry on controlling his fiancée and making sure she didn't disgrace herself. Perhaps he'd asked John and Matt to spy on her. Like that worked . . .

She thinks back, plotting a line through that fateful weekend. Matt had definitely made a beeline for Aoife at the cocktail workshop, and most crucially, John had even had sex with her on Saturday night. Given that Nathan was a close friend – close enough to come over to Spain for John's stag do – why on earth had they behaved like that? Had they acted out of spite or had Nathan himself asked them to put Aoife to the test? Either possibility makes her feel sick.

What if they'd reported back to him that Aoife had failed the test and betrayed him? Dani shudders to think how Nathan might have reacted. He was a vain, proud man who'd treated Aoife as his property. Alternatively, if John and Matt had targeted her as a way of getting some kind of revenge on Nathan, had he found out? And if so, how? Dani certainly hadn't told anyone about Aoife's encounter with John in his apartment, or the fact that Aoife had had second thoughts about the wedding. She'd held her friend's secrets tightly to her chest, determined never to let them go. But it was obvious to all the hens that Aoife hadn't been behaving like your typical bride-to-be: having fun with the girls, yes, but ultimately more excited about marrying the man she loved. Everyone knew something was wrong.

Dani would never have given Aoife away in a million years, but the others might have ... Tiff, for example. She was clearly in cahoots with Nathan. Had he asked her to spy on her old friend and report back to him? He'd also engineered Celine's presence at the hen party and given her those creepy groom masks. Then there was Beth, who was always so correct and had a slight air of moral superiority about her ...

Dani thinks back to that Sunday and the hours before the attack on Aoife – before everything in her mind went blank. The atmosphere at the paella party had been awful. At the time, she'd assumed it was because she and Aoife had refused to leave the club on Saturday night, but now she wonders whether there was more to it than that. Then there was the surprise item that wasn't written into Tiff's meticulous schedule. Why had she missed it off? Dani wonders. Because she didn't want Nathan to know about it, probably. He certainly wouldn't have approved.

In fact, it happened right here on this little terrace, in the blazing sunshine. Dani conjures up the circle of chairs, set out in readiness, and lets her mind roll back.

Chapter Thirty-Five: Then

DANI

The surprise was late. Tiff was in a state of anxiety, tapping away on her phone, walking back and forth to the courtyard to see if it – or he, or she, or they – had arrived. Everyone else went down to the pool to cool off, despite Tiff's warnings that it was too soon after eating to swim. They were going to be starting at any moment, she said with that wringing energy she always used when stressed. Apparently, the surprise wasn't an activity they could do wet.

Dani wondered with only the mildest curiosity what it might be. All she knew was that it involved sitting on chairs. A workshop, then. Please let it not be making a penis out of felt, she thought. Whatever activity it turned out to be, she would have to summon up some enthusiasm for it. That was the pact she'd made with Aoife.

They stuck closely together and pretended they were having an amazing time – despite all the evidence to the contrary. Lunch had been awkward enough, but the atmosphere poolside was just weird. Beth was in the same grump she'd been in over the paella and had escaped to the shady corner of the garden where she was boring her eyes into her Kindle. Celine had just come out of her room and looked thunderous with rage. She plonked herself on a sunbed and lay down fully clothed. Her eyes were tightly closed and she breathed heavily through her nose.

Aoife floated on a lilo while Dani circled her like a shark. 'Your yoga buddy's not looking very serene,' she whispered. 'Maybe she didn't get that job.'

'She wouldn't have heard today.' Aoife looked across the water. 'But you're right, she looks mightily pissed off. Could have had a row with her boyfriend.'

Dani carried on swimming. It was more like treading water, really. Despite the challenges of the weekend and the continuing tension around her, she felt unaccountably happy. No, wrong word. It wasn't unaccountable, it was the opposite. Countable? She laughed inside. Yes, she could count the reasons . . . One, she would have her best friend back. Two, she wouldn't have to put up with Nathan anymore. Three . . .

'He's here!' cried Tiff, interrupting her calculations. She ran towards them, almost slipping on the wet tiles.

Beth snapped her Kindle shut and sighed, while Celine opened her eyes and slowly sat up.

Tiff danced around the edge of the pool. 'Come on! Aoife! Dani! Get out! We've only got an hour.'

Aoife rolled off the lilo. 'An hour for what?' she asked.

'Life drawing!'

Dani should have guessed. They were going to spend the next sixty minutes drawing some stranger's floppy penis.

'Amazing!' said Aoife.

'Sorry, but I'm not feeling it right now,' said Celine.

'You don't have to feel it,' cried Dani. 'You just have to draw it.' She and Aoife erupted in giggles and Aoife laughed so much she nearly sank.

'You can't drop out, Celine,' said Tiff. 'It's obligatory.'

Celine heaved an irritable sigh and stomped off towards the terrace.

'I'm shit at drawing,' said Dani, following Aoife out of the water and picking up her towel. 'But I'll give it a go.'

'Heads-up, he's not exactly what I ordered,' Tiff confessed, checking to make sure she wasn't being overheard. 'I think the photos on his website are about ten years out of date. But he was the only male model who was prepared to come this far out of town.'

'Oh, who cares?' Dani said, doing her utmost to be amenable. 'They all look the same to me.' Aoife burst out laughing again.

Their model emerged from the side of the house. He wore jeans and a white T-shirt, which bulged under a slight paunch. His jet-black hair was greying at the temples and his skin was leathery. He wheeled a trolley, which clinked and squeaked behind him.

'Here he is. Francisco!' Tiff threw in a 'Ta-Dah!' for good measure. She looked extremely nervous.

'*¡Hola!* So-o-o pleased to meet you,' he said, lurching forward and kissing Aoife and Dani on both cheeks. 'I hope you are ready for me.' His eyes twinkled mischievously.

'As ready as we'll ever be,' said Dani.

'Where do you want me? Inside or outside?'

'Inside, every time,' quipped Aoife, getting into the mood.

'*Outside*, actually,' said Tiff sternly. 'On the terrace. We've set up the chairs.'

He gave us a white toothy smile. '*Perfecto*. I have every-

276

thing else. All the girls say I am very well equipped!' He let out a laugh.

Dani sighed. There was clearly going to be a lot of this.

Francisco made a show of going over and greeting everyone. 'Before the class, I make you a nice cocktail each,' he said. 'Get you in a mood!'

Tiff cut in. 'Actually, we should have two cocktails each. I paid for ten people, remember, because it was the minimum charge.'

'For you, everything you want!' he beamed. 'Where can I change, please?'

'Oh . . . um . . . I'll show you,' said Tiff. She led him back to the villa. 'To the terrace, girls! Soon as poss!'

'Jesus! Do we have to?' said Celine as soon as they were out of earshot.

'Yes!' chorused Dani and Aoife.

Beth picked up her beach bag and plodded off. 'You okay?' Aoife asked, catching up with her. Beth shrugged her shoulders. 'Come on, you're good at drawing. It'll be a laugh!'

They took their places on the small square terrace, overlooking the valley. Dani made sure she was sitting next to Aoife, so they could share a laugh. After a few minutes, Tiff joined them, looking even more flustered than before.

'Everything okay?' asked Dani.

'I hope so. He wanted to change in a bedroom, so I had to let him use ours.' Beth looked up sharply. 'Sorry. I'm sure it's okay. He's just taking ages.'

'What's he doing?'

'Getting undressed, I suppose.'

'Hello, girls!' They turned around to see Francisco walking

277

towards them, carrying a tray of colourful cocktails, tiny umbrellas dancing in the sunshine. He wore nothing but a small barman's apron around his waist. He had oiled his body and looked like he was ready to be slapped on a barbecue.

'Oh,' said Tiff. 'I didn't know we were getting a Butler in the Buff too.'

'Penis Coladas, girls! Hah-hah!' Francisco announced, handing them around.

'Not again,' groaned Beth. 'We've had that joke already.'

'Now I bring the paper and the pens, and so we can start,' Francisco said, turning round and slinking back towards the villa, his bare buttocks glowing in the sun. He quickly re-emerged carrying a box of drawing materials and several large pads, which he put on the small mosaic table. He had discarded his butler outfit and was now wearing a short black dressing gown.

'Oh, dear,' said Tiff quietly.

'Where do you want me, girls?' He undid his belt and let the gown slide over his shoulders to the ground.

'I do three five-minute poses first, then a longer one,' he declared. 'Okay, girls. Start sketching!' He gave them his left profile and gazed at the Straits of Gibraltar.

Tiff picked up a pad, took a pencil from the box and started drawing as if her life depended on it. Aoife and Dani chose felt pens and made extravagant sweeps across the page. It didn't take long for them to be convulsed in giggles. Beth doodled in the top corner of her paper – she didn't once glance at Francisco's nether regions. Celine looked equally prudish, as if the activity was way beneath her. Dani noticed that while she *was* drawing Francisco's body, she'd deliberately left out his manhood.

'Aren't you missing the point?' she said. Only Aoife seemed to get the joke.

Francisco adopted a new pose, which was basically the same as the first, just in the other corner of the terrace, where there was some shade edging in. Aoife and Dani got into the swing of it, laughing as they compared drawings, knocking back their cocktails. After the last pose, Francisco insisted they took a group selfie with him in the middle, arms around Aoife and Dani's waists. They held their rather pathetic creations up to his camera and put on cheesy smiles.

Afterwards, Francisco slid into his gown and made them their second cocktail – as per the deal – and included one for himself, which was not part of the deal. Beth didn't drink hers, Dani had it instead. They abandoned their posts and retreated to the shade of the patio.

The hour was up but Francisco seemed to be in no hurry to leave. Aoife jumped up and said she needed a shower. Taking her cue, Tiff reminded everyone that they needed to pack tonight as they had an early flight home tomorrow. It wasn't strictly true – the flight wasn't until the afternoon. She thanked Francisco for giving them such a lovely time, then went indoors, followed immediately by Beth and Celine, each making their own excuses for leaving. Dani was left on her own with him.

Thanks a bunch, girls, she thought.

Francisco leaned over and tapped her thigh. 'One more cocktail?' he said. 'I make it special for you.'

Chapter Thirty-Six: Then

TIFF

'Oh my God, what a slimeball!' I cried as we rushed into our room, closing the door firmly behind us.

'Yuck!' Beth pointed at Francisco's clothes, which still lay on my bed, including his briefs and tiny barman's apron. I regretted letting him change in our bedroom but hadn't known where else to put him.

Beth opened the window as wide as she could to let in some fresh air. 'That's better,' she said, inhaling deeply. She turned back to face me. 'So, Tiff . . . What do we do now? We've escaped, but he's still here.'

'Don't worry,' I said. 'Let Dani get rid of him. Serves her right for flirting.'

'But what if she doesn't *want* to get rid of him? They were looking quite comfy together just now.'

'He won't be hanging around here this evening, I'll make sure of it.'

'Threaten him with a one-star review on Tripadvisor,' Beth said, flumping onto her mattress. 'That should do it.'

'Good idea,' I replied, dragging my suitcase out from under the bed and opening it up. I'd used our needing to pack as a pretext to get away from him, but now I wanted to do it for real. I couldn't wait to take off my Chief Bridesmaid sash and fly home. 'Yet another disaster to add to the list,' I muttered, expecting Beth to tell me it hadn't been so bad and not to keep beating myself up. But she didn't respond. She looked miles away.

'What's up?' I asked, taking my clothes out of the drawer. 'Are you just tired or is it something else?'

She looked cagey. 'Oh . . . I don't know. I've had enough, I guess. Everything's been about penises, hasn't it? The whole bloody weekend.' She lay back and stared at the ceiling. 'I'm sick of it.'

'Well, it *is* a hen party.'

'All this "same penis forever" stuff – it's revolting. Nathan's a person, not a body part.'

'Aren't you taking it a bit too seriously?'

'No.' She sat back up. 'Marriage is about committing yourself to another human being. You can't take it lightly. I'm sorry, but Aoife's behaviour on this trip has been disgusting, from start to finish. Dani hasn't helped either.'

'Personally, I think she's more to blame,' I said, always happy to do a bit of Dani-bashing. 'She encourages Aoife. And they drink way too much when they're together.'

'I don't agree. I think Aoife's been the leader.' Beth clenched her jaw. 'I'm so angry with her I don't know what to do.'

I paused midway in rolling up a T-shirt. This wasn't like Beth. Normally she was so generous and forgiving, she put me to shame. 'Angry about what exactly?' I ventured. 'Do you mean the stuff with the gangsters last night?'

'Yes, and other stuff. Flirting with everyone, left, right and centre. I haven't forgiven her for the game on Friday. That reference to Zach really hurt me.'

'You're not still thinking about that, are you? She said she mixed up the number of truths and lies. I believe her.'

'I don't.' Beth dragged her long auburn hair away from her face and retied her ponytail.

'Honestly, Beth, you're barking up the wrong tree. It was a game, that's all. Aoife was just joking around.'

She made a small disbelieving sound in her throat. 'She wasn't joking with the cocktails guy – she was all over him. It was really embarrassing. And she was flirting shamelessly with John at Supernova. Didn't you see them, grinding their hips together on the dance floor?'

'Yes, it was a bit much,' I conceded. 'But like I said, it's a hen party. These things aren't serious, nothing actually happens.'

'I wouldn't be so sure. Something happened after we left them last night . . .' She paused.

'What?'

Beth gave me a shifty look. 'I don't know exactly, but Aoife got a text this morning. *Last night was hot. Got to see you again.* From someone with a Spanish phone number. What's that about, eh?'

I gave up trying to pack. 'How come you saw it? Did she show it to you?' Beth coloured up instantly. 'Beth? Were you looking at her phone?'

'The message flashed up,' she said. 'I couldn't help but see it.'

'And where was Aoife?'

'In the pool. On the lilo as usual. She didn't see me, and I didn't say anything.'

'Okay. And that's why you're so angry . . . because you think she cheated on Nathan last night.'

'Well, yeah. It's pretty obvious, isn't it? I think it must have been with John.'

'John?'

'He's the obvious candidate.'

'You don't know for sure that she cheated with him. The message wasn't explicit.'

'She gave him her number, that's got to mean something.'

'You don't only give your number to people you have sex with.'

'I *know* she cheated on Nathan. I just know it. I can see it in her eyes.'

'Beth, you can't—'

'She can't love him or even care about him. She just wants his posh flat in Canary Wharf and to go to Michelin-starred restaurants and on honeymoon in Mauritius and—'

'Beth! Slow down. You can't talk like this. Aoife's one of your best friends.'

Beth tossed her head. 'No, she's not. Not really. Not anymore anyway, not since the Zach thing. And I don't like the way she's thrown you aside for Dani. She only asked you to be Chief Bridesmaid because she knew you'd be better organised.'

I stood up and went to the window, closed the shutters. The room was full of hot air now, it would take ages to cool down. Beth was only saying things I'd felt for some time, but it was different hearing it come out of somebody else's mouth. It made it more real, more difficult to deny.

'Why did you come to the hen, then?'

'I don't know ... because Aoife and I go way back, I guess. I also came for you,' she said. 'You were stressed about so many people dropping out and I wanted to give you some support.'

'I appreciate that, but you shouldn't have come if you hate her so much.'

'I don't *hate* her.' Beth looked away from me. 'But I don't think she should marry Nathan. He deserves somebody better.'

That hit me hard. I knew for a fact that he was just as much of a cheat as Aoife was, and there was no proof that she'd cheated on him at all. For some incomprehensible reason, I'd never seen it from Aoife's point of view until that moment. I'd been too wrapped up in my own obsession with Nathan, wanting him for myself, wishing for the impossible to happen, dreaming that he might change his mind and marry me instead. In my fantasies, I slipped so easily into her place, but the reality was murky and too complicated. No good would ever come of my one night with Nathan, I could see that now.

'Okay,' said Beth, coming up close to me. 'I'm going to tell you something. But you've got to promise you won't be angry with me.'

'What is it?' I replied guardedly. 'What have you done?'

'I called Nathan and told him.'

My blood raced. 'Told him what?'

'What's been going on.'

'Meaning what, exactly?'

'You know. I told him about Aoife going off with other guys.'

'You did WHAT? Are you crazy?' She backed off. 'How did he react?'

'As you'd expect, I guess. He was shocked and very angry. He said he was going to sort it. I don't know what he meant by that, but—'

'Oh, God, Beth . . . what have you done?'

'He needed to know,' she replied defensively.

'No, he didn't! He absolutely fucking didn't!' I started to feel panicky. 'She's just been fooling around, having fun. It's all Dani's fault, not Aoife's. She's been leading her astray the whole time. Now Nathan's going to think I've not been looking after her properly, he's going to blame me and – and—'

I couldn't finish my sentence, not without telling Beth the truth. If Nathan thought I'd deliberately wrecked things between him and Aoife, he'd turn against me. He'd made his position very clear. He loved Aoife and couldn't wait to make her his wife. Our encounter had been a one-off, For One Night Only, never to be talked of again and definitely never to be repeated. Now he'd think I'd engineered a split, hoping that we would get together again. Of course, I secretly, shamefully, cherished that hope, even though I knew it would take a miracle for it to happen. Beth's actions had snuffed that light out forever.

'I can't tell you how much I wish you hadn't done that,' I said.

'Well, it can't be undone.' She lifted her chin self-righteously. 'I'm not sorry. I'll take the consequences.'

I gave her a stern look. 'You can say that now,' I said. 'But you don't know what those consequences will be.'

Chapter Thirty-Seven: Now

DANI

'Dani? Are you asleep?'

Dani opens her eyes and tries to shake off the memories of Francisco handing her the cocktail. 'Not really.' She blinks into the sunlight, making out Beth's and Celine's silhouettes. 'What's up? Have you heard from Tiff yet?'

'No, and we're starting to worry,' says Beth. 'It's been hours since she disappeared at the cemetery. It's so unlike her.'

'And she knows we're supposed to be having the ceremony this evening,' adds Celine. 'She's brought some poems to read, and I think she was planning to play some of Aoife's favourite music.'

'Yeah, I have to say, it is weird,' Dani admits.

'I don't want to overreact or anything,' says Beth. 'It's just that, after what happened to you last night . . .' She falters. 'You know, I can't help but think that maybe . . . just maybe something bad has happened to her.'

'I don't think it's an overreaction,' says Celine. 'Especially now we know about John's connection to Nathan.'

Dani stands up. 'You mean, you think Tiff might have been abducted?' The possibility hadn't occurred to her, but it strikes fresh fear into her heart. She remembers the message scrawled on the mirror. Could Tiff be next to be killed? 'Oh, God,' she says, clapping her hand across her mouth.

'We're thinking, maybe we should call the police,' says Celine.

'Trouble is, they're not going to take us seriously,' Dani replies. They walk back to the patio and sit down. 'I don't know what the rules are here, but in the UK, people need to be missing for at least twenty-four hours.'

Celine considers this. 'But if we tell them about the other stuff, then maybe they will take it seriously.'

'True,' says Beth, 'but I'm also worried that it will be worse for Tiff if we involve the law. Somebody has been trying to intimidate us and it's obvious why. They want us to stop digging up the past. If we go to the police that could put her in more danger.'

'Or it could save her life,' says Dani.

'Don't say that!' Beth gasps. 'That's a terrible thing to say.'

'I'm just trying to understand what's going on,' says Dani. 'We could try asking Marta for help, perhaps. She knows more than she's letting on. Or we could go directly to John, tell him we know about Nathan . . . We could threaten to go to the police unless he returns Tiff. Assuming he's got her, that is,' she adds. 'We don't know anything for sure. It's all just guesswork.'

'Oh, I don't know what to do,' says Beth, pulling at her hair. 'I keep having these awful visions of her tied up somewhere with a bag over her head.'

'Don't. She could just as easily be sitting in some hotel with her feet up, sipping a gin and tonic,' Dani says.

Beth frowns at her. 'It's not funny!'

'I wasn't joking. The fact is, we don't know what's happened.'

'I think we should call the police,' Celine says after a pause. 'If she has been abducted, they need to act straightaway. It's called the Golden Hour or something.'

'She's been gone a lot longer than an hour,' mutters Beth.

'All the more reason to contact them.'

'I agree,' says Dani. 'But I think it would be better if I spoke to Inspector Mengual first. I'll explain what's been going on, see what he thinks.'

'That's not a bad idea,' says Celine. 'We're crashing around in the dark, we need some advice.'

'Hmm . . . I still think we should wait a bit longer,' says Beth.

'For how long?' demands Dani. 'What's the cut-off point?'

'I don't know! Another hour?'

'It could be too late,' says Celine. 'Ring him now, Dani. Have you got his number?'

She nods, knowing that there's no guarantee Mengual will pick up. He hasn't responded to her message from yesterday yet. But there's so much she needs to tell him, it's got to be worth another try.

Not wanting the pressure of Celine and Beth overhearing, she goes up to her bedroom, shutting the door behind her. She sits down on the bed. This time, Mengual's number is easy to find. It rings out several times. She can sense him hesitating, looking at her name on the screen and wondering whether to pick up.

Finally, she hears his voice. '*¿Sí? ¿Digame?*'

Talk to me.

'It's Dani again,' she says. 'Daniela Harrington. I left a message on your voicemail.'

'Yes, I know.' His gruff voice is familiar. 'I'm sorry I didn't call you back. I'm not on duty this weekend,' he explains. It sounds like he's at a social gathering. She can hear the tinkle of cutlery, children shouting, guffaws of laughter. 'Is it important?'

'Yes. I think so. It could be extremely important. I'm not sure where to start . . . so much has been happening . . .'

He listens quietly as she tells him about their return to the villa, how she's been trying to remember what happened on the night that Aoife died. 'It's panicked somebody,' she says. 'I think it's John, the owner of Villa Floriana, but I don't have any proof. We were followed yesterday, and last night, I swear this motorcyclist tried to kill me. While we were out, somebody trashed the villa to make it look like the crime scene and they left a note on the mirror in my bathroom. It said "You're Next".'

Mengual's breath catches. 'You should have called the Policía Nacional.'

'I know, but we weren't sure. Marta – John's ex-wife, remember? – seemed to think the message was for her. She didn't want the police involved. I think she's scared of somebody. Maybe John, I'm not sure . . . The other, really big thing I've found out is that John and Nathan, Aoife's groom, are mates.' She tells him about the stag party photo – Nathan in a long black wig, one arm around John. 'None of us knew they were friends,' she says. 'I'm guessing they kept it quiet from you too, yes?'

He grunts sharply. '*Sí*.'

'I don't know if it rings any alarm bells with you, but it seems very strange to me. There must be a reason they kept it a secret.'

'*Claro* . . . Wait, please.' She hears a tuneless chorus of '*Cumpleaños Feliz*', followed by cheers and applause. The background noises suddenly subside. 'This is better,' he says. 'Continue.'

She swallows. 'Nathan was working behind the scenes the whole weekend. We think maybe he wanted John to spy on Aoife – you know, to make sure she behaved herself.'

'This is possible.'

'Or even to test her.'

'Test her? What do you mean?'

'He was very controlling. And John and Aoife . . . well . . .'

'What is it, Daniela? Please, you have to tell me. No more secrets, eh?'

She sends up a silent apology to Aoife before speaking. Sometimes promises have to be broken for the greater good. Mengual listens patiently as she recounts the story of Saturday night. 'Aoife told me that she and John had had sex in his flat,' she says. 'When I confronted John about it, he denied it, but I'd believe Aoife over him a thousand times.'

'Daniela!' he gasps. 'Why didn't you tell me this before? This is important evidence.'

'I'm sorry. Everyone thought it was a burglary, so it didn't seem relevant. I know it sounds ridiculous, but I was trying to protect Aoife's reputation. The media were prowling around, looking for a juicy angle. I didn't want to make it worse.'

'Hmm . . . Did Nathan find out about his friend and his fiancée?'

'No. Aoife only told me, and John certainly wouldn't have said anything. Unless . . . unless it was part of some plan.'

'And your friends – did they know?'

'No. I never said anything to anyone. But they weren't blind, they knew something was going down.' She starts gabbling. 'Aoife was wild that weekend, flirting with everyone, it was pretty blatant – guys at the beach club, some wannabe gangsters we met at Pesadilla, Matt the Mixologist. Oh, yes, he's also in the stag photo. Looks like he's mates with Nathan too. I think he may be the guy on the motorbike—'

'Please, now you are confusing me. What gangsters? Who is this Matt?'

'I'm sorry, I'm sorry.' Her voice starts to waver. 'What we told you about the hen weekend . . . well . . . it wasn't the whole story.'

'I see. Your friend was attacked, killed, and yet you lied to the police?'

'Not lied, as such. We just left a few bits out. Only the embarrassing, unimportant bits.'

'You do not decide what is important,' he says sternly. 'That is *my* job. This is very serious. You can be prosecuted for this, you understand?'

'I know, I get that, but it wasn't deliberate, we didn't mean any harm. And we didn't know about the link with Nathan then. Promise.'

'Hmm. Yes, that is interesting,' he replies, relenting a little. 'Tomorrow, I will make some enquiries. But for now, please don't do anything more. You must stick together and stay in the villa. When do you leave?'

'Tomorrow. The flight's in the afternoon.'

'Good. Travel directly to the airport. If anyone suspicious comes to the villa, or anything else happens, call the emergency number – one-one-two. Now I must go.'

'Okay, there's just one more thing,' she says breathlessly.

He sighs. 'What?'

'Tiff – Tiffany, one of the hens – has gone missing.'

'Gone missing?' he repeats. 'What do you mean?'

Dani explains about their trip to the cemetery, how they split up trying to find Aoife's grave, how Tiff never came back. 'We've been calling and messaging but we're not getting any response. Does that worry you at all?'

'Everything worries me,' he says.

'We're frightened she could have been abducted.'

'Hmm . . . Abductions of tourists are very rare,' he says. 'There could be a simple explanation here. The cemetery visit was upsetting. Tiffany is an adult. If she wants to leave and not speak to anyone, that is her right.'

'I know, but it's out of character. She's not even communicating with Beth and they're best friends. I was wondering . . . would it be possible to contact the local hotels and see if she's checked in anywhere? It would put everyone's mind at rest.'

'Daniela! Do you know how many hotels there are in Marbella?'

'No, but I thought perhaps the police might be able—'

'I am not on duty. Missing Persons is another department. There is a protocol.'

'I know, but you just said you were worried, so . . .'

He sighs. 'Keep trying to contact her. If anything else happens tonight – or she doesn't arrive at the airport tomorrow – call the Policía Nacional directly.'

It could be too late by then, she thinks.

'Okay. Will do.' She apologises once more for disturbing the birthday party and the conversation ends.

Dani breathes out, exhausted by the exchange with Mengual. Relieved too that she has decided to trust him. He's a good family man. She's glad she went to John's flat and found that photo of Nathan. Glad that she finally unburdened herself of the secret about Aoife and John.

'You did good, Dani Girl,' she says under her breath. 'At last, you did good.'

She goes downstairs and fills Celine and Beth in. 'I think he's going to reopen the case,' she tells them. 'But obviously, he's going to need more evidence.'

Celine pulls a face. 'If we have to go through it all over again, I don't think I'll be able to bear it.'

'And what did he say about Tiff?' asks Beth.

'He thinks it's unlikely she's been abducted,' Dani answers. 'Apparently, that doesn't happen very often.'

'But it does happen sometimes,' says Celine. 'I don't like it . . .'

'Mengual said we should wait until tomorrow and if Tiff doesn't turn up at the airport, report it then.'

'Tomorrow?' echoes Beth. 'That's no good. We need to do something now!'

'He's not on duty and it's not his department, so he can't

293

help. I've done what I can, okay?' Dani says irritably. She feels so tired, so confused.

'Okay,' says Celine grudgingly.

'Shall I make us something to eat?' offers Beth. 'We may not feel like it but we should keep our strength up.'

'Yeah, okay,' Dani mumbles. 'Sorry, I need some fresh air.'

She leaves the villa and walks briskly along the track towards the road. Maybe she'll go to the shrine, she thinks, and make an offering for Aoife. Her heart is pounding, armpits sweating. It's late afternoon but it feels like the hottest part of the day. The ground beneath her feet feels hard and unforgiving, there's not a patch of shade to be found.

The olive grove looks cooler, the light softer and dappled. That's where she'll go. She steps onto the dry grass and makes her way down the slope, towards the ridge where the landscape opens out, where she'll be able to see clearly. Think clearly. There's so much to take in and digest.

She slows down. As she weaves between the trees, a memory creeps unbidden towards the front of her mind. She realises it's something she doesn't want to remember, something she's been batting away all weekend. But it nags at her, refusing to leave.

Chapter Thirty-Eight: Then

DANI

He brought out two cocktails, setting one of them down on the coffee table in front of her and holding onto the other. He took a sip of his, then said, 'Are you going to show me around?'

'If you like.' She picked up her drink and stirred it with the umbrella. Looked him up and down. He was still wearing the black silky dressing gown with nothing underneath and a pair of black sliders on his feet. 'Don't you want to get dressed first?'

'No, it's too hot . . . I like to feel free.' Francisco smiled.

Why was he still here? she wondered. Didn't he have another hen party to go to? He'd had a lovely afternoon surrounded by a bevy of females – posing for them in the nude, making sexually charged comments that in any other context would have been viewed as sexist and inappropriate. She couldn't imagine doing this the other way around – a group of stags and a lone female model. But Francisco seemed very happy with his lot. He was lounging on the terrace like he was one of the girls. Tiff had already tried, and failed, to get rid of him. He'd pretended not to understand, but his English was excellent. He was clearly determined to stay as long as he could.

He held out his free hand to help Dani up and she took it. 'Come on. Let's go,' he said, pulling her towards him. They clinked glasses. He stared into her eyes and for a moment she understood what he wanted.

'Okay,' she said. Although it wasn't okay. She knew that. No woman in their right mind goes off with a half-naked stranger, but she couldn't summon the strength to say no. She was swimming in a sea of alcohol. At first, she'd stayed afloat, but now it felt like she was drowning. Sangria at lunchtime, topped up with cava, then three or four strong cocktails. She couldn't remember exactly how many – her own allocation of two, then Beth's. Maybe she drank Celine's as well.

They'd abandoned her one by one, leaving her in the deep end to play with the sharks. They seemed to think it was funny or that she'd deserved it. She didn't know what she'd done. Laughed too loudly at the guy's jokes, perhaps. Maybe they thought – absurdly – that she actually wanted to be alone with him, that she found him attractive. She'd only been trying to jolly things along, to keep the peace and stop Aoife from freaking out.

He was leaning against the wall of the villa. Watching her. 'Drink up,' he said. She took another sip. Insects sang around her head. She felt soft and woozy, like warm dough, ready to be pushed into a mould.

They took their glasses with them. First, to the courtyard, where he'd parked his car next to theirs. They were both white Seat Ibizas. Francisco made a comment about their having the same taste in vehicles, hinting that they were a good match, destined to pair up.

'Didn't choose it,' she mumbled. 'Hire car . . .'

She slurped her cocktail as they walked along the track, arm in arm. This one was different – a Blue Mojito. She didn't like it as much as the Piña – no, Penis – Coladas. That joke had definitely run its course . . . The rum was almost viscous, and the fresh mint had a bitter aftertaste. Even so, she sucked it up through the straw until she hit ice. Francisco took the empty glass off her and tossed it into the bushes. Then he did the same with his own.

'Hey!' she said. 'Whadya-do-that-for . . .' Her words tumbled into each other.

'Can't be arsed to carry them around,' he said. His English was very colloquial. She wondered, in a vague way, whether he'd spent time in the UK.

Without her realising it, the afternoon had slipped into the evening. The sun was lower, but it still felt impossibly hot. Her skin felt dry and itchy, as if somebody had been at it with a cheese grater. She needed to get into some proper shade.

'What's down there?' Francisco asked, pointing at the olive grove.

'Trees,' she said.

'You are so drunk,' he laughed. He steered her off the track, gripping her hand and almost dragging her down the slope. She stumbled over the bumpy ground, ducking under branches, scratching her arms.

'Sloow dooown!' she cried, but it only made him go faster. He dragged her along by the hand, as if she was a reluctant child.

Eventually, they ran out of ground. He stopped just short

of the precipice and let go of her. She stood, swaying, the landscape spinning around her like she'd just got off a merry-go-round. Her vision wouldn't clear. It didn't feel safe. She knew there was a sheer drop but couldn't tell whether it was in front or behind her. Her knees went weak, she could feel herself falling, falling . . .

Suddenly, Francisco caught her in his arms and banged her head against a tree. He kissed her, prising open her mouth and pushing his tongue inside. The smell of his body oil stung her nostrils. She could hardly breathe. He was holding her by the wrists, stopping her lifting her hands.

'Stop it! Get off me!'

'Shut up,' he said.

Now he was chewing at her neck. He let go of one hand but jammed it behind her back, pushing himself onto her. His fingers started crawling slowly up her thighs. She felt repulsed and utterly terrified. He knew she didn't want him, but he carried on. Panic welled inside her. She could hardly breathe. She tried to squirm out from under him, but he wasn't having it. His hard, naked cock pressed against her. He released his other hand and tried to pull down her pants. She fought him off and they tussled for a few seconds, twisting around each other. She lifted her knee sharply and made contact with his groin. He yelped with pain and pushed her away. She lost her balance and started staggering around – close, so close, to the edge. She turned, tripping over the jagged rim of the firepit, a sharp rock slicing into her knee as she fell in.

Francisco was doubled up in pain, cursing furiously at her in Spanish. The only word she could make out was *puta* – whore. He lurched off, still bent over, clutching himself, dressing gown flapping, the belt trailing after him like a tail.

She lay among the charred wood and dirty ashes, too shocked to move, breathless. Her mouth was full of dust. She couldn't speak. The thoughts were there but the words wouldn't form. She had to get help . . . Had to get back to the villa . . . She lifted her head, but she couldn't see properly. It was as if rain was pouring through shafts of sunlight. She tried to shield her eyes, but it didn't help. Her brain was collapsing into darkness.

When she came round, she couldn't tell what time it was, or how long she'd been out cold. Could have been seconds; could have been hours. Time seemed to be expanding then contracting. She was still lying in the firepit like a human sacrifice, waiting for somebody to ignite the flames.

Slowly, she managed to roll sideways, onto all fours. She was dizzy, didn't know if she would be able to stand. She scrambled out of the pit, scraping her knee again on the roughly built circle of rocks. God, it hurt. She made her way back up the slope, crawling through the spiky undergrowth, the ground littered with stones and rabbit holes, gnarled old roots, rotten branches. She felt faint and disorientated. Her knee was torn to shreds.

Chapter Thirty-Nine: Then

CELINE

There were only a few hours of the hen party left. Soon the nightmare would be over and we'd be out of here. I couldn't wait.

After the life drawing class, I escaped to my room, lying down on the bed and staring at the ceiling fan whirring above my head. It had taken all my inner strength not to confront Aoife immediately. Not because I didn't want to spoil the party – I didn't give a shit about that – but because I didn't trust myself not to lose control and do something I'd later regret. Aoife had her friends with her, I had nobody to support me. I didn't want to look at her, let alone celebrate her imminent marriage.

Farrell had warned me not to jump to conclusions. It was good advice, but I felt that I already knew the truth. Aoife was only in her current post thanks to Nathan pulling strings. He was very ambitious for her, but she simply wasn't talented or motivated or hardworking enough to make it by herself. Whose idea it had been to steal the Head of Development job from me I didn't know, but I strongly suspected Aoife was in on it. She'd made a great show of congratulating me on Friday evening to put me off the scent, but hadn't mentioned it since. How she'd thought I would react when I finally found out, I couldn't imagine.

As awkward as the situation was – and that was an understatement – I didn't blame Farrell for telling me. I believe it's always better to know the truth, however unpalatable. And the advance knowledge that I *hadn't* got the job gave me power. I could get my resignation in first, tell my boss Charlie where he could stuff his job. Wild horses wouldn't drag me back to the production company now that Aoife was going to be the new Head of Development. Just the thought of it was absurd.

Anger enabled me to hold it together, but inside I was extremely upset. Until then, I'd respected Charlie and thought he was a good boss. Now I only had contempt for him. I couldn't understand why he was letting Nathan dictate who he should promote. However strong their friendship was, it wasn't fair to push me aside – a long-standing, faithful, hardworking employee – for someone who was barely competent. The only concepts Aoife ever came up with already existed or had been done years ago, which showed how little she actually watched television. I'd helped her out along the way because I liked her, and thought she had potential. But not *that* much potential . . .

I had to have it out with her. I couldn't just meekly stand by and let her trample all over my hard work, my dreams for the future. I'd already started researching how much of a mortgage Farrell and I could raise on my new salary, and we'd been looking at flats on property websites. Also, I wanted to get married. We'd never be able to afford a wedding like Aoife and Nathan's, but with the extra money, we'd be able to have a good party at least. Now I was going to be without a job altogether and all our plans would have to be put on hold. I was devastated. It was as if those twelve years of hard graft counted for nothing, and I was back to square one.

I changed into battle clothes, choosing the black halter-neck jumpsuit because it suited my figure and made me look imposing. I put the straighteners on my hair and paid extra attention to my make-up. We weren't going anywhere tonight, but I still needed to look good. When I'd finished, I gave myself a talking to in the mirror.

'You've got this,' I said. 'Don't let her get away with it.'

Tiff was in the kitchen, scrubbing the hob. 'Ooh, some-body's made an effort,' she said as I marched in. She pointed at a bowl of salad on the counter. 'Take that out, please. Servers should be on the draining board.'

'Where are the others?' I asked, lifting pans and bowls and finally finding a pair of large wooden spoons. 'Are these what you meant?'

'Yup. Beth's sorting out the table. Not sure about Aoife. Dani's still with Francisco, as far as I know. God knows what's going on there.' She pulled a face. 'If he doesn't leave soon, I'm going to have to get tough.'

Tiff wasn't the only one who was going to be throwing their weight around tonight, I thought, as I carried the salad bowl out onto the terrace. The table had been re-laid with bits and bobs left over from previous meals. Beth was making origami swans out of the paper serviettes. She looked up as I appeared.

'You alright?' she asked, observing that I was clearly anything but.

'Hmm . . . looking forward to going home,' I said. 'It's all been a bit intense for my liking.'

'I know what you mean. I've had enough too.'

I looked around shiftily. 'Actually, I wonder if you could do me a favour. I need to have a quiet word with Aoife when she comes down. It's a personal matter. Would you mind . . . ?'

'Making myself scarce? Not at all.'

'And Tiff?'

'I'll try to keep her in the kitchen, but I can't promise anything. I think Aoife's still upstairs. Why don't you just go up?'

'What if Dani's there?'

'She's gone off somewhere with the model.' She pointed to Francisco's clothes which were draped over a chair. 'Tiff brought them out,' she said. 'She doesn't want him to go back into our room.'

At that moment, we heard somebody approaching. We turned to see Aoife stepping onto the patio. She wore a shimmering blue bodycon dress – it was very short and tight, making her long legs look even longer. Her face was thick with make-up, including bright red lipstick. She'd found her Bride-to-Be sash and was wearing it across her chest. Her red Beauty rose was tucked behind her ear.

'How are my lovely hens?' she asked. 'Looking lush, both of you!' She fluttered around the table, skewering olives and popping *rollitos* of ham and cheese into her mouth. 'Don't know why I'm so hungry . . .'

'We're not going out this evening, are we?' said Beth, eyeing the sparkles.

Aoife grinned. 'Well, it's not on The Schedule, but who knows?' She sucked on her cocktail stick. 'I'd be up for one more hit on Banús, how about you? Karaoke at Supernova? Come on, gotta be done.'

'I think I've had enough of that place,' said Beth primly.

'Me too if I'm honest,' I said.

'Oh! Okay. Maybe I'll just go with Dani. Where's the fizz? I haven't had any booze for like . . . an hour.'

I threw Beth a quick glance – here was my opportunity. 'I'll go and get some,' she said, scuttling inside.

We were alone, but I didn't know how long it would last. Nor did I know how to bring the subject up. Aoife seemed restless. A silver balloon had dropped from the terrace canopy and now rolled around on the patio. She picked it up and played with it until it escaped, bouncing onto the grass.

'I hear Nathan's been trying to get hold of you,' I said.

'Yes, I know. Checking up on me. He won't leave me alone for one second. It should be banned . . . grooms talking to brides on a hen. There should be a rule about it.' She walked up and down the terrace in her clopping sandals, running a hand across the bunting. 'How come you know that? No, don't tell me. It was Farrell, right? Nathan told him to tell you to tell me to call him?' She made a growling sound in her throat.

'Apparently, he's got some good news.'

'Really?'

It was now or never. 'About the job,' I said.

She swung her head round to face me. 'Oh, sorry! I thought the good news was for *me*. Wow! You got it? That's amazing, Celine!'

304

I stared at her curiously. What was she playing at?

'No, *you*—'

'Where's Beth with that bloody fizz? Of course, we all knew you were going to get it, but even so, well done. Way to go, eh?' Aoife came towards me, arms open wide, readying herself for a hug.

'Did you hear me?' I asked, backing off. '*You* got it.'

'Don't be daft, I didn't apply.'

'You got it,' I repeated firmly. 'Nathan took Charlie out to dinner last night and sorted it for you.'

She paused theatrically, holding up her hands. 'What! Are you serious? Charlie agreed to give *me* Head of Dev? Oh my God!' A smile started to spread across her face, but she shut it down quickly.

I felt my jaw tightening, teeth grinding against each other. 'What's going on, Aoife? Did you know about this?' I studied her hard. 'You did, didn't you?'

'Sort of,' she replied after several seconds' hesitation. 'I mean, no, not really. Nathan said he was going to ask but I never thought for a second that I stood a chance . . . but shit! I actually got it? That's unreal.'

'It wasn't your job, Aoife,' I said slowly. 'It was mine and you knew it. I'd been working up to it for years.'

Aoife grabbed at the bunting, ripping a piece off. She screwed it into a ball as she talked. 'It was all Nathan's idea. He's always telling me off for not being ambitious enough. Fake it until you make it, that's his motto. When the job came up, I told him I'd give my right arm to be Head of Development, but Charlie would never choose me. "We'll see about that," he said.'

'I can't believe you'd do this to me,' I said, feeling genu-inely shocked. 'I thought we were good friends. You invited me to your hen do, for Christ's sake. On Friday, you told everyone I'd got the job and told me off for stressing about it. When all the time you were plotting to . . .' I was unable to finish my sentence.

'It wasn't a plot – it was just Nathan chancing his arm.' She looked at me wide-eyed, as if she was totally innocent. 'Honestly, I never expected to get it. I'm really surprised Charlie gave in to Nathan. He probably offered to find some investment in return. It's the way business works, I guess.' She walked towards me. 'I'm really, really sorry, Celine. I know how disappointed you must be, but please believe me, it was all Nathan's doing.'

'Leave me alone!' I could feel myself shaking with anger. I sat down and crossed my legs, trying to keep it all in, trying to stop myself from hitting her. How could she be so brazen? Blaming Nathan and Charlie, like it'd been nothing to do with her. Yet, she wasn't planning to refuse the post and was quite happy for me to walk out with no job at all. It took my breath away.

'This is the thanks I get, after all the support I've given you.' I shook my head, remembering. 'You've made endless mistakes. If I hadn't cleaned up after you, you'd have been fired ages ago.'

'I'm sorry, I truly am.'

'No, you're not. You're thrilled to bits,' I said. 'I can see it on your face. Nobody else will accept you – you *do* know that? Charlie will have a mutiny on his hands. People will resign.'

'I'll have to deal with that, I guess. Nathan's always saying it's not necessary to be popular at work.'

'Don't worry, you won't be!'

She groaned. 'Oh, God, this is awful. I hate fighting. Nathan should have kept his mouth shut. He probably forgot you were the front-runner. He doesn't think, just goes all out for what he wants.'

'You're no better,' I snapped. 'People like you make me sick. You're so entitled. I haven't had any of your advantages, I've had to crawl my way up, inch by inch.'

'Yes, I know, I'm sorry. I don't blame you for being angry. The world's unfair, but there's nothing I can do about it.'

'Yes, there is.' I pulled myself up. 'You can withdraw.'

She was about to respond when Francisco came running up the path from the courtyard. He looked flustered and surprised to see us.

'Hi. Your clothes are there,' I said sharply, pointing to the pile. 'Tiff brought them out.'

'Okay, good.' He grabbed his things, dropping his pants and scooping them off the floor.

'Is everything okay?' asked Aoife. 'Where's Dani?'

'No idea.'

'I thought you were with her.'

'No. She showed me the view. I stayed, she went for a walk. To clear her head, I think. She's real drunk! Oof.' He rolled his eyes. 'Okay, got to go. Late.'

'Well, thanks for coming, and thanks for the class,' said Aoife graciously. 'We weren't very good artists, but it was a laugh.'

'Yeah. Bye then. *¡Adiós!*' He rushed off, taking his clothes with him.

Aoife waited until he was out of sight, then turned to me. 'Please let's be friends, Celine,' she said. 'I know it's incredibly awkward, but none of this is personal.'

'Of course it's personal,' I replied. 'It's deeply personal. Real friends don't treat each other like this. I need that job. Without it, nobody will give us a mortgage. We'll never buy a place of our own and we can forget about our own wedding. It'll wreck my life, do you understand? It's *my* job! It belongs to me. If you don't turn it down, I'll – I'll—'

I couldn't imagine what I would do, but I knew it would be bad.

Chapter Forty: Now

DANI

Dani lets her breath out in a rush, gasping for air again as she returns to the present. There's a sick feeling deep in her gut. Her knees weaken and she sinks onto them, hitting the ground and doubling over. Now she understands why she didn't want to enter the olive grove, why the thought of it made her feel so uneasy ... She was assaulted here that Sunday evening. The hands that she feels around her neck in her nightmares are his. It's his fingers that crawl spider-like over her naked flesh. He is the reason she can't bear to be touched intimately anymore.

She kneels in the dirt, heart pounding, a pulse throbbing in her wrist. Everything's falling into place at last. She'd always thought that she was assaulted in the house, although she'd never been sure, but now she knows it happened out here, in the olive grove. The attack on Aoife was separate. How had it become so tangled in her head?

She hears Francisco's voice. 'One more cocktail? I make it special for you.' She tastes the Blue Mojito, sweet yet slightly bitter; sees him throwing her empty glass into the bushes. Of course. That's why the following hours were such a blank.

The bastard spiked her drink.

There's a sudden, wrenching pain in her stomach. With a cry, Dani retches and vomits three years of misplaced guilt into the firepit. She is astonished and shocked by the physicality of it. *I am never sick,* she says to herself. *Never.*

Relief shudders out of her, releasing a tidal wave of emotion that she can't control. She doesn't want to control it. She lets it break over her, succumbs to its strength, her face wet with tears, loud sobs bursting from her chest. The vomit smells rank. She sweeps dirt and ashes over it and crawls away. Her strength fails her. After a few metres, she lies down beneath a tree and curls into a ball, hugging herself, eyes closed, tracing the jagged scar on her knee with a finger. Now she knows how she got the wound. Francisco gave it to her when he threw her down.

She lies there for a while, slowly and painfully extricating herself from the past and coming back to the present. Eventually, she rolls onto her knees and stands up. She drags herself up the slope, leaning on the twisted trees for support, and leaves the olive grove. A feeling of calm returns. Facing up to the memory of the assault was traumatic, but it has given her hope that she can go further, deeper – back to that Sunday evening and Aoife's final hours. One by one, the memories are unshackling themselves. She can sense something happening physically within her – a shifting, a loosening, a giving way. But she only has a few hours left.

Dani enters the villa via the patio doors and goes into the kitchen to get a drink. Her mouth tastes dry and sour. Beth is there, nervously busying herself with food preparation.

'Hi,' she says, chopping tomatoes. 'I was wondering

where you'd got to. Celine's gone to her room – on the phone to her husband. She's really strung out. She wanted to leave tonight, but I reminded her that Inspector Mengual said to stay put. I seem to have been left with making supper.'

Dani surveys the ingredients – Serrano ham and chorizo, cheese, some sardines, olives, a tortilla in an airtight packet, salad leaves, a knobbly cucumber . . . Enough to feed six, let alone three. 'Where did all this come from?' she asks.

'We popped into a supermarket yesterday, when you were in Benahavís. Bought far too much of course. We were going to have a meal as part of the ceremony, remember?' She sighs. 'I can't see that happening now, can you? Not without Tiff. Celine won't want to do it either.'

Dani's stomach feels raw and empty, she has no appetite for food. 'Any word from Tiff?' she asks weakly.

'No. I've tried calling again but it goes straight to voicemail. Either the phone's been turned off or it's run out of juice.' Beth pauses, resting her knife on the chopping board. 'Do you actually think she might have been kidnapped?'

'I've no idea. Probably not, but . . . who knows? Nothing about this weekend has turned out as I expected. Usually, if people abduct somebody it's because they want something in return. They get in touch, make their demands. At least, that's what they do in crime drama. But we've heard nothing. I suppose that's a good sign.'

Beth shrugs. 'I keep veering from being really scared to incredibly angry that she hasn't called in. I don't care if she wants to spend tonight on her own, I just need to know that she's safe.' She holds her hand to her brow. 'I've got such a headache. I think it's partly hunger. Must take some para-cetamol.' Beth nips off to her room.

Dani opens the fridge and is hit by a blast of cold air. As she reaches for the mineral water, her gaze falls on bottles of white wine the others must have bought from the supermarket. She pulls one from the rack, running her fingers across its chilly surface, remembering the sharp, slightly acidic taste.

How easy it used to be to unscrew the cap and pour herself a glass. To hear the glug of the wine leaving the bottle; to take the first sip and feel the alcohol trickling through her system. To sigh pleasantly and think, Ah, now I can relax.

She used to drink for all sorts of reasons – to celebrate, to ease stress, with friends, and sometimes when she was on her own feeling lonely or bored. Drinking was part of her normal, everyday life; she could genuinely take it or leave it. Sometimes she went weeks without drinking. If she had the flu or was on antibiotics she would simply stop. Occasionally, she'd go on a real bender, but only ever at social occasions – clubbing, parties, festivals. At uni, she'd had a reputation for holding her drink, not for losing control. She wasn't one of those women who had to be rescued by her friends and poured into a taxi at the end of the night. If anything, she'd done the pouring.

It was *after* Aoife's death that drinking became a problem. She drank to punish herself. The reason was obvious. If she hadn't been so wasted that night, she might have been able to save her friend's life.

Now the story has changed, the emphasis shifted. It wasn't the alcohol that caused her to black out, but the roofie, or the GHB or the ketamine, whatever that bastard put in her Blue Mojito. And, yes, of course she feels angry. She'd like to kill him for what he did to her that night. But at the same time a strange euphoria swirls through her body. She feels light and free. It's as if she's been lying underground for three years, breathing through a straw, and she's just pushed her head up through the soil, taken her first full gasps of air. Maybe it would be safe now to drink. Just one small glass? As a test?

She takes out the cold, slippery bottle. It's the type that needs a corkscrew. She finds one in a drawer and, cradling the bottle in the crook of her arm, is about to tear off the wrapping when she hears Beth's footsteps in the corridor, coming towards her. Overcome with guilt, Dani stuffs the bottle back in the fridge, taking out the mineral water instead – her heart beating quickly, her palms clammy.

Beth comes back in and returns to her prep. 'Hopefully, the pills will start working soon,' she says.

Dani watches her carefully slice a red onion. 'I had a kind of . . . weird experience in the olive grove earlier,' she begins. 'My memories of last time are returning with a vengeance. Remember Francisco, the life model?' She doesn't wait for Beth to respond but carries on. 'Well, after you all went inside and left me alone with him, we went—'

'I'm really sorry, Dani,' Beth cuts in, 'but I don't think I can listen to this right now. There's enough going on in the present without wading through the past. I've still got this blinding headache – I can't think straight.'

'Okay. Except I think it *is* about the present. It could be connected to—'

'Please, Dani. Just leave it for now.' Beth changes tone.

'Do you mind laying the table? Let's eat inside, it's easier.' She takes four plates from the rack. 'We need cutlery, salad servers, some knives for the cheese.'

Maybe Beth's right, thinks Dani, opening a drawer and taking out some knives and forks. It's not a good time. The atmosphere is tense. They're virtually under siege here. Although she's played down Tiff's disappearance with Beth and Celine, she feels increasingly worried that something has happened to her.

Dani lays the table as instructed, then goes outside and looks up at the darkening sky. Its colour intensifies, purple-blue infused with mauve and pink tones. She looks westward, sees the sun burning defiantly, preparing to dip below the undulating line of the mountains. The lush green forest is in deep shadow and the lake below, so bright and inviting in the day, has transformed into a long black snake. To her left, lights twinkle on the hem of coastline.

She walks across the lawn to the pool, weaving between the parasols and sunbeds until she reaches the furthest limit of the level ground. There's no fence or wall here, just a row of plant pots to mark where the land falls away. The earth is dry and rocky, with only a few shrubs clinging bravely onto the slope. This is where Aoife threw the groom mask. Dani inches closer to the edge and forces herself to look down, wondering whether it's still there. Unlikely after all this time. The mask will have been ravaged by the wind, Nathan's glossy features torn to shreds, bits of nose and mouth flying off and catching on spiky branches. The plastic stick won't have gone anywhere, though. That'll be around forever.

Maybe the cocktail glass is still there too, she thinks, as

the image of Francisco tossing it into the bushes returns to her. It had seemed a careless gesture at the time, but in fact, he was destroying evidence. She'd like to find that glass. She imagines herself in a white paper suit and gloves, picking it up with a pair of giant tweezers, dropping it into an evidence bag. They probably wouldn't be able to find traces of the drug he used. She mainly wants to find the glass to prove to herself that her memory is accurate. Maybe she'll look for it tomorrow morning.

The past creeps up on her again, tugging at her, forcing itself on her, just as Francisco did. Making her watch. Making her listen. Making her feel the pain and the trauma all over again.

Chapter Forty-One: Then

DANI

Blood ran down her calves. Her knee was red-raw, with dry grass and bark stuck to the wound. She tried to pick them out, flinching and eventually giving up as the pain became intolerable. She must bathe the wound. It might even need stitches. She had to get back to the villa . . . Couldn't keep crawling. Had to walk. She put her hand on a tree trunk and slowly heaved herself to her feet.

Her eyes sought out the last vestiges of light. How much time had passed? She had no idea. It was almost dark although the temperature had barely dropped. Looking up, she could see patches of deep blue between the grey-green olive leaves. The sun was setting – trees on the opposite side of the gorge were silhouetted against streaks of purple and gold. The classic romantic vista, she thought grimly as she turned away from the view, hobbling up the slope, grabbing at branches for support as she went.

She reached the track, stopping every now and then to breathe through the pain. Then she turned to her left and set off in the direction of the solid grey shape of the house, its roof like a black cap on a head. Her knee throbbed every time she bent it, each step making her gasp with pain. Why hadn't anybody come looking for her? Didn't they care?

It sounded like the party had already started. She could hear music playing: a pounding bass punching holes in the air. She reached the courtyard, pausing again to rest by the hire car. There'd been another car there before – almost its twin – but it was gone now. Must have been that model's . . . What was his name? Her heart raced as she began to remember. His glittering eyes, his spidery fingers . . . She blocked it all out. Moved on.

She felt her away around the side of the house. Flickering candles were lighting a winding path across the grass. She leaned into its curves, walking towards the noise, as her legs wobbled under her weight.

At last, she found them standing around the pool. They were bathed in floodlights, which made them look like characters on a stage. Aoife, Celine, Tiff, Beth. Three hens and a bride-to-be in full costume. The set was perfectly dressed too. Fairy lights twinkled in the trees, plates of half-eaten food rested on sunbeds, upturned bottles poked out of an ice bucket, balloons drifted idly across the terracotta tiles. A portable sound system blared out a carefully curated playlist.

The much-loved anthem to single ladies filled the air; Beyoncé with a million cicadas on backing vocals.

Aoife and Tiff danced around the translucent blue rectangle of water, singing along, laughing, gesturing wildly with their wine glasses. Beth swayed in time to the music, not quite allowing herself to join in. Celine sat sullenly on one of the garden chairs, not chatting, not dancing, knocking back the fizz like she needed it to dull pain. None of them seemed to have any idea that Dani was there. She tried to call out, 'Hey, girls, it's me! Bet you've been wondering—' But her mouth was dry, and the words clogged in her throat. Defeated, she staggered to the nearest sunbed, crawling onto it and lying down. She closed her eyes.

'Dani! Where the hell have you been?' It was Aoife's voice dragging her back to consciousness, Aoife's warm hand resting on her arm. 'Are you okay?' She only managed to groan in reply. 'What have you done to your knee? Did you fall over? You need to fix that. It'll get infected . . . Hey, Dani Girl! Listen to me. You need to sort that knee out.'

Dani turned away from her friend, scrunching herself into a ball.

'God, you're in a bad way. How much have you drunk?'

Dani could only manage a groan.

'Shit . . . Don't throw up here, Tiff will have a fit. Go back to the house. Get changed, put your face on. It's the final night – party time! I need you with me. Don't let me down.'

'Aoife!' Tiff was speaking now, sounding as whiny as a mosquito. 'We're doing photos.'

'Yeah, in a sec.' She shook Dani again. 'Don't fall asleep. Please. Come on, get up. For me.' Aoife's tone was softer now, more pleading. Dani felt herself being dragged off the sunbed, forced to stand up. The world did a rapid three-sixty around her. It felt like her head was about to come off. She imagined it spinning like a penny on the tiles. Spinning and spinning, then falling flat.

'I want you in the picture,' Aoife whispered. 'Please, Dani Girl. Don't do this to me. I need you tonight.'

Tiff again. 'Aoife!'

'Hold on! Dani's not well.'

'Pissed out of her brain, you mean. It's her own fault.'

'Whatever. I think she wants to be sick – that's, like, unheard of. And she's cut her knee badly. I'm taking her back inside, okay? Going to clean her up.'

'But, Aoife, this is supposed to be—'

'Yeah, I know. Won't be long. Be right back.'

Aoife put an arm around Dani's shoulders. They shuffled forwards, out of sync, like kids losing a three-legged race. She nearly fell a couple of times and Aoife had to yank her back up.

'What the hell happened?' she asked as they reached the edge of the terrace. Aoife lifted her over the bump where the rough grass ended and the smooth tiles began. 'You were gone for ages. I was going to come and look for you, but . . . stuff got in the way. Celine and I had this row.' She rattled on, 'Basically, I got the job. Head of Development. It was Nathan's idea. I don't know how he did it. I told him Charlie wouldn't go for it in a million years, but somehow Nathan persuaded him. Stupid idiot had to go and blab to Celine's boyfriend, didn't he? He told her and now she hates me.'

Aoife's words broke up in her head, Dani couldn't understand their meaning.

'It's really awkward now because of course I want the job, but Celine's saying it's hers and I should withdraw. I think I'm going to, but I still feel so bad about it. She genuinely believes I plotted against her to get it. The other thing is,' she carried on, half-talking to herself, 'if I split up with Nathan, then he'll probably tell Charlie not to give me the job anymore. I might even get fired. It's a mess whatever way you look at it.'

Somehow, they made it into the house. Aoife tried to help

her upstairs, but steps proved impossible. The knee didn't want to know. Dani collapsed at the bottom by the bookcase, curling up on the flagstones beneath the gaze of the Buddha. He observed her without a flicker of judgement, but there would be plenty of judging going on by the pool. Of that, Dani was sure.

Aoife moved her onto a chair and crouched next to her, stroking her hair. 'What happened with Francisco? You were gone for such a long time. Don't tell me you—'

Dani shook her head. She wanted to explain but couldn't find the words. Her tongue felt swollen, her lips were numb.

'Are you okay? What happened, Dani?'

Aoife went into the kitchen and came back with a wet towel. Crouching down, she started to clean the cut.

A ringing sound was coming from somewhere. Aoife got to her feet, crossed the room and picked her mobile off the coffee table. She looked at the screen and rejected the call.

'Nathan,' she announced, returning to Dani's side. She crouched down again, laying the phone on the floor. Dani was vaguely aware that her sparkly blue dress had ridden up, exposing her legs.

'I think we should try to get you into bed,' Aoife said.

The phone rang again. 'Oh, for fuck's sake,' she cried, snatching up the handset. 'What is it?' she said sternly. 'This is my hen. I'm having a *party*, remember? . . . No, I haven't been ignoring you. I promise! . . . There's a really bad signal here . . . It's true! . . . What? . . . Oh. How come? Who have you been speaking to? . . . Yes, I want to know her name . . .' Aoife raised her carefully painted brows. 'Right. Interesting.

I didn't even know she had your number . . . So, what did she say? . . . What?! She said WHAT?'

Dani strained her ears, but she could only hear shouting from the other end of the line. She tried to guess Nathan's words from Aoife's expression. Her jaw had gone slack, her mouth was open in shock. She stood up and started pacing around the room.

'No, of course I fucking didn't! No way!' Her eyes narrowed as she listened. 'Bitch! Beth wasn't even there . . . She left early . . . Yes, we were all at Pesadilla. Some gangsters sent a bottle of champagne over . . . Because they *looked* like gangsters . . . No, I don't know their names . . . No, I don't see how this is humiliating for you. But it doesn't matter anyway because *I didn't do anything*! I certainly didn't go off with them for a fucking orgy . . . What? I'll swear if I want to . . . No! She's making it up . . . How should I know why? You're believing her story over mine, right. That's great. Thanks a lot. I'm only your fiancée, we're only supposed to be spending the rest of our lives together, but that's fine . . . No. I'm not lying . . . I'm *not* lying, Nathan!'

Tell him the truth! Dani wanted to cry out. *It's over. You're not going to marry him. Just tell him the sodding truth.*

Chapter Forty-Two: Now

DANI

Dani paces around the garden, just as Aoife had paced around the sitting room on that night. She can see her friend so clearly – sparkly dress, bare shoulders, blonde spiky hair, eyes on fire, one hand clapping the phone against her ear, the other on her hip. She can hear her voice slashing at Nathan.

The memories are coming thick and fast now, like a tide rushing to the shore. She wants to jump right in and submerge herself. She wants to know. Finally. Once and for all. What happened. She needs to talk to the others, question them again about what they saw and heard. Everyone had pretended to the police that it'd been a perfectly normal hen party, that they'd got along brilliantly and had been having a wonderful time. It wasn't true though. Beth had been in a strange mood on Sunday, Tiff had been jumpy all weekend – bossing them about, sparring with Dani at every opportunity – and Celine and Aoife had fallen out badly over the job.

Dani hears a sound behind her and turns around, just in time to see the back of somebody entering the villa through the open patio doors. From this distance, and in the fading light, it's impossible to make out who it is, but they don't have Tiff's petite shape, that's for sure. It's a man. Who is he? What's he doing just walking in like that?

Her heart thumps as she runs up the garden towards the villa. She slows down as she reaches the edge of the patio, peering into the living room beyond. Nobody has switched on the lamps and it's gloomy. She can't see him.

Her pulse beats in her ears, she feels like she might faint. Where has he gone? She advances carefully, trying not to make a sound, and slips inside.

He's not here. There's only one other place he could be. Upstairs in her room, where she and Aoife slept, where Marta usually sleeps. The message on the mirror flashes through her mind. *YOU'RE NEXT.* Has he come to make good his promise?

She listens for footsteps above her, the creak of floorboards, the opening of a door. There's nothing. Crossing the room, she goes into the kitchen. Beth isn't there. The food is still out, the chopping board covered in bits of tomato, the ham drying on a plate. A fly is buzzing. Where has Beth gone?

She goes through the kitchen and walks down the dark corridor, turning a corner and coming to the two downstairs bedrooms, Celine's first, then Beth and Tiff's. She stands at Celine's door, listening for the sound of conversation, but it's silent. Afraid to use her voice, she knocks as gently as she can, then waits. Is Celine even inside? She tries to press down on the handle, but it won't budge. Something's been put against the door.

'Celine?' she whispers, knocking again. 'It's me. Open up.'

There's a pause, then the handle is released and the door

inches open. But it's not Celine's face in the gap, it's Beth's. She steps aside to let Dani enter, quickly shutting the door behind them and wedging a chair back under the handle. Celine sits on her bed, trembling.

'Did you see him?' hisses Beth.

Dani nods. 'Only from a distance. Who is it?'

'I'm not sure, I haven't seen him for ages, but I think it was John.'

John. Dani squirms inside. He must have realised who broke into his apartment earlier.

'Did he see you?' Dani asks Beth.

'No. He was in the sitting room, rummaging around in a drawer.'

'Maybe he was looking for the spare keys,' Dani replies. 'That's where Marta keeps them.'

'I managed to creep away and came to find Celine. We've been hiding here. Bloody terrified. When you knocked just now, we thought it was him.'

'We heard him in the corridor,' says Celine, picking up her phone. 'Should I call the police? Say we've got an intruder?'

'That's tricky,' says Beth. 'This is his property. You can't trespass in your own house.'

'I think we should go and confront him,' says Dani after a few seconds' thought.

Beth pulls a face. 'Is that wise?'

'I'm not sitting in here all evening, too scared to move,' she says. 'Come on. It's three against one.'

Dani removes the chair from under the handle and opens the door. She walks down the corridor, Beth and Celine following anxiously. The back door has been left ajar. Dani peeps out and sees that the garage door is open.

'We've got him,' she whispers. 'He can't escape.'

They cross the courtyard and stand on the threshold. John must have heard their footsteps because he turns to face them. He's holding a photo album in his hand.

'Hi, ladies,' he says, trying to sound casual.

Dani steps forward. Celine and Beth stand close behind her, blocking the exit.

'Hey, John. We saw you inside the villa. What are you doing?' Dani asks, trying not to show how nervous she feels.

'Er . . . sorting through my belongings. In my own house. Something wrong with that?'

'No, but you don't live here anymore. And you sneaked in, didn't even say hello,' says Dani. 'Why have you got that photo album?'

'None of your business.'

Suddenly, she understands. 'Has it got pictures of you and Nathan in it, by any chance?'

He feigns confusion. 'Me and who?'

'Let's not play stupid games,' Dani replies, finding her confidence. 'Nathan. Your old mate. Aoife's fiancé. You know I was in your apartment earlier. I didn't get a chance to close your photo gallery. You must have realised I'd seen those pics of your stag do.' She points at the album. 'I guess there are hard copies in there. Incriminating evidence. Did you come to destroy it?'

'I don't know what you're talking about.'

'There's no point in denying it. I've already told the police about your secret friendship with Nathan,' says Dani.

He closes his eyes for a few seconds, shaking his head in dismay. 'Inspector Mengual was extremely interested. Said he'd reopen the investigation tomorrow. You might as well 'fess up, now, save everyone the bother.'

'Fuck. Fuck!' John groans. 'You've no idea what you've done. What this means for me. And Marta. She's innocent, she had no idea . . .'

Dani leans in. 'No idea about *what*?'

'I told you Marbs was dangerous, but you wouldn't bloody listen! It's alright for you lot, you're pissing off back home tomorrow, but we're stuck in the middle of this shit—'

'What do you mean?' presses Dani. 'You've got to tell us. What's been going on? Why didn't you tell the police that you and Nathan were mates? What were you hiding?'

'I had no choice but to go along with it. Nathan said it would be easier.'

'Easier how? You were obstructing the enquiry,' says Beth. 'Surely Nathan wanted the police to find out who killed his fiancée?'

'Yeah, he did.'

'So what were you hiding?' presses Dani.

'Believe me, you don't want to know about any of this.'

'Yes, I do. We all do, don't we?' Dani turns to the others, and they nod. 'Sorry, but we're not going to let you out of here until you tell us the truth.'

'I can't tell you the truth because I don't know it.'

'You know something, John. There's a load of stuff you're not telling us,' Celine says, joining in for the first time. 'Are you a couple of criminals?'

Silence.

'What are you involved in?' demands Beth. 'Drugs? People trafficking?'

'No.'

'It's organised crime, right? It has to be. Marbella is heaving with gangs.'

'I just run a bar.'

Dani takes over. 'What about Nathan? What does he do?'

'He's in finance, you know that.'

'What sort of finance? Money laundering?'

Silence again.

'You might as well tell us. Can't you see it's over, John?'

'I needed money to do up the villa,' he says at last. 'No banks would give us a loan. We couldn't get a mortgage. Nate came to the rescue, offered me the cash straight up – no stupid forms to fill in, no credit assessments. We didn't even have to pay interest. All we had to do was make regular instalments into a proper bank account.'

'You must have known it was dirty money.'

'Yeah, of course. It was obvious that was Nate's line of work, not that he ever admitted it. I knew it was wrong, but there was no other option. And Nate was an old friend, he promised it would be fine. And it was . . . until we couldn't pay it back.'

He looks down at his grubby feet. For a second, Dani almost feels sorry for him. Whatever he's got himself into, he's clearly in way over his head.

Beth advances towards him, narrowing her eyes. 'Did you kill Aoife?'

'No!' he shouts immediately. 'Absolutely not. I swear on my life, I had nothing to do with it.'

'But you know who *did*.'

'No . . . I don't.'

'But you have your suspicions.'

He doesn't respond.

Dani cuts in. 'Was it Nathan?'

Yet more silence.

'Is *that* the real reason he didn't want you to say anything to the police about you being friends?'

'Maybe. I don't know. I honestly don't know who killed her and that's God's own truth. Please, leave it.'

But she can't leave it. 'Did you send Matt to Pesadilla?'

'No. Definitely not.'

'So how did he know where to find me?'

'I don't know. You'll have to ask him.'

'Did you tell Nathan we were here?'

John shakes his head. 'He already knew.'

'You've been in touch with him, then?'

'He called me on Friday night. Gave me an earful, like it was my fault you were here.'

'So, when I turned up on Saturday, you pretended not to recognise me.'

'Yes and no . . . I was half-asleep.'

'Why was Nathan angry that we'd come back to the villa?'

'I don't know.'

'Yes, you do.'

'Just keep out of it, Dani. For Christ's sake.'

'Does Matt have a motorbike?'

John hesitates before answering. 'Yes. Why?'

'Just that somebody on a motorbike was following me last night, trying to make me have an accident.'

'That doesn't sound like Matt. He's not violent. More of an errand boy.'

'Does he work for Nathan?' He shrugs a reply. 'I'll take that as a yes.'

'It'll have been Nate on Matt's bike,' John says. 'I know he borrows it sometimes when he comes over. He likes to throw his weight around, show everyone he's the boss, even though he's not. There are people higher up the food chain. But I'm pretty certain it was him who broke in last night and left the message too.'

'Could he have kidnapped Tiff?' Beth asks.

Dani catches her breath. She'd momentarily forgotten that Tiff was missing.

John looks up, his face suddenly flushed with fear. 'What do you mean, kidnapped?'

'We were at the cemetery and she just vanished,' Beth explains. 'It's been hours. We can't get hold of her.'

John lets out a moaning sound. 'Jesus! I tried to warn you off, but you wouldn't listen!'

Beth rushes forward and shakes him. 'Has he taken her? John? Has Nathan taken her?'

'I don't know. Maybe. He doesn't like being backed into a corner. It makes him unpredictable.'

'We should call one-one-two now,' says Dani. 'The police need to find her. We're losing precious time here.'

'No!' says John, raising his voice. 'Please! If Nate's lost the plot, we don't want to panic him. He might hurt her.'

'But what does he want?' cries Celine.

'He wants you to stop digging around and go home.' John thinks for a moment. 'Leave it to me. I'll try calling him. Casual, like. Just to see how he is. Get a take on his state of mind.'

The women exchange glances, not knowing what to think.

'Okay,' says Dani. 'Try and find out where he is, John. Don't mention Tiff being missing.'

He takes his phone out of the large pocket on the front of his shorts. 'I can't do it here. Let me out, yeah? I need to do this in private.' They step aside and he leaves the garage, walking back into the villa. They follow him down the corridor, through the kitchen and into the living room, keen for him not to escape. 'I'll do it outside, okay?' He steps into the garden and walks across the lawn until he's out of earshot.

Dani, Beth and Celine stand watching him from the patio doors, keeping him constantly in their sights.

'He'd better not be tipping Nathan off,' says Beth.

Chapter Forty-Three: Now

DANI

John is still talking on his phone.

'I think we should call the police,' says Celine. 'We don't know who he's speaking to. It could be Nathan or Matt . . . anyone or nobody at all. He could easily be lying to us. We can't trust him.'

'I felt the same about him to begin with,' Dani answers, 'but now I think he's okay. He was clearly worried when we told him Tiff had disappeared. The guy's an idiot, got himself mixed up in something, but I don't think he's totally bad. We should give him a chance. What do you think, Beth?'

She's not listening to them. Dani repeats her name and she finally breaks free from her thoughts. 'What?'

'Do you think we should call the police now or wait for John?'

'I think we should do whatever gives us the best chance of getting Tiff back in one piece,' she replies.

'Okay, let's see what he says when he gets off the phone,' says Celine. 'But if he doesn't know where she is, we have to act straightaway.' The others nod in agreement.

Dani holds her breath for a few seconds, then lets it out in a troubled sigh. 'I can't stop thinking about what John said about Nathan,' she says. 'Do you think he could have killed Aoife? Or sent someone to do it? I mean, that's so extreme. I can't imagine what led him to it.'

Celine considers. 'I always got the impression he was used to having his own way. He's very proud. He'd hate to be humiliated. I don't know whether he was ever violent towards Aoife, but a man like that, operating in that world . . . It's not beyond the bounds of possibility.'

'No, I guess not,' Dani replies, nodding. 'My memories are starting to come back. I remember her arguing with him on the phone.'

'That suggests he was somewhere else at the time.'

'He could have been on his way to the villa.'

'He was in London that weekend,' Beth points out. 'He flew over the following morning, as soon as he heard the news.'

'That's what he said, but he could have already been here. The police might be able to check flight lists – if they still keep records from three years ago.'

'What matters right now is finding Tiff,' says Beth.

'But it's all connected,' says Dani. 'I know it is. If only I could remember what the guy who attacked her looked like . . .' She screws up her face, trying to force the memory out.

'Even if you could, it wouldn't be admissible evidence,' says Beth. 'You can't suddenly turn round after three years and say you saw Nathan attacking Aoife. No court in any country would ever accept that.'

'No, but if there was other evidence to back it up,' says Dani, 'it might count for something.'

'It'll never be proved,' says Beth. 'People like that know

how to cover their tracks. And if John's right and the police here are corrupt . . . well . . . ' She sighs.

'Mengual isn't corrupt,' insists Dani.

At that moment, John walks up the garden towards them.

'Well?' asks Dani, breathlessly.

'Couldn't get through to Nate,' he reports. 'Spoke to Matt, though. He says he hasn't seen Nate for months but I'm pretty sure he's lying. He sounded nervous.' He pauses, looking at each of them in turn. 'So . . . what are you going to do now? Call the police?'

'We have to,' says Celine. 'There's no other option.'

'I agree.' Dani turns to Beth. 'Are you on board?'

'Not sure. I'm worried it might put Tiff in more danger. If Matt *is* working for Nathan, he'll go straight to him.'

'Yeah, that's what worries me too. We could be next,' John agrees.

'We have to *do* something!' cries Dani. 'I'll call Mengual.'

'Shh!' John raises his hand. 'Did you hear that? Footsteps. Coming from the back of the house.'

They freeze, listening to a tap-tap on the tiles, the squeak of a door opening.

'Stay here, I'll check it out,' John whispers. He removes his flip-flops then tiptoes into the kitchen, heading for the corridor beyond.

They wait. Not daring to speak or move. It's so quiet Dani can hear her heart banging against her ribcage, like a small animal desperate to be set free. Who is it back there? she asks herself. Nathan?

She looks over at Beth, leaning against the wall. She's

pink and sweaty, her chest heaving as she fights to control her panic. Celine stands by the dining table, awkwardly posed, weight unbalanced. She looks as if she's been playing Musical Statues and the music has just stopped.

They hear voices, the sounds of a scuffle. A few seconds later, John emerges from the gloom, gripping Tiff by the arm.

'You're hurting! Let go of me!' she cries.

Beth rushes forward. 'Tiff! Oh my God. You're back!'

John releases her. 'Yup! False alarm.'

'Are you okay?' asks Celine. 'Why didn't you answer our calls?'

'I'd run out of battery.'

'Liar,' says Dani. 'You never run out of battery. That's not you.'

'Piss off.' Tiff shoots a filthy look in Dani's direction. 'I didn't want to talk to any of you, okay? Is that a crime?' She rubs her arm as if it's still hurting.

'She was in the bedroom, throwing stuff into a suitcase,' John says.

'What's going on, Tiff?' asks Beth.

'Nothing. I decided I couldn't bear to stay here one more night, not one more moment. I had to get away.'

'But why all the sneaking around? Why didn't you just tell us? Or tell *me*, at least.'

'Because I knew you'd try to make me stay.'

'We've been worried sick,' Celine chimes in. 'We thought you'd been kidnapped.'

'What?' She lets out a nervous laugh. 'I'm fine. Honestly, I'm fine! I've found a little hotel, it's all good.'

'Really?' Celine frowns. 'Everywhere was booked up when I looked. Where is it?'

'Can't remember the name. It's very small. More of a hostel, really. Need to get my things . . . my passport . . .' She turns to go back to her room.

Dani blocks her way. 'Don't go yet, Tiff. We need to talk to you about Nathan.'

Her voice cracks. 'Nathan? What about him?'

'I think you should sit down first.'

'Why? What is it?' She looks at Beth. 'What's going on?'

'Sit down, Tiff,' Beth says, her voice hardening. 'You need to hear this.' She pulls out a dining chair.

Tiff perches on the edge. 'I've got a taxi waiting,' she says, looking nervously towards the outside.

Dani clears her throat, then speaks. 'Nathan's involved in organised crime.'

She laughs. 'No, he's not. He's a businessman.'

'Yes, but it's criminal business. Money laundering. He and John here are mates. Matt too.' She turns to John. 'How long have you known each other?'

'Since school,' he mumbles.

'So, way back. They work together, Tiff, do you understand? It was all part of a plan. Nathan manipulated you into booking the villa for the hen party so John and Matt could spy on Aoife for him.'

Tiff frowns. 'Why would he do that?'

'Nate knows a lot of people in Marbs,' John interjects. 'He was concerned about his reputation. He wanted us to make sure she behaved.'

'Huh, well, you both did a great job of that,' remarks Beth.

'She didn't exactly make it easy. She was throwing herself at both of us. It wasn't normal. We knew something was wrong. I was worried for her. If there's one thing Nate won't stand for, it's being made to look stupid, especially by a woman.'

'So, how did it work?' Dani asks. 'Did you report back on an hourly basis?'

'No, nothing like that. He called me loads of times over that weekend. He wasn't happy. Aoife wasn't picking up his calls. He wanted me to come over and check on her. Then later, on Sunday, he rang me sounding really upset. Somehow, he'd heard she'd gone off with some gangsters at Pesadilla. It didn't come from me. I swear.'

'Then who did it come from? Matt? Another one of his spies?'

'I've no idea. It could have been any number of people.'

Tiff breaks her silence. 'Nathan didn't kill Aoife, if that's what you're getting at,' she says.

'How do you know?' Beth asks.

'Because he loved her. He'd never do a thing like that.' She puts her head in her hands. 'I know him. He wouldn't. It was a burglary. The police said that right from the beginning, it was a burglary!' She starts to cry.

'I never thought it was a burglary,' Dani says.

'Shut up. I don't care what you think, it wasn't Nathan, okay? I know it wasn't.'

Celine looks at her in astonishment. 'Why are you defending him?'

'I'm not defending him . . .'

'That's how it sounds.'

'Oh, Tiff,' murmurs Beth. 'Is it what I'm thinking?'

She nods. 'We've been seeing each other,' she says through a clog of tears. 'Off and on. We're not "together", it's just . . . casual. We leaned on each other after Aoife died. Grew close.'

'When you told him about this trip, how did he react?' Celine asks.

She sniffs noisily. 'He didn't want me to go. Said it would upset me.'

'You called him from Venta El Lago on Friday, is that right?' says Dani, starting to piece the timeline together. 'You told him we were staying at the villa.'

'Yes. I was freaking out. Nathan was already in Marbella – he'd flown out on the flight after ours. He wanted to be available in case I needed him. He's been looking after me.'

'The only person Nate looks after is himself,' mutters John.

Another voice breaks in. 'That's a bit unfair.'

Their heads swivel to see Nathan stepping in from the patio, understated in dark jeans and a crisp white polo shirt.

Tiff starts guiltily. 'I'm sorry, I . . . they wouldn't let me go.'

'It's alright, babe. I heard you speaking up for me. You're safe.'

He walks around the dining table, optimistically laid for four. 'So . . . have you been shooting your mouth off, John? Telling the girls here about our private business.'

'Dani found out about our connection,' he replies. 'She's got a hotline to Mengual. He already knows. They're going to reopen the case. It's over, we can't run away this time.'

'Already knows what?' Nathan interrupts. 'That I lent

you some cash so you could do up an old farmhouse? What's dodgy about that? I was only helping out an old mate.' He turns his attention to Dani. 'But you. You've always been a thorn in my side. *Oh, Dani Girl,*' he sings mockingly. 'That's what she called you, didn't she? Oh, she loved you. You were her favourite.' He glances at Tiff. 'Sorry, babe, but it's the truth.'

'Come on, let's have it all out,' says Dani. 'Did you kill her?'

'No! Of course I didn't. I'm not a fucking murderer!' he spits. 'I loved Aoife. She was going to be my wife!' He prods John in the chest. 'You're the one to blame. Renting out a villa in the sticks, miles from anywhere, no neighbours. No electronic gates, no CCTV. Three years ago, you didn't even have a fucking burglar alarm. Not that it makes any difference. Nobody could hear it ringing.'

'So, it was *you* last night,' says Dani, springing up. 'You trashed the place, left the warning message.'

'You were poking the hornets' nest. I needed you to stop,' he replies.

'You didn't want the police to reopen the case because you killed her. Or had her killed. I'm not sure which is worse.'

'I had nothing to do with it.'

'I don't believe you. You were angry because Aoife had spent the weekend cheating on you with the very guys that you'd sent to spy on her. She had sex with John here, tried it on with Matt too, though he backed off. She was in a bad way. Confused. Sick of the way you always tried to control her. She'd decided she didn't want to marry you. She

338

wrecked the relationship so that there could be no going back. But somehow you found out—'

Nathan listens, wide-eyed. He grabs John by his shirt. 'You had sex with Aoife?'

John squirms. 'No, no. I didn't!'

'That's not what she told me,' says Dani. 'Saturday evening at Supernova, upstairs in the flat.'

'Did you or didn't you?' Nathan growls.

John looks terrified. 'She was all over me, I didn't know what to do, couldn't stop her.'

'That was how you kept an eye on her, was it? That's how you repaid me for helping you out, lending you all that cash? You still haven't paid it back. You fucking cu—'

Nathan throws a punch at John, landing it on his cheek. John staggers backwards into Beth, who screams.

'I know you killed her,' shouts John, trying to get away from him.

'I was in London—'

'You sent someone, then. Who did you send? Was it Matt?'

'I loved her. She was my girl – *my* girl, you understand, not yours! I'm going to fucking make you pay for this.'

'Stop it! Nathan, for God's sake, stop!' shouts Tiff.

But they don't listen, committed now to an ugly, full-scale fight – swiping with their fists, pulling at each other's clothes, locking horns for a few seconds then breaking free, hurtling around, grappling, bumping into furniture . . .

Dani slides down the wall, sinking to the floor. It's like she's watching a film. It feels like she's seen it already, or something very like it, a long time ago. Some of it looks familiar, but she's not sure. The setting is the same, but the actors are different . . .

John is getting the worst of it. Nathan pins him down on the dining table, already laid for supper. As Nathan repeatedly punches John's face, Dani sees him reach for a knife. She gasps as John closes his fingers around the handle, holds it close to his side then suddenly lifts it up and plunges it into Nathan's stomach.

There is a split-second's silence, then someone starts screaming. Tiff, she thinks. Or maybe Celine. John is on his knees. Nathan is lying on the table amid the debris, groaning faintly, eyes rolling into the back of his head.

And there's blood. A lot of blood. So much blood. Blood seeping into the tablecloth, spreading across Nathan's white polo shirt.

John scrunches up into a ball, trying to make himself as small as possible. Tiff is in hysterics. Beth has fallen on her knees and is pressing down on Nathan's wound. Celine has grabbed her mobile and is dialling 112. She goes up to Dani and shakes her. 'Dani? Dani! Don't just sit there, I need you to talk to them.'

But Dani cowers in the corner, pulse racing, ears singing. Everything around her is fading. She's in the same place but being dragged backwards to another time.

Chapter Forty-Four: Then

DANI

'It's over,' Aoife was telling Nathan. 'You and me.'

Dani could hear him shouting down the phone, but she couldn't make out what he was saying.

'Because I've had enough, that's why,' Aoife replied. 'Because you take over, you don't let me breathe . . . You do! You control me all the time. In everything! Now I'm in trouble with Celine over the job . . . Yes, of course I want it, but I don't deserve it . . . It *is* the point. I'm not going to accept it. I can't . . . Yes, she's mad at me. Rightly! . . . No, I'm not grateful, I've had enough. I'm sorry, Nathan, I can't go through with it, can't marry you, can't be with you at all . . . Yes, I mean it . . . I know . . . the wedding . . . thousands of pounds . . .'

Dani sat on the chair, doubled over, head reeling, her bleeding leg outstretched. Aoife had been screaming down the phone but now she was listening. Dani could hear her panting for breath. 'What?' she gasped finally. 'Tiff? You and *Tiff*? I don't believe it . . . When? When did you sleep with her? Oh . . . my God. Well, we're even then. Fine. Best of luck. Marry her instead, you fuck.' She ended the call, flinging the handset to the floor, where it smashed.

'What happened? Aoife, wha—?' Dani tried to speak but

Aoife didn't seem able to hear her. She was in a red mist, picking up objects at random and hurling them at the wall. Ornaments, vases, ceramic bowls and books flew through the air. She took paintings off their hooks and smashed them on the tiles, pushed furniture over, swept a dozen glasses off the sideboard with one hand. It was as if she could no longer see Dani who was in the thick of it, her head buried in her lap, being hit by flying missiles.

She had to calm Aoife down and make her stop. Slowly, Dani lifted her head. She tried to push herself off the chair, onto her feet, but her injured knee buckled beneath her and she couldn't balance properly. Staggering forward, she reached out to Aoife, but missed. She spun around on one leg, dizzy and disorientated, then managed to cling onto a piece of furniture. A sideboard maybe. The back of a chair? She couldn't see properly. Her eyesight was blurry, dark at the sides, she had no peripheral vision at all. She could still hear crashing and breaking glass, but Aoife seemed to have disappeared – gone to find Tiff, perhaps? Dani called her name but only a croak came out.

She made another attempt to walk forward, but the floor was covered in broken glass and pieces of china. She tried to find her way, but the room was spinning so fast around her she couldn't work out which direction she was going in, whether she was on the floor or the ceiling or even climbing up the wall . . .

There was a dark shape by the sofa. Somebody was standing there. Who was it? She blinked but she couldn't make them out. Was it Aoife or was it . . . ? No, surely it couldn't be *him*. She had a sickening flash of memory. She could feel his black silky gown, smell the baby oil on his skin, the sensation of his hands creeping over her. What was he doing here? Had he come back to finish the job? A sudden burst of anger rose within her. Her heart started beating so fast she thought it would explode in her chest.

He came towards her, arms outstretched. She recoiled as he tried to embrace her. She would not let him rape her, she would not! With a loud grunt of effort, she pushed him away, pushed him with all her might. He spun backwards.

Everything went into slow motion. Dani watched Francisco fly through the air. He landed heavily on the coffee table. It shattered on impact, sending thousands of sparkling pieces upwards in a seconds-long firework display before they fell back on him, showering him in glass.

She staggered backwards, losing her balance and collapsing on the floor a few metres away. She lay there for a few seconds, unable to process what had just happened, then turned to look.

But it wasn't Francisco lying there, it was Aoife.

She was lying face up, her legs at strange angles, not moving, groaning quietly. A large shard stuck out of her bare thigh, just beneath the hem of her tight blue dress. Blood gushed forth, spurting like a fountain, turning everything around it to red.

Dani's brain short-circuited. She couldn't understand what she was looking at, couldn't compute it at all. How come Francisco had disappeared and Aoife taken his place? It was an illusion, a magic trick. It couldn't be Aoife. It couldn't. But it was. And Dani had to save her.

She rolled onto her stomach and with a gigantic effort

343

started to crawl to Aoife, inching forwards, wincing as her knee scraped on the tiles. She tried to call Aoife's name, but she seemed unable to speak. The darkness in her head was threatening to engulf her. She stopped, exhausted and overcome with pain.

Then she heard a scream. Celine had come in from the garden. She looked down at Aoife, her mouth open in horror. She started towards her then suddenly halted. Dani waited for her to act but she appeared to be paralysed. Aoife was hurt. Why wasn't Celine responding? There was a thoughtful expression on her face as if she was weighing up what best to do. She seemed unnaturally calm. Dani felt frightened.

Instead of going to Aoife, Celine went over to Dani and prodded her with her foot. Seemingly believing that she was unconscious, Celine walked away. Darkness was descending as Dani watched her make a call on her mobile. Celine started breathing in a way that suggested panic and talking as if she was highly upset.

'There's been a break-in,' she cried. 'My friend has been attacked. She's bleeding to death, please can somebody come? Now! She's going to die!' She pretended not to understand the call-handler, apologising for not being able to speak Spanish. 'It's Villa Flora,' she said, 'I don't know the full address. Villa Flora, can you look it up?'

Villa Floriana, Dani said in her head. *You know full well it's Villa Floriana.*

The call finished, Celine went over to Aoife and kneeled down in the blood. She mumbled to Aoife under her breath. Dani couldn't make out what she was saying, but she sounded angry. There was a strange expression on her face. Her eyes were narrowed and there was a cruel twist to her mouth. She ripped the large shard of glass out of Aoife's thigh. Aoife let out an agonising scream. The wound opened up and blood gushed out even faster than before.

You're killing her, thought Dani. *You're killing her.*

She felt desperate to get across to the other side of the room, to throw Celine off and fling herself on her friend, to press down on the wound with all her strength, but her own body wouldn't move. She had to stay where she was and watch Celine doing nothing to save Aoife. Celine sat amongst the smithereens with her bloody hands clasped together as if in prayer. Her jaw was set firm. There was no emotion in her face. Her clothes were sprayed red, but she didn't seem to notice.

Seconds, maybe minutes, passed. Then Celine stood up, looking dishevelled herself now, and ran out of the villa screaming for Tiff and Beth to come. Moments later, they all rushed back in.

'I've already called the ambulance,' Celine was saying, breathlessly. 'They should be here very soon.'

'Why didn't you come and get us?' wailed Tiff.

'I was trying to save Aoife. I screamed, but I don't think you could hear over the music.'

Tiff looked across at Dani's prone figure. 'Couldn't she help?'

'She's passed out.'

'Fucking useless,' says Tiff. She crouched down in the glass next to Aoife, not caring about being cut. 'Oh, God.

345

This is bad.' She looked up. 'We need to stop the bleeding. Beth, fetch towels from the bedroom or the kitchen ... anything you can find as long as it's clean.'

Beth clutched at her chest. 'How – how – did it happen?'

'She was like this when I found her,' said Celine. 'Somebody must have attacked her.'

'Who? How come?'

'Maybe she disturbed a burglar?'

'Towels!' screamed Tiff. 'Now!'

Beth ran off. Tiff put her mouth to Aoife's ear. 'Aoife! Aoife! Come on ... open your eyes! It's Tiff here. Stay with me, please, the ambulance is on its way, it'll be here any moment, you're going to be okay, but you have to stay awake. Hang on in there—'

Beth came back with a pile of towels, which she threw down next to Aoife. But before Tiff could start applying them, Celine pushed her to one side.

'Let me do this. You're tiny, I'm much stronger than you. You go and meet the ambulance. Make sure they don't miss the turning.' She took a towel and pressed down hard on the wound. The white cloth immediately turned scarlet.

Tiff was trembling. 'But I want to stay with her.'

'She'll be okay. You're more use outside. Beth, you go with Tiff,' Celine barked. 'Use the torches on your phones.'

As soon as she was sure they'd gone, Celine took the towel pad away. She sat and watched as the blood pumped out of Aoife's body at an alarming rate. By now, it was everywhere – on the walls, the sofas, the rug, the chairs, spreading across the flagstones ... Celine seemed unaffected by the horror. She wasn't even breathing quickly. She had no idea that Dani was watching her out of the corner of one eye. Willing Beth and Tiff to return. Praying for the ambulance to turn up, though she knew it wouldn't make it in time. Celine had sent it somewhere else.

Suddenly, Aoife's blood stopped pumping. Celine let out a small cry and slapped her hand to her mouth. Time seemed to stand still. Dani felt a great wrenching inside her, as if her heart had just been torn out. She knew the moment that Aoife was dead.

She wanted to tell them what had happened, but the details were already disintegrating, breaking into the tiniest of fragments, spinning away from her through infinite space. She couldn't catch them, couldn't pin them down. They might be lost forever. Finally, the darkness took over and she slid into oblivion.

Chapter Forty-Five: Now

DANI

The hens are huddled together in the garden, sitting on a low wall by the flowerbeds, not talking, steering well clear of the organised bustle around them. A uniformed officer wielding a gun guards a strip of black and yellow plastic tape, which has been stretched across the patio doors. *Escena del crimen. No cruzar*, it reads. Crime Scene. Do not cross.

Lights are flashing. Several emergency vehicles have parked up in the courtyard. A black motorbike is standing by the wall, two cycle helmets next to it. Nathan must have borrowed Matt's bike for the weekend, she thinks.

A second ambulance is still hanging around, even though they've all insisted that they're fine. Physically, anyway.

John has been arrested and sits handcuffed in one of the police cars. Nathan was whisked off quickly, sirens blaring into the darkness. If he survives, which right now seems unlikely, Celine will be the one he needs to thank. Ironically. She staunched the wound with kitchen towel, used up a whole roll. Everyone else was useless. John was in total shock. Tiff and Beth went into a tailspin. Couldn't deal with it at all. Dani completely gets why they reacted like that. Like her, they were remembering . . .

The past has finally revealed itself to her. Dani's mind

bursts with sensations, words, noises, tiny details, big emotions. Anger, mainly. A lot of anger. For three years she's longed to recapture those vital missing hours, and now she's got them, she doesn't know what to do. There's so much to process, so much to understand.

But for now, they're sitting on the wall. Beth and Tiff are on one side of her, Celine on the other. The four of them in a row, watching insects buzz around a garden light. It must have been like this the last time, hanging around in the dark, shivering with shock even in the night heat. Just the three of them then. Dani had been lying down in the ambulance. The medic dressed her knee but decided she didn't need to go to hospital. All she needed to do was sleep off the alcohol. If they'd taken her in and run some tests, they might have realised she had a date-rape drug in her system.

She stretches her leg out. She was told she didn't need stitches, but even in this ghostly light, the scar is visible. She runs her fingers over the jagged, raised line. It has always felt like a mark of shame. Now it feels like a badge of survival.

Tiff covers her face with her hands. 'Do you think he'll live?'

'Do you actually care?' Beth counters.

'Of course I care! We've been seeing each other for nearly three years.'

'Why didn't you tell me?'

'Because I knew you'd disapprove.'

'Did you know he was a crim—'

'No, of course I didn't!' Tiff wrings her hands. 'I should have gone to the hospital with him. Why didn't I go? That was wrong of me. Poor guy, he's all on his own.' She springs to her feet. 'I'll get a taxi. Do you think they'll allow me to be with him? They can't stop me, can they?'

Beth puts her hand on Tiff's arm. 'Best not to go,' she says quietly. 'You don't want the police to know you're his girlfriend, do you? People might jump to the wrong conclusion.'

'Yeah, good point.' She sits back down. 'I wasn't thinking.'

'It's okay, you're upset.' Beth pats her leg. 'You're alright with us. We won't say anything, will we, girls?'

'I'm not going to lie to the police,' retorts Celine. 'If they ask, I'll tell them the truth.'

'But if they don't ask?'

'They'll ask.'

'Dani?' Beth turns to her. 'You won't say anything about Tiff and Nathan, will you? Tiff had no idea he was into that stuff, she's completely innocent. So was Aoife, I'm sure. We just want to keep it simple.' Dani doesn't reply. She's still got one foot in another time. 'Dani? Are you listening? I'm trying to say something important to you. About Nathan and Tiff—'

'I remember everything,' she replies.

'Okay, but you don't need to volunteer information if nobody—'

'No, I mean, I remember everything about Aoife. How she died.'

'Please don't start on this now,' says Tiff. 'My head's in a spin. Haven't we got enough to cope with?'

'Tiff's right,' says Beth. 'We've all had a shock.'

Dani knows she has to tell them. If she doesn't do it now, she never will. She'll keep it locked inside, where it will eat away at her. 'You need to hear this, it's important.' She inhales. 'I was drugged. Roofied.'

'Roofied?' echoes Tiff. 'How come?'

'The life model guy, Francisco. He spiked my cocktail, took me to the olive grove and tried to rape me. That's why I couldn't remember. I thought the memories had never been made, but they were here all the time, hiding deep inside me. I wasn't able to get them out. It was the trauma of witnessing Aoife's murder, it pushed everything down—'

'You didn't witness it though,' Celine said pointedly. 'You'd blacked out.'

'Not completely. I was drifting in and out a bit, but I was still conscious. I heard Aoife arguing with Nathan on the phone. She told him the wedding was off and he went crazy, said something about you, Tiff.'

She gasps. 'No . . . please, no!'

'Aoife was so angry she completely lost the plot. Started throwing things around, wrecking the place. I couldn't stop her – I was too out of it. I kind of went into some sort of . . . funk . . . I can't explain it but I got confused. I was losing consciousness, hallucinating. I thought it was Francisco in the room with me. I was frightened that he was going to attack me again so I pushed him away. He fell into the glass table. Except it wasn't him.' She pauses, unable to say it.

'It was Aoife?' whispers Beth.

Dani nods. 'I realised at the last moment, but there was nothing I could do. Then Celine came in.'

'Yes, she was the first to find Aoife,' says Tiff.

Dani turns to Celine. 'I saw what you did.'

Celine inhales sharply. 'Like Tiff said, now's not the time to go over old ground. Nathan's just been stabbed, everyone's in shock, it's too much to deal with. Leave it, Dani.'

But Dani can't leave it. She's waited three years for this. 'Why did you let her die?' she continues. 'Was it because she'd got your job?'

Celine stiffens. 'What are you talking about?'

'She'd decided not to take it, you know. I heard her telling Nathan. You killed her for nothing.'

'I didn't kill her,' she bridled. 'This is just ridiculous.'

'You sent the ambulance to the wrong place. You pretended to save her, but you actually let her bleed out. You even pulled the piece of glass out of her thigh, so she would die quicker.'

Beth and Tiff gasp in unison. 'Is this true?' Tiff asks. 'Celine. Is this true?'

'Of course it's not true. I was in shock. We all were.' She makes to get up but Dani forces her back down.

'I didn't kill Aoife, Dani did. She just confessed!' Celine wrenches herself free, stands up and walks away, although where she thinks she's going, Dani can't imagine. The villa is swarming with police, she won't be allowed back indoors tonight. The three of them follow her with their gaze as she strides past the vehicles and goes down the track, disappearing into the darkness.

'Did you definitely see her?' asks Tiff, after a pause. 'Are you absolutely sure?'

'One hundred per cent,' Dani answers. 'She let Aoife die.'

'That's pure wickedness,' Tiff mutters.

'Yes, it is,' says Beth. 'We could have saved her. She could be alive today.'

'I didn't mean to hurt her,' says Dani.

Tiff places a hand on her thigh. 'We know that,' she says. 'You loved her.'

'Yes, I did.'

'Did you have any inkling then that it was you who pushed her? Any at all?'

Dani shakes her head. 'I knew there must be a reason why I couldn't remember those final hours, but I never imagined . . . no, not that.'

'You've been incredibly brave,' says Beth. 'Facing up to your demons.'

'I had to do it,' Dani replies. 'There was no other choice.'

'I'm guilty too,' says Beth. 'I called Nathan and told him what had been going on.'

'Oh . . . I wondered about that. I think I heard Aoife talking about it.'

Tiff speaks. 'And I'm also to blame. I had a one-night stand with him a couple of weeks before the hen party. That's what he and Aoife were rowing about.' She chokes. 'Nathan told me she never found out, but he was lying. It sounds like he did tell her, just before she died.'

'I think so . . . yes.'

'I told myself that he and I were meant to be. I've been so stupid. He's been jerking me around these past three years, popping up to Manchester whenever he felt like some sex. Now I feel even worse. To think that she went to her death knowing I'd betrayed her . . .'

'Look, none of us are blameless. We all played a part in

it,' Dani says, 'and I'm sure we're going to regret that for the rest of our lives. But it was Celine who killed her. You probably can't call it murder, but I know that if she hadn't done what she did, there's a good chance Aoife would still be alive today. Maybe she would have forgiven us, maybe she would have turned against us – trouble is, we'll never know.'

They all look round to see a black BMW drawing up in the courtyard, headlights beaming brightly. The driver's door opens and Inspector Mengual climbs out. He's wearing casual clothes and tennis shoes on his feet. Dani's heart heaves. Of course Mengual would be summoned to the villa. He goes straight up to one of the uniformed officers and they speak to each other. Dani does her best to listen to the Spanish, catching a few words that tell her that Nathan died on his way to the hospital. She looks at Tiff. Somebody will have to break the news.

Dani stands up and walks towards the inspector. Her heart is full of pain, but her step is lighter than it's been for three years. Mengual greets her with a nod of recognition.

'*Buenas tardes*,' she says. 'May I speak to you, Inspector? *En privado, por favor.*'

'Of course, Daniela. About this?' He gestures at the crime scene.

'About everything. You said I would remember one day. Well, I have.'

Epilogue: Six Months Later

DANI

It's early January, yet the sky is clear and it's just about warm enough to sit outside. Dani sits at a table on the pavement. She zips up her jacket and sticks her hands in her pockets. Closes her eyes and lets the sunshine warm her face.

When the coffee comes, she drinks it straightaway, before it has a chance to cool, then orders another. It had been an early flight this morning and she needs the caffeine to help her stay awake. She didn't hire a car this time, it was too expensive for just one person. Instead, she caught the coach from the airport to Marbella bus station, then took an Uber straight to the cemetery. It's open twenty-four hours, but she's not quite ready to enter yet.

Dani contemplates the next few days. She's booked into an Airbnb – an apartment above a gift shop, located a few streets behind the seafront. The Street of Hell is taking a break from its nefarious activities – the bars and clubs are either closed for winter refits or only opening at weekends. It's not hen and stag season. If she's feeling brave, she might take a wander down the second line to see Supernova. Its metal shutter will be down, daubed with fresh graffiti, no doubt. According to Google, the bar is temporarily closed.

Mengual has been keeping her up to date with the investigation. The Spanish system is very complicated, and it'll be some time before John goes on trial. They are still deciding whether the charge will be murder or voluntary manslaughter. Marta is still living in Villa Floriana, but the place isn't available for rentals anymore. Dani has texted her a few times, just to ask how she is, but only ever receives brief, impersonal replies.

Dani will never go back to the villa. She doesn't need to, thank God.

She still keeps in touch with Beth, but strangely, the person she's closer to these days is Tiff. She's suffered a lot, been off work for months with depression. Dani has some idea of what she must be going through and has tried to support her. Aoife would have liked that, she thinks – the two of them finding common ground at last. She imagines a happy photo of the three of them, Aoife in the middle. How it should have been from the start.

As she drinks her second coffee, Dani thinks back six months to the night of Nathan's death. She had asked to speak to Mengual in private. They went to the mirador at the other end of the garden and sat at the same mosaic table as before, only this time the sun was setting and the sky was growing dark. It felt more intimate, like a conversation between friends rather than a police interview. He'd expected her to tell him about the fight between John and Nathan, but she'd only wanted to talk about what had happened three years earlier.

He listened carefully, without taking notes. She was sobbing and shaking, scarcely able to get the words out.

'*Tranquilo*,' he said when she'd finished. 'It's okay, Daniela. I understand what happened. You weren't to blame.'

Then she told him about what Celine had done.

'Maybe it happened as you remember, but also maybe the memory is distorted. You were under the influence of a powerful drug. Your witness statement would be seen as unreliable and it would be impossible to prove,' he replied.

She sighed. 'I know you're right. And Celine will never confess.'

'No. Why would she?'

'I just can't bear the idea of her getting away with it.'

'I understand. But the case is already closed,' said Mengual. 'I can't see any value in opening it again. You've suffered enough, Dani. You were a victim of this Francisco. He's the one we must find and prosecute.'

'But we'll never prove that either,' she said. 'There's no evidence. Just like with Celine, it'd be my word against his.'

But Mengual insisted. Tiff gave him Francisco's contact details, which luckily she had kept. His website was no longer online, he seemed to have vanished. The inspector discovered that he was already in prison, having been arrested a few months after the hen weekend for similar crimes. He was serving a long sentence for several rapes and attempted rapes, all involving spiked cocktails. Dani said she was satisfied that he was no longer free to harm other women and decided not to pursue it. A kind of justice had been done.

She shakes off the memory and returns to the present. Finishing her coffee, she leaves a few coins on the table and walks across the street. It's time.

*

Dani senses Aoife calling to her, guiding her through the white marble maze. She finds the niche straightaway, and stands before it, reading the inscription. Tears well in her eyes. It's okay to cry, she tells herself. Nothing wrong with feeling strong emotions, she can handle them now. She's learned to dive right in and ride the wave. It has taken three and a half years, a load of counselling and self-help to reach this moment, but she's got here, relatively speaking, in one piece.

She inches forward, her lips almost touching the marble. 'It's me,' she whispers. 'Back again. Just me, this time . . . Hey, guess what? I'm three hundred and thirty days sober, that's virtually a year. Sounds unbelievable, eh? But I feel so much better in myself for not drinking. I've got a new job with a charity – just running around doing stuff, but it's good. And . . . you won't believe this . . . I'm seeing someone.'

She pictures Asher in her mind's eye. Tall, bearded, handsome in an understated way, kind, a little vulnerable. He's also a recovering alcoholic – they met at AA. He'd wanted to come with her on this trip, to support her, but she declined the offer. Asher is part of her new life, not the old one – she doesn't want to muddy the waters.

The marble is cool beneath her touch. She traces a finger over Aoife's name, the dates of her birth and death. 'I didn't mean to push you, Aoife. I didn't know what I was doing, I thought you were someone else. As for Celine . . . I'll never understand what made her do it. I guess she wanted that job so much she was prepared to kill for it. She did it for three years, you know, and was incredibly successful. Tiff told me she gave it up. She's at home now, looking after her son. She's lost her career, but is that punishment enough? I hope she feels guilty for the rest of her life.'

She presses her cheek against her friend's name. 'I'm sorry, Aoife. I hope you can forgive me.'

Dani lays a small spray of roses on the shelf. Kisses her hand, then presses it against the inscription. Dries her tears with a tissue. Then she turns and walks back to the cemetery entrance. In her head, she can hear Aoife singing to her, that Irish song she loved so well. She would sing it late at night, when they were lying on the grass, looking up at the stars and the moon. Or in the streets, when they were walking home after a party, arm in arm, barefoot, their high-heeled shoes dangling from their fingers.

> But come ye back when summer's in the meadow,
> Or when the valley's hushed and white with snow,
> 'Tis I'll be here in sunshine or in shadow,
> Oh, Dani girl, oh, Dani girl, I love you so!

Acknowledgements

Firstly, a word of explanation ... The villa of this book does not exist but is a composite of different villas and my imagination. The landscape and some of the venues will be recognisable to anyone who knows the area, but I've played with the geography to suit my story and invented a few places too.

Having never had a hen party myself – or attended one – I definitely needed some help to write this novel. I'd like to thank my researcher, Brenda Page, who always rises to every challenge I set, however difficult and obscure. I would also like to thank my brother Neville and sister-in-law Cherie, who fortuitously live near Marbella and gave me valuable insights into expat life. Particular thanks to Cherie for patiently driving me around as I tried to find the right locations. Thanks to Max Leach – DJ, singer and former mixologist – who told me lots of entertaining stories about hen parties. And to real estate agent Jason Payne, who showed me some amazing villas and was a mine of information about life in 'Marbs'.

Muchas gracias y un abrazo enorme to my Spanish teacher and friend Amaya Moral Garcia, who helped me with the Spanish language elements – if any errors slipped through the net, they are entirely my own.

Huge thanks are also due to the team at Penguin Random House, especially editor Emily Griffin and assistant editor Rachel Imrie. They have been a joy to work with, helping me nurse this book through from conception to final draft. Katya Browne, Lynn Curtis and Sarah-Jane Forder also deserve a mention for their beady-eyed attention to detail.

I'm very lucky to be represented by Rowan Lawton at The Soho Agency for fiction and Christine Glover at Casarotto Ramsay & Associates for film/TV. If anyone ever tells you that agents don't work hard for their clients, they're talking nonsense. These are two incredible women and I'm very grateful for all their endeavours on my behalf, as well as their moral support and good company.

Thanks as ever to my husband David for listening to me banging on about my plot problems as we walk around the park – and for sometimes coming up with solutions! He does a lot more than that, of course. I would hate to be without him.

And last but most importantly, thanks to all my readers. When you enjoy my books, it makes all the hard work worthwhile.